THE DUDLEY FILES

Sold Out Without The Holdout

THE DUDLEY FILES

Sold Out Without The Holdout

Cary Robinson

Two Harbors Press

"Whatever is mine is his."

"The Ballad of Colton and Eli"

To those brave souls who will serve no more
Our fallen heroes lost to war
May you find peace at your journey's end
While at your side stands man's best friend

—Jake Harm and the Holdouts

CHAPTER ONE

It was a beautiful spring day. The weather was just turning from cold to a nice, crisp cool. Everything was beginning to green up. I loved this time of year and I always knew it was coming when my Grandfather's fig tree started to sprout little green points on the ends of the seemingly dead, barren branches that eventually blossom into a lush, green leafy tree. This always signaled the start of a new season.

Maybe that's just what I needed. A new season sounded great to me. I had been feeling kind of down lately, so here it was, spring, a time of rebirth and revitalization. It was time to let go of the gray and gloomy winter that was my soul.

I was sitting on my sofa at Big Rock Lofts in Houston, Texas. My loft is #158. Big Rock Lofts was originally built as a warehouse in the 1950s and was aptly named because the largest rock that had ever been pulled out of the ground in the city of Houston was found while digging the foundation for the building. It's my understanding that it took many sticks of dynamite and several cranes to remove the big rock before the building could be constructed. My windows were as wide open as my mind and I was enjoying a nice big glass of iced coffee brewed with my Toddy coffeemaker. I just loved iced coffee and, with my Toddy coffeemaker, I brewed it cold, which left all of the bitterness locked up in the coffee grounds, unable to be released into the coffee. The bitterness of the long cold winter was now giving way to spring as I discarded the bitter coffee grounds. They were thrown into the garbage along with most of my other possessions I no longer wished to keep. After all, they were just things. Perhaps my own bitterness inside was waning and needed to be discarded as well. I suppose I was having a spring cleaning of the soul, which was probably long overdue.

I've been living by myself for the last year in the warehouse district in Houston, Texas. The warehouse district is located just east of downtown. Houston is quite a large city and for the last several years the up-and-coming "in" place to live was in these large old warehouses on the

1

outskirts of town. The truth is—they were so up and coming that most people who originally inhabited these lofts had already come and gone. The idea of having a mini-New York never truly caught on. Of course the winos, crackheads, and ladies of the evening who lingered on well past my bedtime probably didn't help matters much. Most people move out of Big Rock Lofts within six months, except of course for those who really want to be left to their own accord or who rent out the spaces for art studios. There were plenty of interesting people living in my building.

My super duper, red-and-white HEB telephone (that I received free for shopping at HEB) began ringing. Many people don't know about HEB, a fine Texas tradition. HEB is my favorite Texas grocery store. Over one hundred years ago Charles C. Butt and family started a small grocery store in Kerrville, Texas, with just sixty dollars. It was called the C.C. Butt Grocery Store. The family worked very hard to make it a success. The youngest son, Howard, after returning from World War I, expanded the store and opened another in Junction, Texas, just down the road about sixty miles from Kerrville. Howard's motto, which I believe they still practice today, was, "He who profits most serves best."

In 1971 Howard's son, Charles, became president of the H.E. Butt Grocery Company. The last time I checked there were over three hundred stores, employing over fifty-six thousand employees. Everyone refers to the stores as HEB and the original one, although renovated and expanded, is still going strong in Kerrville. HEB also owns newer, more upscale stores named Central Market.

I just happened to be shopping there one day when they were handing out free telephones for one of their anniversaries. It was a small, rectangular red-and-white phone with a coiled up red cord that is constantly getting tangled. I find myself always having to untwist it, which is fairly tedious. It isn't a particularly good phone but it is pretty cool looking with the HEB letters in white against the red phone. I guess my favorite thing about it was the price. It was free, so it automatically became my favorite telephone.

I debated whether to pick up the phone at all, but after about the third ring it became quite obvious that whoever was on the other end was not going to give up; and the ring became a constant well-timed throbbing sound in my brain, so I grabbed the phone from my desk and answered like any normal American would, "*Bueno*."

It was my friend Birk. "Hey, what's going on?"

I responded, "Same old crap. Who wants to know?" Of course I knew who it was but I was trying to keep my image up as a wise-cracking smartass.

"Careless, it's me, Birk. Don't be a dumbass." Dumbass, smartass, the difference can be so fine that sometimes it isn't always obvious to the untrained individual.

I suppose now is as good of a time as any to introduce myself. My friends all call me Careless. I don't really have many friends and, to be honest, that really doesn't bother me much. In fact, I like it that way. I don't ever have to worry about remembering a lot of names, and when I get pissed off about something I don't really have to stop and think about whom to assess the blame since there are so few of them. Now that I have broached the subject, it may well be that I don't have any friends at all. Still, not a real problem.

My real name is Cary Robinson; although, if anyone ever called me that, I probably wouldn't respond because no one ever calls me that. I'm just not used to it. I have no middle name. My folks didn't see fit to give me a middle name and that was okay with me because, judging from my brother's, sister's, and friends' middle names, it probably would be more of an embarrassment than anything else.

How would you like your middle name to be Leslie, Irving, Rosie, or April? Not that there's anything wrong with that, but it could sure do some damage later on in life, especially at school where everyone learns everything about you, including your middle name. That could be a real problem when all of the school children began chanting, "Ricardo the Retardo," "Bart the Fart," or something of that nature. No, I really didn't need an extra leg up on screwing up my life or having some deep-rooted issues that would cause me later on in life to have to share my feelings with someone or have someone ask me, "How does that make you feel? That will be one-hundred-and-fifty dollars, please."

It was also rewarding not to have two first names strung together. I was very fortunate in that regard. Ron Paul, David Allen, and Richard Lewis, to name a few. I learned from an early age never to trust anyone with two first names. I'm not quite sure where I picked up that trait but it has served me well over the years, and to date I don't believe I have ever been proven wrong.

I first became known as Careless many years ago while in college at Tulane University in New Orleans. I was sitting around with a bunch of my friends and after a few shots of Jack Daniels we started renaming one another. Some of my friends preferred their Jack Daniels mixed with soda and ice, but to me that just seemed to ruin the taste. Why mess with a good thing? I guess I'm just a purist. After the loss of a few brain cells, we all decided to rename one another by adding the word "less" to either our first or last name, whichever sounded better. Of course after a few drinks it was really quite hard to determine what name sounded good, but we muddled our way through nonetheless. There was Zach Shifke. He became Shiftless. There was Scott Hartman. He became Heartless. Jeremy Pantowski became Pantsless. Adam Feckerman became Feckless. Jason Wittinburg became Witless. Josh Worthington became Worthless. Then there was Shamus Ackerman. Yes, you guessed it, he became Shameless, and sometimes I think he was. Last but not least, Cary Robinson was transformed into Careless. There was no looking back after that. Careless was born.

"Hey, asshole, are you listening to me?" the voice on the other end of the phone asked.

"Yeah, yeah, I'm listening, what's up?" I responded.

Just finishing up my iced coffee on a Saturday morning, I was ready for a little something more. As I was speaking, I suddenly realized that I had not added my favorite, main ingredient to my very tasty iced coffee, so I opened the cabinet and pulled out a bottle of Jack Daniels.

I was first introduced to Jack Daniels when I was thirteen years old while on a fishing trip at a summer camp in the most beautiful part of Texas. In Texas, we call that the Hill Country. No, we weren't all just sitting around trying to keep warm. One of my young, goober friends decided he was going to launch his treble-hooked fishing lure out into the middle of the river, but as he reached back he hooked my chin, right before skyrocketing the fishing lure forward. I seem to recall some pain and a few tears. At that moment, I believe I knew just how a fish felt. Yes sir, I can accurately say that I was stuck like Chuck. I'm sure I was quite the sight, but the two very young adult counselors who were on call rushed me over to a little shack on the property and doctored me up. They found a bottle of Jack Daniels in a cabinet and decided to sterilize a sharp knife with it before operating to remove the hook. I remember watching them prepare and I guess I must have turned as white as a ghost because they seemed to be getting a little nervous. I've never really seen a ghost so I don't know if they are actually white but I've always heard people say, "You're as white as a ghost."

At that point they handed me the bottle and said, "Drink this and you won't feel a thing." Sadly enough, I haven't since.

I took a few swigs, they took a few swigs, and a few slices, dices, and bandages later, the operation was a complete success. I suppose fishing led me to drink Jack Daniels. It really isn't a problem and I can quit whenever I want. As a matter of fact I just decided to give up fishing immediately.

It was ten o'clock and my friend Birk was trying his best to ruin my morning. "Are you drinking this early in the morning?" Birk asked.

"First of all, it's brunch time and I need a little something to clear out my sinuses. Why don't you nutshell it for me and tell me what the hell you want this early in the morning?" I responded.

I first met Birk in a restaurant named Dirty's. His full name is Gerald A. Birkenstock. He was originally from Mandeville, Louisiana, just across the New Orleans causeway. Everyone calls him Birk. Of course sometimes I call him other things, but that's okay because he usually deserves it. He was hauling mudbugs when I first met him, but now he works for Coke as a logistics specialist in Houston. Oh, mudbugs, they're really just crawdads the Louisiana farmers raise in their rice fields to sell as delectable treats to fellow Cajuns and seafood lovers.

"Okay, I woke up this morning and I had a great idea! Want to hear it, Careless?" Birk droned on.

"Sure, I've been waiting all my life to hear it. Go right ahead," I said, but I didn't really mean it. I was hoping he'd forget why he called me. Sometimes he does that. Short attention span and all but, unfortunately for me, no such luck this time.

"We're going to the SPCA this morning and you're going to adopt a dog. What do you think about that?"

He was probably hoping for a positive response, but I would have none of that and was most glad to disappoint him. Okay, I'm having my liquid brunch, trying to enjoy my day and my friend Birk is calling me to go to the SPCA with him so I can adopt a dog. I'm thinking to myself, *Why would I want a dog? Do I need a dog? Have I ever expressed an interest in owning a dog?*

It would really be just one more mouth to feed and what about the veterinarian bills? Did I really need more of my valuable time taken up when I could be sitting around doing nothing? Did I really want to clean up after a dog?

The more I thought about it, the more I thought it was probably one of worst ideas I had heard in a long time. "Sure, come pick me up, I'll just swallow the rest of my brunch and we'll ride up there together," I said.

Often times in life you know something is probably not a good idea, so that's when you move forward with it anyway, at full speed. That tends to keep things interesting and, really, who doesn't want that?

CHAPTER TWO

I have no idea why I accepted the offer. I knew it was probably going to be a disaster and I was likely to do something really stupid. The truth is, when it comes to animals, I have a soft spot in my heart—which also usually leads me to having a soft head. How bad could it be? Birk and I would just spend the morning playing with little puppies. It would benefit everyone and, hell, I already had my morning pick-me-up, so I was feeling pretty positive. I was in a good place. Yes, I decided this was going to be good and that I could give back to society by socializing these poor unfortunate dogs that, through no fault of their own, ended up at the SPCA.

I finished my iced coffee and threw the plastic cup into the recycling bin. I always tried to recycle as much as possible. It made me feel good inside, but on garbage day I always emptied the recycling bin into a garbage bag with all of the other garbage and hauled it out to the dumpster in the parking lot. I know it was wrong, but I was consolidating my energy by only taking one trash bag out to the dumpster. I was just trying to reduce my carbon footprint, and you know what they say about a guy that has an unusually large carbon footprint? No need to go any further with that.

Right now, you're probably thinking that I am just lazy, which is true, but I felt kind of like the janitor who refers to himself as the maintenance engineer. That's right, damn it, I'm a maintenance engineer and proud of it. I live in Texas and we don't have global warming in Texas. It's just naturally hotter than hell here. We call it summer.

Birk was about to pull up in his Ford F350, four-wheel drive, dually pickup truck. It was a big, bohunk truck with all of the bells and whistles. It was all white and shiny with running lights on the roof, the mirrors, and on the chrome tubular steel running boards. It appeared to me to be about twenty-five feet off of the ground, twenty-five feet long, and just "sang" of redneck. He pulled up in front of my loft and started blowing his horn.

Maybe it was my imagination, but it sure sounded to me like a freight train was about to run right through my living room. Between the loud rattling sound of the diesel engine and the thunderous horn honking, I thought maybe I had died and gone to the great train station in the sky. *Hmmm*, I wondered to myself, if in fact I ever did make it to the great train station in the sky, which train would I take? Would I take the non-stop express straight to a place hotter than Havana during summertime or would I catch a ride on a comet, taking the scenic route to a place I thought I'd never see?

While I was in deep contemplation, a shrill, piercing sound broke my train station of thought like a damn mosquito buzzing around my ear, annoying the hell out of me. Of course it was Birk, with his famous curbside service, blowing the hell out of his horn.

I stopped what I was doing, which was pretty much nothing but daydreaming, and wandered over to the window to give Birk the salute that he so properly deserved. Since my loft was on the second floor I had a great vantage point to signal to him that I would be down in one minute. I may not have used the correct finger to give him the "just one minute" gesture, but I am certain he got the point.

I left my loft, closed and locked my door, and began making my way downstairs where I ran into Sarge. He was an old classmate of mine at Tulane University, but of course that was a whole other part of my life that right now seemed further away than Uranus, my favorite planet. Sarge was about five-foot-three-inches tall, had a thick head of dark wavy hair, and wore thick black glasses like the kind people used to wear in the 1960s. I suppose he was a throwback to the sixties, but he probably didn't know that. Sarge's real name was Mick Angerman but, unlike his name, he was really slow to anger and was a very easygoing guy. Sometimes he could barely be understood because the words that flowed out of his mouth usually all ran together. Mostly he just walked around saying things like, "Wow, how, how, how, how!"

Like I said, he was still living the sixties.

Sarge had moved into the building before me and it seemed like he was always there. Everyone in the building thought of him as a permanent fixture. He lived in #160 on my floor, so I saw him pretty regularly. True to his form, he was a minimalist. Whenever I visited him, I noticed that his furniture, or lack of, looked like something he acquired from the Starvation Army or perhaps from the curbside of a house where furniture had been used up and left out to be hauled away to the dump. It was quite a simple arrangement consisting of a worn-out sofa with a few noticeable rips here and there, a twin mattress on the floor that was usually not made up, a few lamps made from old milk jugs, a small refrigerator that appeared to be older than I was, and a rickety table more beat up than I was, with two chairs that didn't match.

Sarge is an interesting guy. Some of my friends think he has a split personality. I'm not so sure about that and, besides, if he did have multiple personalities then how would I decide which of his personalities I liked the best? After careful Careless consideration, I decided that I pretty much accepted all of his personalities. Really, what's life without a little variety? It definitely keeps things interesting. But with Sarge it was kind of like pot-luck as to which personality you might get; and, speaking of which, I am pretty sure there was plenty of pot being ingested on his behalf, but that's just a feeling I have. The one thing I can say about Sarge is that he is almost invisible. He moves around from place to place (even in crowds of people) and very few ever seem to notice him. It's really very funny because to me he looks like the elephant in the corner of the room, and yet he just glides by everyone without them even blinking an eye. I've seen it happen dozens of times. He is also very bright, reads ferociously, and has a photographic memory.

"Hey, Sarge, what's up?" I asked. He stopped walking and looked at me because he couldn't believe I noticed him.

I saw those wheels starting to turn behind his glasses and he blurted out, slowly and deliberately, "Mardi Gras 2000!"

After a minute he collected his thoughts and shuffled on up the stairs toward his loft. In the distance I heard, "Wow, how, how, how, how!" Then there was silence.

CHAPTER THREE

I started walking toward the old warehouse front door. The big old iron door with rivets in it looked like it was made during the World War II era by Rosie the Riveter. Rosie the Riveter of course was a cultural icon to Americans during World War II. She represented many women who worked in plants across America, making machinery, equipment, and munitions while our boys were away in the theater. In my mind, I can still see the poster of the beautiful woman with the red-and-white polka-dot scarf on her head, flexing a big sexy bicep muscle. Due to my manliness, I must admit, this did make me a little nervous but she was pretty hot so I got over it real fast. We Can Do It! That's what the slogan on the poster said.

Some people believe that the Rosie the Riveter character was based on a woman from, you guessed it, Texas. I don't like to brag but most really great people either come from Texas or wish they had. Rose Will Monroe was her name, from Coppell, Texas. She was born in 1920 and later became a riveter making airplanes at the Willow Run Aircraft Plant in Michigan. I don't know why but the old riveted iron door to the warehouse just jogged my memory of her. Of course this was probably the only jogging I would do this week. All this jogging really exhausted me.

As I reached for the door, someone from the outside pulled it open and I was getting kind of pissed off because I was sure it was Birk trying to rush me up. On a beautiful day like today I felt that if I wanted to act like I had banker's hours then that's exactly what I was going to do. I started to shout, "Look, Birk...." but then my mouth caught up with my brain and I noticed that it was not Birk at all.

Maybe I was dreaming or maybe it was wishful thinking but the most beautiful girl I had ever seen had just opened the old iron door and was standing right in front of me with a perplexed look on her face. She had long flowing blonde hair kind of feathered back away from her face. I couldn't stop staring at her blue eyes until I looked at her figure and then I couldn't stop looking at her figure. That phrase just kept being repeated over and over in my mind. *We Can Do It! We Can Do It!*

"See anything you want to take home to mamma?" she asked.

Well, even though I consider myself somewhat bold, I was quite embarrassed to say the least. I was still staring at her tatas, but at least I was turning different shades of red, the same red color that matched the red-hot, short shorts she was wearing. "No, I'm good. I'm just socially retarded," I responded.

I have no idea why I said that but unfortunately in my case it happened to be true. She just looked at me with a devilish little-girl grin and said, "Well, at least your half right." While I was trying to figure out exactly what that meant, I quickly realized that she was definitely not a member of the itty bitty titty committee.

So I'm thinking to myself that this could be the start of something really great. "I'm Careless, and you are?" I asked.

"Not interested," she replied with one of the nicest smiles I do believe I've ever been blown off with.

Being a gambling man, I decided to try again. "I'm sorry, I didn't catch your name," I said.

"Okay, Carrot, the name's E.D.—don't ask me what it stands for—I'm moving into a loft in the building. That's my car, Betsy; am I parked in the right spot?"

I started thinking again that I'd like to park in her spot but I just mumbled, "The name's Careless."

"Whatever, Clueless, I'm moving into loft #258; can you show me the way?"

"As luck would have it, you're right above me. Just take two flights of stairs up and turn to the left; you can't miss it," I said.

"That's right, I'm above you and don't you forget it. Now go and get my things from out of Betsy and bring them up to my loft," she rather convincingly commanded.

At least I found out that she liked being on top. It's always good to get to know your neighbors.

Not wanting to piss off my new, very attractive neighbor, I hit the door and went outside to find a dark-blue Oldsmobile and, believe me, she looked plenty old. She was about the size of John F. Kennedy's PT-109 boat. You know the one, the patrol torpedo boat he commanded that was seventy-eight feet long, except this one was labeled eighty-eight not seventy-eight. Both appeared to be from the same vintage era as well and, yes, this probably was your father's Oldsmobile.

Betsy was old to be sure, but she still looked pretty good with a nice healthy shine covering that dark-blue exterior. There were no apparent rust marks. I pulled the door handle and of course it was locked.

"Well, Betsy, it looks like you're not going to get unloaded today," I said as I walked off toward Birk's truck. I guess this will be the first lover's quarrel that E.D. and I are going to have but, honestly, how could she blame me for not bringing her belongings in when she had me locked out like a jilted lover? She darn sure wasn't giving two thoughts to my dilemma. Typical blonde, barking out orders with no follow-up.

"See you later, Betsy," I said.

Betsy said nothing.

CHAPTER FOUR

I grabbed Birk's truck door handle and opened the driver's-side door. I stepped up on the running board and climbed in. This was as hard as it looked. It appeared to be about a twenty-five-foot climb to get in. I imagined that it was one small step for mankind. It would have been nice to have been weightless for the climb up but, being that I had just recharged my battery with a liquid brunch, I made the leap up with no problem.

"What's up, June bug?" Birk belched out.

Before I could answer or completely close the door, he shifted that bad boy into drive and hit the gas. I barely managed to close the door as I attempted to compose myself and strap in. I looked over at Birk and I swear I noticed a little smirk on his face. Birk with a smirk made him look like a jerk. He was trying not to look directly at me, but he really wanted to as he strained his eyes to get a glimpse of my mental condition.

"Birk, in just about a minute you're going to be hurtin' for certain," I said.

At that point the little smirk I detected earlier grew to a big Texas smile and then a great big belly laugh came from right there in the front seat next to me. "Watch it now!" he said, "Careless, we're getting you a dog today. I know you've never really wanted one but, damn it, I've always wanted one; so you're going to adopt the biggest, meanest, stupidest, smelliest, ugliest dog there is, so that I, my friend, can live vicariously through you."

This was definitely the worst idea I had ever heard, *or was it?*

"Oh, yeah, did I forget to mention that it would be a bonus if your new dog's goober mechanism is running on overtime?" he asked.

All the while, I'm thinking about how to explain a furry friend to everyone I knew, but especially to my new, beautiful neighbor, E.D.

We started our long driving journey from downtown toward the SPCA. Of course I knew where we were headed but, being the smartass that I am, I asked, "Birk, where are we headed?"

"What?" he answered.

"You know, what's our heading? What's our twenty? What's our ETA? Where the hell are we going?" I irritatingly asked.

"Careless, you know damn good and well where we're headed. We're going to the SPCA," he said.

"We're going to the **S**exually **P**ermissive **C**arnival **A**ssociation?" I inquired.

"Yeah, that's right, dumbass, and we're almost there," he answered. Birk then explained that he had taken the liberty of calling ahead and spoken to a nice young lady by the name of Karen, who said she would just love to help us out, especially since they appeared to be overbooked at the **S**ocially **P**romiscuous **C**ounty **A**gency.

Birk cranked the stereo while Merle Haggard was playing one of his favorites, "Ballroom Buddies." What a coincidence since that was the song playing the very first time I met Birk at a little-known restaurant and bar named Dirty's. I was attempting to down a three-dollar pitcher of margaritas and chasing them with their world-famous tater tots. In Texas we don't eat Frenchy French fries; we eat a little something called Texas Tater Tots. You know what I'm talking about, Texas Toast, Texas T, Texas Exes. Texas Tator Tots are somewhat similar to other people's tater tots but just bigger and better. That's right; I said it, bigger and better. Instead of "Come and Take It" maybe the Texas motto should be, "Texas, Bigger and Better." And no, we don't all have cactus and oil wells in our front yards. That's just a misconception. The truth is that the oil wells are in our backyards. Let's just set the record straight!

Birk and I were driving down I-10 west toward the SPCA or, as I called it, **S**ilent **P**assive **C**areless **A**ggressive. I have been told by many that I am in fact, the king of being Passive Aggressive. To be fair, this is not something you're just born with. It is a skill that must be finely honed over the years and it's helpful to throw in an Abbie Normal family to kick it into high gear. The Abbie Normal family is of course optional but will greatly enhance your chances of becoming a master like me and, with a little luck, perhaps one day you will.

CHAPTER FIVE

Birk and I pulled up in the parking lot of the SPCA. It was a nice, newish, if not a little Jewish, brick building. There was a big colorful sign right in front painted in pastel colors with a number of animal images worked into the design. To be honest, up until this point I had not been too thrilled to get a pet for all of the reasons I rationalized earlier. On the other hand, after seeing the building and the sign, I was starting to feel a little better about the decision Birk made for me, even though he had not bothered to consult with me beforehand. Oh, well, what are friends for?

Birk turned off the major turbo bohunk diesel truck and I felt a little like someone who had just landed the space shuttle on the runway and then killed the engine. I was just waiting for the rescue trucks to pull up and collect us just like I had always seen on Eye Witless News but nobody came. Just us rednecks and damn proud of it! As I looked around for a ladder to use to climb down from Birk's monster F350 crew cab dually, I became dismayed that one was not available; so I did what any man would do, I turned around and starting yelling like a little girl at Birk about why he couldn't drive a normal car like most fine Americans.

He told me that normally he would, but this was his way to protest global warming. He said we were all going to fry like rats anyway, so he was going to have a little fun in the meantime and, damn it, if he wanted to drive a Cowboy Cadillac then that's just what he was going to do.

After working him up sufficiently, I made the long trip back down to Earth. Once we both had our feet planted firmly on the ground, we closed the truck doors. Birk hit the alarm button, a loud chirp sounded, and a blue light flashed on the windshield. I guess he thought someone was going to try to steal his fine shit-kicker truck, but I honestly couldn't imagine any self-respecting criminal that would drive such a vehicle. It made Birk feel good about himself, so *whatever floats his boat.*

We walked across the parking lot and I must admit that while it seemed very exciting to be adopting and rescuing a pet, I was definitely having second thoughts.

Birk looked at me and said, "Oh, no, get your ass moving. We're on a mission." He opened the front glass door with the SPCA logo on it and swished his arm in a swirling motion beckoning me in, just like a doorman at an apartment building in New York City.

I entered the building and it was very nice, but it was no New York. There was a big sign hanging on the wall with the SPCA logo on it consisting of the letters SPCA with a dog and a cat image intertwined. Birk walked right in behind me to cut off any retreat I may have chosen. I thought to myself that maybe this wasn't such a bad idea. It looked like a nice place and there were people wandering around everywhere with all kinds of animals.

The first thing I noticed was that most of the workers were young ladies, and most of them were quite attractive. Of course this led me to believe I had stumbled into heaven. A place where they take unwanted and abused pets and recycle them to owners who will love, cherish, and care for them till death do them part, and throw in some young hotties wearing aquamarine SPCA shirts—this could definitely be heaven, or at least my version of it. In fact, now that I am thinking about it, I almost felt like I was at a Hooters restaurant.

CHAPTER SIX

Hooters is one of my all-time favorite restaurants. The first location was opened on October 4, 1983. In my mind this should be considered a national holiday. An annual Hooters holiday could be quite beneficial, especially for men and perhaps some women, not that there's anything wrong with that.

I'd love to go up to my boss and say, "Boss man, remember, tomorrow is a national holiday. It's the Hooters Holiday so I won't be at work tomorrow." Of course that would be an excused, paid absence. What would I do without Hooters? I shudder to even think about it. Hooters now boasts that they have over 440 locations spread out in over forty states in America and in twenty-six other countries. My goal in life is to enjoy every single one of them before I get called home. In 2003, Hooters started their own airline; and in 2006, Hooters opened their own casino in Las Vegas. Who in their right mind would not want to fly the friendly, and I do mean really friendly, skies with the Hooters girls, or want to lose their last buck to a Hooters girl at the card table? So what if that happened to be your home mortgage payment. Isn't it great that you made a Hooters girl happy and while smiling at you she accepts your cash donation to keep the rest of the gals scantily clad? Let's face it, they look great and where else can you whisper sweet nothings into your hot waitresses' ear without getting slapped, "Naked and hot!" That's what I always tell the waitresses, referring to how I want my wings prepared of course. Since opening the first location, Hooters has not looked back.

Now I suppose that, much like Hooters, there was no looking back for me at the SPCA. With my friend Birk by my side, we were ushered in by the SPCA Hooters girls.

A cute young lady walked up to us and said, "May I help you?"

Okay, do I use my usual line: "Sure, honey, how about your name and phone number for starters," or do I act like a semi-normal person and ask where the dogs up for adoption are kept, all the while trying not to drool all over myself?

The answer seemed so clear, so I proceeded to say, "Sure, honey, can...." and then Birk swooped in right before I could finish what I was saying and said, "What my friend really wants to know is where are the dogs up for adoption kept because he is a real animal lover and really wants to rescue a dog, giving him or her the great life he or she deserves."

Then a strange thing happened, well actually two strange things. The first was now that Birk had interrupted what I was going to say, I will never truly know what was going to come out of my mouth. The second was when she heard what Birk just said, a big smile slowly developed on her face, and that was very outstanding. It really made me glad to be American.

To add insult to injury, when Birk noticed her beautiful smiling lips curling upwards, he threw in my line, "And your name and telephone number would be most appreciated." This was even better because now I didn't have to make a fool out of myself if she said no, and I could pretend that I would never say something that inflammatory.

It took just a few seconds while I looked on inquisitively and, if possible, her smile got a little brighter and she said, "My name is Karen and I'll be happy to show you the wonderful selection of dogs we are currently looking to have adopted by deserving people. And when you are through looking, please come see me in my office for that other request you made."

Now Birk was a real handsome guy, and ladies always seem to swoon over him, so I can't say I was completely surprised. Birk just looked at me with that "Don't try this at home" look on his face. Oh, how I hate that look!

Karen then said, "You guys come with me and I'll show you where the dogs are. After that, I'll let you look around on your own and see if something comes to you. Are you looking for puppies, small dogs, larger dogs, or older dogs? Our puppies usually get adopted out very quickly but our older dogs take a bit more time and don't have as much luck. Come on, follow me."

Before we could answer, Karen started to walk in front of us and I noticed that, number one, she was definitely hot enough to be working at Hooters; number two, she definitely knew her way around the SPCA; and number three, she genuinely cared for these animals. Perhaps I had made it to heaven. I never thought I would, but it was sure great to be here.

We walked past the front desk on the left and the SPCA gift shop on the right. They were both manned or should I say womaned by very attractive girls all wearing the aquamarine SPCA tee-shirts, and very nice shirts they were. Somehow when you work or volunteer at the SPCA for the benefit of these helpless animals that just want someone's love and attention, it just makes you beautiful, inside and out.

As I walked past the gift shop I noticed a large selection of really nifty items, so I thought I would try to come back later and look around. Don't get me wrong, I'm not a fan of shopping, but this looked kind of interesting and it was for the good of the animals. Usually I'm an in-and-out shopper. I know what I want beforehand, I go get it, and leave as quickly as humanly possible. I feel that shopping, while may be necessary, is a complete waste of time.

Past the gift shop on the right-hand side were little critters in cages that had windows facing outward. There were mice, hamsters, rats, ferrets, and such. There was a cute little family looking at a big white fluffy bunny rabbit. The family consisted of two cute little teenage girls, a mom, and a dad. They were all smitten with this cat-sized rodent and, as I passed by with Birk on the way to the dog section, I looked at him and said, "Man those things are sure good eating!"

Birk just looked at me like I was a dumbass, which was probably true, and the cute little family looked at me in sheer horror as their mouths dropped open, which then made me say, "What? I'm an active member of PETA, People Eating Tasty Animals." I'm pretty sure that Birk was now thinking I was probably a charter member of PETA's sister group, PTAA. People That Are Assholes!

We kept moving forward and the cute little family, after shooting me dirty looks, rushed in to adopt the rabbit and take him or her home. (I can't tell the difference; they all look and taste the same to me.) They saved the bunny rabbit from becoming someone's rabbit stew meal.

Of course I would never harm an animal; I just don't know when to close my mouth and some good actually came of it with the bunny rabbit going to a good home. I just hope they didn't get hungry, but I won't even think about that.

On the left and running through the middle of the building was a cattery the likes of which reminded me of that classic tale, *The Cat in the Hat*. I don't know much about cats and I'm not really an animal person, but there were some very beautiful cats in the clear cages, facing outward so that they could be seen by everyone who passed by. All of them were clowning around, jumping up and down, or sleeping. There must have been hundreds of them. They were all different sizes and ranged from black to white and every color in between. Fortunately, Birk had not brought me there to adopt a cat, but I could tell they were all very friendly and very well taken care of. I felt certain that most of these cats would be adopted by deserving and caring families. That was my hope and if anyone could make it happen then it would be the hardworking fine Americans at the SPCA.

CHAPTER SEVEN

Then the moment we had been waiting for...well I wasn't really waiting for it but Birk was: we had reached the dog section. On the right just after the small critters was a door leading into a separate room where there were at least fifty stainless steel cages stacked four high and built into the wall. They were all filled with puppies and, as with the cats, they were every size and color. Most were sleeping but some were up making cute little puppy dog noises and playing with puppy toys.

I did not come to the SPCA with Birk to adopt a dog, but I now wished I had not entered that room because I just decided right then and there that my life may perhaps be worthless if I did not adopt every single cute little puppy there and bring them all home with me. When it came to dogs, I found it much easier to tell the difference between male or female. Fortunately for me and the puppies, they always get adopted very quickly. In fact every single cage had a manila card taped to it with the puppy's name, rank, and serial number written on it with the word ADOPTED stamped across it in red ink. The puppies were just waiting to be picked up. I was extremely happy to see that these little babies would have a chance to grow old with their new families.

Unfortunately for the older and larger dogs, their fates were not as promising. They were hurtin' for certain because not as many families were willing to give them a chance. In fact, some might never make it out of the SPCA, but I didn't want to think about that. Next stop, older and larger dogs. I did notice that Birk had somewhat picked up the pace on me. I may have some words with him in just a bit.

Karen turned toward us and told us to walk around and look at the older and larger dogs because she had to go take care of a few things. She then turned and walked off. I caught Birk staring at her so I gave him the ole' Careless elbow.

We entered a door in the very back. It felt similar to when I get seated at a table in the very back of a popular restaurant. This of course always happens to me for a variety of reasons. First, I seldom make reservations. I don't really believe in reservations. Where is the fun in that? Then I would always know where I am going to end up for dinner; and, well, that just gets kind of tedious. I also don't believe in waiting in line for food, so if I happen to go to a restaurant that I just happened to not make reservations at, and if that restaurant had a long line to wait in, I would just mosey on over to another fine establishment. I get variety that way. Second, I'm not famous or popular. Sure, I won the spelling bee in second grade at Red Elementary School but that was really a long time ago so almost no one remembers. In the back next to the kitchen is where I usually sit with all of the other no-names. I really don't mind it back there. I always get to meet the chef and all the great aromas come wafting out of the kitchen. Speaking of wafting, as I entered the door in the back of the SPCA, not only was it kind of dark and gloomy, there as a very bad odor on the horizon. Welcome to large and older dogs.

Now Birk and I found ourselves in a small hallway with doors on both sides and of course the one behind us that we had just come through. If I thought the smell was bad then, the growling, howling, whining, and other precarious dog noises were even worse. I couldn't believe my ears, eyes, or nose. I had a really bad feeling about this but I was also feeling somewhat brave since Birk was with me. I opted for door number two.

Birk opened the door to the right of me and, as it swung open, Birk tried to usher me in. When the door was fully open we were hit with a tsunami tidal wave of dog sounds and a smell similar to a water sewage treatment plant. Let's face it; dogs can be a little stinky. But to be honest, I've known people that have been stinkier than dogs. One time at band camp a kid named Elliot had an accident in his pants, and not the good kind of accident. Every time he walked by we all got a whiff, so he became known as Smelliot. He never admitted it but we knew it was him. The smell coming from the large and older dog area was a picnic compared to that.

The room was probably fifty feet long, thirty feet wide, and painted in drab colors, so I'm sure that had some of the dogs making all kinds of unpleasant noises, even if they were all colorblind. Hell, I was wigging out just a little myself and I had only been there for a few minutes.

There were two rows of dog runs facing one another with a walkway in between. There were twenty dog runs in each row, all filled with dogs. Each dog run, made of cinder blocks and mortar, was painted in a bland, boring, monotone beige color and had chain-link gates on the end of the dog run, keeping the dogs from escaping. In the middle of each dog run was a cinder block wall with an opening to another dog run. There was a board connected to a rope that slid down into little slots that were operated by a guillotine-type pulley system. When the board was in the upright position, the dogs could pass through from one side of the dog run to the other. When the board was in the down position, the dogs remained separated. Most of the dog runs were sliced in half by the boards, giving the dogs about a four-by-six-foot area to be bored shitless and use the facilities in. Don't get me wrong, I'm not complaining about the conditions. Most of the dog runs were very clean with cable TV and a wet bar and I noticed several of the young, very attractive volunteers taking the dogs for walks outside on many occasions. The problem was that they always came back to their "new" home, the dog barrio, at the SPCA.

Birk and I walked along the back row. We had dog runs on one side of us and a wall on the other side. The dogs got all excited to see us whenever we stepped in front of their dog runs. The first dog run held a big brown Labrador retriever. He was really beautiful and must have weighed at least one hundred pounds. On each chain-link gate there were quarter-page manila note cards with the words written, I'M LOOKING FOR A NEW HOME, and then gave the dog's name, rank, and serial number.

The big brown Labrador retriever's name was Bubba. I wondered to myself if it were possible that Bubba was related to President Clinton. President Clinton had a brown Labrador and his nickname was Bubba. Nah, he couldn't be related to President Clinton because, according to the card on the gate of Bubba's dog run, Bubba was from Louisiana, and besides he looked like a Cajun. President Clinton was from Arkansas so there was really no way they could be related. When Birk and I got in front of Bubba's dog run, he started jumping up and down like a Mexican jumping bean. He definitely could have played in the NBA as high as he was jumping. He jumped up and looked me right in the eye.

I turned and looked at Birk and said, "Okay, hold the wedding, I want Bubba! Bubba is going to come home with me right now!"

Birk said, "Bubba is just fine and I am sure he will be a great dog, but let's walk around and look at all of the dogs first and, if you still like Bubba, we'll come back and adopt him."

On the surface this seemed to make sense to me but I kept thinking, *What if someone adopted him while we were walking around and my relationship with Bubba would never have a chance to take off and thrive?* I just knew he was the one that was meant for me, which was really silly because an hour ago I didn't need or even want a dog. Something about this place had connected with my heart, mind, and spirit. The funny thing is—I wasn't even sure that was possible before I walked into the SPCA.

We went to the next dog run and a little white foo foo dog was yipping and running around in circles. I didn't bother to even read the manila card on this dog run. I just shook my head at Birk and kept walking. I'm sure someone would love that dog, but it just wasn't going to be me. I think if I had a pesky little dog like that, it would be something similar to a little mosquito dive-bombing my ear while I continually tried to swat it away. Nope, not for me.

As we strolled along we saw just about every mixture of dog imaginable. There were a lot of Labrador mixes of all colors and even two Great Danes. The Great Danes made me sad because they are such noble, gentle creatures, and to be locked in a small dog run was just unfitting and completely unfair. I wondered to myself how anyone could give up such wonderful, majestic animals, but I knew in my heart that they were just too big for me to take home, and I would never be able to take care of them. As I looked at the manila cards on the gate I saw that their names were Bacchus and Rex. Obviously they were from New Orleans where two of the Mardi Gras parades were named Bacchus and Rex. More Cajuns at the SPCA. Then I spotted something that made me feel much better. ADOPTED was the word stamped in big red letters on each of the cards on the dog run gate. Suddenly all was right in the world.

Birk and I had slowly walked down one aisle and were now halfway down the middle aisle. Still, nothing had caught my eye and I couldn't wait to go back to rescue my new dog, Bubba. There were still plenty of noises and lots of dogs barked as we walked by each run. Some jumped in the air and almost did somersaults. Others just jumped up on the dog run chain-link gate and scared the crap out of us. I couldn't blame them. All they wanted was a little love and affection. They all had the funniest names such as Daisy, Duke, Peanut, Cuddles, Jazz, and so on. I wondered how the people running the shelter knew their names when it was obvious that some of them had been picked up off of the streets so I asked a young attractive volunteer who happened to be standing nearby (wearing a lovely volunteer tee-shirt) as to how they knew the dogs' names.

She just smiled a little and said, "If I tell you a secret, do you promise not to tell anyone?"

I was thinking about what she had just asked for a second. I couldn't decide if she was going to ask me out on a date or just make fun of me, but before I could answer Birk stepped in and blurted out, "Sure, we won't tell anybody, Scout's honor."

"Okay then, we just make up the names when they come in unless someone drops them off and tells us their name, which is not often," she said. "Do you know the most popular reason why people drop their dogs off to us?" she asked with a stern look on her face.

Before I could offer up one of my stupid stock answers she gruffly said, "Going on vacation! Can you believe that? Going on vacation!" She turned around and walked over to help another person who appeared to be falling in love with a dog.

That kind of answered it for me, she was definitely not going to ask me out, but it was a nice thought while it lasted. Birk just looked at me and laughed. At least someone was amused. He was being a jackass, but I knew one thing—I would love to be on vacation with that SPCA volunteer.

We finally got to the last aisle and walked slowly down it. I just knew that no dog was going to catch my eye like Bubba had, and I couldn't wait to tell him the good news, he would be coming home with me. We finished up and I looked at Birk and said, "Let's go pick up Bubba."

He said, "Okay, if he's the one then let's go make his day," and we proceeded to go back to where we had started from, Bubba's dog run.

When we got to Bubba's dog run, the gate was wide open and Bubba was nowhere to be found. I thought, *Man, this dog is smart, he let himself out and escaped*, but that's when it finally hit me. I saw his manila card on the gate and sadly for me but great for him; it had big, bold red letters stamped across it, ADOPTED.

My heart sank. How could this be? We had only taken fifteen or twenty minutes to walk around and see all of the other dogs. I was crushed.

The funny thing is that this morning I didn't even want a dog, but now my heart was broken for a dog I didn't even know and yet couldn't live without. This was definitely not the start of something beautiful. It reminded me of a bride grabbing a wedding dress in the bargain-basement sale of a department store just before another bride came along with her sights set on the exact dress, knowing she had waited all of her life just for that one and only dress, but taking just a moment too long to nab it before someone else did. I'm not a woman, but I am in touch with my feminine side (not that there's anything wrong with that), so I'm pretty sure I know how it feels.

"Come on, Birk, let's go home," I said dejectedly.

"Careless, don't worry about it. We'll come back another day and you'll find your special dog. Let's go grab a brewsky. That will make you feel better," Birk said.

Indeed it would, but only after several. Alas, poor Bubba had left the building.

As we were leaving that noisy, smelly room, the young, very attractive volunteer from earlier came walking toward us. I noticed the smell wasn't as bad as it had been. I wondered if it was because they had recently cleaned up or possibly my olfactory nerves were fried. Perhaps it was the young, pretty volunteer who smelled so good that she created a diversion for my nose.

As the volunteer came up to us she asked, "Didn't find what you were looking for?"

Right about then my normal charming self started to surface and I thought about saying, "Yeah, I sure did, how about we hit some lunch?" but instead my miserable honesty took hold of me and I said, "I found one dog I really wanted. He was a brown Labrador named Bubba and he was really cool, but by the time I got back to him he was already ADOPTED. We're going to come back another day."

She just stood there and looked at me like I was an idiot, and truthfully I must admit that most of the time I am. I started thinking again that I might have a shot with her but all she said was, "Bubba was one of my favorites, too. I loved taking him for walks and I'm glad he was adopted. You know, before you leave, you may want to go through the next section. It's just as big and completely filled with dogs."

Birk and I must have looked pretty stupid. Well, definitely Birk did.

Apparently, door number two led to a whole other section with just as many dogs as the one we were in.

I didn't know it at the time but something unbelievable was about to happen and I had almost walked away from it without even an inkling. It's funny how that works; you make what you think is a small, insignificant choice and it turns out that it may or may not have made a huge impact on your life. Sometimes you get lucky and happen into one of those good situations, as I was about to find out.

Birk and I entered door number two and it was identical to the room we had just come from. The noise and smell were just as bad and the dog runs with the gates and dividers were exactly the same. The only change was a different young volunteer was working on this side and there were a whole bunch of other dogs we hadn't seen yet. Don't get me wrong, this volunteer was just as hot and just as nice as the last one. Of course, I had about the same shot at going out with this one, and that was zero, but that certainly wouldn't stop me from trying. I had my work cut out for me because I needed to practice all my lines and moves to use on my new neighbor, E.D., once I got back to Big Rock Lofts.

We strolled up and down the aisles just as we had done on the reverse side, and there were some really great dogs with some really cute names. Most of them were Labrador mixes but there were some poodles, bloodhounds, a few boxers that were really cute and playful, and even a basset hound with little short stubby legs and ears that dragged the ground. The basset hound was really funny and there was a boxer named Crash crashing into the gate because he wanted out of the joint. I can't say that I blame him and I would definitely keep him in mind, but since I had seen Bubba, nothing really floated my boat.

We finished walking down the first aisle with no luck and had the same results with the second aisle. We got to the third aisle and I guess my mind and heart just weren't into it because I didn't see any dog I was drawn to. Sure, most of the dogs were barking or howling when we walked by and a lot of them jumped up on the gates, but I just wasn't interested. The magic was gone, or so I thought.

I looked at Birk and said, "Let's get out of here."

CHAPTER EIGHT

We were at the end of the aisle next to a window with light streaming in. As Birk and I turned to leave, a warm feeling suddenly came over me, and I felt like I was being watched. This was very strange and when I looked around, I saw in the very last dog run a large, skinny, fawn-colored dog. He had a big head and the most beautiful brown, expressive eyes I had ever seen. He was a large dog but he was quite skinny and I wondered if he was getting enough to eat. It hadn't hit me yet but we were going to meet each other and fall in love.

I continued to walk with Birk and we were going to leave, but something made me look back at that last dog run that was bathed in glowing sunlight. The dog had pressed his body very tightly up against the chain-link gate. His coat was shimmering in the sunlight. He wasn't carrying on like the other hooligan dogs that were making all kind of noises. He just pressed himself up against the chain-link gate, stayed silent, and stared me right in the eyes.

At that point I had not noticed it, but my feet had stopped moving and something was pulling me back to him. Birk walked on ahead and kept our conversation lively but some kind of force or power pulled me back to this dog, and I was compelled to follow it. I don't really know if there is such a thing as divine intervention but this was probably as close as I would ever come to noticing it.

Instinctively, I reached down with both hands and started rubbing the dog's back as I stuck my fingers though the chain-link gate. His short, fawn-colored hair was somewhat coarse and yet soft to the touch and very shiny, almost like gold. I could tell it made him feel good and I realized that all he wanted was for me to come over and pet him. He just wanted to be touched by me and was acting beautifully. I could also tell that, once I started rubbing him, his whole body seemed to relax almost as if a big sigh was coming out of him. No barking or jumping. It didn't take but ten seconds for me to fall in love with him.

I looked at the manila card fastened to the chain-link gate. It read, Name: Dudley, Breed: Boxer, Great Dane mix. Eats dry food and is good with children and other dogs. Primarily kept outside and loves people, likes to play, and ride in car. Loves to snuggle and is very friendly. The card indicated that he was between six and eight months old.

Birk was still walking ahead and chatting with me, even though I hadn't been with him for the last several minutes. I wondered just how long it would take him to figure out that I wasn't walking alongside him anymore. Apparently it didn't take that long because I saw him starting to walk back towards me with a perplexed look on his face.

While rubbing Dudley through the chain-link gate, I looked at Birk and then shifted my gaze back down to Dudley who hadn't broken eye contact with me since the moment I laid eyes on him.

Even though this was much different, I didn't want a repeat of what happened with Bubba. Bubba was okay but he was definitely no Dudley and he was now in the past. I looked back at Birk as he nodded his approval, then looked back at Dudley as he nodded his approval, so I snatched his manila card off of the cage so no one would be able to take him away from me.

It was a weird feeling because I had cared for other animals before but this was different. It was as if the forces of the universe were flowing through us, or I guess it could have just been a bad case of gas, but either way I wasn't letting Dudley out of my sight. I was exhilarated, anxious, and downright scared, but I knew it was the right thing to do. I felt really good about it and I could tell by the look on Birk's face that he was in agreement but still he tested me.

Birk said, "I'm sure he's a fine animal and if you really want to adopt him then that's fine, Careless, but the SPCA receives tons of dogs in here every day and this isn't something you should rush into. Maybe we should think about it and come back tomorrow."

At that point I was clutching Dudley's manila card so tightly in my hand that no one except perhaps God would be able to pry it from my kung fu grip. I firmly told Birk, "Dudley's not an animal, he's my friend and I'm not leaving here without him!"

With one hand on Dudley's back and the other squeezing the manila card, I stood there and stared Birk down in defiance. He finally shook his head up and down and acknowledged that Dudley was the one. A young couple walked by and stopped to look at Dudley. They looked nice enough and I'm sure they were very deserving of a great pet.

Dudley growled somewhat under his breath and I said to them, "He's taken, move along, nothing to see here!" I said it in the nicest way possible but forcefully enough so they got the point. They just frowned a little bit and Dudley helped them along their way with a series of low growls, which they seemed not to appreciate at all. I must admit that Dudley and I were laughing a bit inside. Once they had completely passed by, he became passive again and looked at me as if I were the only person or thing in the room. I'm pretty certain he only had eyes for me and wouldn't be happy until I brought him home.

I was ready to bring him home right then and there, and believe me he was ready to go. He had already packed his bags, locked the door, and fired up the old automobile. Too bad E.D.'s car, Betsy, wasn't here. I know Dudley would have tried to make a getaway in her. Oh, who am I kidding? I knew full well that Dudley's driver's license had expired during his stay at the SPCA but, being that we lived in Houston, I figured if all the illegal aliens drove without a license, then Dudley could as well.

I reached for the latch on the gate and was about to release Dudley from his prison when I heard a voice behind me say, "Hold on, sir, what do you think you're doing?"

I looked back and it was Karen, the young lady who had greeted us when we first entered the SPCA. Should I be clever and try to finesse her or should I just be straightforward and explain to her that my friend had spent enough time in this no-tell motel and that we were going to make a break for it.

Before I could say anything, she said, "Sir, if you want to take him outside or in one of our get to know you rooms," and she stopped speaking and held her hand out, indicating that she wanted the manila card that had previously been on the cage.

I didn't want to let it out of my grip but since I was holding it so tightly that my fingers were turning purple, and since she had a very authoritative and determined look on her face, I relented and reluctantly handed it to her, but only because she was beautiful and smelled so good.

Then she began speaking again, "If you want to take DUDLEY," strongly emphasizing his name while staring me down, almost as if she was undressing me with her eyes, which was quite all right with me and most likely wishful thinking on my part, "then I will have to let him out of his cage for you and walk him to wherever you want, but before I do that you will have to fill out a registration card and pay a sixty-five-dollar fee at the adoption desk," she said.

I didn't want to do this just in case someone adopted him while I was busy filling out paperwork. I wasn't sure my heart could take that.

I was about to explain to Karen that I did not want to miss my opportunity to adopt Dudley while I was filling out forms. I pulled out my pretty thin wallet and offered her a twenty dollar bill to look the other way while Dudley and I made a prison break but she was having none of that.

She told me she would take the manila card to the adoption desk where I had to be interviewed, fill out some paperwork, and pay sixty-five dollars for Dudley. Little did I know this would probably be the best sixty-five dollars I would ever spend.

I looked down and told Dudley I had to leave, but that he shouldn't worry and I'd be right back. He looked a little bummed out and kind of made a bitter beer face. Then he moaned a little bit. It was hard for me to walk away from him but I did so knowing I would be coming right back to get him, and thankful that dogs don't think in terms of time like humans do, so if I was gone for one minute or one week, it would all feel the same to Dudley. He just knew I was gone.

Karen sensed I was uncomfortable leaving Dudley so she told me she would handle the adoption personally instead of leaving me with a total stranger who could never fully understand the deep relationship Dudley and I had. Birk, Karen, and I walked off to get things done. Dudley just stared at me and moaned a bunch. I turned and smiled at him and he smiled back.

We walked through one door and then another to get back to the main part of the building. We walked past the cattery and, just before we reached the front desk, we hung a right, which put us in a small conference room directly behind the front desk. We all sat down at a table and Karen handed me some papers to fill out. It took several minutes but was relatively easy. It was a little easier than a second grade math quiz so I breezed right through it and even answered the extra credit questions. I slid the completed forms across the table to Karen. I was anxious to have my assignment graded so I could go get Dudley and start our lives together. My life of course, was already just dandy without Dudley but I felt like he would really add something to it that had been missing without me even being aware of it.

Little did I know how right I was. What was in store for us was something unbelievable, but I'll get to that later.

Karen took the forms and started looking them over, just as I was looking her over. I couldn't help it; I'm a man. That's my nature. She put the papers down and caught me off guard. I don't remember what I was thinking about exactly at that time but, whatever it was, I knew enough to know I should be embarrassed and turned a bit red for good measure. Karen raised one eyebrow at me and pursed her lips. Birk kicked me under the table and I got semi-normal real fast.

"Mr. Robinson, I see that you have never owned a pet before," she questioned with a puzzled look on her face.

I responded, "That's not exactly true. When I was a freshman in college my roommates and I had a pet cat, although later on that year it was pointed out to us that it was really a rat. We named him Jambalaya. To be fair, we really didn't know the difference until he grew quite sizeable; and you can call me Careless, everyone else does."

"Well, Mr. Robinson," she said, as I broke in right then and exclaimed, "Careless."

She resumed, "Okay, Careless, and what happened to Jambalaya, the rat?"

"Well, once we learned he was a health hazard we went ahead and microwaved him," I said.

At this point Birk broke out in laughter. Now Birk didn't have just any laugh, he had a certified, bonerfied, Cajun laugh. It sounded a little like a chicken getting his neck rung by Granny just before Fried Chicken Sunday. It might have been an octave or two higher but it was every bit as annoying and just lingered on.

Of course I was just kidding about the microwave; it was really a convection oven. Okay, I was kidding about that as well. At this point, Karen was just horrified and had a shocked look on her face. She was about to send me to time-out when I told her I was kidding, that we had really trapped Jambalaya and set him free in a wooded area up the road a ways.

She was not amused and, thankfully, Birk had stopped his hyena laugh.

"Okay, Careless, other than Jambalaya the rat, who I'm going to assume that you and your buddies DID set free, have you ever owned or taken care of another pet or animal?"

Well, now I felt as if I were in front of Judge Karen being cross-examined, which really was not the way I had envisioned being examined by her so I quickly blurted out, "You know, we're all God's creatures, including our pets, and I can assure you that once Dudley and I are together he will be treated as such."

Having said that, Karen's scowl, which she was wearing ever so nicely, began to fade and I do believe that her frown turned upside down. I could tell she was playing nicely into my hands, which was okay because the truth of the matter was that I had already fallen in love with Dudley and I knew he would live as well as I did, which may or may not be a good thing, depending on how you look at it.

Birk was just sitting there in amazement. He couldn't believe how the mood had just changed with that one statement. We're all God's creatures. So true!

"Well, Careless, I see you want to adopt Dudley," Karen said. "Dudley is a large dog. Do you think you will be able to handle such a large animal? Will you be able to exercise him enough and care for him the way he should be cared for?"

I was going to use my stock answer of "We're all God's creatures" again, but I thought playing that card again wouldn't go over too well, so I answered, "I sure do!"

"Okay, Careless, I've got a form here with some questions on it. I'm going to read the questions to you and I want you to really think about them and give me your best answers," Karen said.

I responded, "Are they multiple choice?"

"Not hardly, now let's begin. Careless, what vet will you be bringing Dudley to for his health needs?" she asked.

This was bad. I was getting stumped on the very first question but I couldn't let her know that because I didn't want anything screwing up my adoption of Dudley. He was counting on me and I did not want to disappoint him. I looked Karen right in her very beautiful green, cat-like eyes and said, "Honey, I don't have a vet right now because frankly I have never owned a pet, discounting Birk of course, but he is more of a friend rather than a pet. I was really hoping you would recommend a vet who you approve of so my dear friend Dudley can receive the very best care."

Not only did her standoffish nature disappear, but her very beautiful and delicate lips began to form a smile. Now, Birk was sitting there, rolling his eyes, but Karen didn't even notice him. She was focusing only on me and my answers, which is how it should be. In fact, I was being honest even though I was on my most politically correct behavior.

"Okay, Careless, I like a lot of veterinarians, but I think you and Dudley may be best suited for the Westbury Animal Hospital. One of my favorite veterinarians works there. His name is Dr. L.D. Eckermann and he volunteers a lot of his time here. He is a big supporter of the SPCA and an all-around good guy. One of the benefits of adopting an animal at the SPCA is that your first visit to the Westbury Animal Hospital is free of charge," she said.

I really admired that. It was a wonderful thing the vets did by volunteering. It lowered the cost to the SPCA and helped to get animals adopted to good homes.

Karen continued, "In fact, he may be the one that neuters Dudley."

"Whoa there, slow down a minute, he will do what to whom?" I asked.

"Well, Careless, it is the policy of the SPCA to spay or neuter any animal before it can be adopted. There are so many unwanted animals around that we do not want to contribute to the problem. If you want to adopt your good friend, Dudley, then he will have to first be neutered," she explained in a very serious tone.

"But what if he doesn't want that?" I asked.

"And how would you know that, Careless?" she inquired.

Birk was now getting a little nervous. I could tell he was probably thinking I was going to blow it.

"Well, I asked him just before I left him in Motel Hell and he said he definitely did not want to be neutered, and besides who in their right mind would want to be neutered anyway?" I replied. As I spoke I saw the little smile that had appeared on Karen's face was slipping away along with my chances of adopting Dudley.

"Look, Careless, it's a relatively painless procedure," she said.

I questioned, "Painless for whom?"

"Careless, not only is it painless, it won't affect Dudley at all; and honestly it is the best thing for him. Not only will he be following our procedures and not procreating, thereby not adding to the overpopulation of unwanted pets, it could also very well be saving his life down the road because a neutered animal is much less likely to come down with cancer. If you're not going to breed Dudley, and you're not," she said while staring me squarely in my eyes, "then this is the most humane and healthy choice for him."

Finally, there was a glimmer of hope I could cling to in making my decision about Dudley's yikies while still allowing me to adopt him and get him out of this dreary, drab place. "Are you sure it's painless and that he won't notice that his hoohaas are gone? Are you sure he won't miss them and that the other dogs won't make fun of him?" I asked.

Now Karen was looking at me like I was speaking Chinese, which reminded me, I was getting kind of hungry. All this dog shopping was really wearing me out.

"Careless, Dudley will be just fine; now, can we proceed?" she asked.

I nodded my head yes but I can honestly say that I wasn't feeling good about it. I felt like I was selling my friend down the river, but it was the only way we could be together. If I didn't do it, either he would get adopted by someone else, which I couldn't bear; or if he didn't get adopted in a timely fashion then he may even have to be put down, which was not an option for me. That's a little something they call giving the dog the "blue juice" to make it not sound so bad. I call it the waste of a perfectly good life.

Birk was watching the whole thing in amazement. I am sure he never thought I would make it this far in the interview.

Karen read off another ten questions or so dealing with health issues, food issues, exercise, and wanted me to know that for any reason if Dudley didn't work out I would have to bring him back to the SPCA. I wondered how it would be possible for it not to work out since Dudley and I were made for one another.

I agreed to all of the terms, signed the contract, and paid the sixty-five dollars, which was a real bargain, considering I was getting a new friend and especially since I didn't have many to begin with. I whipped out my wallet and opened it up to put my money to good use.

It is often said that money can't buy you friends, but now I think that might be wrong and it made me revise that Beatles song, "Money CAN Buy You Love." After we finished up and were going our separate ways, I returned to the back part of the shelter where the large and older dogs were kept, to see Dudley one last time before his "operation" and to let him know the really great news that he was coming home with me, and the not-so-great news that part of him would not be coming home with me.

As I approached his jail cell I noticed he was just sitting there as if he were waiting to go. Boy, did he have a disappointment coming to him. As soon as Dudley saw me, he started wagging his tail very quickly in clock-wise large circles, like a helicopter getting ready to take off. This was most unusual because most dogs I have seen wag their tails from side to side, some faster than others, but Dudley's tail was wagging in a complete circle. I had never seen this before. If he rotated his tail any faster, I was worried that we might have lift-off and he would escape before ever making it home with me. Then he did what he had done the last time I saw him. He pressed his body up very closely against the chain-link gate so I could pet and rub him. It was amazing that all this poor animal wanted to do was be loved. He started his low, under-the breath growl, which he had never done to me before. This was odd because I never thought he would act that way toward me, but right then Birk started speaking. He must have snuck up behind me without me noticing while I was tending to Dudley. I really didn't mind that he growled at Birk because, honestly, I did that on a pretty regular basis myself.

I proceeded to tell Dudley the great news and the not-so-great news. He was very excited that he would be coming home with me, but not too thrilled about losing something he had become so attached to.

Birk was getting kind of restless and was ready to get going. I told Dudley goodbye and I would be along tomorrow to collect him from The Bates Motel. I withdrew my hand and started my retreat, which was really not very easy.

Dudley just stared at me and gave a sigh and moan while starting to sit down. I knew he was sad and I wanted to rush over to console him but I knew it was time for me to leave. Besides, I would be back in just one day to take him home.

Birk and I walked through both sets of doors to get out of the area that held the large and older dogs and started to make our way toward the front of the building and on to the parking lot. We passed by the puppy room on the left side and the cattery on the right. As we passed the rabbits and rodents Birk said, "You know that dog sure is skinny. We're going to need to fatten him up."

I nodded my head in agreement. I didn't feel much like talking. I felt kind of guilty, but I knew that was just my guilt gene kicking in overtime so I chose to ignore it. We left the building.

Karen was leaning her super-fine body up against a stone wall outside in front and waved to us. I guess she was on a break so I decided to try one last time just in case she had changed her mind and had finally realized that she couldn't live without me. Birk told me later that everything I had said to her came out sounding like Mush Mouth on the *Fat Albert Show*. Am I able to still use the word fat? I'm not really sure anymore so I'll just say *The Weight-Challenged Albert Show*. I hope she had a secret decoder ring. I did however manage to blurt out my telephone number to her in broken English. So much for public speaking.

She told me she was not really interested but did appreciate that I had adopted Dudley. She told me that, sadly, Dudley and others like him were scheduled to be put down in two more days to make room for a bunch of new arrivals, and I had literally saved his life. Mentally, I was trying to determine as to whose life had really been saved, mine or Dudley's. Only time will tell.

I said goodbye to Karen and noticed by her facial expression that she was deep in thought. Perhaps she was memorizing my telephone number I had just given to her. A guy can dream!

CHAPTER NINE

Birk and I walked across the parking lot to his own personal bus, the Cowboy Cadillac, the Ford F350, Super Cab, Long Bed, 4 X 4, dually pick-up truck. As I climbed up without the help of a much-needed stepladder, I kept looking around for the tanker to pull up alongside us to fill up the truck so it could continue to run. Birk climbed in, buckled up, strapped on his aviator sunglasses, and cranked that truck right up. It belched out a puff of gray smoke from the oversized dual chrome tail pipes as he slammed it in gear. Away we went, and I must admit, I was a little sad to be leaving the SPCA empty-handed. That would change soon enough.

Birk cranked up the radio and off we sped back to my loft. A local band was playing one of their new hit songs, "Goodbye Kate." The band's name was Jake Harm and the Holdouts. Birk got all excited and started singing along with the radio. Now his laugh was bad enough, possibly causing global devastation, but his singing, well let me just say that it was unworldly and very, very hard on the ears.

"Excuse me, Birk, but would you please yank out my fingernails rather than make me listen to that excruciatingly painful noise emanating from your mouth?" I asked. "It's making my ears bleed." My ears were definitely hurtin' for certain.

Birk got annoyed and glanced at me, asking, "Okay, fine, you want to be that way? I have tickets to go see Jake Harm and the Holdouts at the Houston Livestock Show and Rodeo that only comes once a year. They're playing on the field level at The Hide Out in the Astrodome and the tickets are sold out. I was going to take you with me but now I'm not so sure about that!"

At that point he wore a very smug look on his face as if he had just told me off. I decided to ignore him since he was being a jackass. There was very little traffic so it only took us about twenty minutes to get back to the loft. It is very amusing to see how regular cars, and by that I mean normal-size cars, quickly shimmy to one side or the other when they see an oversized Cowboy Cadillac barreling down on them. It certainly does cut down on your driving time. I guess that is definitely one advantage to driving a school-bus-sized pickup truck. At least I knew if we ever had an accident in Birk's truck, there was a ninety-nine-point-nine-percent chance we would live to tell about it.

We pulled up in front of Big Rock Lofts and I reached for the door, opened it, and I started my climb down to leave. Birk looked at me and asked, "Well, you want to go or not?"

I was thinking about telling him where to go, but I played along and asked, "Go where?"

He got all bent out of shape and said, "Haven't you been listening to me? I have tickets to see Jake Harm and the Holdouts in the Astrodome!"

I replied, "How could I hear you when you shattered my eardrums with that thing you call singing?" Then I cracked a big smile on my face. Sometimes I can be quite funny, or so I thought.

"Very funny, Careless, are you in or out?" he asked.

"Wouldn't miss it for the world. Thanks for thinking about me," I said.

Once I was safely back on the ground, Birk hit the gas before I even had a chance to close the door. The centripetal force from the acceleration closed the door just fine as Birk sped off, listening to more of Jake Harm and the Holdouts.

As soon as the dust cleared I made out a silhouette of a person up ahead standing next to E.D.'s big blue Oldsmobile submarine named Betsy. I wondered why in the world someone would name their car, and if they were to name their car then why would it be a stupid name like Betsy? Why not name it Cher, Susan, or Lisa? I'm sure Betsy felt funny about her given name and would love to go down to the courthouse and legally change her name to something a little more normal. I know that's probably not going to happen. Was E.D. already getting her car broken into on the first day she moved in? That would be novel.

As I cautiously approached Betsy to see what was going on, I noticed a cute little person wearing tight little red shorts, leaning halfway in the car, pulling out boxes. As it turned out, it was E.D. unloading her car. She backed out of the car with a box in her arms. She had changed clothes or at least had shed some, which was just fine with me. She had pulled her long flowing blonde hair back in a ponytail and, in addition to wearing her short little red shorts, she had on a matching red bikini top and was wearing a pair of leather sandals, all of which were extremely revealing.

She looked up at me and said, "Careless, now I know I told you to unload Betsy for me. Do you have a hearing problem or are you just a dumbass?"

"I'm afraid a little of both, but I will say that I am enjoying your over-the-shoulder boulder holder," I responded.

"Don't worry, you're never going to see the girls," as she gestured downwards, tilting her head somewhat. "Now get off your ass and grab some boxes so we can get Betsy unloaded today," she barked.

I tried to explain to her that I intended to unload Betsy earlier but she had left the car doors locked. E.D. was having none of that. I wanted to grab something else but instead she handed me a box she had pulled out of the backseat of the car and then turned to grab another one. With a large box in her arms she walked toward the loft, and I followed her. Honestly, I never really cared for manual labor but the view behind E.D. made it a little more tolerable. This really was not going to be as bad as I thought. Hell, I might be able to do this all day.

Without turning her head around, E.D. said, "Quit staring at my ass. And don't say you're not, because I know you are!"

I'm not sure exactly how she knew that and, while I was trying to think of a snappy come back, I couldn't because I was too busy staring at her ass.

I carried the box behind E.D. to the third floor. Her loft was literally right above mine. The door was cracked open a bit and when E.D. got to it she gave it a kick with her foot and it swung fully open.

I walked in behind her and, to my surprise, most of her furniture was already in place. There were several boxes of things scattered all around the loft. The layout was very similar to mine. There was one large room as you walk in and a small bedroom off to the left. "Don't worry, Careless, you won't be spending any time in there," E.D. said, laughing as she noticed me checking out her bedroom.

Off to the right was a small kitchen area and small table with chairs for dining. In the middle of the large room she had placed a nice-looking gray sofa just big enough to sleep on, with a coffee table in front of it smattered with a few books no one would probably ever look at. I did not notice a television. There were two great big old windows looking out to the front of the building just as I had in my loft. It appeared that over the years the window frames had been painted over, so I was reasonably sure she wouldn't be using these windows any time soon.

"Careless, why are you just staring out of the window when I have so much work for you to do? Now, let's get busy and when I say 'let's' I'm referring to you!" she barked.

I left her loft and trudged down the stairs to empty out Betsy and bring her contents back up to E.D.'s loft. I made at least ten trips back and forth and then I started remembering why I hated manual labor so much. I couldn't believe how much crap she had stuffed into her car or where she was going to put it all. Hell, her damn car was almost as big as her apartment. Then I started thinking crazy things like, she could have saved a ton of money and just lived in her car instead of leasing a loft. Of course the obvious two things wrong with that were: number one, no indoor plumbing, and number two, I would not be able to check out the hot girl who just happened to live above me. It's really a bonus for me when I think things through to their natural conclusions.

I brought the last box up and E.D. had me place it in the bedroom. "All finished, darlin'. I'm ready for my tip," I said.

"Here's a tip for you, Careless: next time get paid in advance," E.D. said. She walked over to me, placed both her arms over my shoulders, and kissed my cheek. "Now run along and play."

Good enough for me. "Paid in full," I informed her.

She released me and stated, "I just knew you were going to work cheap. Don't you worry, I'll have plenty of more jobs for you."

I started to walk out and I turned just a bit and looked back, "Hey, E.D., I didn't catch your last name," I inquired.

"That's right, now get moving before you irritate me," she said.

I knew enough to know neither of us wanted that, especially me. I left her loft and started down the stairs but as I got closer to my loft I started hearing familiar wailings coming from a distant place, a place somewhere back in time…, "Wow, how, how, how…, yeah, heh, heh, heh, heh!"

Of course it occurred to me that it was just Sarge probably making a new discovery for mankind.

CHAPTER TEN

I walked up to my door with the number 158 stenciled on it with white spray paint. Nothing fancy here but you do get what you pay for. Big Rock Lofts is ideally located so that I could get to all my destinations in Houston rather easily. I can get on any major freeway from my loft within five minutes and could be at most sporting events, concerts, restaurants, or movies in five-to-ten minutes. I drive an old Dodge Power Wagon, similar to the one my very dear friend, Floyd Potter Sr., used to drive. It is really just a half-ton pickup truck with a locking camper shell on the back. Mine is a four-wheel drive model and kind of a tan color. It has been through the wringer, but is still very sturdy and solid as a rock. It has a really cool, shiny silver ram's head with big curled buck horns mounted in the front on top of the hood. The ram is about the only thing shiny on the truck, but it drives just fine and even has air conditioning and heat. It has limited power steering and manual windows, but that doesn't bother me because I have a killer stereo in it and I wasn't really trying to impress anyone anyway, except for maybe E.D.

I had my first encounter with Floyd when I was a child attending a ranch camp for boys and girls in Medina, Texas. It was called Echo Hill Ranch, named after the hill the cabins and main flat backed up to. It was remote and didn't offer any fancy things. The children were offered a variety of activities such as swimming in the chilly, spring-fed Wallace Creek, horseback riding on multiple trails in the untouched wilderness, riflery, archery, hiking, and arts and crafts. There was indoor plumbing but no air conditioning or heating, no telephones, no computers, or electrical gadgets of any kind.

At camp everyone learned how to live off of the land and become self-sufficient while preserving the environment. One of the camp mottos was, "Always leave a place cleaner than you found it." We called that the law of the West. I'll never forget the first day I arrived at the camp. I was six years old and took a four-hour bus ride from Houston. I got off of the bus at the camp, but we arrived early so only a few kids were there. My counselor showed me to the meager bunkhouse and told me to grab the bed of my choice and to throw my bags on it to mark it as taken. I did that and walked out of the bunk to have a look around. I was curious and of course a little bit nervous, especially since I had never been to camp before, much less slept anywhere except my own house.

I started to walk across the flat. Everything looked so large to me. I thought to myself that this was the biggest place I had ever seen. There were several buildings across the flat just on the edge of a ravine that led down to Wallace Creek. Wallace Creek ran through the property and was also where I hoped to swim one day soon.

I couldn't decide which building to go explore first so I just chose one at random. I walked into a hut that had no doors and no back walls. It smelled kind of strange and there were cages lined up on tables with shelves stacked three high, running all the way across. The cages all had glass fronts and of course I moved in as quickly as possible to see what was in the cages. Well, I got so excited I almost fell out. Just about every cage had some type of reptile in it, the majority of them being snakes. I did not know it at the time, but many of the snakes were poisonous, very poisonous. The only snakes I had ever seen in the big city were people, so this was a new experience for me.

I had never seen anything like this before. As I approached the first cage, which I think may have been just a modified fish tank with a lid on it, the snake in the cage started vigorously shaking his tail back and forth. To my amazement I heard a loud and vigorous rattling sound. To say that I was a kid in a candy shop would not do this situation justice. As I looked around, I noticed all kind of snakes—some very beautiful in color. There was even a Gila monster, which is one of the most beautiful lizards I have ever seen. Gila monsters can grow up to two feet in length and look like they are made up of tiny little orange and black beads. Although they are pretty, they are venomous. With childish stupidity, I slowly drew my hand back and made a fist to knock my knuckles against the front glass of the cage just to see how the noisy snake would respond. As my hand started forward I heard a booming voice behind me ask, "Can I help you?"

I froze and at first I thought maybe God was talking to me, similar to the way he spoke to Moses at the burning bush. The voice seemed to be coming from above and I hadn't seen anyone in the hut with me so that sounded about as good of an explanation as any. Since I wasn't really that religious anyway, I decided to turn around and see if I could find where the voice was coming from.

I had quite the scare when I found a large muscular man standing directly behind me. I had no idea where he had come from because I certainly didn't see him when I first walked in. I think I would have noticed a man of his stature but maybe I was so excited to see all those animals I had overlooked him. He had short-cropped, dark-brown hair that was neatly combed back. His eyes were brown behind thick black-framed glasses similar to the ones Sarge wears. He was wearing a white tee-shirt that had a round Echo Hill Ranch emblem on it with a sticker that said, Hello, My Name Is: Uncle Floyd. His light brown hiking shorts were held up by a belt with a triangular Echo Hill Ranch emblem on the brass belt buckle, and he wore brown, leather hiking boots with ankle-high socks. There was a small portion of an unlit cigar hanging out of his mouth, which he was chewing on. He seemed larger than life and his presence filled the little shack.

"I'm Uncle Floyd, and you are?" his booming voice echoed while he waited for my answer. I didn't speak at first because I wasn't sure what to say and I thought I was probably dead meat on a toilet seat. I was sure I was in big trouble by being somewhere I was not supposed to be, plus I was just about to do a knock-knock joke to something I later found out was a rattlesnake.

Finally, I mustered up enough courage to tell Uncle Floyd that my name was Cary and I was from Houston, Texas.

"Well, Cary, we don't tease animals. It's wrong to do that and you could get hurt very badly if you don't respect them. This is the Nature Shack and I will be teaching you about animals. These particular snakes are all poisonous and just one bite could even kill you. That is a rattlesnake you were about to anger, and it strikes at anything that moves. If you make him really angry he might strike the glass cage hard enough to break through it. Then it's just you and the poisonous rattlesnake. You wouldn't like that now, would you?" Uncle Floyd asked.

I said nothing and just shook my head to answer no.

Floyd was an amazing man. All of his collected snakes in the Nature

Shack came from the wild. He caught all of his own specimens. Later that summer while I was on a nature hike in the woods with Uncle Floyd in the lead and seven other campers, he came to a dead stop. He held his hand up for no one to move and told everyone to hold still and be quiet.

He went back to where we had all just walked and stopped, reached his hand down, and pulled it back up holding onto a six-foot-long Eastern diamondback rattlesnake. It had been covered up with leaves and twigs, and we all had just walked right over it and not even seen it.

Uncle Floyd matter-of-factly placed the serpent into a pillowcase he had looped around his belt, and we continued our nature hike. He was pretty amazing and never showed fear of anything.

As I walked along our nature hike, I kept hearing bells. *Ring ring, ring ring, ring ring.* My daydream came to an end and I realized that so had my time with Uncle Floyd, because he had been called home many years ago. I was sad about that, but I was sure happy to be able to dream about a time when things were a little simpler. It seemed so real. Who knows? Maybe it was real and I'm just dreaming now.

CHAPTER ELEVEN

Ring ring, ring ring. It was just my trusty red-and-white HEB telephone. I picked it up and answered, "Crisis Hotline, please hold for someone who cares."

"Mr. Robinson? Mr. Robinson? CARELESS!" a voice from the not-too-distant past came blaring out.

I poured myself an iced coffee and sat down. "This is Careless, you may begin speaking at the beep," I clowned around.

"Careless, it's Karen from the SPCA," the voice continued.

I knew it! I knew she wanted to go out with me and that she couldn't keep her hands off of me. "Yes, Karen, you don't have to ask me twice, I'll go out with you," I blurted out.

"Careless, that's just not going to happen, but thanks for thinking of me," she quipped. "I have some news about Dudley."

I sat up straight and took notice. "Is Dudley all right? Is everything okay?" I'll admit that I was a little concerned.

"Everything is just fine, Careless," she said.

"Fine for a standard lopit-offa-me operation," I softly muttered. "Is Dudley ready to go? How's he feeling? Has he asked for me yet?" I inquired. Even though I had only met Dudley briefly, I was really missing him and couldn't wait to bring him home.

"Careless, give him one day to recover from the surgery. Just to be safe, we'd like to keep our eye on him for a day; then he'll be ready to come home," she said.

"May I come visit him in the meantime because he phoned me just before I took your call and told me the hospital food there sucks?" I asked.

"Careless, I recommend that you don't visit him because he'll get all excited and we don't need that. Just wait a day and come pick him up," she said.

"Okay, that's fine but where would you like me to take you out for dinner tonight?" I asked.

"Careless, we're not allowed to date clients, I'm sorry," she said.

46

"But once I get Dudley, I will no longer be a client," I lawyered her.

"Oh, okay, in that case, NO, but thank you anyway. I'll see you when you pick up Dudley tomorrow. Come see me and I'll get you checked out. Bye, Careless," she said.

Of course I wasn't listening because mentally I was busy checking her out. Something about a girl with dark hair and green eyes captured my imagination but then all I heard was a dial tone. I guess that was a no.

I was sure excited to be bringing Dudley home the next day. I started cleaning up my loft and moving everything around to make it perfect for Dudley when I heard a knock at the door. Should I answer it or not? I couldn't decide. Nobody likes unexpected visitors. Then there was another knock and that's when I heard, "Yeah, heh, heh, heh, heh."

Sounds like Sarge to me. I started walking toward the door. *Knock knock knock!*

"Okay, Sarge, I'm coming. Keep your pants on," I shouted. I opened the door and there stood Sarge. He was wearing his usual, which was a plain white tee-shirt with a large peace sign in the middle, ragged cut-off blue jean shorts, and leather sandals.

"What's up, Sarge?" I asked.

"Hey, man, han, han, han, han, han, I need to go to the library, man. Can you give me a lift man, han, han, han, han?" he asked.

"Sarge, I'm kind of busy right now. Is it really important?" I asked.

"Well, man, I need to check out some new books. I've finished the ones I got last week," he said.

I had forgotten Sarge read so much. The funny thing is, he is a true wealth of knowledge. It seems all he does is read books and eat. He doesn't even own a television. It isn't because he couldn't have one, he just doesn't believe in television and has no desire to own one. It's not like he couldn't fit one in his apartment with his lack of furniture and décor. He often referred to television as the work of the devil and that it would be the ruination of mankind as we know it. Yes, Sarge is a very deep thinker.

I looked him over closely and he was begging me with his beady little dark eyes from behind those black thick-framed glasses. I really didn't want to go as I was busy dog-proofing my loft. I turned away from Sarge for a moment and let my gaze wander out through the window for a while as I thought about whether I should take Sarge, and about how much he would guilt me if I didn't. I was just preparing to turn around and tell him no when a funny thing happened. The old iron front door of the loft burst open and the most beautiful girl I had ever seen sprinted out of the building in, shall I say, very skimpy jogging attire.

With her beautiful, long blonde hair pulled back in a ponytail, she loped off like very well-developed thoroughbred. Suddenly it hit me that it was E.D. going for a jog. At that moment I got my memory jogged and remembered Sarge was still in my apartment and he wanted to go to the library. He sure was being awfully quiet, but I hatched a plan that on the way to the library, we could "coincidentally" meet up with E.D. since she was jogging in that general direction and as a nice gesture I would happen to have a nice cold bottle of water for her. We would have to do this fast so I didn't lose track of her. I can't believe I moved my butt so quickly for a pretty girl. Maybe for Dudley I would move this quickly but, for a girl, I just couldn't believe it.

I certainly could never tell Birk about this since he would laugh me off the face of the earth. I rapidly turned around to put my plan into motion and started telling Sarge to get ready because we were going to make a trip to the library. After all, a mind is a terrible thing to waste. "Sarge, get your things together and let's get a move on. I'm not getting any younger. Let's hit the library."

While I try not to make a habit of it, I was talking to myself. Sarge had sat down, leaned back against the wall, and gone to sleep. He was definitely in his happy place. There was never a dull moment with Sarge.

"Sarge, Sarge! Wake up, Sarge!" I shouted. "Let's get going to the library. You're not getting any younger," I joked. I clapped my hands together as loudly as possible to make him wake up and to get him moving.

Finally I heard, "Wow, how, how, how, how, how, how," come out of his mouth. We were almost at go time.

"Let's go, Sarge, chop chop," I said while clapping my hands together.

Sarge started to slowly stand up and move toward the door. Where was Dudley when you needed him? This definitely would not have happened on his watch and I was so looking forward to picking him up tomorrow.

Sarge finally made it to his feet and I gently grabbed him by the arm and herded him toward the door. I wasn't going to miss a chance to see my new friend and beautiful neighbor, E.D.

"Yeh, heh, heh, heh, heh, heh, let's go to the library," Sarge muttered. Sarge left my loft and quickly went to his loft right next door to grab his library books so he could return them and check out some new ones. I grabbed a cold bottle of water from the fridge and walked out of my loft. Sarge rejoined me in the hallway with a stack of four or five thick hardbound library books.

We made it down the stairs and out of the old iron door that slammed shut behind us. Sarge and I walked up to the Dodge Power Wagon as I fumbled for the keys. I finally got them in my hand, unlocked my door, got in, and unlocked Sarge's door. Sarge got in and ever so carefully placed his library books on the backseat. We both strapped in and I turned the ignition key, pumped the gas pedal a couple of times, and cranked her up. She started right up with a loud thundering boom followed by a nice, deep, throaty purr. You just can't beat a fine automobile like the Dodge Power Wagon. They definitely don't make them like this anymore.

Dodge started building the Power Wagon for local consumption in 1946 but in fact it had been used during World War II and the Korean War. It was built on a three-quarter ton army truck chassis and had an eight-foot cargo box on the back. They weigh about eighty-seven-hundred pounds and can carry up to three thousand pounds of payload in the bed. It was really more like a tank on wheels. Dodge eventually fazed them out because they didn't comply with new federal safety regulations for light-duty trucks. Of course, nothing about this truck was light, and safety features, there were not too many—other than nobody would be stupid enough to hit a vehicle of such proportions. It was a real shame they are no longer made because they are one bad-ass truck and tough as nails. In my opinion, you just can't find quality like that anymore. It was an oldie but goodie.

Right then I decided that if E.D. could name her car Betsy, I could name my Dodge Power Wagon. I thought about it for a while and decided to name him Clarence. Clarence was a good name, a sturdy name. I remembered that Clarence was the name of an angel in the classic Christmas movie, *It's a Wonderful Life*. How many times have I seen that movie? Way too numerous to count.

Clarence was also one of my favorite characters on *Leave It to Beaver*. On that show, Clarence was one of Beaver's brother's friends. They called him Lumpy for short, but I digress. Beaver's brother's name was Wally and

I wondered why any parent would stick his kid with a name like Wally. You know Wally probably got beat up every day or stuffed in a locker at school just because his name was Wally. Perhaps he even received the classic swirly.

Regardless, I just knew if Betsy met Clarence, they would probably fall in love, and of course E.D. would then follow suit and have no choice but to fall in love with me so that Betsy and Clarence could spend some quality time together. This really could end up being a great romance novel, or how about a hit movie, *When Clarence met Betsy*. It could happen. I hope Sarge didn't want me to help him with his library books. Maybe he could just leave it to Beaver.

CHAPTER TWELVE

Sarge and I rolled down our windows and I cranked up the radio. The Jake Harm and the Holdouts song, "The Ballad of Colton and Eli," was playing as we drove off. It told the story of a young American hero lost to war and how his best friend, Eli, a service dog, was decommissioned by the Marine Corp to live the rest of his life with Colton's family. It was a really touching song that spoke to the heart. We continued on as I began looking for my true love, E.D., while Sarge was looking for his true love, library books. I wondered if either of us would ever find true love and, if so, how long it would take. I was certain Sarge would be the first, and so he would as we drove toward the library.

While driving I was looking high and low for E.D. but I didn't see her anywhere. I continued to scan for her as we drove. We drove up and down just about every street, and a few more we shouldn't have, to catch a glimpse of E.D. While I wasn't quite ready to give up, Sarge finally piped up, "Hey, man, han, han, han, han, I think the library is in the other direction. Do you know where you're going, man, han, han, han?"

"Yeah, Sarge, I was just taking the scenic route. Keep your pants on," I said. To be honest there wasn't anything scenic about it, just some office buildings and a few homeless people scattered here and there. The only thing that could make this route more scenic would be a beautiful blonde girl in jogging attire moving gracefully through the streets, but as luck would have it that was not going to happen today.

My plan had failed miserably as is often the case. We pulled up in front of the downtown library as I negotiated a parking spot. Sarge was getting a little glimmer in his eye. I could tell he was happy, and I determined that maybe my plan had worked after all. I didn't get to see E.D. but I did do a good deed and it was obvious I made Sarge's day.

Sarge and I exited the Power Wagon, I locked the door, and we started to walk in. The Houston downtown library is really an amazing place—a beautiful, three-story, modern brown-brick building. Located at 500

McKinney, it is on the outskirts of downtown right next to the Ideson building, which was the home of the first Houston Library until it became too small. The Ideson building was named after Julia Ideson by the Houston City Council in 1951. Julia was born on July 15, 1880, in Hastings, Nebraska, and moved to Houston when she was twelve years old. In 1903 she was hired as a librarian at the Houston Lyceum. She traveled extensively and was the first woman in Houston to be listed in *Who's Who in America*. She was also a suffragette and brought many speakers to the city of Houston, some being quite controversial for the time. Julia was called home on July 15, 1945. She had been in charge of the Houston Public Library for forty-two years. A historical marker was placed in front of the Ideson building in honor of Julia's contribution.

This fantastic library was completed in 1975 and opened in 1976. In 1989 it became known as the Jesse H. Jones Library in honor of gift endowments from Jesse H. Jones. Jesse H. Jones was born the son of a tobacco farmer on April 5, 1874. When he turned nineteen he moved to Dallas to manage his uncle's lumberyard. From there, he moved back to Houston in 1898 where he started the South Texas Lumber Company. He also built and sold homes. In 1907 he built the ten-story Texaco building in downtown Houston and built the seven-story Bristol Hotel. Later he built the Houston Chronicle building and the Rice Hotel, which at that time was one of Houston's finest hotels. He also built several large office buildings in downtown Houston. Jesse was very accomplished and later became chairman of the Texas Trust Company, president of The National Bank of Commerce, and a majority shareholder in Humble Oil & Refining and the Houston Ship Channel. He was very active in politics and the American Red Cross. Jesse became chairman of the Reconstruction Finance Company that helped support many American businesses and helped finance many public works programs. He was also involved with the Federal Loan Agency, Federal Housing Authority, and the Home Owners Loan Corporation. In 1940 Jesse became the secretary of Commerce and remained very active. On June 1, 1956, Jesse was called home, but schools, parks, bridges, and even the Houston Symphony Hall were named after him.

Sarge and I walked into the library through automatic doors like the kind found at supermarkets. After we entered, the doors started to close behind us, and Sarge turned around and became very interested in watching them close. That was probably just a nervous reaction or some sort of compulsive fascination he had developed over the years.

Sarge finally snapped out of it and we walked up to the front desk where an elderly woman looked over her glasses and down her nose at us. With a stern look on her face, she asked if she could help us.

"Yes, ma'am, my friend and I would like to know what section the new release movies are in, preferably ones with a lot of action," I inquired, being the smartass I was while Sarge's mouth dropped open in disbelief.

The good librarian then went on to tell me that while this wasn't Blockbuster Video, in 1995 the entire library catalog had become computerized and not only could we find whatever we were looking for on the library computer, but we could also have access by computer to the complete collection from any other Houston library branch. She seemed quite proud of that and indeed it was a great accomplishment.

I thanked the librarian for the great news and told her my friend was ready to turn in some books and to check out some new ones. As I turned to look at him while motioning him forward to place his books on the countertop to be returned, he still had his mouth wide open and had a bizarre look on his face.

I said, "Look, Sarge, I'm sorry about the Blockbuster Video crack. I was just trying to make a joke at someone else's expense."

"No, man, han, han, han, han, you don't understand," he said as he pointed up to the second story with a stupefied look on his face. There was a big opening between the floors at the second and third levels of the library that allowed them to be seen through from the bottom floor. As he pointed to the second floor I could see he was eyeballing a rather attractive young blonde-headed girl in jogging attire. Her back was turned to us.

Could it be? Did I drive all up and down the streets of Houston looking for E.D. and it turns out she is right here in front me? If this were really her, then what was she doing here? And since I had been looking high and low for her, could this be a sign from above that we were meant to be? It didn't really matter because in my mind, that's exactly how I rationalized it.

I turned to Sarge and now he was staring off in the distance at something he loved even more than beautiful women, and that was library books. Sarge had the need to read and he retained everything he had ever laid eyes on. It was quite amazing. I had heard about people like Sarge but he was the first person I actually knew that had this remarkable ability, or affliction, depending on how you look at it.

"Sarge, why don't you let me turn those books in for you so you can pick out some new ones," I coaxed him. He looked a little puzzled and rightly so for Careless had a plan.

Sarge looked at me, then down at the books he was meant to turn in, and then behind him where three stories of books were just waiting for his perusal. This went on three more times. After the fourth time and possibly a case of whiplash I sternly looked at him and yelled, "Sarge, snap out of it!"

It was as if someone had flicked him in his temple and his thought process was looping over and over. Finally, he extended his arms and started to hand me the books to be turned in. I extended my arms in kind and as he began placing them in my arms they "accidentally" slipped right through and smacked the floor just right to make the loudest slapping sound you have ever heard. It reverberated around the very quiet library through all three floors. Suddenly, my mind reverted back to summer camp in Medina, Texas, listening to the happy children's voices echoing off of the surrounding hills.

That thought process didn't last too long because Sarge was looking at me in horror. That nice, sweet, seasoned citizen behind the library desk was not too amused either. I quickly assessed the situation. The books were completely undamaged other than the thunderous slap that was still echoing its way around the entire library. That's when I kicked my plan into high gear. I quickly composed myself to look as cool as possible, if indeed that was even possible. Just as the loud noise from the books was echoing around the library, I adjusted my hair just right, did a package check, leaned slightly back on the library counter and looked straight up at E.D. with a large, boyish, shit-eating grin on my face. The acoustics in the library were spectacular.

She was already looking in my direction and, right then, our eyes met. She began to giggle and placed her hand over her mouth ever so slightly so as not to let on that she was amused, but she couldn't quite contain her glee or her beauty. She looked around quickly to make sure nobody was watching her looking at the idiot that had just created a sound that could possibly have been a four-point-five on the Richter scale.

After carefully surveying the landscape, E.D. moved her hand away from her mouth and motioned for me to come up to where she was. She still had a smile as big as Texas plastered across her face. I bent over and quickly gathered up the very loud books. I told Sarge how sorry I was and that it was just an accident, but he was already in La La Land, eyeballing a bunch of books and, for all I knew, he didn't even know that anyone else was in the library with him.

I turned and gently handed the books to the slightly irritated, impatient person working behind the counter. She was impersonating a librarian. I apologized rather profusely and I think she may have forgiven me. All I heard was *hmmmph!* I was going to take that as a good to go. She placed the books down and just before I left to go join my true love, E.D., I pulled my arm into my shirt like a turtle pulling his arm back into his shell and proceeded to polish the front cover of the top book. It was an old completely worn out copy of the 1950's Ayn Rand novel, *Atlas Shrugged*. I cracked a half smile and raised one eyebrow, hoping to elicit a response, and the very nice librarian behind the counter shook her head a little and made an abbreviated smile as if to say *Okay, you're forgiven now get out of my face while you go find your true love.* That's the way I saw it. She was really just an old-fashioned romantic, so I proceeded on.

Sarge had already disappeared, searching for books he had not had the pleasure of being introduced to yet, but I was hopeful of getting him out of the library before closing time. I looked around and found an escalator ascending to the second floor. I walked over and began my ride up to heaven or at least my version of it.

E.D. was waiting for me at the top. "What the hell are you doing here, Carrot?" she asked.

"That would be Careless," I corrected her.

"Whatever," she exclaimed.

I quickly looked around and surveyed the surroundings. My keen intellect told me there was a photography exhibit about to open on the second floor; and since it appeared that E.D. was there directing where all of the photographs were to be hung I assumed that: one, either she was the artist; two, she was the director of the library; or three, she was the artist's agent. Since I was certain she was not the director of the library, I had a fifty-fifty shot at which remaining deduction was right, so I went with the most obvious. "Well, as matter of fact, I heard there was going to be a photography exhibit by an excellent, up-and-coming artist and there was very little I could do to keep myself away," I chirped.

Right then E.D. got a perplexed look on her face so I knew I had hit the jackpot and made the right call. Now, not only was she going to fall head over heels in love with me, she was also going to think I was some sort of psychic genius or something.

"That is so kind of you, Careless. Thank you so much, but how did you know about my show when it hasn't even been announced yet and I myself have told no one?" she asked inquisitively.

She paused and was studying me, waiting for what type of a response I would give. In my mind, I was thinking I had to take the good with the bad. On one hand, I had nailed the call that this was E.D.'s photography exhibit, and on the other hand she had me dead on about how I could possibly know about her exhibit when it had not even been announced yet and there was also the little fact that she had told no one about it. Facts are stubborn things, as John Adams once said.

Anyone else might look at this as a dilemma, but not Careless. "Well, if you must know, my powers of deductive reasoning are always on red alert. For instance, when you moved into the loft I noticed as I was carrying in your complete belongings that you had several perfectly framed black-and-white photographs. This was a tale-tell sign that: one, either you are a collector; two, you are a photographer; or three, you are both. I also noticed, again while I was bringing up your entire life's belongings to your loft, that as you were unpacking, you hung up a worn khaki vest with a lot of pockets in your closet. This told me you were either a fisherman or a photographer. Since you did not smell fishy, I cleverly assumed you were a photographer. I also noticed the very tip of your right index finger was slightly more calloused than your other fingers, indicating that you use the tip of your right index finger more so than any of your other fingers, most likely to depress the shutter button of a single refractive lens camera. How am I doing so far?" I asked as I watched her mouth drop open with an even more puzzled look on her face.

"I also noticed that as you are going about your everyday business, you occasionally do a double take, which indicates to me that you are framing up a photograph in your mind and you are concentrating so hard on that image that nothing else is registering with you at that time," I said.

Now she was like putty in my hands. She quickly gathered her wits about her, gave a curt little smile, and said, "Nice try, Car Lot, but I know that was just a lucky guess."

Was it? I wonder. How did I know all of that and why did I not think of it sooner so I could have used this information to benefit myself? Maybe I was keenly aware of the details surrounding me and just never realized it. "That's Careless," I said quietly as I was deflated after E.D. brought me back down to Earth.

Once we both got over my keen intuitiveness, E.D. showed me around her photography exhibit. Her work took up almost all of the walls on the entire second floor of the library and even though I didn't know much about art or photography, I had to admit that E.D.'s work was nothing short of spectacular. She had at least twenty photographs on the walls and they were taken of anything from nature shots to buildings and structures. Some were rendered in black and white, which made them look almost antique and nostalgic, and some were rendered in full color, using every vibrant color of the spectrum, almost as if they had been painted on a canvas.

I was literally stunned at how fantastic E.D.'s photographs were and at how she caught life and images with her camera that most people just simply passed by and missed. Talented and beautiful, that's why she loved me so much, or would one day.

As we walked from photograph to photograph she explained each one to me, where it was taken, and what she was thinking at the time she viewed the image and shot the photograph. I was actually learning a lot about my future bride, but as we got to the last photograph I must admit that it caught my attention. It was an enlarged photograph of the Astrodome printed in black and white with the sun setting right behind it. The sunlight at that certain time of the day made all of the little side-by-side-windows that made up the roof of the Astrodome sparkle, making them look like twinkling stars in the night sky, except of course, it was daytime.

I noticed that one of the little windows was not sparkling like the others, but I didn't give it a second thought until much later. The photograph was framed and matted beautifully in black and white as well, and it was simply majestic. Something about this beautiful photograph really garnered my attention, something I couldn't quite put my finger on, but for now I focused my attention on E.D. It was strange that as many years as I had lived in Houston, I had never seen the Astrodome before in that manner. That really opened my eyes as to what I could possibly be missing as I trudged through life in Houston, Texas.

CHAPTER THIRTEEN

The Astrodome in Houston was dubbed as the "eighth wonder of the world" by Judge Roy Hofheinz back when it was opened on April 9, 1965. Judge Roy Hofheinz was probably the largest driving force behind having the Astrodome built along with what he called the Astrodomain, which included a baseball and football stadium called the Astrodome, a large arena called the Astrohall, a theme park named Astroworld, and several hotels surrounding the area. Roy Hofheinz was born on April 10, 1912. His father was a laundry truck driver who died while the judge was still a young boy. Afterwards, he went to work to help support his family while receiving an education from Rice University and later from the University of Houston, and the University of Houston Law School. Later he became a Texas Harris County judge, a controversial mayor of the City of Houston, a campaign manager for President Lyndon B. Johnson, a United States congressman, and a United States senator.

Judge Hofheinz was flamboyant and a terrific orator. He helped create the National League baseball team, The Colt .45s, that later became the Houston Astros. He was a developer and avid sportsman. The judge helped pioneer FM radio and held interests in several FM radio and television networks. He even co-owned Ringling Brothers and Barnum & Bailey Circus at some point in time. For all of you Bubba's out there, he helped develop Astroturf for the back of your pickup trucks. The judge had a very interesting life. He was called home on November 22, 1982.

On January 3, 1962, after three bond issues to build the world's first domed, all-weather stadium, and many lawsuits later, the groundbreaking ceremony took place. Many Harris County commissioners fired Colt .45 handguns filled with blanks into the ground at the ceremony to commission the Astrodome and to welcome the Colt .45 baseball team to Houston. There's nothing like giving handguns to a bunch of politicians! There's a thought that we could probably all do without.

The actual construction of the Astrodome began in July of 1963. It was an interesting construction site that drew a lot of fanfare and media. Large cranes erected steel beams, and the outline of the world's first domed stadium started to take place with eighteen stories of arches. Soon enough the Dome Dogs would be cooking, and Dome Foam would start flowing. In 1965 that is just what happened in the first home opener game where the New York Yankees were beaten by the Colt .45s. The reverend, Billy Graham, said that the Astrodome was "a tribute to the boundless imagination of man."

The judge had luxury boxes built into the Astrodome and boxes just for the sportscasters. He extended the seating area behind the dugouts to get the fans a little closer to the players and, to top it off, he had a two-million-dollar scoreboard put in, the most expensive of its kind at that time. The Astrodome shaped up nicely and held baseball and football games, concerts, rodeos, boxing matches, tennis matches, soccer matches, bull fights, motorcycle races, car races, and destruction derbies.

The judge was rumored to have cleverly built himself a residence in the Astrodome to live in and, in fact, was said to live there for several years. His quarters were said to be three stories in height and built right into the Astrodome wall about seventy-five feet above right field. If true, his view from his perch would have been the whole baseball field covered in Astroturf.

The judge was also rumored to have a lavishly decorated office, a one-lane bowling alley, a movie theater, a putting green, a barbershop, and a billiard room, and it was rumored that President Lyndon B. Johnson slept there on occasion. The judge was rumored to live in this large, well-decorated area for many years and very few were ever able to have even seen it, if indeed it truly existed. Most people had never even heard the rumors of its existence. An elevator would have been needed to get to the judge's abode, and the entrance was said to be cleverly hidden behind a door in a food court area of the Astrodome. My guess is that the elevator had a note affixed to it that read something like: Danger—Service Elevator—Out of Order. That would be fitting, seeing that he was a judge.

CHAPTER FOURTEEN

After I had finished the grand tour of the photography exhibit on the second floor of the library with E.D., I told her that her work was just lovely and that she was very talented. I told her it was amazing to me that someone as beautiful and talented as she was would even be interested in me. She, of course, agreed wholeheartedly, although I'm not quite sure what that meant. Perhaps I would have to use my powerful psychic abilities to figure this one out, but I'm pretty sure it wasn't going to be good for me. Regardless, I felt the time was right so I was just about to wrap my arms around E.D. and give her my finest bear hug. I could see in her eyes that she wasn't going to shoot me down this time. For once, something positive was going to happen. I started moving toward her and she was not backing away, until we both heard, "Yeah, heh, heh, heh, heh, heh! All right, man, han, han, han, han, han, han!"

Sarge had appeared from out of nowhere and startled the bejesus out of both of us, causing us to lose our train of thought. Hell, for a moment I forgot where I even was, but it became clear to me, I was now standing in line waiting at the bus stop of lost opportunities. That's the way Sarge always played it. You never really knew where he was until you knew where he was, or until he wanted you to know where he was.

"Thank you, Sarge, Carefree was just coming to find you so this time he can carefully help you with your library books and to give you a ride back to Big Rock," E.D. said.

I looked longingly into E.D.'s beautiful blue eyes, ready to rekindle the moment but, sadly for me, that bus had left the bus stop of lost opportunities and rarely, if ever, were you able to catch the next one. I said, "That's Careless, darlin'."

Both Sarge and E.D. looked at me and in unison said, "Whatever!"

Sarge and I proceeded to the escalator and went down to the front desk where my favorite sweet little librarian was waiting graciously behind the counter to help Sarge check out the books. He had only six books and, since E.D. just shot me down, it appeared that thankfully I would not have to make another spectacle of myself. It turned out that Sarge was a favorite regular of the library and if they gave out frequent flyer mileage for library usage, Sarge and I could probably take several first-class, round-trip vacations to Australia or perhaps Hawaii; but for now the only exotic trips to be taken were in Sarge's mind as he read his library books.

After checking out the books, Sarge and I returned to the Power Wagon for our short journey home. We made it back in no time and Sarge eagerly got out of the passenger side of the Power Wagon, slammed his door shut, and moved very quickly toward the old iron door of the building to enter and begin his mental journey.

Suddenly he stopped in his tracks, stood there in silence for a moment of contemplation, turned and looked at me, and said, "Careless, thanks, man, han, han, han, han, han!" He turned back around and scurried off to his loft like a little squirrel that had just found some nuts to bring home for the winter.

I got out of the Power Wagon, gently closed the creaky door of my old friend, and proceeded to the old iron door of Big Rock Lofts. I bet Sarge used his imagination to pretend he had gone through an old iron gate of a castle. I really admired Sarge for the way his mind took him on journeys. I however was not that lucky. My imagination was about as long as a trick-or-treat bag of candy lasting on All Hallows Eve once the little munchkins brought it home and began devouring it all. I used my key to unlock the front door and entered the building. I walked through the tastefully done entryway and I started my hike up the stairs to #158.

I got upstairs just fine and entered my loft. For some reason it seemed as if something was missing. I couldn't quite put my finger on it and I keenly observed that nothing was out of place or missing, but in fact something was missing and it was right under my nose, or to be more precise not right under my nose when it should be. "Dudley," I exclaimed. The loft and I were missing Dudley.

To be honest, we were probably missing Dudley for the longest time but just never really knew it. You know how sometimes when you are leaving a place and you keep asking yourself what you are forgetting? You know it's something but you just can't quite remember what it is. I felt like I was missing Dudley for the longest time and I was getting very excited to pick him up. I turned on the television to watch absolutely nothing, perhaps just to hear a voice. Being alone would just not suffice anymore. I thought to myself that no one should be alone, not even me. I poured myself a nice big glass of freshly cold-brewed iced coffee, added my special ingredient, Jack Daniels, threw a few ice cubes in for good measure, took a few sips, and laid back on the sofa. Even though I had a pretty good and eventful day I found myself wishing that it were already tomorrow. I closed my eyes and soon enough it would be.

At 5:00 the next morning, I cracked open one eye just to scout around before I allowed both eyes to jump open and surprise the hell out of me. It appeared I had sat down to watch some television and Rip Van Winkled my way into tomorrow, which technically was now today. The reason my eye was giving the loft the once over is because my brain was registering something, and curiosity got the better of me. I was hearing a noise that sounded vaguely familiar. A barking dog sound was coming from my loft and for just a brief moment I thought maybe, just maybe I had already sprung Dudley from the Island of Misfit Toys even though I didn't remember doing so.

No such luck. I left the television on from the night before and the local news channel, Eye Witless News, was doing a segment on a local dog shelter. They were showing the "Pet of the Week" and it was barking its head off. Then I opened both eyes and began warming up my brain so that I may actually be able to use it.

After a couple of minutes of the start-up procedure, it dawned on me that today was my lucky day because I would go pick up my new friend, Dudley. It also dawned on me that I needed to drain the main vein and that I had an unusually bad case of cotton mouth. Once I had my motor running I got up off of that sofa and proceeded to take care of business. Being that the loft was an efficiency, I thankfully didn't have to go far, because, frankly, my eyes were beginning to float.

CHAPTER FIFTEEN

I did everything I could to make the time pass quickly. The SCPA was not open until 9:00 a.m. Several hours passed but, no matter what I did, everything was moving in slow motion. Whenever I find I'm doing something enjoyable, I never bother to check the time, and time is the one thing I never seem to have enough of. But when I'm bored or have to wait for an event I really want to happen, I tend to be a clock watcher and all I can hear is Ben Stein saying as slowly as humanly possible, "Bueller, Bueller, Bueller, Bueller," as he did in the movie, *Ferris Bueller's Day Off*. "Bueller, Bueller, Bueller, Bueller."

I stopped looking at the clock and decided to use my time constructively. I began to clean the loft and dog-proof it. I had never owned a dog before and, little did I know, although I'd soon learn, there is no such thing as completely dog-proofing your place. I picked up my dirty clothes and placed them in my laundry basket. All the empty cups made their way into the sink. Some empty beer cans and plastic cups found their way into the recycling bin. Hell, I even got out the vacuum cleaner for the first time and attempted to use it. I say attempted to use it because it took me twenty minutes to locate the on/off switch and an additional twenty minutes to figure out that the vacuum cleaner needed to be plugged into a power source before it could make itself useful. "Bueller, Bueller, Bueller, Bueller."

Once the countdown was over and ignition had been achieved with the vacuum, I proceeded to vacuum the entire loft, and may I say that I did a great job for a beginner, and the loft was looking good in the hood. At that point in time it was eight o'clock. I still had a little time to kill and that's when my little red-and-white HEB telephone starting boiling over. I wasn't really expecting any telephone calls and it was still a little early for someone to be calling, but I picked it up anyway and asked in a very concerned manner, "Crisis Hotline, how can I help you?"

"I'll tell you how you can help me, Clueless, you can stop running your vacuum cleaner at seven in the morning when most normal people are still asleep. That's my crisis; you think you can fix that?" a familiar voice asked.

Of course I knew it was E.D. from upstairs, so I replied, "I'm sorry but I believe you must have the wrong number and it's Careless not Clueless."

"That's real funny, Careless, but the next time you wake me up early again, that vacuum cleaner is going to find its way to a place you wouldn't think humanly possible. Do we understand one another?" she retorted.

"Well, you don't have to be so anal about it. Did I hear you say you wanted to go grab some breakfast with me? Is that what I heard?" I asked.

Click! That's all I did hear as she hung up on me to get back to La La Land. Her loss because everyone knows that breakfast is the most important meal of the day.

"Bueller, Bueller, Bueller, Bueller." I started to think maybe Ben Stein had a better shot at E.D. than I did.

After being so rudely rejected, again, I had a look at the clock and, low and behold, time had finally moved forward. I suppose all that excitement with me having to read the *Learning to Vacuum for Dummies* manual, and with E.D. professing her love for me, I had forgotten to watch the clock and now the moment I had been waiting for: I was going to give Dudley a get-out-of-jail-free pass. Free for him, not for me, but that was going to stay my little secret. He would never find out. It was now 8:30 and time for me to hit the road for the SPCA.

I took one more look around the loft and it did look spotless. Careless had made the loft spotless. I liked that. I walked over to the television and turned off Eye Witless News. Then I walked toward the door, turned out the lights, and walked out. I locked the door and started down the hallway to the stairs. After making my way down the stairs I pushed open the old iron door at the entrance and let the sunshine in. It was a glorious day. The weather was perfect, the sun was up, and the birds were chirping. I was definitely in my happy place until I got the you-know-what scared out of me.

"Where you headed, dipshit?" I heard from directly behind me.

At that point I jumped like Michael Jordon stuffing the basketball in the bucket because I wasn't expecting anyone to be there, let alone sneak up behind me and start talking. For God's sake, it was only 8:30 in the morning. Who would be awake and outdoors this early in the morning? So much for my super-keen observation.

After gravity finally brought me back down to Earth, and before I could turn around and face my stalker, I noticed Birk's behemoth white Cowboy Cadillac pickup truck parked in front of the loft next to the Power Wagon. I put my hand over my heart to indicate to him that he almost gave me a heart attack and to make sure my heart was still beating. I turned around and said, "Birk, DO NOT ever sneak up on me like that again. You have no idea how close you came to losing your life."

Birk got a big smile on his face and broke out laughing. He said, "Yeah I was a little nervous when you started flying around like Icarus, but tell me, how were you going to reach me from up there. I didn't know a home-boy like you was even capable of jumping like that." He began belly laughing away at my expense of course.

I was about to get mad at him but it was funny so I starting laughing as well and without missing a beat I gave him a wedgie. "Laugh that one off, Birk," I shot back at him.

"Okay, okay you don't have to get personal," he said. We were both still laughing as Birk untucked himself. He obviously had been leaning up against the loft and when the old iron door opened outward he was shielded from my view. Otherwise I should like to think I would have spotted him right away.

"You didn't think I was going to let you pick up Dudley by yourself, did you?" he asked. "What kind of friend would I be if I let you do this all by yourself? No sir, we're in this together, Careless," he said.

"So in other words, you think you may have a shot with Karen, the girl at the SPCA? That's all I heard you say," I quizzed him.

"No, that's just one of the many reasons I wanted to go. I'm a very complex man, as you know, Careless," he answered.

"I know, Birk, you're really complex," I chuckled. We started walking toward his truck.

As I started my uphill hike to get into Birk's humongous truck, I kept thinking we just couldn't move quickly enough to get Dudley. It was as if we were moving in slow motion in a black-and-white dream. I have always heard that dogs only see in black and white. I wonder if that is true. I suppose I will just have to ask Dudley when I see him. I'm sure he will set me straight. I finally came to rest in my seat as Birk hopped in the truck. We buckled up and Birk hit the ignition as a loud belch sounded followed by a plume of noxious gas streaming out of the dual, very large chrome tail pipes of his Ford F350 4 X 4 dually pickup. Birk threw it into gear and put the pedal to the metal with his lead foot.

Even though I was sure we were moving along at a very good clip it still felt like I was moving in slow motion. Maybe I was just excited about getting Dudley, but no matter how fast we went it wasn't going to be fast enough. I kept thinking to myself, *Would Dudley really like me? Would he like the loft? Would he like my friends? Did I have any friends? What would he like to eat? Was he housetrained?* These were some of the questions I suddenly realized I had no clue about. Why had I not bothered to think about any of these concerns?

I felt a little sweat beading up on my forehead, kind of like when I used to get in trouble during high school while getting sent to the coach's office for "bad behavior." It was really hard to anticipate how many pops I was going to receive. *BOHICA!* Bend over, here it comes again. I still remember Coach Macy with his paddle that had holes drilled in it for extra velocity and stinging power. Of course Coach Macy was from Poland so when I finished receiving my punishment I stood up straight and said in my very best Polish accent, "Thanka you, Coacha Macy!" Then of course I proceeded to get several more pops. I was a very slow learner back then and suddenly my butt started having remembrance pains. *Oh, the joys of my youth*, but my thoughts abruptly turned back to Dudley at the SPCA.

Birk and I were now closing in on the SPCA since it was not far from Big Rock Lofts. Birk did a boot-scoot right, over two lanes, to exit the freeway. Afterwards he used his turn signal. I just looked at him like the road-rage road-hog he was. He probably just thought he was the king of the road. Either way he glanced over at me giving him the look, and asked, "What?" in an impish, irritated manner.

He knew what he did, and I wasn't about to mix it up with him. "Hey, I used my turn signal; that's all that matters," he rebutted to my silence. We made a couple of turns and rolling stops at some red traffic lights and stop signs before finally screeching to a halt in the SPCA parking lot.

The powerful diesel engine of the truck was turned off and Birk began strapping his parachute on for the long jump down. I just sat there staring ahead as if in a dream. I knew I wanted to go get Dudley, but when the moment of truth arrived, my control over my bodily functions seemed to have waned. I was so excited I just wanted to take in the moment, for a moment, but Birk was having none of that. "Hey, June bug, you coming or what?" Birk asked as he knuckled the passenger side window a couple of times.

That broke my concentration somewhat and my motor functions suddenly returned. I opened the door and proceeded to jump to the ground. Birk and I walked swiftly across the parking lot to the front door of the SPCA. I felt like I was about to win the jackpot lotto and perhaps, just perhaps, I was, although it could just be life's lotto. I would soon find out. I felt my heart racing just a bit as we entered the SPCA and we went up to the front desk.

A nice older woman and a twentyish-looking man were working behind the desk. They were both volunteers. While we were waiting in line I looked at Birk and asked, "Hey, Birk, did you know that both of those people working behind the desk are volunteers?"

Birk said, "Careless, you couldn't possible know that. How could you know that? Don't be a dumbass!"

"Keen deductive intuition," I answered with conviction.

The person in front of us finished up and a volunteer from the back of the SPCA brought up a little black dog similar to Toto from the classic movie, *The Wizard of Oz*. I kept looking around for the wicked witch of the West or Glenda the beautiful, good witch, but sadly none of us were in Kansas anymore. I just had to write that because I pretty well say it at least once a day and it blurted its way out of my mind. I hope you will forgive me. As we both stepped up to the counter we were greeted by the mayor of Munchkin Land or maybe it was Mayor McCheese from McDonald's. They look awfully similar.

Either way, I kept expecting someone to break out in a rendition of "The Lollipop Men" song while spastically twitching their arms back and forth and kicking their legs up like a pissed-off donkey as they did in the 1939 movie based on a novel written by L. Frank Baum. You know the one, Dorothy, the farm girl from Kansas, flies off in her house to the Land of Oz, and meets up with the Cowardly Lion, the Scarecrow with no brain, and the Tin Man with no heart. Throw in a few witches, a great, powerful wizard, and a dog named Toto, and you have yourself the makings of a fine film. But we weren't here for Toto. We were here for Dudley, who by the way was probably somewhere over the rainbow, thinking there was no place like home. There would be no lollipop men dancing around. Nope, it just wasn't happenin', Captain.

CHAPTER SIXTEEN

The two fine SPCA volunteers looked us up and down and asked how they could help. Of course Birk noticed that both of the volunteers were wearing aquamarine SPCA tee-shirts. When the lady turned around to get something, he also noticed the word "volunteer" plastered in big letters across the back. Birk fake-punched me on the arm and muttered, "Keen deductive intuition, my foot! Nice going, Shitlock Holmes!"

I began to smile just a bit. Birk was a little slow on the uptake but eventually made his way to the party.

"Yes, my good sir, we are here to pick up my friend Dudley. I believe Karen is expecting us," I stated with conviction. I have found that often when you know someone of influence and you need to have something done, then in that instance it is okay to use that name accordingly to your advantage. This time it didn't turn out as well as I had hoped.

The young man asked, "Dudley?" as if quizzing me on my eighth grade math problems. Then the young man looked at me and waited for my response.

"Yes, that would be Dudley S. Robinson. His limousine is waiting just outside the front door over there," as I pointed toward the front door. "He does not like to be kept waiting, if you know what I mean. The limousine charges by the hour," I explained to the inquisitive young man while Birk looked on and acted as innocent as can be.

"Well, I do see that Dudley has been paid for and it says here he was recently altered, and the owner, a Mr. Careless, will be called when he is ready to go," the young man informed me. "I don't show that we have called you yet, Mr. Careless. We like to keep the altered pets for at least two days so we can monitor them. I'm sorry, Mr. Careless, you're going to have to come back tomorrow for Dudley," the disagreeable volunteer said.

"First of all, it's Careless, not Mr. Careless, and second of all, my friend Dudley wasn't altered, he had a special procedure done called a "Lopit-offa-me." Lastly, the big cheese around here, Karen, personally called me

70

and told me to come pick up Dudley. She said he was feeling better, wanted to go, and that he was very dismayed at being cooped up," I replied.

The young man picked up the telephone, which of course is exactly what he should have done in the first place and punched a few buttons to ring Karen's extension. After about five seconds he said, "I'm sorry, Mr. Careless, but she's not in. You can wait around for her or come back tomorrow, but I have no idea when she will be back. There is nothing I can do about it," he said.

I said, "That's Careless, and would you mind trying Karen once again?" I inquired. He picked up the telephone dialed a couple of numbers and then hung up.

"I'm sorry, Careless, but she doesn't seem to be in and I am going to have to help the next person in line," he said.

I looked behind me and sure enough there were several people in line, waiting to adopt a pet so I moved aside and looked at the young man and said, "That's Mr. Careless to you," as I stepped out of line and began walking across the entryway and towards a small hallway on the other side of the building. I motioned for Birk to follow me as the less-than-eager volunteer turned his smile upside down with a puzzled look on his face.

Birk looked a little confused as well but little did he know that I had asked the young man at the front desk to ring Karen's extension a second time for a very good reason. Birk and I walked across the entryway and about halfway down the hall when I abruptly stopped and held up my hand in front of Birk, palm out, which is the universal hand signal for stop or talk to the hand, dumbass, whichever you prefer. I ordered, "*Alto!*"

There were several doors down this hallway, all marked with different nameplates. In front of us was a door marked assistant director of volunteers. Much to the chagrin of the young man behind the desk and to the bewilderment of Birk, I began knocking on the door. After several seconds the door opened and Karen popped her head out. She got a great big smile on her face when she saw me because she knew that one of her residents was going to a new, loving, and permanent home, but also because I was so handsome and amusing. I am almost certain it was the latter.

"Careless, I am so glad you're here. Dudley is doing great and is in very fine spirits right now. In fact, he is a little too spirited and probably needs to go home with you right away without any delay," she said.

Of course Birk was standing there with a confused look on his face, which was fairly normal for him. I, on the other hand, thanked Karen and cocked my head around to look toward my less-than-helpful friend behind the counter across the entryway. I was sporting a look of confidence and satisfaction. Mostly satisfaction.

Karen asked us to wait in the entryway while she personally went to spring Dudley. As soon as she left us, Birk grabbed me by the arm and asked, "Careless, you are really starting to scare me. How in the hell did you know Karen was here? And how on God's green earth did you know where her office was? Karen's name isn't on any of these doors. What the hell's going on?"

I just smiled slyly and said, "Elementary, my dear Birk, elementary."

After several minutes of cajoling, Birk finally got it out of me that I had found Karen's office by having the young man behind the counter call her a second time while I carefully listened to which office the telephone ringing sound was coming from, even if it was behind a closed door. Coincidence, I think not, and neither did Birk who was very impressed with my skills.

What I neglected to tell him was that Karen told me where her office was when we spoke by telephone the day before and that she would be there most of the day. My guess is she was probably on another call when the young man was ringing her up or she was too busy to pick up the telephone; but Birk didn't really need to know everything, and he didn't.

Karen came back from the holding area where the "altered" dogs were kept and observed. She told me Dudley was very anxious and excited to see me and that he should be right out. I guess he was getting all gussied up to make a great first impression. It was a little late for that because my first impression couldn't have been better.

Just then, two full-length swinging doors busted right open as if a tornado had blown through them and the young man who had previously been behind the counter and who had been "helping" us came running out with Dudley. Actually, Dudley was running, the young man was just trying to keep up with Dudley's brisk pace. The young man was holding on with both hands and shuffling his feet as fast as humanly possible. He was yelling something, but it was hurried and sporadic so I couldn't quite make out what he was saying. I gathered from his body language that it was probably something to the effect of, "Dear God, please forgive me for all of my sins. I promise to do better. Please just let me live through this." Something like that. Unfortunately for the young man there was no such luck. Finally, it all broke down and went to hell in a handbasket. The young man was unable to keep up with Dudley's pace and tripped as Dudley started dragging him across the smooth, slick concrete floor, straight towards me. That's when all of the squealing and crying really began, and not just by the young man skimming along the floor.

I really thought this might be the end of my life as I knew it because Dudley was about to freight train me into oblivion; but, as luck would have it, he came to a screeching halt right before I was about to get clobbered. The young man slid to a stop and tried unsuccessfully to compose himself. He got up, dusted himself off as much as possible, and tried to make polite conversation to distract us from his little mishap. "Mr. Careless, what did you say Dudley's middle initial of *S* stood for?" the young man asked.

I just looked at him and replied, "Steamroller!" Oh, how we laughed while Dudley sat right by my side without moving a muscle. He appeared to have a devilish grin on his face as he stared into my eyes, just waiting for me to give him a command and I did.

"Let's go home, boy," I said, and we proceeded to leave.

CHAPTER SEVENTEEN

Dudley, Birk, and I walked toward the front door to begin Dudley's life of freedom. He was very handsome, and when leaving the SPCA with an animal that will be going to a new home, everyone gets a warm feeling in their heart. And why not? Dogs are people too. People waiting in line or just walking around came up to us and wanted to pet Dudley because he looked so adorable with his long floppy ears, big jowls, beautiful coat, big square head, and beautiful expressive eyes.

Of course Dudley was having none of this. Whenever someone walked toward him, he was in stealth mode until they got just close enough, and then he growled under his breath. It gradually got louder as the person came closer. If they hit the jackpot and actually got close enough, they might receive a bark and some major league goobering. Needless to say, he deftly fended off several well wishers on the way out. I had him on a leash the SPCA provided as he walked right by my side and didn't pull whatsoever. I kept thinking this was too good to be true.

We went outside and walked toward Birk's school bus. While Dudley was in the sunlight I noticed a couple of things. His coat was very beautiful, shiny, and almost golden. He had short, coarse hair that glistened in the sunlight, and I noticed that Dudley was a little on the thin side. This made his large beautiful head look even bigger than it was and almost not in proportion to the rest of his body.

The SPCA paperwork stated that Dudley was a stray found wondering around in Katy, Texas. Katy was just west of Houston. Along with his big head and huge jowls, he also came equipped with a long tail that spun around in a circle like a helicopter rotor, not back and forth like most dogs. It was very funny to watch. I knew I was going to have to fatten him up.

We all walked across the parking lot to Birk's truck. Birk hit his keychain alarm button and the doors unlocked. Since his truck had four doors, I opened the back door and Dudley hopped right up into the backseat. It looked like riding in a truck was not going to be a problem for this big fella.

Birk and I opened the front doors and climbed into the front seats. Once we were buckled in, Birk cranked her up to begin our journey home to Big Rock Lofts. Dudley moved from the backseat to standing on the center armrest console. He placed his head on my shoulder and starting purring like a cat. I removed his leash so it wouldn't get caught on anything.

Birk didn't like Dudley putting his big head in the front seat with us, so I told Birk to open the sunroof. His truck had every gadget and feature known to man. It was a beautiful day and the weather was nice. As soon as the sunroof opened, Dudley stood tall and poked his big head out of the truck for a look about as Birk hit the gas. Dudley really seemed to enjoy this. Here we were, two hillbillies riding around in our pickup truck with a big old hound dog's head poking out of the sunroof. If only I had a camera! It reminded me of Jed Clampett's dog in the sitcom, *The Beverly Hillbillies*. Dudley was really amusing us.

When we got on the freeway his big jowls started flapping around in the wind. It was quite a sight. He almost looked like a test pilot trying to see if he could withstand the G-forces of a jet airplane or space shuttle. Jowls and teeth—that's all we could see. Everyone we passed was smiling and pointing toward us, and because of Birk's need for speed, we passed almost everyone. That Dudley was a real cut up.

We exited the freeway and headed to the loft. Birk pulled up right in front where we were lucky enough to find a parking spot, especially one that could accommodate his Cowboy Cadillac.

I was deciding what to do with Dudley and whether to put his leash back on. Of course it would be irresponsible of me not to put him on a leash just in case he started running around like a wild animal. He could really get hurt or possibly hurt someone if he escaped. Before I had the opportunity to put a leash on him, Birk went ahead and opened the driver's side backdoor and Dudley flew out of the truck, almost knocking Birk over.

Birk lost his color for a moment and I believe I overheard him say, "Damn dog!" before he regained his composure.

Dudley loped his way around the backside of the truck, which took a little while because of its mammoth size, and stopped right by my side. As he sat down I realized he probably wouldn't need a leash because he wasn't going to run off. Later on I would find out just how wrong I was.

As we approached the big old iron door to the loft, Dudley stopped and did his business. I took this as a good sign that I would not have to be cleaning up after him in the loft, which was great because this was one of the mysteries I did not know about him yet and, even worse, I've had an aversion to number twos since childhood so I sure didn't want to be cleaning those up. As it turned out, he was completely housetrained. I wondered if someone had gotten rid of him or if he had just wandered off while no one was looking. At this point it didn't really matter because we were together now and I couldn't imagine anything changing that.

Birk hopped back up in his truck, cranked it and his tunes up, waved goodbye, and sped off. I guess he had other fish to fry. It was just as well because Dudley and I needed to have some bonding time together and this was a great opportunity for him to get comfortable in the loft without any more distractions.

I put my key in the old iron door and unlocked it. I opened the door and started walking forward. As if on cue, Dudley followed right by my side and didn't waiver whatsoever. I could definitely get used to this. I started my climb up the stairs to the second floor and there was Dudley walking right next to me, negotiating the stairs like a champ. He must have been very grateful to me for getting him out of doggie prison because he was on his best behavior. Whenever I stopped walking, he stopped, sat, and looked up at me to see what I was going to do next. We walked down the hallway together and I couldn't have been more proud. Finally we reached #158 and I took my key out of my pocket, unlocked the door, and welcomed my new friend into his home.

He walked right in as if he had lived there for a long time. He explored for a few minutes, sniffed everything, hopped right onto the sofa, curled up, and took a nap. I knew he was sleeping only because I saw his jowls inflating and deflating like a clown blowing up a balloon at a children's party. Then came the soft snoring so at that point I was certain he was asleep and he felt at home. I figured he had a ruff couple of days with his jail break and elective surgery, although he and I had not "elected" for him to have it; but still, it was a surgery. I let him rest and went about my business.

First, I called the Westbury Animal Hospital for Dudley's first checkup. I definitely wanted to make sure he was healthy, especially since he was a stray and seemed so skinny. He would also need a follow-up exam after his lopit-offa-me operation. I dialed the Westbury Animal Hospital number on my trusty red-and-white HEB telephone.

"Westbury Animal Hospital, would you please hold?" I was asked by the young lady who answered the phone.

Before I could say yes, I was already on hold. I waited for a couple of minutes and she came back on and asked, "I'm sorry for the wait, how may I help you?"

I said, "Yes, ma'am, I need to make an appointment for my new friend, please," as I pointed over to Dudley who was curled up on the sofa as if she could see my hand gestures over the telephone.

Dudley was still lying there but he now had one eye open and was watching me as I was talking on the telephone. It was almost as if he knew I was talking about him.

"Yes, sir, have you been in to see us before?" the young lady inquired.

I explained to her this would be my and Dudley's first visit, that I had just picked him up from the SPCA, and he needed his first check-up. I also told her Dudley wanted to see Dr. L.D. Eckermann who had come highly recommended by the other inmates at the SPCA.

She giggled a little but then it was right back down to business. She told me that Dr. Eckermann, or L.D. as some referred to him, was very busy and it would be at least a week before he could see Dudley. She asked if I wanted to wait that long.

That seemed kind of a long time to wait but the young lady did inform me that there were several other very good vets who would be just thrilled to give Dudley the once over. I told her Dudley was dead set on seeing L.D. so I asked her if Dudley could speak with L.D. to request an earlier appointment.

This time she burst out laughing and told me that even though it was Sunday, Dr. Eckermann was at the clinic making rounds. She said she would talk to Dr. Eckermann to see if he would squeeze Dudley in, especially since Dudley was so insistent about the appointment. "I will have to call you back, is this your correct number on the caller I.D., Mr. Robinson?" she asked.

I said, "Honey, the name's Careless, and yes that is my correct number. Dudley and I will be anxiously awaiting your phone call." I hung up my trusty red-and-white HEB telephone and went to sit on the sofa with my soft and furry friend.

As I sat down with him he stood up on the sofa and turned himself around to face me. I wasn't quite sure what to make of this because I had never owned a dog before, and I certainly never had a large dog face to face with me while in the reclining position. I was getting a wee bit nervous and I didn't know quite what he was doing. He laid back down on the sofa right next to me, pressing his body against me but positioning his head so it was right on top of my chest. He kind of shuddered a little bit and started making some tiny noises under his breath that really almost sounded like a cat purring.

I wasn't quite sure what to do so I put my hand on his big head and started gently rubbing his ears. He kept on purring and then repositioned himself again so as to boot-scoot even closer to me, if that was possible. He leaned in and pressed himself up against me again while laying his head back down on my chest. I guess I was being spooned by a dog. How sad my life had become to be spooned by a dog rather than a good woman. I suppose this was the next best thing. I rationalized that it could be worse somehow but that was going to take a bit more thought and, as luck would have it, I had plenty of time on my hands to do just that.

Dudley moaned and groaned and ooohed and aaaahed as I believe I detected him going through several different octaves. He promptly went to sleep in that position. I was sure he was asleep because while he stopped making all of those peculiar noises, he started softly snoring again and his jowls were going up and down again while filling and deflating with the air from his breath. This was a new experience for me and one I thought I could most definitely get accustomed to. It was about that time of day for me anyway so I put my arm around Dudley's chest and proceeded to shut my eyes. At that point we were both sawing logs and it was all good in the hood. Dudley and I were now in our happy place, which was with one another.

CHAPTER EIGHTEEN

I believe what happened about an hour later could only be described as a wet dream. I don't really remember what happened in the dream but I am certain I won't soon forget how I was awakened. I opened one eye and saw a big red gooey object headed right towards my face. My immediate thought flashed back to the 1958 movie classic, *The Blob*, starring one of my favorite actors, Steve McQueen, God rest his soul.

If you are much younger than I am, let me recommend that you watch this movie so you know just how I felt at that particular moment in time; but to nutshell it, a big red gooey blob from outer space came to Earth and was swallowing up everything in its path until the hero of the movie, an amazing actor the likes of which we rarely see today, saved the day and the planet. This would be an easy deal for Steve McQueen. Terrence Steven was his given name and he was born in Beech Grove, Indiana, on April 24, 1930. His father, who was a stunt pilot, left his mother and Steve when he was just an infant. Steve definitely felt the need for speed as he raced motorcycles and cars. He later served his country as a United States Marine. He was married three times, had several children, and was called home at the age of fifty on November 7, 1980, from a form of cancer known as mesothelioma. During his acting career he was known as the "King of Cool" and, although he made many fine films such as *The Magnificent Seven*, *The Great Escape*, *Bullitt*, *The Getaway*, *Papillon*, and *The Towering Inferno*, it was *The Blob* I remembered him in. I probably need therapy but I digress. Perhaps it's a good thing I am not a professional movie critic.

Thankfully, I was not swallowed up by the blob. In fact I was not having a wet dream at all. I would describe it as more of a wet nightmare except that by now I was wide awake. As it turned out, my face was very moist from that big red gooey thing I'll just refer to as Dudley's tongue. He was licking my face over and over. He had a huge tongue. I had never really noticed that before, but it seemed like it was almost the length of the Great Wall of China.

Apparently my friend was through taking his power nap and thanking me with Dudley kisses for breaking him out of the joint. I bet Steve McQueen could have broken him out much easier than I did and with no one knowing the better, but that mission fell upon me; and judging from the way I was going to need to towel off my face, it appeared the jail break was a job well done.

At that point I started trying to push Dudley away. He was now practically on top of me. Thank God, E.D. or Birk weren't here to see this. It was funny but enough was enough and, as I started to gently push Dudley away from me, he leaned in more by using his strong and well-developed leg muscles to offset my effort to separate us. The more I pushed, the more he countered with his resistance. That's when I had a flashback to high school, "For every action there is an equal and opposite reaction."

I may not have been a great student but this lesson was definitely coming back to haunt me. I could just read the newspaper headlines now, "Recluse dies in his apartment alone, spooned and survived by his dog," and further down in the article Sarge would be quoted as saying something like, "He seemed like such a nice neighbor. He always kept to himself and was very quiet, except for that one time in the downtown library."

No, it wasn't going to end that way for me. I finally mustered up enough strength and wiggled my way out of Dudley's kung fu grip all the while saying, "No, Dudley! Stop, Dudley! Enough, Dudley!"

I got up from the sofa and wasn't quite sure what had just happened but I damn sure wasn't going to tell anyone about it. Frankly, I'm pretty sure Dudley wouldn't like it if I were to kiss and tell. As I began walking away, Dudley leapt off the sofa and trotted toward me. Between us was a pretty good-sized wooden coffee table I had acquired from the last tenant of #158. Actually, I didn't really acquire it; I think the last tenant left it because it was so old, ugly, and heavy that he just couldn't bear to take it with him. I guess you could say I inherited it. I watched in amazement as Dudley did his best impression of the island dance, the Limbo, as he scrunched down and walked right underneath that coffee table. The only problem was that before he reached the other side, he decided to stand straight up and when he did the whole coffee table lifted off. Eh, Houston, we have a problem.

Since Dudley wanted to be by my side, I was now watching a pretty good-sized coffee table moving toward me with four long golden legs underneath it. At first I didn't know what to do because I was beside myself, but after a few moments I realized that Dudley was building up ramming speed and perhaps an intervention was necessary. I decided right then to get a hold of myself much like the great entertainer, Michael Jackson. "Dudley, stop," I commanded.

Sure enough he stopped just before I was about to get kneecapped. "Stay, Dudley," I commanded again as I walked over to him and lifted one end of the table up high enough for him to escape. He bolted out from under the table and, as I placed it back down on the floor, he came up to me and sat down right by my side. I just looked at him looking at me, and I really tried to get mad at him but I just couldn't. He had a big smile on his face with those big jowls hanging down.

While we were having "our moment" I said to him, "You know, Dudley, this would make a great mystery novel and I already have a fitting title for it, *The Case of the Walking Coffee Table.*"

Just then I heard a throaty *mmmmmm* sound emanating from him and it changed pitches ranging from low to high. We just looked at each other and oh how we laughed. Yes, he was quite the cut up!

Dudley was a bit surprised when my super-duper, deluxe, free, red-and-white HEB telephone went into action and started doing its thing. He stood up and walked over to the telephone where he turned his head sideways and looked curiously at this new thing that was making noises at him. He turned his head sideways and back several more times as he studied the telephone while deciding what course of action needed to be taken next, Dudley style. He looked at me and looked back at the telephone and he let out a mighty, ferocious bark, the likes of which I can only describe as the mighty roar of a dominant male lion protecting his pride in Africa. It was impressive.

I was about to move toward the telephone to answer it when Dudley gobbled it up in his mouth and started making some kind of throaty grunting noise while shaking it around from side to side and then up and down. As I walked closer to him I could hear a voice on the telephone say, "Hello, hello, Mr. Robinson?"

Of course this could have been many a different people but when I heard, "Mr. Robinson," I figured it had to be either the Westbury Animal Hospital or the IRS. I was shooting for the Westbury Animal Hospital since I didn't have enough coin for the IRS to take notice. "Dudley, give me that phone, you big goofus," I commanded.

He stopped shaking the telephone around, looked at me with my hand outstretched, and flipped his head toward me while opening his very large mouth. The telephone came flying toward me and thankfully I caught it with one hand because it had definitely been slimed, Dudley style. I didn't really care for Dudley goober on both of my hands. At this point I just looked in amazement at Dudley. I was stunned. How did he know to give me the HEB telephone or did he know at all? I wondered.

Either way, I imagined he most likely did not like telephone solicitors, and he certainly lacked basic phone skills. We would probably have to work on that. While I was giving him the eye and trying to figure out if this was just a random act, he just sat there with a big smile on his face as if to say, "Yep, that's right, I did it."

If only I could teach him to beer me from the refrigerator. Now that would be a neat trick.

"Hello, hello, Mr. Robinson," a slightly muffled voice was coming from my hand, muffled from the goober. I remembered I was still holding the telephone in my hand and after wiping it down the best I could on my shirt, which was disgusting, I put it up to my ear. "House of pain, how can I help you?" I responded.

"Yes, well, Mr. Robinson, this is Laura from Westbury Animal Hospital and I spoke with Dr. Eckermann. He said since he is here making rounds anyway and since Dudley is a new patient from the SPCA, he would be happy to see you both today. Does 2:00 work for you?" she asked.

I said, "Sure, honey, that would be just fine with me but let me just check with the big guy real quick like." I put the phone down and looked at Dudley. "Hey, 2:00 okay with you for your first check up?" I asked him.

He just looked at me and started mumbling something about seeing a man about a horse or something like that so I took it as a yes.

"He says yes but wants to know if you give lollipops for good behavior and, by the way, the name's Careless," I told Laura.

"Okay Mr., I mean, Careless, we'll see you at 2:00. Do you know where we're located?" she asked.

"Nope, sure don't," I said.

"We're located at 4917 South Willow. Do you need directions?" she asked.

"Nope, I'm good. I'll find you, I have GDS," I responded.

"You mean GPS? What's GDS?" she asked.

Of course I told her, "Global Dudley Systems. What else could it possibly stand for?" In parting I said, "Tell L.D. we'll see him at 2:00," and I hung up the telephone or what was left of it after Dudley had swished it around in his very large mouth a few times.

We still had a couple of hours to kill until it was time for Dudley's check up so I decided to take him outside to drain the main vein. Before I could get there, a knock, knock, knocking came from the door and it definitely sent Dudley rocking.

He bounced up, trotted over to the door, and stared at it. I noticed that his short, coarse, golden-color hair along his back, starting at his shoulders all the way down to his tail had formed a thin line and was standing straight up. After marching over to the door, he stood erect as if he were frozen in time like a stone lion statue in front of a home, protecting it.

As I passed Dudley on the way to the door to see who was there, I placed my hand on his head, looked him squarely in the eye, and said, "Good boy," very enthusiastically as if to reward him for watching over the loft.

I suppose he already thought of the loft as his turf, which was just fine with me. He took his eyes off of the door for one moment to acknowledge my praise and gave me a quick glance before fixating his gaze back on the door.

I unlocked the deadbolt lock on the door and proceeded to open it. Much to my pleasant surprise, E.D. was standing there, looking more beautiful than I had even remembered. She was wearing a beautiful yellow-and-orange sundress that started at her shoulders and stopped just above her knees. It was a great fit in all the right places. Her golden, flowing hair just seemed to blend into the sundress.

I tried to say something but she was looking so fine that I became confused as to what language I spoke. At that point I probably could have used some of that down-home bilingual edumacation the local public school districts are always pushing because all I could do was mumble some sort of haiku that was pretty much unintelligible.

After my severe loss of words, thankfully E.D. took verbal charge and said with a devilish grin, "What's the matter, Careless, cat got your tongue?"

I just knew she was in love with me, but at the present time I was the only one of us that realized it. I kind of smirked as she let herself in because the joke was on her. I didn't have a cat. I had a dog named Dudley and he was still frozen there, not moving a muscle. I closed the door behind her and it was as if the room brightened up as she made her way in.

She looked a little confused as she finally noticed Dudley sitting there watching her every move. She started cracking up laughing, looked at me, and inquired why there was a huge animal in my loft. She asked if I had gotten a dog or was it just a statue because he wasn't moving a muscle. She was staring at me, waiting for my answer, and Dudley was staring at her, waiting to see what she was going to do.

I completely lied and responded, "Honey, that's not a dog, that's Melvin, the rat; he lives in the building and travels from loft to loft, stealing cheese from all of the residents. Are you telling me you have never seen him before?"

E.D. and Dudley started laughing. She walked over to him and gave him a big hug. I was waiting to see how Dudley would react because this was a new thing for the both of us. He definitely did not disappoint.

When E.D. finished hugging Dudley, she turned and walked toward me. Dudley began making the most unusual noises, some I had not heard come from him yet. It was kind of like a quick, repeating low-pitched rumbling, grunting noise.

E.D. and I laughed but I can't decide if what happened next was funny or perhaps a little bit strange. Dudley unfroze himself and bolted toward E.D. who was unsuspecting because she was walking toward me with her back to Dudley.

He lowered his head like a charging bull that had just seen red, got right up to her, and slid to a stop with three quarters of his entire rather large body coming to rest under E.D.'s pretty little sundress.

I must admit at this point I was a little embarrassed and perhaps a little jealous because Dudley was putting the move on my main squeeze before I even had the chance. I was looking down at Dudley's rather awkward entrance into E.D.'s private estate and as I raised my gaze a little higher I noticed E.D. was now staring at me, wondering what I was going to do about the situation.

Just as I thought it couldn't get any worse, I noticed E.D.'s beautiful sundress started moving around back and forth and side to side almost as if she were Marilyn Monroe standing over a subway vent, and the noise that followed was somewhat disturbing. Like me, it seemed that Dudley had a hankering for beautiful blondes and had latched onto one of E.D.'s legs with his front legs and was kind of humping it while making the most bizarre type of grunting noises.

E.D. was not amused. "Careless, you had better get your critter off of me or you can be pretty sure you will never get as far as he has," she pledged.

I decided to be funny and said, "That's not what I call my critter. I call him Big Pete." She was having none of that.

At that point, I stopped laughing and bent down to attempt to get Dudley to remove himself. I raised her dress slightly so I could see what Dudley was doing. Sure enough he had his two front legs wrapped around her right leg. He looked at me and the only way I can accurately describe him is having a bitter beer face, all scrunched up with his eyes semi-rolled back into his big head.

I yelled at him, "Dudley, Dudley, stop that right now!"

He got all ashamed, stopped making noises, put on his regular face, let go of E.D.'s leg, and came out from underneath E.D.'s sundress.

I just sat there in disbelief, but found the whole thing humorous.

E.D. looked at me and told me that it would now be quite all right with her if I turned her dress loose and let it drop back down to its normal position. She said the show was over and, I guess, indeed it was. Dudley was now waiting patiently at the door and sitting very quietly. E.D. didn't seem to care that much about what had just happened. She still had a big, beautiful Texas smile on her face.

With that unpleasant incident behind us, I told E.D. I needed to take Dudley downstairs to go outside to drain the lizard. She explained to me that she had come over because she needed a couple of heavy boxes moved around in her apartment, and seeing that my name was Careless she would like for me to take "care" of that for her. I told her I would, as soon as I took Dudley downstairs and outside where the back portion of the property was completely fenced in so he could take care of business.

That was fine with her and she accompanied Dudley and me out of the loft, down the stairs, and out the backdoor where Dudley bounded away to go check out everything. There was a six-foot wrought iron fence surrounding the back side of the property and the only way out was a small gate that always remained closed unless someone entered the top-secret code of 1, 2, 3, 4.

Dudley ran around like a mad man, sniffing and raising his leg up on just about anything that didn't move. He was having a blast and completely forgot about me just as I did with him so I could concentrate on E.D. who was watching Dudley's antics with the cutest little girl's smile on her face.

"So, you come here often or not at all?" I started my classic pickup line of questioning. Funny how that never seemed to work but I always tried it just in case, and was hoping she was not too mad about Dudley's little episode, because he pretty much had his way with her.

Strangely enough, she seemed okay with it as she turned toward me. Outside, the sun really brought out her natural beauty. She was almost glowing in the sunlight. To be honest, neither of us could really be angry with Dudley, seeing that like me he had great taste in women.

E.D. asked me what my story was. I knew then that she was interested in me. Why shouldn't she be? I am a handsome, funny, and talented guy. I also possess a great dog who had literally been around almost all of the bases with her. I told her I had graduated college with an advanced degree of B.S. or something along those lines and I was working at our family steel business where I had worked since I was practically in diapers. I told her I was searchin' for a person of her caliber and beauty to marry and take care of me in the manner in which I was not accustomed to yet, but was hopeful.

She just kind of giggled and said, "Careless, perhaps it would be a good idea for you not to quit your job at the family steel business."

I could now tell this might not be going the way I and the good Lord had intended, so I told her I routinely paid the poor man's tax by playing the lotto and that once I hit it big I would sweep her off her feet and make all of her dreams come true. She told me that first of all, I was indeed poor and second of all, she didn't know what the hell I was even talking about, which, she explained, were two things that would not get me very far with her.

I tried to tell her I didn't plan to remain poor for the rest of my life but that it was just a phase I was going through, kind of like adolescence.

She told me that when I finally reach adolescence to let her know because, until then, she may have to just phase me out.

I told her not to worry because when I grew up I was sure she would be very proud of me but that she probably shouldn't expect miracles. I wasn't through talking to E.D. but it suddenly occurred to me that it had become very quiet and as I looked around I didn't see the smallest hint of Dudley. I was getting a little nervous. E.D. and I scoured the property in search of Dudley. What should I do? I only had Dudley for a few hours and he had already taken off. Nobody had entered the gate so unless he had managed to open the gate by punching in the code and turning the doorknob with his paw, I was going to have to rule out a gate escape similar but not exactly like Steve McQueen in the movie, *The Great Escape*.

E.D. and I walked the whole inside perimeter of the property several times while calling out Dudley's name. I thought perhaps if I tapped my heels together three times, thought of Dudley, and exclaimed that there was no place like home, he would magically appear; but E.D. was standing right there watching me and she would definitely think that I had gone gay on her, not that there's anything wrong with that. If that ever did happen in front of E.D., I was certain that door would slam shut and be closed to me forever, so I wisely decided against it.

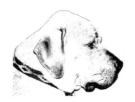

CHAPTER NINETEEN

I was really getting worried about Dudley and so was E.D., but she told me she had an appointment she had to keep with a gallery owner for her next show so she had to leave. I knew she felt bad about it and she promised to help me search some more as soon as she was finished with her appointment. She said she would look for Dudley while she drove to and from her meeting. I thought that was nice, especially in light of the precarious way Dudley had introduced himself to her.

Once again, I was all alone. Why did I ever let Birk talk me into getting a dog? I did realize that at some point it would end in a heartbreak, but I never thought it would be this soon. I did not like this at all. I looked around for thirty more minutes inside the gated area and all around the outside, but Dudley was nowhere to be found. I started to wonder if this is how he ended up on the streets of Katy, Texas, all alone with no one to take care of him. Then I must admit for the first time I started to get a little angry with him because I couldn't believe he would just up and leave me. I would never have left him. I started rationalizing that he was just a dog and he had probably moved on to greener pastures and probably wasn't coming back. I began to feel that he probably enjoyed his freedom more so than my companionship. Even if he wanted to come back, I hadn't had enough time to even buy him a necktie to put his SPCA identification tag on him. Not a good day for Careless.

I called out Dudley's name several more times and then entered the back door of the loft to retire and think about what I had done wrong. I walked up the stairs and into loft #158, but I must say I was feeling quite alone. I mixed up a batch of my special cold-brewed iced coffee with a smidgen of Jack Daniels to lessen the blow.

After enjoying my beverage, perhaps a bit too much, I called the Westbury Animal Hospital on my trusty red-and-white HEB telephone and explained that Dudley and I had a slight change of plans and I had to cancel our appointment with L.D. I felt really bad about that because he made special arrangements to see us on a Sunday, but I thought I would look pretty stupid showing up without a dog.

The young lady on the telephone was very sympathetic and wished me luck. She said if we decided we needed another appointment we should not hesitate to call. I told her I would and to please thank L.D. for me. Now if I could just find my dog, I would be in great shape. Knowing him, for as little time as I did, I assumed he was probably halfway back to Katy, Texas.

I called Birk and told him what happened and thanked him for the heartache. He couldn't believe it and said he was coming over to check it out for himself. "Careless, have you been putting too much Jack Daniels in your coffee again?" he asked.

The answer was probably yes but this time it had nothing to do with Dudley going missing. I wondered if he found someone he liked better or maybe he found a garbage bin somewhere that was filled with all of his favorite foods. Either way, I was pretty sure he wasn't coming back, and even if he wanted to, he may not be able to find his way back.

Sadly enough, this appeared to be a recurring theme in my life. When I was five years old, my mother was called home and at that point in my life I couldn't quite grasp what had happened and thought she had abandoned me and my brothers and sister. To add insult to injury, my father remarried and moved on to greener pastures as well. History, while trying to repeat itself, can sometimes be painful and even though you may want loved ones to return, most of the time it's just not possible. Regardless, Birk was on his way to oversee operation Hoududlini.

I went downstairs, alone, to meet Birk when he arrived. He would be here soon with the rocket speed he used to drive with. Birk had two speeds: fast and extra fast. I got down the flight of stairs and was about to go out to the front of the building through the old iron door to meet him when something made me do a U-turn to check the fenced-in back area of the property once more. As I exited to the back, I almost fell out from fright as the backdoor closed behind me. The backdoor immediately opened back up again and Birk came through it. He had obviously hitched a ride into the building when another tenant opened the old iron front door that always remained locked except to those who had a key. I also got quite a jolt when I saw Dudley tooling around in the fenced yard smelling everything and doing his business just as I had left him before he disappeared. I could not believe my eyes and Birk walked right up behind me and started asking me if I needed glasses or was just a dumbass.

I answered, "Possibly both!"

Just then, Dudley caught me in his eyesight and came running toward me. I didn't realize how much I missed him until just now. I thought for sure he was gone and was not coming back, but there he was just as plain as day. Dudley ran right up to me, stopped, stood up on his back legs, and threw his front legs over my shoulder. He curved his paws around to get me in his kung fu grip and licked my face non-stop. I guess he missed me as well.

After about five minutes of this lovefest reunion, I finally had to tell Dudley to stop as I began using my shirt for a bath towel to dry my face.

Birk chirped in with, "Hey, why don't you two get a room?" There you have it, my good friend already starting with the jokes.

Birk told me he had to leave and after I had a long talk with Dudley about running off, we left as well. Birk went out of the front old iron door and Dudley and I started our climb up the stairs to get back to our loft. As we were walking I heard Birk crank up his diesel Cowboy Cadillac and, with a quick couple of honks of the horn to say goodbye, he sped off.

Dudley's escape and return was really bothering me. Maybe I had too high of an opinion of my skills of observation and deductive reasoning but still this was one mystery that at least in my mind needed answering. I kept playing it back in my head as Dudley and I approached the door to #158 but still I had no clue as to how he escaped and just as mysteriously returned. I know E.D. and I had walked the inside perimeter many times with no sign of any openings, so either he managed to exit through the locked gate or there had to be a secret passageway. Neither of these ideas sounded very sane to me and as we entered the loft I decided to give it further scrutiny at a later time.

I then realized Dudley and I had just enough time to make his appointment at the vet if they would still let us come in, so I grabbed my trusty red-and-white HEB telephone, punched in the telephone number to the vet, and cradled it between my head and shoulder.

"Westbury Animal Hospital, how may I help you?" the voice on the other end of the line asked kindly.

I explained that Dudley had been a bad boy but he was sorry and wanted to know if L.D. would still see him this afternoon. I was placed on hold for a moment and the young lady came back on the telephone and said L.D. would love to meet Dudley and for us to come in at our original appointment time.

Before hanging up I told her Dudley wanted to know whether he would get a lollipop if he behaved himself during the examination. She laughed a little and told me that while they didn't really give out lollipops for good behavior, they did expect good behavior from both of us, and if Dudley played his cards right he might receive a dog biscuit, and if he was extra good he might even receive a rawhide dog chew.

I told her I was just hoping Dudley wouldn't chew on the doctor, thanked her, and told her to have no fear, we were on the way. I hung up the phone and turned around to tell Dudley, but it was too late because he had overheard the entire conversation and was already starting to goober. I began to think to myself that this was going to be easier than I had imagined. Incorrecto was I.

After I hung up the telephone on the weather-beaten wooden desk I had rescued from a dump many years ago, which for some reason now had goober marks on it, the ringing immediately began again. This was a little unusual but maybe the Westbury Animal Hospital had forgotten to tell me some urgent piece of information they really needed me to know before I unleashed Dudley upon them.

I answered the telephone, "Crisis Hotline, state your problem, please, and for your protection this line may be recorded."

This never really worked but I always thought one day that whomever was calling would forget where they were calling and start blabbing away about all of their problems so I could pretend to care and possibly use it against them for at least the rest of their lives, but probably no longer than that.

"Carefree, E.D here, did you ever find that serial molester you call a dog?" she asked me.

"The name's Careless and I believe the term is serial thriller. I know you were really worried about his safety. He actually just came back from his sabbatical and he is all rested up and ready for another go round. What time shall I tell him you will be arriving?" I asked.

"Careless, before I come back over there, you had better learn how to treat a lady, especially one of my stature. Do we understand one another, Careless?" she asked.

"You can't teach an old dog new tricks," I hap-heartedly muttered.

"I wasn't talking about you, Careless. I was referring to your new roommate. I feel certain you are beyond help at this point," she shot back at me as she threatened to hang up.

At least both E.D. and I agreed upon something so maybe fate was starting to move E.D. into my corner of the boxing ring. Hope is a very powerful emotion, almost like a potent drug and yet after a while they both wear off and seem to fade into the distance. Realizing at that moment that anything was possible and I might have to slightly modify Dudley's behavior around beautiful young women, I said goodbye to E.D. and told her I would definitely take this high-priority matter up with my superiors.

She was not amused but frankly if I could get away with Dudley's behavior with the excuse that I was just a dog and didn't know any better, then I probably would. After being disconnected, I placed the red-and-white HEB telephone back down on the weather-beaten, Dudley-goo-bered antique desk.

It was becoming quite obvious to me that Dudley had no idea he was a dog. Then I heard the television turn on. Confused at first, I looked over to find Dudley sitting on the sofa, watching television. He looked at me lov-ingly and turned back toward the television. I actually learned two things just then: one, he liked the Animal Planet channel; and, two, he was sit-ting right on top of the remote control, thereby turning on the television.

Needless to say I was a little relieved. I certainly did not want a dog who was more intelligent than I was. Almost as intelligent, but not more so. I never did learn how to program or use that television remote control. Perhaps Dudley would help me with that later. The instructions were in Chinese. I wonder if Dudley understood Chinese.

At that point I told Dudley to turn off the television because we were going for a nice little ride. Sure enough, right on cue, as he lifted his big golden buttocks off of the remote and the sofa, the television turned off. Together, Dudley and I walked out of the loft and I closed and locked the door. I placed the keys in my pocket and we started moving toward the stairs. Dudley didn't budge from my side. He was very, very loyal.

As we walked we heard a faint voice off in the distance, "Yeah, heh,

heh, heh, heh, heh, heh!"

It was Sarge, probably talking to himself again or perhaps daydreaming while taking a journey in one of his books but, needless to say, Dudley did not approve of it and he surprised me as his golden hair stood straight up from his neck down to his tail and along his back as he started growling in his low-talking voice.

I assured him that everything was just fine as we went down the stairs to the entryway. I opened the old iron front door and Dudley and I left the building. We headed for the Power Wagon. I opened my door and he hopped right in and made himself at home in the passenger seat. I cranked up the mighty V-8 engine, which in my opinion had way too many horses for this vehicle and, I must admit, did manage to get me into trouble a few times while exceeding the speed limit. Often times, whenever I was stopped for going a little too fast, I always (most of the time unsuccessfully) explained to the fine officer who had stopped me that the posted speed limit was really just the recommended speed limit, and it didn't apply to a competent driver such as myself.

They usually smiled briefly as they wrote and handed me the ticket. I suppose I would have to slow it down a bit now that I had precious cargo in the truck with me. Dudley was his name and goober was his game. I opened both windows up and, as we drove off, Dudley stuck his big, beautiful, golden head out of his window. It was go time.

As we drove along, I noticed his big floppy ears caught the wind like two big sails and his jowls flopped up and down in the wind. Several people behind us on the freeway were turning on their windshield wipers while the sun was out. This really made no sense to me until I realized the wind was carrying Dudley's goober all the way from his jowls to the unfortunate driver's windshields behind us. Needless to say, they were not pleased. Being the positive person I am, I just thought of it as a free car wash for others, compliments of Dudley.

93

CHAPTER TWENTY

As we were driving, I found out that Dudley really dug country music. I cranked up the stereo for him and he was just in hog heaven or, should I say, dog heaven. Jake Harm and the Holdouts came on singing their new hit song, *Wild Turkey at Sunrise*, and I'll tell you what, Dudley's starting shaking his tail around in a big circle. He was definitely ready for a boot-scoot.

I exited the freeway and drove for a few minutes until we arrived at the Westbury Animal Hospital. I pulled up in the parking lot and was just amazed at what a nice building it was. It was made of a beautiful gray stone and glass, and was a very modern-looking building. I stopped the Power Wagon and slapped a leash on Dudley because I wasn't really sure how he would act around other dogs. I opened my door and we both jumped out at the same time. I slammed the door shut behind me and we started walking toward the entrance.

Along the way, Dudley stopped and smelled all of the landscaping while checking out everything. "Come on, Bella, let's go," I heard a woman say to what I can only describe as a rather large fluffy cottonball with four teeny weeny cottonball legs.

As I looked over, I saw a woman picking up her foo foo dog to take into the vet. She was eyeballing Dudley and then me as if Dudley was going to make a morsel out of her Bella. Of course she had no way of knowing Dudley was a lover not a fighter. I kind of gave her the Texas wave and she just looked at me like I was an idiot and perhaps she was right. In addition, I gave her my very finest fake smile as she turned around with Bella and walked through the front double doors of the clinic. Dudley was all excited to see another dog so he marched right in behind them. He looked a little confused when he arrived in the lobby because Bella was nowhere to be found.

A very cute, young, perky girl at the front desk asked, "Hello, welcome to Westbury Animal Hospital, how may I help you?"

"Dudley, party of one for L.D.," I told her.

"Oh yes, we have been expecting you, Mr. Robinson. Please fill out these forms and we'll get a weight on Dudley," she said while handing me the obligatory clipboard loaded with several pages of forms and a pen.

"Ma'am, the name's Careless and I'll be glad to do all that but where is the scale?" I inquired. She then directed me to an area behind a wall just in back of the lobby where there were all kinds of goodies for Dudley to get into. Bella was there as well. Mystery solved.

Dudley went right up to Bella and they started sniffing one another. They hit it off just fine but Bella's owner looked at me with a bit of a frown and I gave her my second-best fake smile and started pointing back and forth in Bella and Dudley's direction as if to announce a prearranged marriage and that frown turned upside down.

"The doctor will see you now, Mrs. Silverman," another young lady behind the desk said as Bella and her owner walked off toward one of the examining rooms. Dudley was a little bummed out but he was still exploring around and at least I now knew he was fine with other dogs. I sat down in a chair and began to fill out the tedious paperwork for first-time users.

As I began to write, Dudley hopped up on the chair next to me and sat there like a person. I had to tell him a couple of times that I didn't like people reading over my shoulder. It wasn't like he needed to check the accuracy of what I was writing so I told him to knock it off. He just started licking my face. It was always something with him.

Let's see....patient's name. I wrote in Dudley but there was no place for the middle name. I turned to the patient and asked him what his middle name was. Of course being the ham he is, he answered by grumbling under his breath, "Errrr, mmm, ahhhh, errrr."

"Okay, okay, you don't have to be embarrassed about it. I was just asking so I could write it on the form," I explained to him. At that point it was getting out of control and unbeknownst to us we were being watched by Dr. L.D. Eckermann, who had been standing there, witnessing the antics.

While Dudley was still sitting in the chair next to me, he picked up his front long leg and placed it around the back of my neck. He then leaned into me and placed his head on my shoulder while looking upward into my eyes. He had me now, so I couldn't get mad at him or tell him to stop goofing off. He was quickly becoming my best friend and confidant.

"Excuse me, Mr. Robinson, do you two need a private moment to-gether? I can come back in a few minutes," a voice from across the room said.

It just dawned on me that Dudley and I were not the only two people in the room and I became slightly embarrassed. Dudley and I both turned a nice shade of red and quickly separated. At least L.D. didn't ask us to get a room like Birk did. That could have been a little more awkward. We dusted ourselves off and tried to act as normal as humanly possible. "No, no, we're good," I said as I looked up and saw a nice-looking middle-aged man wearing a white doctor's jacket with the name L.D. Eckermann sewn in blue letters on the left side at chest level.

"Mr. Robinson, why don't you bring Dudley to exam room number three and we'll have a look at him," L.D. said.

"Okay, Doc, but the name's Careless," I said as Dudley and I got up and began walking toward exam room number three.

"Okay, Careless, you can call me L.D.," the doctor said.

"You got it, L.D.," I said. I just wanted to try it on for size. L.D. was good. I liked that name. It rolled smoothly off the tongue as I said it and it also sounded pretty cool. I thought back once again to my early childhood habit of not trusting people with two first names but I did like and trust people with two initials as their name. L.D. and E.D. both came to mind. Judging from his appearance, L.D. seemed like a stand-up kind of guy as he followed us to the exam room.

Just before the exam room L.D. asked me to weigh Dudley on the scale in front of us. The scale was pretty cool because it seemed like part of the floor as I had Dudley stand still on it for a few moments. I did notice when L.D. walked right next to him, Dudley didn't utter a peep. Usually anyone, except for me, who gets near Dudley got a warning growl or grunt. He's not much of a people person and I really have no idea where he gets that from. But he must have liked L.D. because he just eyeballed him with no sound effects. Needless to say, L.D. and I were quite pleased with Dud-ley's weight as he turned out to be eighty-eight pounds.

All three of us entered the examining room and L.D. shut the door be-hind us. It wasn't very large but it was roomy enough and nicely decorated. There was another door directly in front of us just like the door we had just passed through. I believe it led to the lab and operating rooms. There were several diplomas on the wall from Texas A&M University where L.D. had graduated from. If you were going to be any kind of vet in Texas or anywhere else in our great nation then Texas A&M University was the place to train and graduate from. By the way, do you know what you call someone who graduated from Texas A&M? Answer: Boss.

Texas A&M University was first established in 1862 by the Congress of the United States and was built and opened on October 4, 1876, in College Station, Texas. Originally called the Agricultural & Mechanical College of Texas, it was founded to educate farmers and military personnel. When first started, the University only had forty students and six faculty members. By 1963, as the college grew larger, the Texas Legislature re-named the college from the Agricultural & Mechanical College of Texas to Texas A&M University. The university campus is now the seventh largest in the United States with approximately forty-eight thousand students, and boasts having over 5,200 acres of main campus as well as being the home of the George H.W. Bush library.

There are many time-honored traditions at Texas A&M University, one of which is that everyone says howdy to one another when they meet. As annoying as that may be, it is a tradition, and when someone says howdy, you can bet they will be receiving a howdy right back. Until recently, the students of Texas A&M University have held a bonfire every year during the weekend of the Texas A&M, University of Texas football game. This is a longstanding tradition that dates back for over ninety years. They call themselves the Aggies, and the bonfire, which is usually about four stories high, is called the Aggie Bonfire. It is massive and is built by the engineering department using a crane and a lot of students. They currently participate in the Big Twelve Football Conference and have a renowned marching band known as the Fightin' Texas Aggie Band, the world's largest military marching band. They are known for their precision timing and are a real treat to watch. The University is also well known for the cadet core that has supplied military officers for World War I, World War II, and many other conflicts since. Texas A&M University is on the cutting edge of plant genome modification to improve food sources for people and animals and has successfully cloned cattle, goats, pigs, deer, horses, and cats. The veterinary and engineering schools are ranked as some of the best in the world. It is a great honor and accomplishment to graduate from these schools. You can bet that if your vet has a diploma from Texas A&M University hanging on the wall, your pet will be well taken care of and your vet has had the best available training. I must admit that my mind was placed at ease once I saw the diploma on the wall made out to L.D. Eckermann.

"So, I see you are an Aggie, L.D.," I said.

"That's right, class of 1973," L.D. replied.

The examining room was decorated with warm colors although I didn't know why because it was my understanding that dogs do not see colors. I was going to ask Dudley about that but he was busy eating a dog treat L.D. had cleverly hidden in his hand. That was just great, now I knew Dudley could be bought off by a simple morsel of food. This was a secret I would keep to myself. There were several shelves and cabinets in the room with all kinds of gizmos. Other than the treat jar I had no idea what I was looking at. I did notice several of L.D.'s framed awards hanging on the wall next to his diplomas. One of them was from the SPCA showing L.D. as a board member who donated his time to help the animals that, through no fault of their own, came to live at the shelter. This was called the "Angel Among Us" award.

There was another nicely wood-framed document with L.D.'s name on it showing he was once the president of the Texas Veterinary Medical Association. Right next to that was an award for the Practitioner of the Year from the American Animal Hospital Association. The last one hanging on the wall was the Companion Animal Practitioner of The Year award from the Texas Veterinary Medical Association. L.D. was certainly highly decorated and had a wealth of experience. I decided right then that he was the right choice for my new friend, Dudley.

"Right after I graduated from Texas A&M Veterinary School I moved back to Houston and started working for the Westbury Animal Hospital, and in 1976 I became a partner and have been here ever since," L.D. informed me.

"Okay, L.D., you're hired," I said as I gave him the thumbs up hand gesture.

L.D. told me he wanted to get Dudley up on the table to examine him. He then called a vet tech into the room to manhandle Dudley onto the table and to keep him in position to be examined. Mistake number one!

Dudley was doing just fine until a young man walked into the room, wearing green medical pajamas.

As soon as Dudley spotted him, which was almost instantly, I noticed a pool of water on the floor. I looked up and saw there was no water or rain leaking from the ceiling and in fact when Dudley and I drove over from the loft I hadn't noticed a cloud in the sky. No, it was more like the scene from one of the scariest movies I ever had the misfortune to see. It was a misfortune because it was so good and so scary that I hardly slept for a week after watching it. That movie was *Alien*. Several times in the movie when the weird alien life form was about to eat someone, saliva would appear in the scene, or what could be referred to as the money shot. This was the signature money-maker scene because whenever there was dripping goober on the floor right next to someone, that person was usually written out of the movie in an extremely gory fashion. As I was having my flashback experience to *Alien*, the vet tech was about to be written out of the exam by Dudley or so he probably would have wished. The next thing I saw was Dudley's big goobering jowls curling up and then I began to hear it....

It was a soft, very low-pitch, menacing, monotone growl. I knew this was not going to end well but, being brave, the vet tech just kept inching toward Dudley as the very low-pitch, menacing, monotone growl got progressively louder. As the vet tech was about to reach down with his hand and try to calmly pet Dudley, I decided this would be a great time for me to intervene and step in between the two before the vet tech ended up like dead meat on a toilet seat.

Just as I did, L.D. asked the vet tech to wait outside and said to me, "Dad, why don't you bring Dudley in the back?" as he opened the door in the back of the room. He led us into another big room filled with an operating table, several other exam tables, x-ray and imaging machines, and cages occupied by recovering animals.

L.D. directed us into the large room and stopped right at an examining table. L.D. talked to me about Dudley's appearance and told me that he seemed a little skinny. He asked me if I could get Dudley up on the examining table and I told him that would not be a problem.

I bent down and told Dudley that everything was going to be okay as I hooked my arms underneath him and hoisted him up upon the examining table. L.D. quickly went to work on him without a peep from Dudley.

I found this a little unusual because Dudley didn't really take kindly to strangers and usually didn't take to anyone except me. Yet, there he was just acting like his normal, nice, goofy self.

Seeing that Dudley was my first real pet, I had never been to a vet before and I could not believe the onceover L.D. gave him. He listened to Dudley's heart very carefully with his stethoscope, looked in his ears, looked in his mouth, checked his teeth and gums, and turned him upside down and all around. He pinched, pressed, and prodded even in some places I could tell Dudley wasn't too happy about, but still not a peep from him. I guess he knew we were there to help him and I'm pretty sure dogs can pick up on human feelings and intentions a lot better and quicker than people actually do.

L.D. started examining Dudley's jowls and stretching them back with his hands. I told L.D. I thought he was a very brave man and he just laughed. He told me he wasn't afraid of this big ole' boy, and that this dog probably would never bite anyone.

I hoped he was right. He seemed confident enough. As he continued inspecting Dudley's teeth, L.D. told me that indeed Dudley was somewhere around two years old and, while he was in pretty good shape, he was slightly malnourished.

I told him that was probably because he was running around wild with nothing to eat and no one to care for him. L.D. agreed.

When he listened again to Dudley's heart he said Dudley definitely had a heart murmur and he would talk to me about that later. This made me a little nervous but L.D. assured me it was probably nothing. He took a few samples of bodily fluids and looked over the stitches from Dudley's operation. Just when Dudley and I had almost forgotten about that ordeal, L.D. told me some of the stitches were about to come undone and needed to be restitched. He told me Dudley had been a little overactive. Good thing he didn't know about the incident with the lovely E.D. That would be our little secret. This time he would have steel stitches and there would be no way Dudley would be able to hurt them, but I found out I would have to come back in about ten days to have them removed.

L.D. said, "Dad, why don't you hold Dudley still while I stitch him back up. Try to keep him nice and calm."

I told him that would be no problem and it wasn't. L.D. quickly put on some disposable rubber gloves and started sewing Dudley back up with the steel stitches. As I stroked Dudley's head to keep him calm, I asked L.D. what was taking so long and also mentioned that if he was sewing a shirt or sweater, "I take an extra-large. Yes, that's right, I'm extra-large and in charge."

Neither L.D. nor Dudley were amused. Dudley wasn't feeling a thing and the restitching only took about ten minutes. Once finished, Dudley stood up and jumped off the operating table. I guess we were ready to go. L.D. took off his disposable rubber gloves, put his hand on my shoulder, and told me he was glad to have met me and glad to have Dudley as a patient.

I don't know if he was telling the truth about Dudley; but if he was, then he was definitely a saint. He told me someone from the clinic would be calling me in the next couple of days with the results of all of the tests they were going to run and he would talk to me about Dudley's heart murmur when we came back to have the steel stitches removed. L.D. walked us out and Dudley and I went to the desk to check out.

"Sir, may I help you?" asked a young lady behind the counter.

"Yes, ma'am, Dudley and I just finished up with L.D. and we're about ready to take off," I replied. Just then, quicker than a lightning strike, a golden-tan flash sprung up from below, grabbed a bag of dog treats from the countertop, and left only a trail of goober. That's when all of the noises started, as well as my extreme embarrassment and amusement. Moaning, groaning, grunting, growling, and loud moist eating noises were emanating from below. One of us was definitely having a lip-smacking pleasure and I was pretty certain it was not me.

"Sir, what was that?" the young lady asked.

"What was what?" I shot back at her.

"Sir, did your dog just eat a whole bag of treats?"

Okay, so here's where I panicked just a little bit and replied, "Honey, the name's Careless, and no speaky English!"

"Okay, Careless, since this is your first visit..." Then the noises got really loud, crunching and munching along with all kinds of moans of ecstasy while I just pretended there was something very interesting up on the ceiling and craned my neck upward as if to observe whatever it was in a classic case of misdirection. "Anyway, as I was saying, since this is your first visit with us and with Dr. Eckermann, and since Dudley was adopted from the SPCA, there will be no charge. On the other hand, I will have to charge you ten dollars for that bag of treats Dudley just inhaled," she said as she started to type up the bill on the computer.

At this point, everyone in the waiting room was cracking up laughing and waiting to see what the king of clowns would do next. One thing was definitely certain, he had more antics to share with the class. Fortunately for me, the bag of treats was keeping Dudley busy so he didn't really have the time or energy to do any more damage.

Standing just behind me, L.D. told the young lady that the visit as well as the bag of treats were "on the house" and there would be no charge.

I turned and thanked L.D.

Dudley just looked up at L.D. and me and let out a huge belch. Well, that brought the house down. Everyone in the building began to chuckle at that point.

L.D. said, "Dad, why don't you go ahead and take Dudley home and I'll call you later in the week with the results of the tests."

I turned around and noticed my very good and presently inexpensive friend was lying on his back with his long golden legs sticking up in the air while gravity had his rather large jowls forming a very nice crocodile smile. I also noticed he had a slight dog-treat-induced bulge in his stomach. He was definitely going to have to loosen up his belt a few notches and it wasn't even Thanksgiving yet.

After a few choice words to coax him to stand up, I hoped he would behave himself as we walked toward the door to exit the building.

"Thanks, L.D.," I shouted and waved with my free hand while holding onto Dudley's leash with the other. Dudley had definitely left the building.

CHAPTER TWENTY-ONE

When we got outside, Dudley was back to his old self and never left my side as we walked toward the Power Wagon. On the way, he sniffed just about everything, and when we got to the passenger side I opened the door and Dudley jumped in. I cranked the window down and walked around to the driver's side. I strapped Dudley in with the seatbelt and did the same for myself. He didn't complain but I could tell he didn't like it much. I told him it was for his own good and it would be really good practice for him to get use to the constraints of "workin' for the man."

Dudley was not amused, but as we drove off, his nose kicked into high gear and he forgot all about it. He began sniffing away trying to determine what all of the smells were and where they were coming from. I knew this would keep him busy until we got back to Big Rock, but what I didn't realize was that a person with an interesting dog is also a person of interest to the ladies. I figured that if I got second looks from the ladies just because of my friend Dudley then pretty much anyone could, not that I'm not a handsome, rugged individual—because I am, if I do say so myself, and most importantly I can honestly say that Dudley agrees.

We navigated our way back to Big Rock and I stopped in front of the building. As I shifted Clarence into park I noticed Dudley's tail began spinning around again like a helicopter rotor. I was puzzled at first but as I looked ahead I noticed E.D.'s big blue Oldsmobile, Betsy, as she called her, had just pulled up and E.D. was exiting the car. I unstrapped Dudley from his seatbelt restraint and, before I knew it, he managed to jump his big butt through the open window and was trotting toward E.D. with a big smile on his face.

"What's the word, Thunderbird?" I inquired of E.D.

"Careless, this serial thriller of yours is on his way towards me so I hope the two of you had a nice long talk and at least one of you knows how to treat a lady," she exclaimed.

Before I could reply or think of a snappy comeback, I noticed that in fact Dudley had slowed down his approach toward E.D. and was acting like a gentleman.

She knelt down and began petting and rubbing his big head. She grabbed his ears and began rubbing them. To my amazement he sat down, lowered his head, and his eyes started going back in his head like he was so relaxed he almost appeared to be going to sleep. Well, I had never witnessed anything like this before; but in my defense, I was a rookie. I just looked at the two of them in amazement.

E.D. noticed my bewildered look and asked, "What, you don't know how to handle dogs? They like it when you rub their ears; it relaxes them. I grew up with dogs. Careless, am I going to have to teach you how to care for your dog?"

"Yes, Mommy, you will, and I have some other things I will need your personal instruction with as well. Will you be available, say, around 6:00 tonight for some tutoring?" I inquired.

"Nice try, Carwash, but you and I both know that simply is not going to happen. You can send Dudley over for a visit now that I see he can control himself," she said. Just as she finished speaking Dudley began trying to hump her leg.

I was about to say, "The name's Careless," but instead all I said was, "Never mind," and the funny thing was that she said, "Never mind," at the very same time. Strike up another one for the great timing of Dudley. I couldn't really blame him. He did have exquisite taste in women.

E.D. finally managed to remove Dudley from her leg and charged off. All I saw was the old iron front door slamming shut behind her. Dudley and I just looked at one another as I shrugged my shoulders with a grin on my face. I suppose I would just have to live vicariously through him, for now.

Dudley marked his territory the whole way up to the old iron front door. Once inside, we scooted past the entryway and up the staircase. When we made it to #158, I unlocked the door and we both proceeded to go inside. I closed and locked the door behind us. It had been a ruff day at the office so I put some dog food down for Dudley.

I made myself an iced coffee with some Jack Black and stretched out on the bed to rehash my adventurous day. Note to self: we're out of coffee so stop by Dunkin' Donuts tomorrow and grab a couple of bags of their famous coffee. I find it to be much tastier than Starbucks and according to Dunkin' Donuts' own advertising they have America's best coffee. If it isn't the best, then it is pretty darn close.

Ah yes, my favorite coffee from Dunkin' Donuts. I never really cared for those other foo foo coffees. You know the ones, with all of the fancy names and sizes with something other than the metric or English systems of measurement. To me, the fancier the name and cup design, the more I was certainly going to have a financial mishap and be separated from way too much of my money when I purchased it. I'll just simply stick with the working man's coffee, the everyday, ordinary coffee. The taste was good and the price was right.

Dunkin' Donuts was originally founded in 1950 by a gentleman named Bill Rosenberg. The first store was opened in Quincy, Massachusetts, and quickly became a hit. Besides the amazing coffee, who among us could deny the irresistible aroma and taste of those fresh hot donuts? I'm not sure I have many weaknesses, but I would be hardpressed to not take a bite of the sugary goodness they call donuts. By 1954 five more Dunkin' Donuts shops were opened, and in 1955 Dunkin' Donuts franchises were sold. There are currently over 9,700 Dunkin' Donuts shops worldwide in at least thirty-one countries. With items like delicious coffee, fifty-two varieties of donuts, bagels, muffins, pastries, and even breakfast sandwiches, it is no wonder that more than three million people make purchases from Dunkin' Donuts every single day. Dunkin' Donuts coffee can now be purchased in many stores. It could be that I have just gained five pounds thinking of those delectable donuts, so perhaps tomorrow I'll just stick to thinking only about the coffee.

CHAPTER TWENTY-TWO

As I laid there dozing off, I put my coffee down and heard some crunching noises going on pretty close to me. Dudley had taken a mouthful of his food and brought it over close to my bed. He dropped the food he was holding in his rather large mouth onto the floor and was pushing it around with his nose. He looked around in all directions, looked at me as if waiting for the all clear signal, and then ate it a few morsels at a time.

I told him to quit playing with his food because somewhere in the world there was a starving dog but he just kept right on goofing off with his food. *Crunch, crunch,* he ate one or two morsels at a time. I must admit that while it was amusing, it did become slightly irritating. He finally finished his whole bowl of food and turned his attention toward my iced coffee with the rocket fuel additive. I started to close my eyes to go where the grass is always greener. Before I completely zonked out I heard a large slurping sound coming from right next to me. Someone, other than me, was partaking in my Dunkin' Donuts and Jack Daniels iced coffee. I was just too tired to take it away from him and there wasn't that much left anyway so I let him go to town. I shut my eyes and was off to La La Land.

I was definitely somewhere other than La La Land, but where? Everything was so green and peaceful and there he was walking up to me. None other than the first love of my life and no, it was not E.D. and it certainly was not me. It was Eagle, the horse who became my friend and first showed me how to open my heart and how to love. Sadly for me, Eagle had been called home many years ago.

It finally dawned on me where I was and what I was supposed to be doing. I think this may be what the Native American Indians referred to when they designed and built their dream catchers. I never really owned a Native American dream catcher but nevertheless, my dream catcher was my heart. I suppose I would figure out later what to do with the rest of my body parts, but for now Eagle was here, just as plain as day, and he was waiting for me.

Eagle pranced right up to me, stopped in front of me, and placed his head in my outstretched hands, just like in days gone by. As hundreds of times in the past, I placed one hand just behind his chin and with the other hand began gently rubbing his forehead between his eyes, or as the child of my dear friends once called it, his "five head," but that's another story for another day. Eagle and I were together again and that was all that mattered.

As strange as it seemed, I was now back at Echo Hill Ranch, the boys and girls camp in Medina, Texas, in the heart of the Texas Hill Country where I spent all of my summers as a boy and a young man. Somehow I knew, whether good or bad, I had become the man I am today partly if not mostly from my living, learning, and loving experiences at Echo Hill Ranch. I started off as a young boy or a rancher as one of the owners, Tom Friedman, used to call us. We were really more like campers but I must admit that, at six years old, it was pretty cool to be a rancher.

One of my favorite counselors at camp was a man named Jack Slaughter. We called him Cowboy Jack and he was the head wrangler for the horseback riding expeditions we took on trails through pretty much untouched valleys and hills. Jack had long, straight blond hair and piercing blue eyes. He always wore a cowboy hat and had a gentle and kind voice. His sidekick was a dog named Kroger. Kroger was a fawn-colored Rhodesian Ridgeback, the type of dog known to hunt lions in Africa. We never really saw Kroger during the daytime but he occasionally came around during our feeding times until one day he got banned from the dining hall after that terrible incident occurred when he grabbed a whole loaf of freshly baked bread and swallowed it down before anyone could catch him.

During the day, Kroger mostly slept under one of the bunks but, boy howdy, he came alive at night. He was hardly seen at night but he was sure heard. He was a silent and almost invisible hunter when the sun went down, but when he did occasionally bark, it echoed around the surrounding hills many times. He had one of the most booming barks I have ever heard. Sadly, Jack and Kroger now both live only in my dream catcher but, oh yes, they did live!

Eagle was the horse I rode at Echo Hill. As I stood there with him, he began slowly moving his head up and down and stomping one of his hooves on the ground. Eagle was a beautiful stallion, about sixteen hands high. He was chestnut in color with a jet-black mane and tail. After I was a rancher at Echo Hill, I became a counselor in training, and then I became the head wrangler, just like Cowboy Jack, many years before. Early every morning before sunrise and before the ranchers woke up, I got ready to ride, walked out of my cabin door, and whistled for Eagle. Then I walked over to the corral as Eagle came galloping up from wherever he had been.

The camp was on four hundred acres and Eagle and the other horses pretty much had the run of the place. I brushed and groomed Eagle, fed him, saddled him, and rode off to round up the other sixteen horses along with a donkey named Lucky. Nobody ever rode Lucky. He was kind of like the camp mascot. He was a funny, nice little donkey. The other horses were usually in two or three places, so it wasn't very hard to find them, especially when the horse you were on could run like the wind.

I usually found the other horses and Lucky in places on the ranch known as the South Flat, the East Flat, Big Foot Falls, Chalks Bluff, Three Rivers, or the Gypsy Campfire. Eagle and I rode until we found the other horses. I loved rounding up the horses and watching the sun come up as I drove them back to the corral. It was such a free and liberating experience being alone out in the middle of nowhere, just me and nature.

Of course sometimes nature took it course in dangerous ways. I will never forget riding down the South Flat and almost running over a pack of coyotes. They were so silent I didn't even know they were there until I was almost on them. Eagle knew they were there well in advance because he could smell them. I noticed him acting a bit skittish, but fortunately for everyone the coyotes were more scared than we were and scattered off into the woods until they disappeared from sight. Eagle and I kept a look out for them regardless. They never came back.

There was a time, many years ago, before my and Eagle's time, that Charles Hart, also known as Chuck the Wrangler, was riding on a trail to a site known as Three Rivers. He was alone early that misty morning in search of the other horses when he had a slight brush with fate. He had just ridden into an area where there was a canopy of overgrown tree branches when his favorite horse, Shalom, (meaning peace in the Hebrew language) started wiging out and sidestepping. Chuck was at a loss as to the behavior of Shalom, but before he could do anything about it a huge bobcat he had not yet seen (and perched on a limb only about ten feet off of the ground just above him) let out a huge roar and leapt off a branch right over his head coming to a soft landing on the other side of the trail to disappear into the woods.

Being a wrangler was a blast but it certainly did come with its dangers. I had been bitten, kicked, stepped on, and even thrown once, but I wouldn't have traded it for the world. As the Peter Gabriel song goes, *"Eagle flew out of the night,"* and as I was hugging him again for what I hoped would not be the last time, I noticed a throaty, grunting noise in my ear.

I started swatting at my ear to shoo away whatever was making that noise and I am pretty sure Eagle heard it as well because he started bobbing his head up and down at me as if to say something, as if to say goodbye. His eyes were my eyes as we stared at one another. I hopped on Eagle and we took off in a full gallop toward the South Flat. Careless the Wrangler didn't want to leave but nature is something even Careless can't control so my dream catcher awaits me for another time, another place, and it wouldn't be soon enough. Goodbye, old friend.

CHAPTER TWENTY-THREE

I opened my eyes and was still stretched out on my bed. What a great trip it had been. I did notice something in my left ear making weird noises, something wet and cold. As I pointed my eyes in that direction, I saw Dudley lying right next to me with his nose as scrunched up to my ear as close as humanly possible. I couldn't even begin to describe the type of noises entering my head via my eardrum, but I did notice Dudley was wide awake and staring right into my eyes while his head rested motionless on my pillow.

Somehow, somewhere still far away, tucked in my heart, I felt as if I had just seen that same look, same eyes, and same expression. Now the only positive thing I could think of at this point was that I probably wouldn't need to go for my annual hearing test since Dr. Dudley had just performed one on me.

"Ha ha ha ha, now that's rich," I heard Birk laughing boisterously. "If I only had my camera," he complained. Apparently Birk had let himself in with my extra key I had given to him but I didn't hear him come in because I had been someplace else, someplace where we'll all hopefully reside at some point, in another one's heart.

Dudley got up and went into protective mode. He stood at attention on the bed between Birk and me and gave a little snarl as if to tell Birk to shut up and approach no further. Finally, all those years of medical school really might just pay off for Dr. Dudley because if Birk was not careful he would be in need of a doctor very soon, especially if he moved much closer.

"Good boy, Dudley, it's okay now," I reassured him. I sat up and placed my hand on his shoulder, which is when his whole body began to relax as he stood down from red alert.

"Hey, you've got work tomorrow so I thought we'd go have a late lunch and then go to the bookstore. What do you say?" Birk asked.

"I say you're buying and what are we waiting for?" I answered.

Dudley hopped up and went to the door because he needed to go outside to do his thing. I told Birk to take him downstairs and let him out back in the gated area but to keep an eye on him so he wouldn't ruin my day by making one of his great escapes again.

Birk opened the door but Dudley didn't budge. He looked back at me, waiting for some type of command. I told him to move his butt and take care of business, but he wasn't going to leave unless I went with him.

I got out of bed, cleaned myself up, drained the main vein, changed my shirt, and walked out with my boy at my side, which was just as it should be. Birk walked out behind us and I shut and locked the door. We went downstairs and were about to go through the back door to the gated area for Dudley to stretch his legs and relieve himself.

Before we did I told Birk I wanted to do an experiment and that I needed him to go through the front entrance of the loft and walk around to the outside of the gated area in back. I told him to be silent and wait there until he saw something out of the ordinary. He looked puzzled but did as I asked.

Dudley and I went through the back door of the loft and he went romping around inside the gated area. I pretended to turn my back to him and sure enough he disappeared again but this time I had Birk waiting for him. Birk discovered that Dudley had managed to squeeze his somewhat skinny body in between a steel fence post and the corner of the building. I had seen this small space earlier after the last time Dudley escaped but I didn't think he could fit through it.

Thankfully Birk sent Dudley back through the opening and back to me, although I was certain he would eventually have returned just like he did the last time.

Birk found an old four-by-four lying on the ground and wedged it in the space so Dudley would never be able to escape again. Mystery solved.

I did have to go to work the next day, which was unfortunate because I really wanted to be independently wealthy just like most other independently wealthy people. Sadly, I had to work for a living, but one day I plan to write a book about my adventures with Dudley and think of some witty title that will catch many readers' attention so they can experience Dudley as well. I haven't really thought of a title yet but it's definitely going to be a good one. After that, when nature takes its course, I hope to be independently wealthy like so many other great independently wealthy people. If you don't mind, I'm going to quit writing the phrase independently wealthy now even though my goal is to become independently wealthy.

While I was watching Birk (who will most likely never be independently wealthy) watch Dudley run around like a maniac with his head in the air, smelling, and sniffing everything like a crack addict, I began to think about what I should do with Dudley during the work day. I didn't know what to expect from him while I was away but it was getting close to the time I would need to make some sort of decision.

I really had only three options available to me that I could think of and those were: one, take him to work with me; two, leave him in the loft by himself during the work day and hope that he didn't get bored or anxious and destroy what little I owned; or three, which was really just a variation of two, leave him in the loft during the work day with a babysitter or someone who would continually come over to check on him.

Seeing that, yes, you guessed it, I'm not independently wealthy, option number three wasn't really a good one for me. I liked option number two but wasn't quite sure how Dudley would handle separation, and my fear was that he might possibly take it out on the contents of my loft. The contents of my loft, while meager, were innocent and did not deserve the harsh tooth-thrashing, mouthing, and overactive goobering they would most probably receive, so in my mind I elected to choose option number one.

Now, being that I didn't work alone I was going to have to get creative if I was going to walk into my office with Dudley the following morning. I was pretty sure he would be okay going to work, but I worked with my Grandpa and my brother so I wasn't sure they would be too keen on having another mouth to feed at work.

CHAPTER TWENTY-FOUR

Robinson Pipe & Supply was established long ago by my grandfather, Ben Robinson. Ben has a heavy Russian accent since he was originally from the mother country, but left with his brothers and sisters many years earlier due to the oppression by the central government that controlled virtually everything but did virtually nothing for the people. He and his brother Isadore started two separate scrap metal companies when they arrived in the good old U. S. of A. They lived out of their offices and traded for just about anything people wanted to get rid of. Think of the sitcom *Sanford and Son* and you can somewhat visualize their businesses.

Ben started with nothing and with a little luck and a lot of elbow grease his business grew and became quite successful. After making it through the depression, Ben eventually moved out of his office, bought a larger scrap yard, got married to his lovely bride, Rose, who was from Germany, and started a family. He later left the scrap metal business behind, "Lamont, you dummy!" and became more specialized in the steel pipe business. He brought my brother and me into the business to start modernizing it and to keep it moving along for the next generation, whenever that may be.

My grandfather definitely had a vision. The pipe distributed from Robinson Pipe & Supply can be found all over the world in most freeways, bridges, buildings, mass transit systems, water and sewer systems, telecommunication lines, flag poles, airports, and sign poles, some even sporting a buck-tooth animal on top of them along many Texas highways. To be sure, there were hard times and my grandfather often told me that during the Great Depression he didn't even know there was a depression. He just went to work every day, worked very hard, and before he knew it the Depression was over. He said he just chose not to participate. He told me that and many other stories for a reason—and that was because he wanted me to understand that nothing was ever free and nothing ever came easy. To get something, hard work was required.

I learned my lesson well while he was busy brainwashing my brother and me by waking us up early at 5:00 a.m. every Monday through Friday, cooking breakfast for everyone, and then driving us all to work. Eggs, sausage, toast, and even cereal for those who dared to eat healthy. He also made coffee the old fashioned way with an old percolator coffeemaker, which I am pretty certain he smuggled over from the old country. It looked like it might take a rocket scientist to load it up to make the coffee but the coffee it produced was pretty good, even if you had to floss a few coffee grinds out of your teeth afterwards. Really, that just added to the flavorful experience.

I remember all of his teachings now because we repeated them so many times it was just hard not to remember, and in fact had become a way of life for my brother and me, so I suppose he was successful in the brainwashing—or as I think of it now that I am out of puberty, the life lessons. He is a wise man but how will he react when he sees my new, dear friend, Dudley? I guess I will just have to find out tomorrow.

Dudley was through exploring and goofing off so he came loping back up to me. He had a beautiful gait. He was graceful and was starting to put on some weight, which made him even more handsome. He was almost regal but he never acted snobby like some of those Frenchy French dogs. He was a man of the people and it appeared he was ready to go out to lunch and the bookstore.

I looked at Birk and he was shaking his head from side to side to express his extreme displeasure at the idea of Dudley tagging along with us to lunch and the bookstore. I must have been hanging around with Birk more than I realized because he somehow knew what I was going to suggest before I even had a chance to open my mouth. That's just when I cracked a big toothy smile, as well as did my friend who was sitting right by my side, and we both began to gush that boyish charm we so cleverly possess. It just came naturally oozing out.

I must say I was kind of proud of Dudley. *Like father like son*, I thought.

Birk kept shaking his head from side to side, which either meant he really didn't like the idea of Dudley attending or he was having some sort of rare seizure. I wasn't quite sure which. In my defense, it was hard to tell with Birk.

Birk finally relented and we headed back into the building and out to the front through the old iron door. All three of us made our way to Birk's

Cowboy Cadillac. I opened the back door for Dudley and he hopped in with ease. Birk and I climbed up into the front seat, closed and locked the doors, and Birk cranked up that bad boy.

He looked at me and asked, "The Usual?"

I just nodded to him and Dudley licked him from ear to ear with his slobbery and, may I say, quite large tongue.

Birk's eyes rolled back in disgust as he turned his head to look at me to complain, but I was having none of that. Before he could start whining like a little girl I just shrugged my shoulders, gestured with both hands slightly held out with my palms facing upward, and matter-of-factly, even unemotionally, said, "You know, they say a dog's mouth is even cleaner than a human's mouth."

Secretly, deep down inside, Dudley and I were laughing hysterically but we dared not show it. I am sure Birk would not take too kindly to that. I looked at Dudley and he sat down on the backseat. I told him to click it or ticket, to be safe; and after an extensive face sleeve-wiping experience, Birk threw it in reverse and let her rip.

We pulled out of the parking lot going fifty miles per hour. I thought to myself that someone must be a little hungry.

Birk and I decided to go to one of our favorite restaurants and it just so happened it was only a couple of miles away. By my public school math calculations, we should be there in about just enough time for me to get my seatbelt fastened. As I reached down to do just that, Birk brought the truck to a screeching stop.

Perhaps this might be some of that fuzzy math because we got there sooner rather than later. Birk must be slowing down a tad because usually by the time I blink my eyes we are at our destination. In Texas, we call that high-speed transportation.

We don't need a bullet train because we all drive like a bat out of hell. Sure enough, we were now in the parking lot of a Houston landmark. China Gardens claims to be the home of the best egg rolls in Houston and also the notoriously famous dish, lemon chicken. I wasn't sure how it was accomplished but those chickens sure did taste lemony delicious.

China Gardens is located in downtown Houston on Leland Street. It was founded by Marian and David Jue in 1969. I wonder if they may be Jueish? Back in 1969, there weren't many buildings surrounding the restaurant and frankly there probably weren't that many Jueish people around as well, but if you go there now you will notice it is right across the street from the Toyota Center where the Houston Rockets and Houston Aeros play. Many people eat at China Gardens and then walk across the street to watch a basketball game.

China Gardens is now mostly run by the offspring of Marian and David. Their son Richard works there every day along with their daughter Carol. Richard's daughter has been working there it seems since she was out of diapers. They are a very hardworking, goal-oriented family, and they run a tight ship as well as provide excellent food and service.

When you walk in, you will most likely be greeted and seated by Marian herself. Once you have been seated, she might call you "baby" and sit down with you to impart some of her Chinese wisdom, most of which will come from her life experiences of hard work and good decisions. She is probably one of the most hardworking, brightest businesswomen I think I have ever met, but that's not all. She'll even give you advice on family, personal, business, and health matters. If you are really lucky, she may actually stand up and start massaging your neck and shoulders while continuing to talk to you. That will get you nice and relaxed in preparation for the extremely delicious meal you will have. I have been eating at China Gardens since it opened. My grandfather started bringing me there when I was just a lad.

CHAPTER TWENTY-FIVE

After the truck was shut down and parked in the parking lot, all three of us jumped out of Birk's truck and headed toward the entrance. Richard was standing outside talking to someone and, as we approached him, his conversation with the man he was standing with abruptly stopped and he focused his attention solely upon the three of us. He looked right at me and said, "How do you want him prepared? I'm thinking of stir fried with a nice hot dumpling sauce."

We all burst out laughing except for Dudley who was not at all amused.

I asked Dudley what he thought about that and of course he said something as he muttered unmentionables under his breath. But once he knew we were all joking, he simmered down somewhat. I didn't have the heart to give him my stock answer about how they eat dogs in China. I didn't want to give him nightmares.

Richard waved us in and said he would watch Dudley while Birk and I dined. I didn't want to leave him, but since dogs were not allowed in the restaurant I tied Dudley to a pole in front of the restaurant with a leash I had but rarely used. I told him that, if he acted nicely and stayed right there, I would bring him back a fortune cookie. He reluctantly agreed and sat down next to where Richard was standing. Richard and his friend had already resumed their conversation but they were speaking softly so as not to let anyone overhear them.

Birk and I went in the front door of China Gardens. It was a very interesting place. As you walk in on the right, there is a full bar with a television in the corner to watch sporting events and, believe me, every time there is any kind of game or event, you can bet during working hours that the television is turned on. It's probably on even after working hours. In fact, I'm not sure it ever gets turned off. There is a little desk on the left where the bills are paid and where takeout orders are picked up. Many people order takeout food for lunch and on the way home for dinner. Those darn workaholics!

My goal is to someday be a retired workaholic and possibly independently wealthy. I'm not allergic to work or anything like that but everyone has to have a goal. Am I right? Don't answer that; I know I'm right. Even a blind squirrel occasionally finds an acorn, so I'm definitely right.

"Hello, Careless," I heard a voice from behind the desk say, "Table for two?"

It was Carol and she grabbed a couple of menus and started to walk us to our table. Not only is Carol hardworking and very nice, but she is very attractive. She is a real sweetheart. Apparently Birk took notice of her so I had to give him the old elbow to the ribs as we were walking. I can't blame a guy for looking but it just seemed wrong; and if Birk didn't deserve my elbow yet then he soon would, so I was definitely justified.

He just gave me one of his looks and we proceeded on. All of the tables were immaculate with red-and-white tablecloths diagonally one on top of the other, and silverware, napkins, and water glasses placed ever so perfectly and precisely. The restrooms were on the left and all along every wall hung huge sculptures made from different shades of green-colored jade.

Jade is a beautiful green-colored stone revered by the Chinese culture for over twelve thousand years. Jade is known for its strength and ethereal power. It is believed by some in the Chinese culture that jade allows them to communicate with spirits that inhabit the earth. It was, and probably still is, believed the jade stone protects the mind, body, and spirit of the living as well as those who have been called home. Many of the jade sculptures hanging on the walls at China Gardens depict scenes from different times in Chinese history. They are beautiful and make eating there even more enjoyable, if that is even possible.

Hanging on a wall in the front of the restaurant are pictures of celebrities who have dined at China Gardens. Marian is well known for her hospitality and good food but she is also very bright and well connected in the business and political community.

"Hello, baby! Where your granddaddy?" I heard a familiar voice say as Birk and I were being seated at our table. Marian sat down with us as Carol walked off to seat another customer. Marian had a big warm friendly smile and she was wearing her big dark-framed glasses slightly down on her nose and a little crooked for good measure. "How you doing, baby?"

she asked.

I told her we were doing just fine and I went on to tell her about my new friend, Dudley, who I was excited about joining me in my life travels. She smiled and handed me a little bamboo plant in small blue-and-white ornate porcelain pot with little white rocks in it instead of soil. It was growing in the shape of a heart. She told me it was for me and my new friend because she knew how much I loved him. "Sometime you find true love and your heart full. You lucky!" she said.

I must admit I was a little puzzled because there was no way she could have possibly known about Dudley before I arrived at the restaurant or that he was sitting right outside, being watched, I hoped carefully, by her son Richard. When I inquired about it, she just looked at me while still smiling and raised one eyebrow as if to say, "Really! Is there anything in Houston much less the universe that I don't know about?" You know the look I'm referring to—the one a mother gives her son when he thinks he has pulled the wool over her but in reality she knew what he was doing all along. I remember that look vividly and was seeing it just now.

I didn't know whether I was a little nervous nelly or glad that I had such a good and powerful friend in Marian; but I did notice she was wearing a small, round jade necklace with some Chinese writing on it. I wondered if she was in touch with Dudley's spirit. Surely if she was speaking to my spirit, I would know about it. Frankly, I wasn't sure I even had a spirit but I remained ever hopeful. Perhaps the only spirit I thought I might have came out of the neck of a Jack Daniels bottle when I poured myself an iced coffee.

Marian saw me looking at her necklace and did a little half nod with her head, confirming something, but I wasn't quite sure what. She stood up, walked behind me, massaged my shoulders for a moment and said, "You have good lunch, baby, and you know what? In China they eat dog." She started laughing profusely and deeply while walking off.

I knew she was joking about the dog comment, or at least I hoped so, but I was feeling a little weird about what just happened. Of course it was nothing a great Chinese meal wouldn't help me forget.

"Birk, did you see that? Did you hear that? That was really bizarre and I'm just a little wigged-out right now. What did you think about that?" I asked. I turned my attention toward Birk who was holding his menu in front of his face, oblivious to what had just transpired. It was as if time had just stopped and Marian and I were the only ones in the restaurant during our conversation.

Birk finally lowered his menu to acknowledge that I was speaking to him but he couldn't manage to talk because he had just stuffed a hush puppy into his mouth and was trying as hard as he could to masticate. He really was a habitual masticator. At least he was good at something. He finally managed to choke out a few words after he downed the hush puppy and said, "I know, there are so many good things on the menu. What are you going to order?" as if he hadn't even been there when Marian visited our table.

China Gardens is also famous for their hush puppy appetizers that they serve in little red plastic baskets on top of thin white paper napkins that separate the hush puppies from the basket. It is probably done this way to have a nice presentation while soaking up the extra oil they were deep fried in. They are superb and come out steaming hot. I haven't figured out why they are so good, but Richard always tells me it is because of his top-secret ingredients. I think his top-secret ingredient may be TLC (tender loving care) but, with that in mind, I decided to just enjoy the hush puppies and not inquire into their tasty goodness. Hush puppies are rolled up little balls of corn meal, deep fried, and served hot. While tasty, they are probably not very good for you. Since we've all got to go sometime, I might as well enjoy myself, so on with the hush puppies.

Birk and I polished off the whole basket of hush puppies and ordered some hot and sour soup, egg rolls, and the famous lemon chicken from our waiter, who had been working at China Gardens for at least twenty years. China Gardens probably makes the best hot and sour soup I have ever tasted. It is very peppery with lots of fresh vegetables and eleven herbs and spices, which is just the way I like it.

I realized after enjoying the crunchy, hot, delicious hush puppies that Birk and I should probably not still have an appetite but after all it was Chinese food so I figured that by the time the main course had made it to us from the kitchen, we would be hungry again. As usual, my mental prowess was correct because when we actually received our food twenty minutes later, we opened the hanger and made it all gone.

When we finished our meal, we got up and walked to the front of the restaurant to pay our bill. Richard's daughter was manning the cash register. What a hardworking, great kid! We paid our bill and started toward the door.

Marian was sitting at the bar, waiting for us. She waved as she said, "Bye, baby, see you next time. Tell granddaddy hi."

We waved back and thanked her. As we passed by she put a fortune cookie in my hand and closed my hand around it. She said it was for my "friend." I really had no idea how she knew I had promised Dudley a fortune cookie, but rest assured, she knew. I was thankful because after that fine meal I had completely forgotten I told Dudley I would bring him a fortune cookie. Birk and I walked out of China Gardens.

I didn't know what to expect from Dudley when we were out of the restaurant because I had never left him before, but what I saw next really floored me. Dudley was belly down on the sidewalk in front of China Gardens with his legs stretched out in front of him, looking almost like an ancient Egyptian sphinxter. He was very regal and handsome; then I noticed he was no longer tied up to the pole where I had left him. He was just sitting there, facing Richard who was no longer talking to the gentleman he had been talking to earlier when we walked up. He was now sitting on the sidewalk facing Dudley and having a conversation with him.

It turns out that Richard was a real schmoozer. I didn't want to interrupt this tender moment, but Birk and I were ready to go so I called to Dudley and he looked at Richard who nodded his head in affirmation. Dudley got up and ran toward me. He stopped and sat at my feet. He was very excited, as if he were seeing me for the first time in weeks.

I told him to simmer down and began massaging his big golden head. He turned his head sideways in approval and then I unwrapped the fortune cookie Marian had given to me for him. I took the paper fortune out and tossed the cookie to him. He caught it in his rather large mouth and began crunching it. As the ear-shattering crunching noise continued, Richard said, "He really loves you," while handing me the leash that appeared not to be needed. I looked down at the fortune in my hand and read it: In order to make a friend you have to be a friend. Fortunately for me my friend was sitting right next to me.

When I inquired as to how Richard knew that, he told me Dudley told him when they were talking while Birk and I were in the restaurant.

I just kind of laughed because I was sure he was kidding, but then he gave me the look I had just seen thirty minutes earlier from his mother, Marian. Now it was starting to get a little weird and, when I looked over to ask Birk if he had noticed this, he was busy bent over and facing the opposite direction while pulling a *Greensheet* newspaper out of a newspaper dispenser.

The *Greensheet* is a newspaper full of advertisements from people who are either looking for something or trying to get rid of something, so I felt as if this was fitting because Birk was also full of something and I was constantly trying to get rid of him as well. He was always up to something and rarely very observant. It worked out well for him as he glided through life.

This reminded me of what my grandpa, Ben Robinson, always told me, which was that everyone has their place in the universe, but the trick is to find out where that place is and to get yourself there as quickly as possible before you're called home. Birk obviously had found his place at an early age, God bless him.

We walked back over to the Cowboy Cadillac and all three of us hopped in. Dudley jumped into the backseat and was ready to go. I think he thought someone may have actually wanted to try to stir fry him because he seemed a little cranky.

I assured him we were not in China and, regardless, most of us now use microwave ovens because stir frying takes way too long.

Once again, he was not amused. I smiled at him and placed my hand on his golden-colored head. He got over it pretty quickly and looked at me with his loving eyes.

Birk abruptly hit the gas and we sped off. The lovefest ended.

CHAPTER TWENTY-SIX

Birk opened the sunroof while driving. He turned to me and told me we were now heading to the bookstore. He wanted to let me know his favorite author and country music legend, Kinky Friedman, had just released a new book and since Birk had read and adored all of Kinky's books he was really hot to pick up Kinky's latest.

He got all excited describing the new book he wanted to purchase. I could tell this from the little vein slightly protruding from the side of his neck, which was readily visible to the naked eye. I could be wrong however because it was entirely possible that Birk was just having his normal reaction while driving aggressively. It could also be that he was possibly stroking out, but to be honest I wasn't really sure I could tell any difference.

Many people, including myself, have recommended to Birk that he take a defensive driver's safety class but thankfully he has chosen not to at this point. Believe me, he could use the class, but I was fearful that he would get completely frustrated and either kill the instructor or one of his potential classmates because like me he would probably try to prove to them that the speed limit wasn't really the maximum speed allowed by the authorities, but was merely a recommendation for those drivers who felt like they may not have the same super motoring skills he possessed.

You see the problem there, don't you? I happen to be a much better driver than Birk as evidenced when he then turned his head sideways instead of watching the road and, while facing me, asked if I wanted to get Kinky's new book at the bookstore. While we were driving along at ridiculous, breakneck-redneck speeds and with him not looking ahead, he asked me again if I wanted to pick up a copy of Kinky's new book at the bookstore.

While I should have recommended to him that the only place we were probably going would be the hospital because of his foolish driving habits, I couldn't answer him because I was only thinking about one thing right then and, no, it wasn't E.D. My mind was stuck on identifying the man Richard had been talking to in front of China Gardens. I am the kind of person who just likes to, and really has to, reconcile things in my mind. I like to think of myself as slightly more social and possibly a little more handsome than the character played by Dustin Hoffman in the movie, *The Rain Man*. In that movie two brothers went on adventures together. One of the brothers was a two-bit hustler and the other brother, an idiot savant, was being used to hustle people.

It was an entertaining film but in fact I was having a "Rain Man" moment. That man who was talking to Richard looked very familiar. I wasn't quite sure who he was but my brain was now locked in on trying to place and identify him because I was sure I had seen him before. While I was mentally visualizing this person, I came to the conclusion that it was quite possible this man was wearing a fake beard. He was also wearing sunglasses and a ball cap. In fact, I was almost certain the man in question was wearing a fake beard because the color of the beard was just slightly different than the color of the hair on his head and the coarseness was different as well. It was not very noticeable but for some reason my brain was vapor-locked on it. He was impeccably dressed, wearing nice jeans, a black button-down shirt with white mother of pearl snaps instead of buttons, and a nice chocolate-colored, light mid-length Western-style jacket with some fancy stitching embroidered on the back in a lighter-colored brown thread.

I was certain I knew who he was but this was one of those moments like when I sat down to write this book but just couldn't force my mind to give me the words to fill the pages. You have to be in the moment and when you're not, try as hard as you may, your mind may not cooperate.

Of course, the harder you try to force your brain into telling you the words you're looking for, or remembering remote, forgotten details, then the more it may try to hide them away in some little room off to the side behind a locked door labeled "Do Not Enter." Then one day when you are not even thinking about it, when least expected, it hits you smack between the eyes and is revealed. It's really strange how that works.

"Hey, are you listening to me? Did you even hear a word I said? Careless, Earth to Careless, come in, Careless," Birk barked out at me.

At that point my concentration was broken and I realized I would just have to revisit the mystery of who the man talking to Richard was at a later date. I suppose I could just do the smart thing and ask Richard, but something told me he was going to give me a fortune cookie answer and confuse me even further, so I decided to not think about it for a while and hopefully, as if by magic, the answer would come to me. It sounded like a good plan and I wanted to respond to Birk before he went into convulsions and killed all three of us with his erratic driving.

"I'm sorry, are you speaking to me?" I asked Birk, which completely irritated him.

"Well, I wasn't talking to your new soulmate sitting there in the backseat if that's what you were thinking," he shot back.

That's when Dudley, who had been relatively quiet and behaving himself, with his head sticking out of the sunroof to drink in the afternoon activities through his nose, gave out a few grunts and a couple of growls while eyeballing Birk.

I said, "Well, you may have been better off talking to him."

Birk quickly turned his head for a brief second to face Dudley, who had managed to maneuver his massive golden head just inches from Birk's face, and Birk asked, "Dudley, what do you think, should we go to the bookstore to get Kinky's new book?"

Of course, Dudley said something, but we just couldn't be sure of what.

Birk asked me again if I wanted to get Kinky's new book. I finally told him I'd consider it. He was very happy with himself. I asked him if he wouldn't mind stopping to pick up Sarge on the way to the bookstore. I could tell he wasn't too excited about doing so but he agreed to anyway. It wasn't that Birk and Sarge didn't get along. They did get along just fine. In fact, if I had to make a judgment about the two of them, I would have to say Birk and Sarge were probably two of the most annoying, irritating individuals one could meet. They are both very nice, and most of the time mean well; but they can be most tedious at times while not even trying that hard, so it stands to reason that they should like one another.

Birk agreed to swing by and extract Sarge. While driving, Birk asked me all excitedly if I knew that Kinky Friedman, author extraordinaire, had autographed copies of his new novel for sale at the bookstore. It appeared to me that Birk was in a big hurry to purchase an autographed copy of Kinky's new book and begin reading it immediately, if not sooner. It reminded me of kids wanting the long-awaited, newest edition of a comic book that had just come out, or perhaps waiting in line for the next book in the Harry Potter series, or maybe even waiting for the next greatest electronic gizmo or video game to be released.

I could see the dilemma Birk was having. Take an extra three-point-five minutes of his time to go pick up Sarge or save the extra three-point-five minutes and quickly scurry over to the bookstore to nab his autographed copy of Kinky's new book.

Sarge loves books and hence loves bookstores. We would probably have to pry him out of there when we were ready to go, but I thought it would be nice to take him. Sarge might actually be a "Rain Man" idiot savant but I just wasn't sure of that. I was probably only half right.

Birk simply couldn't contain himself and inquired again if I knew Kinky Freidman had autographed copies of his newly released book at the bookstore. Of course he already knew the answer to the question before he lobbed it at me.

I simply mumbled a purposely unintelligible answer but for some reason that didn't stop Birk from hearing the answer he wanted to hear. I had no way of knowing what he thought he heard but it really didn't matter because he then said, "That's right, and do you know what the name of Kinky's new book is?"

Again, I mumbled something unintelligible as if to pretend to not hear or care about what Birk was talking about, but once again he replied, "That's exactly right. It's titled *The Christmas Pig*. How on Earth did you know that, Careless?"

I looked at him and said, "Well, I simply deduced that in fact, you are a pig, and Christmas does come once a year so it made perfect sense to me."

That's when Dudley started nodding his head up and down in an affirmative action. I wasn't sure if Dudley had benefited in his past from affirmative action but it wouldn't have surprised me, knowing Dudley the way that I do.

Birk asked, "Hey, what did you just say?"

"Nothing," I responded. "Just get us there in one piece."

Dudley and I started laughing outright. Birk was not amused.

CHAPTER TWENTY-SEVEN

We came to a screeching halt in the parking lot in front of Big Rock Lofts. I opened my door and Dudley jumped over from the backseat. As I exited the vehicle, I felt a little nudge behind me. It was Dudley trying to exit the truck. I wasn't sure if he just wanted to be with me while trying to avoid a bout of separation anxiety, or if he just didn't want to spend some quality alone time with Birk. Either way, it didn't matter to me. I was happy to have him by my side, which is where a true friend rightly belongs.

Dudley and I made our exit from the truck and I closed the door behind us. As we began walking up the sidewalk to the old iron door at the front of the building, Birk blurted out, "Will you guys please hurry it up? I don't have all afternoon."

While continuing to walk forward we did not bother to give Birk a response even though he certainly deserved one, and not the one he was probably expecting. Dudley and I just looked at one another and I'm not sure but I believe his eyebrows were raised in the same aggravated manner mine were, using facial body language to indicate that Birk was a dumbass who didn't require any type of response.

Dudley stopped to drain the main vein, which completely irritated Birk but it did let me know how Dudley really felt about the situation. To make matters worse for Birk, this was one of the longest evacuations I had witnessed from Dudley.

Just before Dudley finished up, Birk honked the horn, stepped on the gas to rev up the engine, and started yelling something neither Dudley nor I could make out. It sounded a little like Hungarian, but since Dudley and I don't speak Hungarian, we just continued on our way, completely ignoring Birk.

I swear I almost detected a little smirk on Dudley's face as we continued walking, while back in the truck Birk was getting histrionic. I laughed inside a little for a job well done. Sure, it was funny, but I didn't want to outwardly encourage Dudley for his behavior. His behavior and results should prove to be encouragement enough.

I whipped out my keys and unlocked and opened the old iron door. It creaked just a little bit, but it was nice and solid so I wasn't worried about its sturdiness. I did think the next time I came downstairs I should give it a little spritz of WD-40 or some kind of oil to lubricate the hinges.

Dudley and I passed through the empty entryway and began climbing the stairs up to the second story. Dudley turned out to be an excellent stair climber, much better than I was. To me, climbing stairs is a little like exercise and I'm just not too fond of exercise, not that there's anything wrong with that, it's just that I am allergic to it. Every time I ever tried it, it made me break out in a sweat and sometimes even affected my breathing. While I'm sure it didn't bother Dudley, I didn't much care for it.

I haven't really noticed Dudley being allergic to anything except possibly criticism, but who isn't? No, exercise is just fine for those who enjoy it, but I get most if not all of my exercise from life. I exercise my way through life every day so therefore I receive plenty of it.

Dudley and I finished climbing up the stairs to the second floor and began walking down the hallway. This sure seemed a lot like exercise. I hope I didn't start exhibiting the symptoms of an allergic reaction. Once we were in front of loft #158, Dudley stopped at the door and sat down. He was waiting for me to unlock the door and enter. I was really amazed at how he had so quickly come to call the loft his home and that he already knew which door was his. All of the doors looked the same so it was interesting to me how he could pick out the correct door. He was one smart cookie but this time I tricked him and walked past #158 to Sarge's loft, #160. It took Dudley only a split second to snap to it because he quickly turned his head to investigate why I hadn't stopped. His whole body followed his head and his legs as he stood up and quickly joined me at my side.

There's just not enough that can be said about having your best friend always by your side with never a worry about being alone, having someone to chat with, or having them watch your back, while at your side. I'm pretty sure someone can watch your back while at your side. I'm not certain if it is physically possible; but I know if anyone could pull it off, it would be Dudley.

As Dudley and I arrived at loft #160 I noticed his nose had kicked into high gear and he was sniffing away. He didn't smell or track things like most dogs. Of course, he was not like most dogs and perhaps even a bit more human than dog. The way Dudley picked up a scent and tracked things was to raise his nose in the air and sniff away. This way he could determine what the smell was, and from which direction it was coming from. It was really amazing to watch him in action, singling out smells and following just the one and only scent he had separated from the others. Once he latched on to a scent, he wouldn't stop tracking it until there was no longer a trace of the scent or the object creating the scent was found. I was pretty sure it was usually the latter. In this case he really didn't have far to go because we were standing right in front of the origin of the aroma he had picked up with his super keen, hound dog nose.

I finally looked down and noticed smoke pouring out from under Sarge's door. I was a little concerned but I remembered that Sarge happened to be a smoker and really enjoyed rolling up and smoking a big fat one from time to time.

I was never quite sure what exact ingredients he was using in his smoke but suffice it to say that his stash probably had a label on it that read something like *SSS*, the abbreviation for Sarge's Secret Stash, and it most certainly left him feeling jolly. Ho, ho, ho, ho..., which was very close to what I heard next, which was, "Yeah, heh, heh, heh, heh...."

I then realized Sarge was probably okay and did not require the assistance of the Houston Fire Department.

"That's all folks. Nothing to see here; just move along," I jokingly told Dudley as I looked down at him sitting next to me with his sniffer in the air going full blast. He was not amused and was impatiently waiting for me to knock on the door, which I promptly did.

"Wow, how, how, how, how, how, how," I heard as the door opened up with Sarge standing there wearing his wife beater undershirt and shorts. He was just raising his dark rimmed, thick, 1960's style glasses to his face so he could actually see with whom he was speaking. He finally managed to place them on his face and as they came down to rest on the bridge of his nose he said, "Wow, man, han, han, han! I am so glad to see you, man, han, han, han. How have you been man, han, han, han? Come on in, man, han, han, han."

At that point I was about to answer him back but he bent down and started petting Dudley who promptly started to grumble just a bit, but his tail did start swinging in a circular motion as he stood up and started to walk into Sarge's loft.

Obviously Sarge was talking to Dudley and I was beginning to feel left out like a lonely single totem pole. It was really okay with me because after all, it would have been completely rude for Dudley not to go into Sarge's loft once he was invited in. It's not like he was a vampire waiting to be invited in or anything like that, and yet he did have some unusually large and pointy canines which looked very similar to fangs. I started to think about getting a mirror to test if Dudley actually had a reflection, but I decided that would just be just silly and, Lord knows, I don't need any help looking silly, especially with Dudley around.

I went ahead and followed Dudley and Sarge into the loft even though neither of them bothered to invite me in. Thankfully, I wasn't a vampire either so I could enter without being invited in. As I entered, I noticed nothing was really out of place but there was a "hot pot" with something boiling in it on a creaky old metal table next to the door we had just come through. It appeared the smoke had been coming from the hot pot, and not pot or something else Sarge may have been smoking.

That was a load off of my mind. It was probably a good thing Sarge never bothered to replace the battery in the smoke detector in his loft or we really might have had a visit from the outstanding and for the most part underpaid men and women of the Houston Fire Department.

Dudley looked at me and then back toward the hot pot. He walked toward it and sat while watching it intently. He didn't budge an inch. Sarge finally noticed me and said, "Hey mannnnnnnn, han, han, han, han, how's it going?"

I smiled at him and told him it was all good in the hood and that Birk, Dudley, and I were thinking about going to the bookstore and wanted to see if he wanted to join us.

"Are you serious, mannnnnnnn? Hell, yeah, I want to go. Thanks, man, han, han, han, han, han, han," he gleefully responded. "Let me just turn off the chicken I was boiling in the hot pot, and we can go."

Now it made perfect sense to me. Dudley had smelled what he thought and most likely hoped was his next meal, which was boiled chicken. I had to hand it to him; he probably ate better than any of his hoodlum friends on the street when he was catting around unattended in Katy, Texas.

Sarge reached over and turned the dial located on the bottom portion of the hot pot to the off position. The boiling stopped almost immediately.

He then turned quickly and walked toward his bed, which consisted solely of a mattress on the floor. It didn't look like a particularly comfortable bed and if I had to guess, it was probably a hand-me-down or perhaps something he had salvaged off of the street. While it didn't look too appealing to me I'm certain it was much better than sleeping on the floor. I'm pretty sure I saw Dudley eyeballing it when he walked into Sarge's loft earlier, but once he located the chicken in the hot pot his attention got immediately diverted. Food promotes a very strong thought process in Dudley. If only Sarge's bed could talk, oh, what a tale it could probably tell, but it was only a bed and frankly I'm probably better off not knowing.

When Sarge got to the foot of the bed, he reached down and grabbed a wadded-up wrinkled shirt. At first I thought he was just going to throw it on over his wife beater undershirt but no, I was mistaken. Sarge raised the shirt up to eye level, holding it with both hands, and tried to gently shake out the wrinkles. After he repeated this process several times, he brought the tee-shirt closer to his face where he positioned it right next to his nose. With his nose just inches from the armpit of the shirt I heard a *sniff, sniff.*

Dudley must have heard it as well because as soon as the sniffing sounds started, he cocked his head around to see what the heck was going on. As Dudley and I stared on with curiosity, Sarge repeated the whole ritual with the opposite side of the tee-shirt. He looked at the two of us, then back at the shirt and said, "Yeah, heh, heh, heh, heh…smells okay to me."

His face quickly disappeared for a moment as he slipped the "okay smelling" shirt on over his head and his wife beater undershirt. It was a white tee-shirt with a big multi-colored peace symbol in the middle. That was pretty fitting for Sarge and it did fit him rather well even though it was probably vintage 1960s.

"Give peace a chance," I shot off at him while holding up my two fingers forming the letter V for victory or peace, whichever your choice may be.

He just smiled and said, "Right on, man, han, han. Right on."

Honk honk, honk honk was the next sound I heard. Outside, Birk was laying on the horn of his Cowboy Cadillac. Someone was getting a little teensy weensy impatient. Sarge heard it as well so he walked over to a shelf, grabbed some spray-on deodorant, stuck it up under his shirt, and began to melt the polar icecaps by creating a hole in the ozone layer. Global warming, Texas style! Sure, we were all going to fry like rats but there's nothing quite like the fragrance of Old Spice spray-on deodorant and B.O. mixed together. Manly, yes, but I like it too, not that there's anything wrong with that.

Sarge stepped into some old beat-up leather sandals and he was good to go. He walked toward the door and since the hot pot had been turned off and cooled down, he grabbed a piece of chicken and flipped it up in the air over his shoulder without even looking where it came to rest, which was right smack in the middle of my friend Dudley's overly large mouth.

I wasn't quite sure how Dudley coordinated that move, but it was reminiscent of something I had seen the Harlem Globe Trotters do when I was a young lad, acting bad.

CHAPTER TWENTY-EIGHT

In a former life when I was much younger, my grandfather used to take me to see the Harlem Globetrotters play basketball in an arena named the Summit. It wasn't just a basketball game, it was really a magical show put on by very athletic comedians. For an hour or so all of the cares and woes that were so important at the time seemed to magically slip away as the Globetrotters showed their true genius, working their magic in the confines of a basketball game in a basketball arena.

Looking back, I can remember quite clearly all of the faces in the crowd, young and old, trained on the Globetrotter players as they skillfully mastered their basketball opponents while bringing smiles and enjoyment to all those who were privileged to be in the audience. The old gag of the water bucket being thrown on the crowd seemed timeless. When one basketball player got a paper cup of water thrown on him by another basketball player, the recipient of the water grabbed a bucket of water from the sideline and chased the other basketball player all over the court until he had him cornered right in front of some amused but alerted onlookers. They were alerted because they just knew when the water in the bucket would get launched, they would get soaked. To the surprise and laughter of the fans the bucket of water always turned out to be paper confetti. This never failed to be one of the highlights of the show.

The Harlem Globetrotters appeared to be the creation of Abe Saperstein in Chicago sometime in the 1920s. Their famous theme song was a whistled melody named "Sweet Georgia Brown" composed by songwriter, Brother Bones. Most of the original Harlem Globetrotters attended Wendell Phillips High School in Chicago when they formed the team, The New York Harlem Globetrotters. Originally the Globetrotters were a regular basketball team in the World Professional Basketball Tournament where they went on to be defeated in the championship game by the New York Rens. They eventually came back to beat the New York Rens the following year and won their championship by beating the Chicago Bruins and Minneapolis Lakers.

Once the Globetrotters perfected their skills, they became master entertainers and never lost another game. When they worked in comedy, dribbling routines, specialty plays, and shots, there was no looking back for these ambassadors of good will. Some of the most talented, entertaining, and memorable players were Wilt Chamberlain, Lou Dunbar, Meadowlark Lemon, Fred Neal, Reese Tatum, and Marques Haynes.

Wilt "The Stilt" Chamberlain was number thirteen and was signed just out of the University of Kansas. He was seven-foot-one and once played in a Globetrotter game hosted by the then USSR in Lenin Central Stadium. "Sweet" Lou Dunbar was number forty-one and had worked with the Houston Rockets. He also played a game with the Globetrotters in Rome. Meadowlark Lemon was number thirty-six and was one of the most cherished players by the fans. He was funny, athletic, and a delight to watch, earning his well-deserved nickname the "Clown Prince." He was also inducted in the Naismith Memorial Basketball Hall of Fame. Fred Neal, number twenty-two, was simply known as Curly, which was humorous in itself because he had no hair; he was completely bald. He was probably one of the best shooters and dribblers the Globetrotters ever had on their team. Curly reminded me a lot of my friend Birk. They were both avid dribblers.

I am pretty sure I have seen Birk dribble a river but, moving on, Reese Tatum known as Goose was number fifty and played with the Globetrotters for over twelve seasons. He was very funny and kept the crowds in stitches. Marques Haynes was number twenty and was also a phenomenal basketball player. He was inducted into the Naismith Memorial Basketball Hall of Fame as well. The Globetrotters are world renowned and have been on television shows and cartoons such as *The New Scooby-Doo Show*, *Harlem Globe Trotters*, *The Super Globetrotters*, *Gilligan's Island*, *The White Shadow*, *The Simpsons*, and *Futurama*. The Harlem Globe Trotters represent all that is right in America.

If one day I am fortunate enough to have children, preferably with someone like E.D., I will definitely take them to see the Harlem Globetrotters. The shows are just good clean fun and have entertained families for generations. Young, old, and in between can be seen leaving their sorrows, cares, and worries behind while watching the Harlem Globetrotters play basketball, even if for just an hour or so.

As we all walked out of Sarge's loft he closed the door and continued on. Using my keen powers of observation I said, "Hey, Sarge, you gonna lock your door or what?"

It's not as if he had a lot to steal but still, better safe than sorry. Probably his most prized possession he had in his apartment was his book collection that he loved so much.

"Yeah, heh, heh, heh, heh, man, you're right. Thanks, man, han han, han, han, han, han, I keep forgetting to do that," he said as he did an about face and took a large wad of keys from out of his pocket.

I had no idea why he had so many keys or what in the hell they could be used for, but with Sarge you just never knew. For all I knew, he used them as wind chimes. Always a mystery, that one! I finally did ask him why he had so many keys.

He explained to me that over the years he had moved from place to place and had locks on various things, but he never weeded through any of his keys or thrown the old ones out. He didn't remember which ones were which, so he just kept them all.

My thought process didn't allow me to really understand that because he could simply just try all of his keys on what he currently had and where he currently lived and discard any key that didn't fit. By the way, if it doesn't fit, you must acquit. I always loved that catchy phrase but for the life of me I don't know why. I guess if it wouldn't have been used to benefit someone that had taken a life, I probably would have liked it even better. Regardless, when I told Sarge what I was thinking, he looked somewhat perplexed.

He looked at me and said, "Wow, how, how, how, how, how, man, han, han, han, han, I just never thought of that."

It appeared the earth had just moved for Sarge, but I also knew deep down inside he would probably never go through his keys or get rid of the ones that were no longer useful, perhaps because he hoped to possibly use them again someday. I do have to give him credit because I think for some people, what was once useful may have some other purpose, or perhaps they just hope it may become useful again someday. Perhaps similar to a girlfriend you couldn't stand all the while you were with her—until one day you woke up and she was gone and you just figured out that you had made the mistake of a lifetime by letting her walk out of your life, and your soul was so lonely for her that you would beg, borrow, or steal your way back into her heart, only to find out she was already with another guy who absolutely knew she was the greatest thing in the world until death do them part. I'm certainly not admitting anything here. I'm just drawing an analogy for those who do not have the pleasure of knowing Sarge.

I guess we all may have our own keys that unlocked something dear to us at one time or another, perhaps in our hearts or our minds, that we are reluctant to let go of. I can't really fault a person for that.

"If you see me walkin' down the line with my fav'rite honkytonk in mind, well I'll be here around suppertime with my can of dinner and a bunch of fine." This is how I was just daydreaming about Sarge with some lyrics from the ZZ Top song, "Beer Drinkers and Hell Raisers."

With a "Wow, how, how, how, how, man," Sarge locked his door, slammed the unusually big wad of keys back into his front shorts pocket and off we walked, down the hall, past my and Dudley's loft and towards the stairs. I wanted to ask Sarge if he was just happy to see me or was that a big wad of keys in his shorts pocket but decided to leave well enough alone, not that there's anything wrong with that. Some things are really best left unanswered.

There we were, the three of us, walking into the great unknown and believe me between Birk and Sarge it was definitely going to be unknown and for me, probably not so great; but you play the cards you're dealt. Off we went strolling down the stairwell.

Dudley was being unusually quiet and walking right by my side. I think he was watching my footsteps to make sure he was moving stride for stride with me. I remember thinking he would be a great police department K-9 Unit dog. He appeared to be very observant and noticed anything that moved or was out of place. He certainly had a good honker on him as evidenced by the way he zeroed in on Sarge's hot pot. I guess he was probably also a good judge of character. Only time will tell, but he did pick me as a companion so he must know what he is doing. Either that or he was just fat and happy from being fed a piece of chicken from Sarge's hot pot. What a crock!

Downstairs, Dudley pranced right over to the old iron door, ready to travel with his homeboys. I opened it and Sarge, Dudley, and I headed toward Birk's Cowboy Cadillac.

Birk looked none too happy. He had a slight grimace on his face and was waving us to move quickly forward with his hand gestures. Birk, The Magnificent, was summoning his subjects. He was really getting a little agitated because apparently we weren't moving quickly enough. "Come on, you guys move slower than molasses," he shouted out of his open window.

We all quickened our pace. We briskly power walked to Birk's truck, the Ford F350, 4 X 4, crew cab, long bed, dually, diesel, which was something Birk liked to call the "King of Trucks" but I just call the Cowboy Cadillac. Perhaps that's why his majesty, Birk, thought of himself as royalty, able to summon us forward with a mere hand gesture; but he most likely just had indigestion from eating Chinese food.

The three of us reached the truck just in time because he had already cranked it up, was revving the engine, and had another Jake Harm and the Holdouts song blasting. *"Wild Turkey at Sunrise. Wild Turkey with tears in his eyes. Rocking back going nowhere fast. Just out of reach with my heart in the past...."*

It sounded like a real uplifting song and as we jumped in the truck Birk started singing along, which was what I can only accurately describe as chicken cackle. I was now sitting in the front seat with my seatbelt firmly holding me in while protecting me from the G-Forces Birk's driving skills, or lack of, were going to exert upon me.

Sarge was seatbelted in the back directly behind Birk, and Dudley had assumed the position where he had his two front feet resting on the center console between the two front seats, and his two back legs bracing his muscular body on the backseat. It just wouldn't have been normal if Dudley's head wasn't jutting out of the sunroof. That boy loved the sunroof!

Birk hit the gas and off we sped like a runaway Noah's ark but, instead of a giraffe head sticking out of the top, it was more of a large, shiny, golden, fawn-colored hound dog with big floppy ears and even bigger jowls that were flopping around in the wind like sails with sea spray misting off of them or, as I like to refer to him as my friend Dudley.

CHAPTER TWENTY-NINE

We traveled from downtown for about the time it takes to say one Mississippi and before I knew it we were pulling into the parking lot of the Barnes & Noble bookstore. It was quite a large superstore with books galore that could fill the imagination of most people, but there were also music CDs, movie DVDs, worldwide and local periodicals, and magazines for sale. It was truly impressive and I did notice Sarge's lips were quivering ever so slightly in anticipation of losing himself in such a setting.

I was glad we stopped for Sarge even if Birk thought of it as a waste of time in his haste to buy the new Kinky Friedman book. I was actually looking forward to a nice iced coffee at the coffee shop conveniently located in the bookstore just inside to the right of the entrance.

We began to jump out of the truck when I turned to Dudley to tell him he had to wait in the truck. He was none too pleased and began verbalizing such with some low-pitched throaty rumbling noises. I tried to explain to him there were no dogs allowed in the store but he was having none of that and did not want to be separated from me.

Birk started laughing and asked me why I didn't just pretend he was a service dog or my seeing-eye dog. He did however stop laughing when I told him the only reason I even needed a seeing-eye dog was because he was so butt ugly that it blinded me to have to look at him. His smile then turned upside down and it didn't look to me like he was having a nice day. Dudley and I on the other hand started chuckling a little under our breaths; and when Birk got a load of that, he was really not amused as he stormed off across the parking lot to enter the bookstore.

Since Dudley seemed to be in a little better spirit I explained to him again that he had to wait in the truck until we got back. The weather was nice and cool and we would leave the windows and sunroof open so he could get some fresh air and bark at people if he so chose. He seemed to understand he would not be attending the party so I closed the door, leaving him in the backseat. He looked a little sad and kind of pitiful.

I must admit that I think we both were having a tad of separation anxiety even if it was for just a short time, but before I could do something stupid, Sarge walked around the back side of the truck and came up to me while putting his hand on my shoulder and said, "Look, man, han, han, han, han, han, han, he's going to be fine, hine, hine, hine, hine, hine. He'll be just fine, hine, hine, hine, hine, hine, hine. Let's go read some books, man, han, han, han, han, han."

We said goodbye to Dudley. It was hard to leave him sitting there by himself, and all the way to the bookstore entrance I glanced over my shoulder to see him look longingly at me as if begging me to come back, but off I went like a trooper without him. I knew we wouldn't be in the bookstore for long so Dudley would just have to wait until we came back to retrieve him. I couldn't have been more wrong.

Sarge and I walked in the double glass doors of the bookstore and sure enough we spotted Birk thumbing through Kinky's new book, *The Christmas Pig*, which he had picked up from a large, rather neatly stacked pile of books on a big solid wood oak table in the very front of the store.

I started to wave to him to tell him we had made it into the store but he was off on another planet somewhere. Probably Uranus. I don't really know how anyone feels about our solar system but I am of the firm belief that the name of the planet, Uranus, is just not utilized enough in every day conversation. Uranus. Stop the tape now and say it along with me. Uranus, it just rolls right off the tongue. While I may never be able to prove it, I would hazard a guess that one of the first words spoken by man was probably something like Uranus. Of course, early man probably never visited Uranus but Uranus was probably a nice place to visit. That is however just sheer speculation on my part, but enough about Uranus.

Birk obviously had no intention of breaking his concentration while perusing his new book to acknowledge that Sarge and I had both made it safely into the bookstore, so we continued onward. I turned to Sarge to lodge a complaint about Birk being such a space cadet but as I began speaking I noticed I was standing by myself. I sure hope no one was watching me. That's just what I needed, the crazy man talking to himself, getting bounced out of the bookstore by security guards.

Apparently Sarge had meandered off to lose himself in either his first, second, or third favorite pastime, one of which was reading. I don't really need to inform you of his other two pastimes or which order they came in, that is where your imagination will have to come into play. Alone, I wandered over to the right of the bookstore to grab an iced coffee from the coffee shop. Too bad they didn't have my favorite pastime to pour into my iced coffee. A little bit of Jack Black would have done me just right and definitely would have simmered down my nerves about leaving Dudley in the Cowboy Cadillac.

I waited in line for a few minutes behind a couple of people. Once they ordered their foo foo double frappe crappe latte without a shotte they moved to the side to reveal probably one of the most stunning beauties I had ever come across, other than E.D. or Dudley. E.D. and Dudley both had golden-blonde hair but this girl was completely different. She had long, thick, dark hair. Her eyes were even darker, large, and very expressive.

"Sir, sir, sir! What can I help you with?" she questioned me over and over.

I finally snapped out of the trance her beauty had placed me in and realized she was trying to take my order, and several people standing in line behind me were listening and becoming slightly agitated with my lack of a response. I may have been under her spell, but my mind was still racing and noticing every little detail around me in the background.

"Yes, ma'am, I'd like a large iced coffee, decaf of course, with a neat shot of Jack Daniels to take the edge off," I finally responded once I had made my return trip from Uranus. There's that planet again. I just love that planet.

"Sir, I'm sorry but we don't serve alcoholic beverages here. Would you like me to leave room in your coffee for some cream or sugar?" she inquired.

My brain finally began recovering from my beauty-induced coma and I informed her that I liked my coffee just like I liked my women, strong and bitter. She cracked a little smile and told me my total was three dollars and fifty cents.

I pulled my wallet out of my back pocket, opened it, and whipped out a five-dollar bill without ever taking my eyes off of her or, for that matter, even blinking. I told her to keep the change. I was trying to impress her but, let's face it, I wasn't having back problems due to a full and heavy cash-laden wallet in my back pocket weighing me down and causing a strain on the ole' back. No sir, I didn't have that problem at all.

She took the five-dollar bill and thanked me.

"So, Maria, may I call you Maria? The name's Careless. I'm guessing you are originally from Mexico City, you are twenty years old, and are here in the United States on a student visa, is that right?" I asked. At that point, the expression on her face went blank.

I continued, "Just how long have you been a practicing Buddhist?"

She then turned a bit pale, her smile flattened out a bit, almost turning upside down, and her lovely dark eyes widened just a little. They were truly the most beautiful eyes I had ever seen. They were as pitch black as nighttime in the countryside when there are no lights, moon, or stars. I again felt myself losing my thoughts in the abyss of her beauty, but I did notice she and possibly some of the waiting customers were getting a little impatient and perhaps thinking they might be dealing with a stalker.

I was sure someone this beautiful probably had many admirers and on-lookers, and was now probably thinking, *Stranger danger, stranger danger.*

CHAPTER THIRTY

It was now put up or shut up time. Would I dazzle Maria with my charm, good looks, and amazing powers of deduction or would I end up being thrown out on the sidewalk by the security guards? I figured I had a fifty-fifty shot either way.

"Well, I surmised your name was Maria from your nametag. Your dark hair, beautiful dark eyes, and dark complexion, along with your accent placed your origin to be central Mexico so I assumed you were from Mexico City, and as far as practicing Buddhism...," I said, while I could clearly see she was becoming intrigued when she raised one eyebrow slightly higher than the other just over those exquisite coal-black eyes, "and as far as being a Buddhist, when I paid you with the five-dollar bill, I noticed when you reached for it, your long sleeve from your shirt raised just slightly above your very attractive wrist for a mere moment where I instantly discovered there was a small, but colorful tattoo of Buddha on our wrist. You know," I continued, "it is customary to rub Buddha's belly for good luck. Shall I have a go of it?"

By this time the customers in back of me were keenly listening and didn't seem overly concerned to be waiting in line. Of course some people are entertained rather easily. I was now happy to see that instead of thinking *stranger danger, stranger danger*, Maria had turned that frown upside down while smiling at a clown, yours truly.

"That was so amazing, how did you do that? That was very impressive," she said excitedly.

"Thank you, Maria, it was really quite simple. I just used my powers of observation and would you like to marry me?" I asked.

She started sniggling a little and shouted, "Next in line."

It looked like Careless' time was over and so I nodded my head in approval of her beauty, grabbed my coffee, and proceeded to move on to the periodical and newspaper section. I guess there will be no bilingual babies in my immediate future. *Dios mio!*

142

There were ten wooden racks in the magazine section, just loaded with newspapers from all over the world and magazines about every subject you could possibly imagine, and then some. Something felt very wrong as I started to peruse the *Up Close with Biker Chicks* magazine. You don't see that every day and, being a self-educated man, I began my reading of lesson plan one in the magazine.

I was still sure something just wasn't right. Perhaps it was just that my coffee was a little off because it was missing the special ingredient. It certainly was not good to the last drop without my companion, Jack Daniels, in it. Well, I simply had to make due but something didn't feel right. I was holding up the educational magazine, *Up Close with Biker Chicks*, in front of my face and reading it, but I felt like I was being watched. You can always tell when you're being watched because you feel like you're being watched. That's just a little trick I learned along the road of life. You can thank me later for teaching you one of my secrets.

While pretending to be reading I slowly lowered the magazine just below my eyes and started nodding my head up and down and using facial expressions to look as if I were really interested in the articles. I'm sure some people passing by probably thought I had a nervous facial tick, but I'm pretty sure I didn't have one. I really only read magazines like that for the articles. How many times have I repeated that line in my life? That was a rhetorical question but the answer is: too many to count. As I was being too clever by half, I slowly turned my body from side to side and peered out among the people in the bookstore to see if anyone was watching me.

I saw Sarge about twenty paces away from me with his head buried in a book that was actually as large as his head. He had quite a few books stacked up in the waiting so it appeared he was definitely thinking of pulling an all-nighter. He didn't notice me looking at him because I was very cleverly disguising what I was doing. He didn't notice me or anyone else for that matter, because he was mentally off on planet Uranus or perhaps somewhere else in his imagination while reading books.

I turned just a little and looked down the long rack of magazines but nothing unusual stood out. I turned a little more and there was dear sweet Maria still serving coffee and still not contemplating marrying yours truly. Maybe one day in a galaxy far, far away. Perhaps even somewhere close to Uranus. Later on, I really should edit out most of the references to

Uranus, but as you can see Uranus is still prominent in this tale. Besides, there's really nothing wrong with Uranus, but it's somewhere I definitely have never been.

I turned a little further and noticed Birk impatiently waiting in line to buy Kinky's new book. He was twitching just a bit and looked at his watch several times, which I found odd because I never knew he could actually tell time. He was never on time anywhere he went, so I just assumed he probably never learned what the big hand and little hands were doing on his watch. I turned a little further and looked back to Sarge who must have been on his third book because two books were already stacked up next to his other pile of must reads. Nothing appeared to be out of the ordinary but my Careless senses were still tingling. I repeated this whole process over and over but I discovered nothing out of the ordinary. That was about to change.

After doing the whirlybird several times, I suddenly came face to face with the manager of the bookstore. He was a quiet little devil. I didn't even hear him sneak up on me but in my defense I was concentrating on other more pertinent matters. He was about five-foot-ten, clean-shaven, and had short-cropped curly brown hair. He was wearing some nice tan slacks and a crisp white button-down shirt with a little tag pinned to it with the words Store Manager written on it.

He looked at me and I looked at him for a minute and I finally said, "Hello, Mr. Manager, or may I call you Store?"

I waited for his serious look to lighten up but that never happened.

"My name is Seth and yes I am the store manager and your name is?" he inquired.

"The name's Careless," I responded.

"Sir, we have a serious problem," he stated in his official capacity as store manager.

"When you say we, who are you referring to? Do you have a mouse in your pocket?" I asked.

"No, Mr. Careless, but I am going to have to ask you to remove your animal from the bookstore," he responded.

Now I definitely knew something was wrong, and those bizarre feelings that I had of someone watching me were real. "It's actually just Careless and I know that my friend Birk is getting slightly agitated because he has been waiting in line for so long to buy his book and he hasn't shaved in a couple of days but there is really no need to refer to him as an animal. Are we not all animals? Are we not all people? Can't we all just get along?" I asked.

Seth, store manager, didn't appear to be amused, but all the while that Seth, store manager, and I were becoming best friends forever, I was still scoping out the bookstore to see who was watching me, and I got a real shock when I turned my head slightly to do some more checking, while still pretending to listen to Seth, store manager.

There in the corner of my eye I saw what I can only describe as a golden-colored flash moving so fast it was almost a blur. When I looked up from my magazine there was nothing but when my vision was blocked by the magazine, the golden flash reappeared and slowed down. Boy, *Up Close with Biker Chicks* Miss March was looking pretty fine, but back to the mysterious golden flash that had been spying on me, or as I will now refer to him as Dudley.

I will admit that he was pretty clever. He had obviously escaped out of one of the windows from Birk's Cowboy Cadillac and used his very sensitive nose to track me into the store. He was also very clever, watching me closely, and every time I started to turn in his direction to spot him, he dashed down a different isle of magazine racks, avoiding detection. When I glanced away, he returned and started watching me again. Very clever indeed! I bet he learned that from one of the inmates at the SPCA.

I suppose Seth, store manager, being the very clever store manager he was, noticed Dudley was eyeballing me and assumed he was my "animal." Finally, I reluctantly put the magazine down, which really did have interesting articles, and said, "Dudley, get over here right now. I know you're in the bookstore."

With my index finger extended, I pointed down to a spot right in front of me and didn't have very long to wait. He darted out from behind one of the other magazine racks on another aisle and came trotting up to me where he stopped and sat down right in front of me.

With his eyes staring into my eyes, he was awaiting my next command.

I said, "Good boy, I missed you so much," while I started rubbing his very beautiful golden and rather large head.

He started mumbling something in short grunts under his breath to show how much he missed me as well and I told him how sorry I was to leave him in that mean old Birk's truck. I guess I forgot where I was for a moment but then Seth, store manager, pretended to clear his throat and said, "Can I get you guys a room or do you want to take it outside? There are no animals allowed in the store."

Dudley's and my head swung around in unison to look at Seth, store manager, to show our disapproval of him. Dudley growled at him and I myself snarled just a bit. When Dudley starting goobering, I'm sure Seth, store manager, felt a smidgen of fear and starting backing up somewhat. While walking away from us in a quick but steady pace, he said, "The store policy is that there are no animals allowed in the store. I'm going to get security so I suggest that the two of you leave the store immediately."

Dudley and I turned and walked past the coffeeshop where we both waved goodbye to the lovely Maria, who was giggling because she had just witnessed Dudley's shenanigans, and we walked out of the front door to take our business elsewhere. We didn't need a rock from Uranus to fall on our head to know when we're not wanted.

CHAPTER THIRTY-ONE

Just a few yards away, there happened to be a James Coney Island hot dog restaurant. I wasn't really that hungry and yet I found myself envisioning a chili cheese dog with onions. James Coney Island really did make the most magnificent hot dogs. While Dudley was certainly no wiener dog, I felt pretty certain he could put away a few hot dogs. I was sure hot dogs wouldn't be bad for him. Hell, people eat them, why can't Dudley?

As we were coming in for a landing at James Coney Island, I looked at Dudley and asked him point blank, "One dog or two?"

Of course, I expecting him to say nothing but as I had come to realize with him, he definitely said something. "*Urrrr, ruff, urrrr, arrrrr,*" he vocalized.

"So you want two, is that correct?" I clarified.

As soon as I said that he started rubbing his head on the side of my leg in affirmative action. I just knew he was a product of affirmative action. I wasn't quite sure how or even if he understood me but he was definitely trying to tell me something. I just assumed he liked James Coney Island as well so I opened the door and we both strolled in together. Like a good friend, he never left my side. It wasn't very crowded in the restaurant and there was no one in line at the counter where the orders were taken. A very nice young man wearing a blue collared shirt with a white James Coney Island logo on it and a white, pointed, paper, James Coney Island hat, walked up to us and asked if he could take my order.

James Coney Island was founded in Houston by two Greek immigrant brothers, James and Tom Papadakis, who were searching for the American dream and they certainly found it. The very first location was on Walker and Main Street in downtown Houston. It was said that the brothers flipped a coin to see who the restaurant would be named after. They were known for their delicious sandwiches, hotdogs, and chili. The restaurant was wildly successful and expanded in later years. James was called home in 1968 and Tom was called home in 1974, after which several of the sons and some family members began running the business. In 1990 some Houston investors purchased the business from the family and continued the great tradition of delicious food and hot dogs. There are currently over twenty locations. For hot dogs, James Coney Island can't be beat.

I told the young man behind the counter that I wanted his finest hot dog smothered with his best chili, cheese, and onions. I also asked him for two of his finest hot dogs just plain, with only the wiener and bun for my friend.

"Sir, are you okay? You're the only person standing in line," he mistakenly informed me.

Not too observant this one! I guess he thought I was a whacko from Waco but that thought didn't last very long because, while being blocked by the counter, Dudley had been out of the young man's eyesight, but when Dudley suddenly leapt up on the countertop and rested his front legs on it while looking this very nice but not very observant young man in the eye, he quickly took the order of the chili cheese dog with onions and the two plain hot dogs with just wieners and buns.

"Don't be nervous, son, he only eats people when he doesn't get what he wants," I explained to the young man behind the counter.

Dudley and I quickly turned our attention away from the young man behind the counter, glanced at one another for a brief moment, and smiled a bit; but the young man then informed us that there were no dogs allowed in the restaurant unless they were service dogs or seeing-eye dogs. He told me my total was eight dollars and forty-five cents.

I put on my sunglasses, asked for a copy of the bill in braille, and then asked Dudley if he would mind terribly to guide me over to an unoccupied table so we could enjoy our nice, wholesome, healthy meal together. I whipped out my wallet and extruded a ten-dollar bill from it. I held it up to Dudley's very handsome face and asked him how much it was. He grunted something, grabbed the money from my hand with his overzealous, goobering mouth, and again jumped up on the counter coming to rest on it with his two front legs.

I think he may have startled the young man behind the counter because he took a couple of hasty steps backwards and I could see the whites of his eyes. I was reasonably sure Dudley would never hurt anyone, but he was definitely full of surprises and he could be somewhat intimidating.

Dudley placed the ten-dollar bill down and grumbled something I thought sounded like, "Keep the change."

Sure, it was so easy to be a big spender with someone else's money. He just smiled and off we went to go have a seat at a table for two while we waited for our hotdogs. Me and my seeing-eye dog, Dudley.

Our number finally got called and I walked up to get our order. The young man asked me how I was able to get to the counter without my seeing-eye dog. It seems I had forgotten my clever rouse and left Dudley sitting at the table anxiously awaiting his hot dogs. At least he was watching my every move so I knew if a problem did arise he was available to pounce.

Now, since I made a slight error, I would have to think quickly on my feet. I explained to the young man behind the counter that I had an excellent memory and sense of smell so it was in fact quite easy for me to find my way back to the counter. I may have great powers of observation but my acting skills left much to be desired and the young man wasn't buying it. "You can really see, can't you?" he asked.

I pulled out my wallet and whipped out another ten-dollar bill. I held it up around eye level in between the young man and me and said, "Son, help me out, how much is this?"

He took the ten-dollar bill from my hand folded it up neatly and placed it in his front pants pocket. The young man then said, "Have a nice day, sir."

While I hated to blow the money, I really didn't feel like getting kicked out of another fine establishment today. I must say that taking your friend out for a meal was sure getting expensive. This place has sure gone to the dogs.

I walked over to the table, sat down, and placed Dudley's two hot dogs in front of him. I reached down to grab my hot dog (no, reader, my James Coney Island hot dog), and picked it up to take a bite out of it. As it approached my mouth, I noticed Dudley was staring at me as if he wanted a bite. Upon closer inspection, I noticed his hot dogs were no longer in existence. He must have consumed them both in under five seconds. His eating habits reminded me of Birk's driving. Quick and to the point.

As I was finishing what surely had to be one of the four basic food groups, I heard someone impatiently honking his horn very close to the window where Dudley and I were seated. I was finishing up but Dudley had finished light years ahead of me. As I suspected, it was Birk revving up his engine by pressing down on the gas pedal and waving his hand sporadically as if to tell us to hurry up and move our butts. Someone had bought his book and was getting a little impatient.

Dudley and I napkinned off, stood up from the table, and walked out of the door toward Birk who thankfully was still there.

"Let's go, grandma," Birk hurled an insult at me. Just to irritate him further, I began walking in exaggerated slow motion as Dudley matched my pace.

I could see by Birk's facial expression that we had the desired effect on him as he was none too pleased. Once we reached the Cowboy Cadillac, I opened the back door and Dudley hopped in. He assumed the position, where his head was sticking out of the sunroof and his back legs rested firmly on the tan-colored leather backseat while his front legs rested on the center console between the two tan-colored front seats. He was ready for takeoff.

I opened the front door, jumped in the front seat, and buckled up for safety reasons. After you have driven with Birk a couple of times you know you really do need to strap in and hold on for dear life. It was very similar to the Texas Titty Twister, the looping, very steep, mega G, roller coaster ride that was once at Astroworld.

Astroworld was a theme park situated on fifty-seven acres of land off of Loop 610 in Houston, just across the street from the Astrodome. It was officially opened in 1968 by Judge Roy Hofheinz and was said to complete the package of what he referred to as the Astrodomain. Astroworld was home to many great rides including the Astroneedle, The Viper, The Batman Ride, Greased Lightning, The Texas Cyclone, Excalibur, and many others. During Halloween, Astroworld transformed into a haunted scary theme park aptly named Fright Night and even had a haunted hayride as well as several haunted houses. Astroworld was sold to Six Flags Over Texas in 1975 and, like most good things in life, came to an end when it was closed down and demolished in 2005. Now all that's left of Astroworld are a lot of Houstonian's cherished memories and an empty field of grass.

CHAPTER THIRTY-TWO

As we started our trip back to Big Rock, I noticed Dudley was all alone in the backseat. I looked at Birk with a puzzled look on my face and he asked me, "What?"

I explained to him that besides him being a little light in the loafers, the backseat appeared to be a little light as well. Unless Sarge had shrunk down to a size undetectable to the human eye, then he was not in the backseat of Birk's Cowboy Cadillac with my friend Dudley. "Birk, what the hell did you do with Sarge?" I asked him.

"Oh, he said he wasn't ready to go and since you and your hound dog homeboy got thrown out of the bookstore and I had already purchased my book, I told him I was ready to make like a tree and leave. He told me to go ahead and that he would find a way home. He looked like he was really into reading the books he had picked out, so I left him there. He'll be okay; don't worry," Birk said.

I just loved it when he rationalized things to allow him to do something he knew he shouldn't. I didn't make a big fuss about it because it just wasn't worth it. I decided I would just have to drive back to the bookstore later to see if Sarge needed a ride home. Problem solved.

In less time than it takes a middle-aged married man to spot the hottest young, bikini-clad beauty on the beach, Birk had us in front of Big Rock Lofts. I'm not sure if any of the three of us knew how we got back so quickly, yet we were there. Everything in between was just a blur. Birk came to a screeching stop while Dudley and I prepared for extraction. I unstrapped myself in the front seat. Boy, I hope that seatbelt doesn't leave a mark.

I noticed as I was exiting the truck that another Jake Harm and the Holdouts song, "Where'd You Go, Brother Joe," from their new CD was playing on the radio. He sure seemed popular. This little ditty was about Jake's oldest friend that went missing one day and was later found in a dumpster. That must have been a sad day for Jake. I walked over to the back of the truck door and liberated Dudley. He in turn, jumped out and liberated himself all over the grassy area that led up to the old iron door at the front entrance to Big Rock Lofts.

I closed the door and Birk rolled down the front window. "Can't you control that weasel dog of yours? He's starting to remind me a little of you," Birk said gleefully, and so he was.

"Birk, you're a real wordsmith," I told him jokingly. "Hey, isn't that Jake Harm and the Holdouts?" I asked him while pointing at the radio.

"Yep, and guess what, Careless? I still have four tickets to see him play live at The Houston Livestock Show and Rodeo for this week. Two for you and me, and two for the lucky gals who will be attending with us," he said, while smiling.

It appeared that he was pretty proud of himself. "Hey, Birk," I said.

"Yes, Careless," he answered.

"Just who are the lucky gals you are referring to that will be going with us to see Jake Harm and the Holdouts perform? And um, I don't recall seeing Jake Harm and the Holdouts in the lineup of entertainers for the Houston Livestock Show and Rodeo," I pointed out to him.

"That's right, numbnuts, that's because he's not playing the main show, he's playing in the Hide Out and you need to have special tickets to get in to see him. It's very exclusive," he said.

If it was that exclusive then I wondered how Birk got tickets. My first guess is that he sold his blood and my second guess was that he made a donation at the sperm bank, but then again, I'm pretty sure Birk gave at the office and often. After I thought about it a little further, which believe me was mentally painful and I definitely didn't want to, I couldn't think of how Birk purloined the Jake Harm and the Holdouts concert tickets or how he would get any self-respecting female to attend the concert with him. So, this will thankfully have to go down as one of those unsolved mysteries. "Okay, Birk, you see what you can do about rustling us up some dates," I said as I walked off with Dudley by my side. I was pretty sure I could get a date; but with Birk, well, he might just have to go out with his old standby, Veronica, the blow-up doll.

In 1931 the Houston Fat Stock Show organization was formed, followed by the first Houston Fat Stock Show in 1932. It was very popular and drew big crowds. In 1961 the name was changed to the Houston Livestock Show and Rodeo. This event has been held at many locations over the years, some of which were the Sam Houston Coliseum, the Astro-dome, the Astrohall, and finally now at Reliant Park. Many people show livestock; there are horse shows, rodeos, exhibits, food stands, electric bull riding, a huge outdoor carnival, live bands, wine competitions, Go Tejano Day, and even Oreo cookie pig races. Many cowboys go on long trail rides that conclude at the actual site of the Houston Livestock Show and Rodeo. The first annual Barbeque Cookoff Contest was started at the Houston Livestock Show and Rodeo in 1974 and is one of the largest of its kind. It is extremely popular with Barbeque Cookoff teams the likes of Asleep at the Grill, Blowin' Smoke, Texas Trail Tramps, Road Kill BBQ, and one of my favorites, Bun Stuffers.

I love to barbeque and get most of my recipes from my favorite cook-book, *Kill It and Grill It*, written by Ted Nugent and his lovely wife, Sh-emane. The Houston Livestock Show and Rodeo sponsors art programs and gives school scholarships to very deserving young men and women. It occurs for almost a month every single year during the months of February and March in Houston, Texas (where else?), and provides a huge benefit to the Houston economy, as well as creating many jobs. The whole com-munity pitches in to put on this larger-than-life production and a lot of the people you see working there are volunteers helping out by giving their time and service. Some famous musicians that have visited in the past are Gene Autry, Charlie Pride, ZZ Top, Kiss, and Elvis Presley. President George H. W. Bush has even made an appearance. If you have never been to this event, I recommend you give it a try. It is a lot of fun and very en-tertaining. I didn't know it at the time, but it would also be the scene of a mystery I would happen into and help solve. You'll find out more about that in short order.

CHAPTER THIRTY-THREE

Dudley and I walked up the sidewalk to the old iron door entrance of Big Rock Lofts. I unlocked and opened the door; we walked in, went up the stairs, and arrived at #158. I took my keys out, unlocked the door, and Dudley and I went in, closing the door behind us. I poured myself a nice cold iced coffee, added a couple of shots of Jack Black, and sat myself down on the sofa. The next thing I knew, Dudley was sitting right next to me. He pressed his eighty-eight-pound muscular body up against me and laid his head down on my shoulder.

"Hey, I'm not that kind of a guy," I told him. Or was I? I tried to push him a little away from me but every time I started pushing him he stiffened his legs up and shifted his body weight forward. Apparently he must have studied about Sir Isaac Newton in doggie school because for every action I took to push him away from me, he had an equal and opposite reaction and kept pressing up against me. I suppose it could be worse. I took a few sips of my super-charged iced coffee, set it down, and closed my eyes for a little down time while my guardian angel, Dudley, watched over me.

I really don't remember ever waking up, but I must have sleepwalked into the shower because my face was all wet. I reached for the shampoo but got a handful of a big furry face. I then realized I hadn't woken up at all but Dudley was up; and when Dudley was up, everyone was up. I grabbed the bottom of my shirt and began drying off my face. Dudley had been licking my face non-stop.

When I held up my hand, palm out in front of him and told him to stop, he started licking my hand. When he finally finished I took a look at my watch and it was already after seven. I jumped up because I just remembered that Sarge was still at the bookstore and would probably need a ride home.

I gathered my wits and turned to Dudley and asked him if he wanted to go with me. Of course had he been a regular dog he would have said nothing but, oh no, not Dudley. He started mumbling something and walking toward the door. Off we went as I opened the door and we walked out of the loft. I closed and locked the door behind us and we walked toward the stairwell.

As we walked down the steps together we ran into E.D. She was looking particularly super fine with her long golden hair pulled back, and wearing running attire. She did not even notice us. She was standing very still while reading a piece of paper that had two fold marks in it. It appeared to be a letter and she was clutching it with both hands very tightly. She was sporting a determined but stern facial expression.

I pretended to clear my throat a couple of times but still nothing so much as a hello. I started waving both of my hands in front of her face and jumping up and down like a marionette but still nothing. Something did finally get her attention though. Dudley had skulked his way right up to her and did what any normal red-blooded American male would do. He buried his head right in her crotch and began feverishly humping her leg while letting out the most precarious of grunting noises.

Oh, what I wouldn't give to be a dog right now. I'll just have to live this moment vicariously and precariously through him. "What the hell's wrong with your mangy mutt?" she exclaimed.

"Well, for one thing, he has exquisite taste in his women. You can't really fault him for that," I retorted.

"Well, he's about to get my foot up where the sun don't shine if he doesn't back off," she explained.

I told Dudley to come and sit by my side and once he dismounted that's just what he did. He really must have a thing for blondes, especially good-looking ones with the name E.D. She was busy reading what now appeared to definitely be a letter, and she was ignoring us again. I cupped my hand partially over my mouth to block her view, even though she wasn't looking, and whispered to Dudley, "Good boy!"

I approvingly placed my hand on his head as he looked up at me and smiled. He really was a good boy and had a nice toothy grin, similar to that of a crocodile.

"I heard that, Witless," E.D. said. I guess she was paying attention after all.

"That's Careless, honey, and may I ask what you are doing?" I inquired.

"Well, if you must know, I'm reading a letter. Is that okay with you and your serial thriller dog, Careless?" she shot back.

"Is it a good letter?" I asked.

"Aren't you supposed to be some kind of super detective or a spy or something? Why don't you tell me what you think it is?" she said.

"Well, E.D., first of all, I am not a secret Asian man, I am just a regular guy with overly, well-developed observational skills as well as another overly developed feature if you know what I mean," I went on as I raised both my eyebrows to exaggerate my boast.

At that point she stopped looking at the letter, looked up directly at me, and gave me a look that, since it is family hour, I probably shouldn't describe right here.

She appeared to be in no mood to be toiled with so I continued on. "Okay, E.D., you are reading a letter you just retrieved from your mailbox from your boyfriend who in fact lives in this very city and you have just come to realize he is your former boyfriend. He wrote in the letter that he no longer wants to see you and that he is moving on and hopes you will do the same. There's probably some generic excuse about it being him and not you and he is really sorry, 'have a nice life.' I believe, if I'm not mistaken, that this is a Dear John letter. If it's any consolation to you, I think he's a complete fool. How'd I do?" I asked. It was a rhetorical question; I already knew how I did.

Her icy stare started to melt just as tears began to melt from her eyes. She began crying and then there was silence. Once again, Careless to the rescue! Always leave them crying, that's what I always say. I didn't know exactly what to do because frankly, I'm somewhat socially retarded; but since the word retarded can't be used anymore for politically correct reasons, I'll just refer to myself as socially challenged. Happy now?

Dudley and I just looked at each other. He was as clueless as I was.

E.D. walked forward a few steps and stopped right in front of me. She placed her arms around my neck and laid her head on my shoulder.

Dudley didn't like this at all and started to grumble a bit but I waved him off with a look and some hand gestures. He settled down pretty quickly.

E.D. said, "You're one hundred percent right. It is a Dear John letter from my boyfriend, Burt, or I guess my ex-boyfriend, Burt."

"Oh, I loved him in the *Smokey and the Bandit* movie," I said.

She giggled a little.

"How in the world did you know all of that?" she asked.

"You know us CIA agents, ma'am, we are trained super observers," I said.

She then asked me if I worked for the CIA and I told her I certainly did, the "Certified Idiots Association."

She continued to sob with her head on my shoulder.

"E.D., the guy's obviously an idiot, you're better off without him. If it makes you feel any better, I'll take you out to dinner some time. Would you like that?" I asked.

"When?" she questioned.

"I don't know," I answered.

"How about tonight?" she asked in a determined manner.

I noticed her voice actually sounded a little more chipper and her melting tears had stopped flowing. Careless to the rescue. I know; I'm good! "Tonight it is, but right now I have to go pick up Sarge at the bookstore before someone mistakes him for a homeless person," I said.

"No you don't, Careless, I saw him downstairs when I was getting my Dear John letter from my mailbox. What time should we go tonight?" she asked.

"Meet me at eight on the stairwell and I'll take you to a nice Italian restaurant," I said.

She said, "Oh, I love Italian."

"Did I ever tell you I was Italian?" I joked.

She removed her arms from around my neck, gave me a kiss on my cheek, and forced a little smile as she said, "I'll see you at eight and I still want to know how you knew about the letter. You can tell me later at dinner. Be on time and don't keep me waiting!"

I probably wouldn't tell her how I knew about the Dear John letter but it was really quite simple. I knew it was a letter because it had been folded in thirds to fit inside of a standard number-nine envelope people most commonly use to mail letters, and the crinkled up envelope it came in was shoved carelessly in her shorts front pocket with enough of it sticking out so I could make out that it indeed was postmarked in Houston, Texas.

I was able to make out the name and return address in the top left-hand corner as well. By her earnest look and the way she was grasping the letter so as to not let go of it, it appeared that she was also not really prepared to let go of the relationship. It clearly had to be a Dear John letter. Her eyes betrayed her and that was when I knew it was a painful letter for her to read and yet she couldn't put it down. No, I certainly would not tell her of my methods. Why should I make her relive her pain and, as a bonus, I could remain a devilishly handsome source of mystery and intrigue to her.

"Come on, boy, let's go find Sarge and make sure he's all good," I said to Dudley. We trotted down the stairwell together. It was almost as if we had been side by side all of our lives. I was afraid to admit how comfortable I was with Dudley always right next to me. I was afraid because I couldn't remember how it was before he was with me and likewise how it would be one day when he wasn't. I dare not think of that day and I hope it doesn't come any time soon. At the bottom of the stairwell, we found Sarge sitting on the sofa in the entryway, reading a book.

"Sarge, I'm so glad you made it back. Dudley and I were just on our way to retrieve you from the bookstore. How did you get back?" I asked.

"Hey, man, han, han, han, han, han, han, this foxy lady asked me if I knew you and I told her I did. She gave me a ride home when the bookstore closed man, han, han, han, han, han, han," Sarge said.

You can now probably guess Sarge's age because I really don't recall the last time I heard someone use the word "foxy" to describe a girl. Sarge was definitely living in the past, but what's wrong with that anyway? The past is always someplace you wish you could get back to and, hell, Sarge is the only person I know who has managed to at least visit there, if not live there.

"That's great, Sarge. What are you reading? Did you buy a new book?" I inquired.

"Wow, how, how, how, how, how, how, no man, han, han, han, han, han, han, I totally forgot, that foxy lady that gave me a lift home handed me this book and told me to make sure to give it to you the next time I saw you so here you go man, han, han, han, han, han, han," he said while getting up from the sofa and handing me the book.

He patted Dudley on the head while Dudley growled just a smidgen. He then disappeared up the stairwell. I held up the book. It was actually very heavy and quite thick. The title was *The Complete Tales of Sherlock Holmes* by Sir Arthur Conan Doyle. Of course I knew of Sherlock Holmes but had never read any of the stories about him. I knew he was a legendary crime and mystery solver but that was the extent of my knowledge. The book had a beautifully illustrated, colorful cover with a picture of Sherlock Holmes on it and it appeared to be pretty old. I opened it up to quickly glance through it.

I certainly did plan to read it but I opened it because perhaps it's just human nature to open a book once it is presented to you. When you open the book, you open the mind and when the mind is open, the world is open to make all things possible. I turned to the first page, which was the dedication page, and I was floored to read a note in very beautiful and meticulous handwriting, written in dark black India ink, in the top left corner of the page. It read: To Careless, one of the most insightful and observant men I think I shall ever meet, and also the most handsome. Okay, I made the handsome part up but continuing on it read: Put your talents to good use. Until we meet again. Love, Maria.

I was stunned. I did not expect that. I smiled and was surprisingly happy for a change. I turned to share what had just happened with Sarge. I felt like I should share it with someone, but he was out of sight, out of mind, and long gone. This was very interesting indeed. I rarely get surprised but as with all things, I was sure it would not be the last time.

I clutched the book in my right hand and cupped my left hand to match the shape of Dudley's very large head as I began to pet him on his head. As always, he was right by my side, which is how it should be. I told him to come with me and we walked back up the stairs to #158. I took out my keys, unlocked the door, and we both entered. I closed the door behind us, put the book down on the coffee table, and prepared to take a shower. I had to get all gussied up and put on my smell-good for my dinner date with E.D. tonight, if she actually showed up; but all I could think about right now was Maria, and that book she sent to me.

I got undressed, pulled the shower curtain back, and turned on the water. After what seemed like a fortnight, the water began to warm up. I stepped in and closed the shower curtain behind me. I stuck my head under the warm water and with my eyes closed reached over for the shampoo bottle. As I usually do, I just feel around until I feel the shampoo bottle. I was groping around for the shampoo bottle and my hand experienced something unusual and very large. If you thought I was going to get crude here, think again. My hand came across a big, wet, hairy mass, and it appeared to be moving around. Still, not going to get crude.

Even though I suspected what this new sensation was, I wiped the water away from my eyes and looked down. There he was in all his glory. Dudley had pushed the shower curtain aside just enough to stick his big head in the shower almost all the way up to his shoulders. I just looked at him like he was a big goofball and, in fact, he was. I finished up, turned the shower off, and toweled off both of us. I started getting myself ready and slapped on some smell-good. Then I looked at Dudley and slapped some smell-good on him as well. He appeared to like it. We were using Aqua Lavanda cologne, which was the same cologne rumored to be used by Frank Sinatra, Chairman of The Board, ole' Blue Eyes himself. At this point Dudley was very proud of himself. He is a real classy guy, that Dudley.

Frank Sinatra was born as Francis Albert Sinatra in December of 1915. He was an amazing singer, with very popular songs like "Strangers in the Night," "My Way," "Witchcraft," and "New York, New York." He appeared in several films such as *The Manchurian Candidate* and *From Here to Eternity*. He began singing in the 1930s and later received an Academy Award, a Grammy, the Presidential Medal of Freedom, and the Congressional Gold Medal.

Sadly, he was called home in May of 1998, but he had a long and fulfilling career, and his music is still popular. He is missed but not forgotten, and Dudley and I were now wearing what was rumored to be his favorite cologne. We both smelled good and looked even better.

CHAPTER THIRTY-FOUR

It was quickly approaching the witching hour, so I told Dudley I had to leave him for a while. He said something which led me to believe he wasn't happy. I could tell he wasn't very thrilled. "Look, I left some food and water out for you and, if you get tired, take a nap on that lovely yellow-and-orange sofa right there," I said while pointing at the lovely yellow-and-orange sofa. "If you really get bored then you can order a movie on cable TV and if you eat all of your food and are still hungry, I left a twenty-dollar bill on the coffee table for you. You can order a pizza or something," I said. That seemed to lift his spirit a little but the joke was on him because I didn't have cable TV. What Dudley doesn't know won't hurt him, or so I thought. I would find out later that the joke was on me.

I got dressed, put on my boots, slid my wallet in my back pocket and hugged Dudley goodbye. I told him I would be back soon. I just hoped he wouldn't miss me too much.

I did a quick package check and headed for the door. Dudley was sitting on the sofa, watching me, and wearing his sad face. I thought twice about leaving him but I didn't want E.D. to be mad at me, and I sure didn't want to "keep her waiting."

I opened the door, closed it behind me, and locked it. I slid my keys back in my front pocket and headed for the stairwell. It was exactly seven-fifty-seven. Not one minute later, E.D. came waltzing down the stairs in a very tight but elegant mid-length red dress. Of course, the power color. Her hair was long, flowing, and golden. I knew she was very beautiful but I had no idea she was this beautiful, and for just the second time in years I was at a loss for words.

"Careless, you clean up pretty well," she said.

I tried to verbalize a snappy comeback but my brain was pretty much shut down so no thoughts were being processed and my mouth didn't appear to be moving.

"Problem, Careless?" she inquired. "I know, I know, you're struck by

161

my beauty. It's really a curse, you know. Just nod your head up and down a couple of times to let me know you comprehend what I am saying; and, as a benefit, it may get your blood flowing to your brain again," she said.

I just nodded a few times and my thought process did actually start to return. We began walking down the stairwell together. I have always heard that one can get blinded by beauty but this time it had left me blind, deaf, and dumb, at least temporarily. As we walked along, I regained some of my composure and told E.D. that I had actually been daydreaming, and that she looked very beautiful.

She just smiled and laughed because she knew I was lying. We made our way through the front entryway and I opened the old iron door for her. We left the building and the door clanked shut behind us. When we got to the Power Wagon I opened her door for her as she scootched in. She buckled up and I closed the door. I went around to the driver's side, got in, and cranked her up. The engine was quite muscular sounding and I do believe E.D. was impressed. I turned on the radio and off we went to a restaurant named Lucio's.

Things were going very well. So far I hadn't screwed it up, so I would have to give this date a thumbs-up. E.D. wasn't talking much but she seemed to be relaxed and having a good time. I had never received a Dear John letter or even a Dear Jane letter for that matter, but I was sure it probably wasn't much fun. A few minutes later, the sun was on its way down and we arrived at Lucio's. There were no parking spots in front of the restaurant so I offered to drop off E.D. in front while I attempted to go park the Power Wagon. She happily agreed so I dropped her off and swung around to the other side of the street to find a parking spot. There was a doorman in front of the restaurant and he opened the door for E.D. and let her in. I was sure this happened for her all of the time as well as probably receiving a lifetime supply of free drinks. As luck would have it, I found a parking spot directly across the street from the restaurant.

I pulled up and backed right into the spot with a very clever parallel parking maneuver I like to refer to as the Careless Crossover. I closed and locked the door and started to walk across the street towards the restaurant. When I got about halfway there, I noticed the doorman was giving me a funny look. He was a large, muscular, handsome man, probably in his mid-twenties with a full head of thick brown hair. By the way he was eyeballing me, I was preparing myself for trouble or at the very least not to be allowed in the restaurant.

I was quite surprised when his eyes lit up and he started speaking in my direction, "Damian! Is that you, Damian? I haven't seen you in years. How have you been?"

I was more than a little shocked so I quickly glanced over my shoulder and looked behind me to make sure he wasn't talking to someone else. No, there was no one behind me so he was definitely talking to me. "Damian Mandola, come on over here. You are Damian Mandola aren't you?" he asked.

I thought carefully about it for a moment. I mean, do any of us know who we really are? Maybe I was Damian Mandola and had been just dreaming I was Careless this whole time. Nah, that could never happen. I was definitely Careless, so of course I did what any honest person would do, I responded, "Of course, I'm Damian, who else could look this good?"

I smiled and the rather large doorman moved toward me. That's when I thought the jig was up and I was probably going to hit the pavement. The doorman was only two inches in front of me and hugged me. Then I heard him say, "I knew that was you, Damian. I sure have missed you."

It turned out the bear hug was just an overly friendly hug from one *paesano* to another. "Come on, Damian, let me get you a table," he said as he led the way to the restaurant door.

He opened the door for me and I walked into the restaurant. There was a sea of people crammed together waiting to be seated, and E.D. was in the middle of that sea. I guess reservations probably would have been a good idea if I had bothered to make them. E.D. looked at me and I could see from her facial expression that she was quite displeased. I suppose she was not the kind of gal who liked to wait for things, and in her defense, with her looks, she probably never did have to wait for anything. This would be no exception.

My new long-lost friend, the doorman, came up behind me and, somewhat like Moses, parted the sea of people. He said, "Out of the way, Damian Mandola is here."

Sure enough, just like the Red Sea, the crowd of people parted and there was now a clear trail to the other side of the restaurant as we were led to our table. As soon as we sat down, the path closed back up in sardine can fashion. If the Egyptians would have been there they would have surely been swallowed up. That's what they get for having slaves!

After we were seated, my new friend, the doorman, waved goodbye and I heard him tell all of the wait staff that Damian Mandola was in the restaurant so the service and food must both be impeccable, and it was.

It is said that everyone has a double somewhere. I have no idea what Damian Mandola looks like, but obviously he must be very handsome. I did know who he is because I had eaten at his restaurant, Damian's Cucina Italiana, several times. Damian Mandola opened his first restaurant while he was a senior in high school. His family was originally from Italia, then moved to Louisiana, and finally settled in Texas. He was a co-founder of another fine Houston tradition, a restaurant named Carraba's. Damian's Cucina Italiana is located not far from Big Rock Lofts, in downtown Houston, and focuses on traditional Italian cooking. It just happens to be one of my favorite restaurants and their spinachi gnocchi is outstanding.

E.D. smiled and looked at me. For once, I think I pleasantly surprised her. She asked me what all the commotion was about and wanted to know how I procured a table when there was a one-hour wait. Obviously she had inquired and put her name on the list but, unfortunately for her, she was no Damien Mandola; but then again, neither was I, but she didn't know that.

Luckily for me, she had not heard the exchange between me and my new friend, the doorman. I went on to tell her that when you have the great looks and personality I have, things just fall into place and I receive special treatment wherever I go.

Of course, she knew I was lying and one of her very cute little eyebrows started to rise just a little higher than the other one, showing her skepticism. Before she could utter another word, several waitresses starting buzzing around our table like busy little bees, placing sparkling water, wine, bread, and an assortment of appetizers on the table. E.D. just looked at me again and I could tell she was puzzled, but happily so. We had not even ordered anything yet and the table was filled with food and drinks. I don't get special treatment in restaurants very often; but when I do, I prefer to be Damian Mandola. Sometimes it pays to be someone else and sometimes it doesn't. This was one of those times it did.

Our waiter poured two glasses of red wine. I was pretty sure at this

moment in time, E.D. wasn't thinking about her Dear John letter anymore. We toasted one another with some mighty fine wine. As we began
talking, our waiter walked over with some menus. He must have been very
happy because he was singing jubilantly. I admired that because I couldn't
sing worth a damn and I had never really been jubilant. Hell, I rarely even
use the word jubilant. I would be more apt to use the word Uranus.

"*Buena note*," he said in a singsong voice. I knew then we had trouble
on our hands. He went on to welcome us to Lucio's and started to list his
favorite items on the menu. Apparently they were all his favorites. Oh,
but the fish of the day, when he got to that, he was so excited I thought he
would rise off of the ground like the Mighty Mouse helium balloon at the
Macy's Thanksgiving Day Parade in New York. He called it the *salamone*
with an emphasis on the long *A* sound at the end. I didn't really know how
it was prepared because after the first glass of red wine and hearing the
word *salamone* instead of salmon, nothing else seemed to matter much.

E.D. and I both had another glass of wine, toasted one another again,
and ordered the special *salamone* with the house salad from our happy waiter who we had almost forgotten was still standing there. He smiled, took
our menus, started singing again, and waltzed off toward the kitchen.

Things were going pretty well and I could tell E.D. was no longer hurtin' for certain, at least for right now. I asked her if she would excuse me
because I needed to go drain the main vein. She thought that was amusing
and I excused myself. I went across the restaurant and into the men's room.
It was pretty nice, made out of green marble and gold. I made my way to a
stall and was standing in front of it when I heard a squeaky, high-pitched
voice just to the side of me in another stall say, "I'm going to put it in now."

Immediately following that I heard another, more powerful and lower-
pitched voice say, "No, do not put it in!"

Then the squeaky voice said, "I am, I am going to put it in!"

"No, do not put it in," the lower voice said.

"I am going to put it in," the squeaky voice said.

Once again, the deeper voice said, "Do not put it in!"

This went on several more times and finally I finished my business,
flushed the toilet, zipped up, and preceded to back up to see what the
heck was going on next to me. My imagination ran wild and I thought it
was going to be something disgusting. You always hear those stories of

what goes on in restrooms but you never expect it to happen while you are there. As I backed away and glanced to the left of me I noticed a little boy who couldn't have been more than six or seven standing in front of a toilet with his father right next to him. The kid was holding a small stuffed animal that looked a bit like Bullwinkle the Moose. Bullwinkle the Moose was a cartoon character from the 1960s and his name was derived from the last name of a friend of one of the creators, Jay Ward.

The little boy was holding the stuffed moose close to the water in the toilet and pretending to dip it into the water while saying, "I'm going to put it in now."

His father, who actually needed to use the restroom, was finishing up and told him again, "Do not put it in!"

I started to laugh out loud and the little boy turned, looked at me, and started to laugh mischievously as well.

Dad was not amused.

I turned around, washed my hands, dried them, and went back out to join the lovely E.D. who was being entertained by several of the wait staff. While on the way to the table, the swinging kitchen door quickly flung outwardly open and our very happy, singing waiter came flying out with a tray of food held with one hand at shoulder height. I quickly ducked and missed having my head taken off by mere inches as the tray of food came rapidly toward my neck. I was a little anxious about it but chose to say nothing. The waiter never even noticed me. I walked behind him on the way to the table to find E.D. cracking up laughing because she had witnessed the whole thing. I suppose it was funny, even though her amusement was at my expense.

The happy waiter served us our meal. The house salad was wonderful and had all kinds of green and purple lettuce in it as well as walnuts, goat cheese, and craisins sprinkled on top for good measure. The *salamone* was grilled on a plank and looked delicious.

E.D. and I began talking about places we had been. Her photography career had taken her on assignment to many countries and added to her extensive and expensive photography portfolio. She told me she had been to China, Japan, Vietnam, Turkey, Israel, Egypt, Spain, and Italy. I, in turn, told her I had been to Houston, Dallas, Austin, San Antonio, and Medina, Texas. It was clear she was more well-rounded than I was and that she was a seasoned traveler. As we ate, the conversation changed to places we wanted to go but hadn't been to yet. She rattled off England, France, and Africa. I rattled off my stock answer, Uranus.

She smiled a bit and told me to get serious. That's when I went through my whole list of why going to Uranus was great, it seemed nice, not many people go there so it wouldn't be too crowded, the inhabitants were supposed to be nice, and I heard the food was pretty good and reasonably priced. Now I was getting the go "f" yourself look, but I was saved by our happy waiter who had just moseyed on up to our table without either of us realizing it. He sure was a happy little fella, not that there's anything wrong with that.

Just when E.D. was about to let me know I was dead meat on a toilet seat, the waiter chimed in, "Oh, I hope you don't mind but I overheard your conversation and I just have to say that I *love* astrology. My favorite planet is also Uranus."

Now he was directing his stare right at me. *Awkward!*

E.D. and I looked at one another and started laughing hysterically. Out of the closet and into the frying pan. That's what I always say. We finished our very delicious meal, thanked the waiter, and asked for the check. I was informed (or actually Damian was informed) there would be no bill. That's a little something I like to call, "On the house."

We left the restaurant with full bellies and warm hearts. E.D. was doing much better now than she had been earlier in the day while reading her Dear John letter. In fact, I was pretty sure she didn't remember it at all.

E.D. and I left Lucio's and we walked toward the Power Wagon. We made small talk along the way and she told me she had a great time and appreciated that I had taken her mind off of her problems. Finally, she was starting to realize what a great guy I was. I was successfully not screwing this up when the doorman waved and shouted, "*Ciao*, Damian."

E.D. was puzzled and looked at me for an explanation. I just shrugged and told her I didn't speak Italian so I had no idea what the doorman said. Dodged another bullet.

We walked up to the Power Wagon and I opened the door for her and closed it once she was safely in. I walked around the front and opened the driver's side door, climbed in, closed it, and cranked her up. I was about to put it in gear when I noticed E.D. was looking at me. I asked her what she was thinking and she asked, "This is where he sits, isn't it?"

"I have no idea what you are talking about," I replied. I absolutely did know what, or should I say who, she was talking about, but I didn't want to ruin the moment.

"You know exactly what I am talking about. I'm talking about that overactive serial humper of a dog of yours. What's-his-name, you know: Dude," she said.

At this point all was lost so I reverted to the truth and said, "Yes, if you must know, that is where he sits and his name is Dudley, but I do like the name Dude. Maybe that could be his nickname, and he only humps you so it probably has something to do with your animal magnetism. You can't really blame him for that."

"You love him, don't you?" she asked.

"Well, love is a very strong word. Let me use it in a sentence to illustrate my point. I love you and will you marry me?" I asked.

Normally that would have pissed her off but since I had been on my very best behavior all night she just smiled and said, "Home, James."

She was right. I do love him with all of my heart. What's not to love? Several minutes later we pulled up in front of Big Rock Lofts. We exited the Power Wagon and I escorted E.D. through the old iron door. In the entryway, Sarge was on the sofa reading a book and didn't even notice us.

As we started up the stairwell, I asked E.D. if she was going to have me up for a drink. She kissed me on the cheek, smiled at me, and said, "Not on your life, Witless, but thank you for a wonderful evening."

She quickly turned and scurried up the stairwell. It all happened so fast that I forgot to use my stock answer of, "That's Careless," so in this particular case I may have actually been Clueless. I had still done a nice thing, so all's well that ends well. I turned to go up the stairs to check on "The Dude," and, as I did, I heard Sarge's voice behind me say, "Shot down, man, han, han, han, han, han, han. That's a bummer man, han, han, han, han, han han!"

Indeed it was, but not as big of a bummer as what I was about to find waiting for me in loft #158.

CHAPTER THIRTY-FIVE

I made my way up the stairwell and to my door. It seemed quiet in the loft so I assumed Dudley was behaving and was probably just resting until I came home to provide entertainment for him. This time when I assumed, I just made an ass out of me.

I took my keys out and unlocked the door. I tried to open it like I normally do but it became lodged up against something on the inside of the loft and only opened about a quarter of the way it should normally open. It was really stuck like Chuck, so I gave it a shove with all of my might and it moved just enough for me to stick my head in to see what the malfunction was. There, up against the door was my yellow-and-orange vinyl sofa.

I don't know why, but all I could now think of at this point was that song by Ray Wylie Hubbard, "Up Against the Door, Redneck Sofa." "*Sofa that I'd come to know so well.*" Unfortunately, Dudley had dragged the sofa from clear across the room and it appeared that the only thing that stopped him from going any further was the door. This was not one of those new cheap, lightweight sofas either. I bought it from my roommate in college, John Fisher, and he got it as a hand-me-down from his mom. I had moved it several times since college and it always took three or four guys to lift it because it was so heavy. I don't know how that dog was able to move it. Powerful indeed he was. The force must be with him.

The problem was that Dudley hadn't just dragged it across the room; he had also stripped it down to its original components. The only thing left of it was the wooden frame and some steel springs. All of the vinyl and stuffing was scattered all around the loft. While I can fix almost anything with duct tape, this time I don't think it was going to do a sufficient repair job. That sofa purchase was probably the best twenty-five dollars I had ever spent, and now it was gone, just like that. I would have to thank it for its many years of service before I sent it off to the great sofa graveyard in the sky.

I summoned up some more strength and pushed the door (and the sofa) open enough for me to get into the loft. What a mess my friend had made. I called out to him and he came flying out of the bedroom. He was probably pretty tired after demolishing my sofa and had gone to take a power nap on my bed. Destroying a sofa can be hard work so I could see where he might need a little rest. He ran up to me and jumped up to give me a big hug. It kind of reminded me of the hug I had received earlier by the doorman at Lucio's. Now I began to wonder if in fact Dudley may be Italian. I'll have to think about that for a while.

I was really going to reprimand Dudley for tearing my sofa a new one but once he started hugging me, looking at me with those big, kind eyes, and licking my face like a hyperactive child licking a lollypop, all I could say was, "I know, I know, I missed you too, boy!"

After what seemed like a couple of hours, I was ready to get a bath towel to dry off my face and I was going to tell him to knock it off; but before I could, he stopped on his own and went racing toward the door. With all of the excitement, I had accidently left the loft door open. Standing in the doorway was the lovely E.D. She was still dressed from our dinner date and if possible looked even better than before. It doesn't take a detective to figure that out and, believe me, I notice details like that. She was holding two wine glasses and a bottle of a nice Merlot from Fall Creek Vineyards produced right here in Texas.

Yes, we make our own wine in Texas. In Texas, we don't rely upon the Frenchy French or the Californians to make foo foo wines. Texas is well known for making some of the finest wines on the market. In Texas, we also produce very fine tequilas, vodkas, bourbons, and beer. Just like throughout history, we don't have to rely on others for our basic needs. E.D. caught me off guard because I wasn't expecting to see her this soon but I tried not to act too surprised and said, "So, you just couldn't get enough of me, isn't that right?"

Her reply was pretty simple, she said, "Hapless, I have no idea why, but I was actually thinking about having a drink with you and thankfully this scene just jarred me back to my senses. Now, your mutt better not be eyeballing my leg or I may have to make a hot dog out of him."

Yes, indeed, Dudley was quickly and silently sneaking up on E.D. and was preparing to mount her leg. When he heard the hot dog threat, his ears perked up a bit and he stopped dead in his tracks. I called to him and he trotted back toward me.

"That's Careless," I said as E.D. did an about face and marched back up to her loft.

Note to self: interestingly enough, E.D. looked just as fine when coming or going. I didn't consider it a total loss when I learned something new like that. I like to think positive.

It was then and there that I made a Careless executive decision. I didn't make them often so, when I did, I preferred to take it seriously. I knew now there was no way I could ever leave Dudley in the loft unattended for long periods of time. I didn't have much furniture but what I did have, I really wanted to keep or at least keep in one piece. I decided Dudley would be going to work with me tomorrow morning and every day thereafter.

I picked up what remained of the sofa's innards while walking toward the loft door. I closed and locked the door and started to place the skeletal remains of the sofa into garbage bags. I looked around for Dudley, but he was long gone. He was busy sawing logs on my bed. I wasn't sure how he managed it but his body was completely under the sheets with his head sticking out, resting on my pillow. I rolled my eyes. I guess he did have an exciting day so maybe he was in need of a good nap. I got undressed and slid into bed, pushing him to one side. One thing I was now sure of, when you lie down with dogs you don't wake up with E.D.

CHAPTER THIRTY-SIX

Ring ring, ring ring, ring ring. I kept hearing bells. I opened my eyes half expecting Dudley to be eyeballing me, but he was still sleeping. There's really just no way I can accurately describe what it's like to get spooned by a large hound dog named Dudley. You really have to be a dog lover to tolerate that. I pushed him away from me but as much force as I used to push him away, he Newtoned me again and pushed back with an equal and opposite force. Finally, I managed to roll out on my side of the bed.

"House of Pies," I said as I answered the red-and-white HEB telephone. "You coming to work today or are you on vacation?" a voice on the telephone asked.

"Who the hell is this?" I asked. I knew full well who it was.

"It's your boss, Ross the Boss," the voice said. It was my brother, Ross, Ross the Boss. It was 5:00 a.m. and he wanted to know if I would be at breakfast. We normally ate breakfast together with Pappa every weekday morning before work. None of us particularly functioned too well early in the morning but it was good family time and it had turned into a daily ritual. We broke bread together (which was important), grunted a few times, and proceeded to the office.

I told Ross the Boss I was skipping breakfast today and would see him at the office. He inquired as to why so I told him I had a big surprise for him and I hung up the telephone. I got dressed, cleaned up, grabbed an iced coffee for the road and ran out of the loft. About two seconds later, I kept thinking I had forgotten something. That's when it hit me. I had forgotten Dudley. I made a U-turn and headed right back into the loft where Dudley was waiting patiently by the door. He was just sitting there as if he knew I would return in rapid fashion. I may be a slow learner but he did teach me a lesson with the sofa, so I definitely wasn't going to leave him there alone. I didn't know how exactly I was going to explain him to everyone at work but I was sure I would think of something by the time I got there.

Dudley and I left the loft in a hurry. Fortunately for me, I only lived five minutes from my office, which was just east of downtown. I opened the old iron front door and we trotted across the front lawn to the parking lot where the Power Wagon was waiting for us. Dudley stopped for a moment to do his business and I wanted to tell him to hurry up but it's hard to rush that sort of thing. I opened the Power Wagon door to let Dudley in on my side and he jumped over the middle console and into the passenger's seat, his seat. I buckled us both in and fired her up. We sped off to work. I was feeling a little hungry so we made a pit stop at Whataburger.

Whataburger is an orange-and-white-striped hamburger joint founded in Corpus Christi, Texas, in 1950 by Harmon Dobson. There are presently over seven hundred locations, they are open twenty-four hours a day, and they make really delicious hamburgers and breakfast tacquitos, which are warm flour tortillas stuffed with eggs and most any other breakfast food items.

Dudley had never been to a drive-through, so he remained interested. I waited our turn in line and pulled around to the outdoor speaker. When we were asked to give our order, Dudley leaned over, looked out of the window, turned his head sideways, and raised one of his eyebrows. This new experience really had his attention. I ordered two potato-and-egg tacquitos and we whirled around to the pickup window.

When the young lady at the window asked for the four dollars we owed, I started to hand it to her. As she reached out to take it, Dudley lunged forward and scared the ever-loving bejesus out of her. He sure was getting protective.

I apologized profusely and held Dudley back with my right arm while paying the young lady with my left arm. She timidly handed me the tacquitos and we were off to the pipe yard.

My grandfather, Ben Robinson, started up our business over eighty years ago. He literally brainwashed us when we were kids by waking us at 5:00 in the morning, making breakfast, and then taking us to work by 6:00 a.m.

Of course that was many years ago and now my brother Ross and I run the business. My grandfather had groomed my brother and me to carry on in the family business. I always felt deep in my heart that I wanted to be a writer and write books people would enjoy, but destiny is a funny thing.

You can't fight it, you can't control it, and yet it's always right there in front of your face, even if you refuse to see it; so it was off to the pipe yard.

We call my grandfather, Pappa. He is an astute businessman, but he is definitely "old school." Sometimes being old school is a good thing. He is well respected in the business community and has many business relationships that continue to benefit us daily. Ross brings him to work every morning and he walks around and inspects everything, talks to everyone, and points out how he feels improvements can be made. He runs a tight ship and taught us everything he knew, and everything we know, but he doesn't stop us from modernizing the business and thinking outside of the box. He wants us to succeed and carry on the business for future generations. We have a pipe yard just down the street from the Houston Ship Channel and not far from the Anheuser-Busch Brewery. It is called Robinson Pipe & Supply and is one of the oldest, third-generation steel businesses in Houston.

The Houston Ship Channel was the brainchild of some sailors traveling up the naturally occurring Buffalo Bayou as they sailed toward the City of Houston many years ago. Houston is also affectionately known as the Bayou City. Once it was confirmed that the city of Houston was a viable port, the Port of Houston was officially established in 1842. Since then the Port of Houston, or as I refer to it, the Houston Ship Channel, has been widened and deepened many times to support larger ships, using a process known as dredging.

Dredging a ship channel entails using a machine to pump dirt and debris from the floor of the ship channel, thereby widening and making it deeper. The removed materials are deposited at some other location. This allows many more ships to come into the channel at the same time. The Houston Ship Channel is one of the busiest ports in the world and boasts more than seven thousand ships per year move through it. It was even used for ship transports during World War II. Many oil refineries, holding facilities, and trucking companies line the banks of the Houston Ship Channel. Sugar, oil, steel, cotton, produce, and many other commodities and items move daily through the port and are offloaded or loaded onto ships. The Houston Ship Channel is said to be some 530 feet wide and about forty-five feet deep. A bird's eye view can be had while passing over the Jesse H. Jones Memorial Bridge, or as it is most commonly referred to, the Ship Channel Bridge. For a great view of the Houston Ship Channel, a boat, named the Sam Houston has been giving daily tours since 1958.

The Anheuser-Busch Brewery on Gellhorn Drive was opened in 1966 and sits on 136 acres. The brewery began its long history in Saint Louis, Missouri, in 1860 by Eberhard Anheuser who was originally from Germany. His son-in-law, Adolphus Busch, became the president of Anheuser-Busch in 1880 after Eberhard was called home. Many brands of beer are made by Anheuser-Busch, such as Budweiser, Bud Light, Michelob, Michelob Light, and Ziegenbock.

Anheuser-Bush sells their products internationally and became the largest beer brewer in America somewhere around 1957. They used to routinely give factory tours and serve pitchers of beer at the end of the tour, which was one of my favorite parts. They even used to keep some Clydesdale horses at the facility.

In 1971 the Anheuser-Busch Brewery opened Busch Gardens—a forty-acre theme park built alongside of the brewery with animal attractions such as monkeys, elephants, tigers, deer, bears, and so on. There was even a large pagoda and a boat ride. Sadly, the beautiful theme park was short-lived and closed in 1973. Now it only remains a fond memory tucked away in a young man's heart. Thankfully, the beer is tasty, cold, and still flowing. That's also important.

CHAPTER THIRTY-SEVEN

Dudley and I rolled up to the parking area and we quickly ejected ourselves from the Power Wagon. Inside the office Pappa was sitting in his chair, waiting for us and smoking a big old stogie. He always had a cigar in his mouth, even when he went to sleep at night, which certainly could cause a problem as you may well imagine. He looked at me and said, "Good morning."

Pappa was originally from Russia and had come over with his twelve brothers and sisters. He and his brother Isadore started steel scrap businesses. They worked hard and in the beginning even lived at their offices. Pappa's company branched out and transformed into mainly a pipe yard, but still processed some scrap steel. As Dudley and I walked in together, Pappa just looked at me like I was an idiot, which was probably true. He shrugged his shoulders, and we kept on walking.

I sat down at my desk and Dudley parked himself right next to me. I knew he wanted his tacquito because he was goobering up a river. I unwrapped his tacquito and placed it on the ground in front of him. He inhaled it before I could even blink. He seemed happy to be at work and jumped up on a green leather sofa next to my desk, sat down, and watched my every move.

I started going over some purchase requisitions for some pipe coming in, when Ross the Boss strolled into my office. He was a nice, skinny little man with a lot of energy. He walked right past Dudley without even noticing him. He sat down on the green leather sofa, looked at me, and said, "It's about time you got here."

He received a wet willy from someone acting silly. He got a little scared as evidenced when he jumped about five feet straight up in the air. "What the hell is that?" he squealed. "Are you out of your mind?" he shouted.

I told him that indeed, I was out of my mind and he should meet Dudley, our new silent partner, although he was anything but silent as he began mumbling about something. If Dudley played his cards right at work we may even promote him into our collections department.

Ross the Boss proceeded to tell me for the umpteenth time about how this was a place of business, and no place for pets. I tried out the seeing-eye dog routine that had not worked too well at James Coney Island but Ross the Boss was having none of that. He wasn't easy to fool, this guy. I told him Dudley would be no trouble and I couldn't leave him at my loft unattended because of the sofa he had made a snack out of.

At this point, Pappa walked in smoking his cigar. He had heard the whole conversation and started chuckling when I got to the part about the sofa that had been eaten alive. When Ross the Boss saw Pappa chuckling, he began smiling and laughing just a little bit. That's when I started laughing and then Dudley started laughing. Oh, it was just a laugh riot.

Pappa stopped laughing, took a puff of his cigar, exhaled a plume of white smoke, and told everyone to get back to work. He left my office and walked back into the front office where he would greet people as they walked in. He was a real people person and customers genuinely loved to stop and chitchat with him. He placed his hand on top of Dudley's head as he walked out and patted him a couple of times.

I couldn't believe it but Dudley tilted his head up to allow Pappa to pet him and he didn't utter a sound. Pappa was a real public relations bonanza. After that, I got back to work reviewing our purchase requisitions. It was a little boring but I was good at it, and it needed to be done. I should be good at it, I had been doing it most of my life. In our small family steel business you do whatever needs to be done; so one minute you may be purchasing material and the next thing you know you may be selling, collecting money, or hopping on a machine to load or unload trucks. Everybody works hard and that's just the way it is. Pappa, Ross the Boss, Dudley, and I had no problem with that.

After a few hours, Dudley wanted to go outside to drain the main vein. I took him outside in the pipe yard, and it was clear he wanted to go exploring around the entire five acres. I really didn't have time for that but he did need to stretch his legs and relieve himself from time to time. Maybe Ross the Boss was right. Maybe the workplace wasn't conducive to having a pet. I just couldn't leave Dudley at home unattended. Lord knows, there might not be a building left standing by the time I got home from work if he was left alone for that long.

Using my powers of imagination, I began to think of a solution. What would Ross the Boss do? For that matter what would Jesus do? Jesus was the outdoor groundskeeper of Big Rock Lofts. He was pretty practical. Light bulb! Dudley needed a fenced-in dog run he could access whenever he needed or wanted to without me having to take him out or worry about him running around the pipe yard and getting hurt by one of the eighteen-wheeler trucks or front-end wheel loaders. I also didn't want him to be able to see the welding and fabricating we were doing on the large billboard sign poles that would be installed all along the highways. The arc of the welding machines could severely injure his eyes or even blind him.

I looked around the pipe yard and found the perfect little spot for him. It was right in the front of the office building along the McCarty Street side, and it was already fenced on two sides with the office building on the third side. I would only have to put up one side of a fence to have a nice enclosed dog run for Dudley. It was about thirty feet long and twenty feet across. It was perfect except for one thing. It was being used as a pipe rack to store twelve lengths of forty-eight-inch-diameter pipe. That presented a bit of a problem but I was determined to work through it.

Dudley finished up meandering around the pipe yard and was ready to go back in the office, see Pappa and Ross the Boss, and take a snooze on his newly discovered green leather sofa. I didn't think he would be eating this sofa because I sensed that he liked it too much, but I wasn't taking any chances. At least if he was attached to it, he may not slice and dice this one. Still, I would keep my eye on him just in case.

We walked back into the office and Dudley went right up to Pappa and Pappa started petting him. Dudley's tail began wagging around in helicopter fashion. Oh, Lord, I hope that didn't mean I was becoming a helicopter parent. That's just what I needed to add to my list of character flaws.

After a few minutes of stroking, Dudley walked back into my office as I sat down at my desk and looked over some figures. No, not E.D.'s figure, some sales figures. Dudley sat down on his green leather sofa, rolled over on his back, stuck all four legs straight up in the air, closed his eyes, and started snoring. If anyone walked by that didn't know him, they would certainly think that rigor mortis had set in. He was definitely executive material.

After getting my work done, I called Ross the Boss on the telecom and asked him to come to my office. I would have asked him to bring me coffee but since he was Ross the Boss it seemed somewhat inappropriate. He came in and sat down in a nice cushy circa 1930's leather chair in front of my desk.

At this point Dudley hadn't moved but he did have one eye open, so I knew he was listening. I asked Ross the Boss if he would please take the Caterpillar 928H front-end wheel loader and move the rack of forty-eight inch diameter pipe to another location in the pipe yard so I could make a fenced-in dog run for Dudley, letting him go in and out as he pleased.

Ross the Boss hemmed and hawed but finally agreed to it. I watched as he went outside, climbed up the ladder to the cab of the front-end wheel loader, and then I heard the powerful diesel engine crank up. The two mounted forks on the front were raised up, and Ross the Boss drove over to the rack of forty-eight-inch diameter pipe or, as I now refer to it as, Dudley's Happy Place.

The Caterpillar 928H front-end wheel loader is a big industrial yellow tractor with two forks on the front that can go up and down and tilt forward and backwards. It can lift all types of pipe weighing up to eighteen thousand pounds and in various lengths and diameters. It has four very large all-terrain tires that are about the same height of an average human being, and a steel ladder attached to it leading up to the enclosed cab where it is operated from. It has air conditioning, AM and FM radio, and drives much like a car on steroids with a big steering wheel and several controls to operate the forks.

Ross the Boss picked up and moved all of the forty-eight-inch-diameter pipe and placed it on a different rack in the pipe yard. There were forty to fifty racks of pipe, separated by size, neatly arranged in uniform lengths all around the pipe yard. You know what they say guys, "size matters." He came back in and told me he was finished and I thanked him.

Now my job was to level out the ground, plant some grass for Dudley, and fence in the remaining open side. I also had to find an entry and exit point to install a doggie door so Dudley could go out and come back in. I got up from my desk and as I walked past Pappa in the front office I told him I'd be right back. He just waved and I saw a big plume of white cigar smoke rise up toward the ceiling. He is a very calm and patient man. Not much seems to bother him and thankfully that keeps Ross the Boss, me, and our business on an even keel.

I walked outside and around the perimeter of the office where the new dog run would soon be. Our office was state of the art in the 1950s when it was built. We like to refer to it as the Taj Mahal of pipe yard offices. Nothing too fancy but it gets the job done. One day we hope to build a new office, when this one burns to the ground or gets blown down by a hurricane. Until then, we'll just make due.

Most of the outside of the office building is made from brick but I did find one small section made out of some type of old wood paneling. Using my amazing powers of deduction and, since it would be no easy task to cut through brick to install a doggie door, I knew the doggie door would have to be cut out of and installed into the section of the office with wood paneling on the outside.

I stepped off the distance from the end of the office building to where the wood paneling started. It was exactly twelve paces. Now I just had to go back inside of the office to step off the same amount of paces from the end of the building on the inside, and see where the doggie door needed to be installed.

I went back into the office and Pappa waved me in while still smoking his stogie. El Producto was his brand. He was our official receptionist, greeter, and chief. He may not be young or pretty but he gets the job done and is an institution at Robinson Pipe & Supply, not to mention being the founder. I walked through my office, through Ross the Boss's office, and to the back side of the building.

Dudley was through Rip Van Winkling and was now by my side. I walked a few paces and Dudley walked a few paces. That's when I decided to have fun with him. I quickly stopped to see what he would do and he quickly stopped. I took one step back and two steps forward. He did the same. It appeared I could not fool him so I quit clowning around with him and went back to the end of the office and stepped off twelve paces. Dudley was walking in lock step with me.

There appeared to be one small problem. The twelve paces landed us right smack in the middle of the only restroom in our office. That was the only place the doggie door could be installed without having to bust through brick on the outside of the building. I went back to my office and called for an executive family meeting to discuss the installation location of

Dudley's doggie door.

No meeting took place. Once I told Pappa and Ross the Boss what I intended to do, they informed me that Dudley was good to go as far as staying at the office and his official doggie door could be installed wherever he wanted, even the restroom. I called one of our employees into my office and explained to him what I needed. His name is Hammer and, wearing his tool belt, he immediately walked into the restroom with his T-square, pencils, and tools, so I began to think maybe I had made a hasty decision. He took some measurements, made some calculations, and left to go to a pet store just up the road to purchase a doggie door. When he got back it was Hammer time and he was about to put the hammer down on the project and hammer through the office wall.

As you can probably tell, I like writing the word hammer almost as much as I like writing the word Uranus. About thirty minutes later, after a lot of banging and power tooling, the mission was deemed a complete success. Hammer walked into my office and told me the company doggie door was officially open for business.

In the meantime, Ross the Boss had taken the liberty of having some of the other employees that work in the pipe yard throw sand down and plant grass in the area where the forty-eight inch diameter pipe used to call home. They also planted a skinny little oak tree firmly in the ground in the middle of the new dog run, which was okay because being that Dudley was also a little skinny, he probably wouldn't need much shade. My job now was to fatten them both up, Dudley and the tree, and in no particular order. In the meantime Dudley could get a sun tan on his big frame or rest comfortably in the shade of that skinny little oak tree. Maybe in about ten years the tree would be big enough to offer a great deal of shade. I suppose you have to start somewhere.

The employees also fenced in the one remaining open side of the dog run and the new Dudley playland palace was complete. Dudley hadn't tried it out yet. He was taking another power nap on his green leather sofa. It was, after all, his first full day of work at Robinson Pipe & Supply, so he was pretty tired. At least he was being productive. I really think he is going to become a valued employee.

A few hours later we had finished up our work and it was lights out at Robinson Pipe & Supply. Ross the Boss left with Pappa to drive him home while Dudley and I locked up.

I locked the door to the office, we walked side by side through the parking lot, and I opened my door to the Power Wagon. Dudley jumped in and moved over to the passenger seat. He was ready for a cold one after his long day at the office. I got in, cranked her up, and we drove to the front gate of the pipe yard. I hopped out, closed the door behind me, and closed and locked the sliding chain-link front gate used by eighteen-wheel trucks to enter and leave the pipe yard. It was a pretty wide gate, probably sixty foot across to get those big trucks in and out.

I got back in the Power Wagon and started driving toward Big Rock. I decided to take a detour and head back over to the bookstore to thank Maria for the Sherlock Holmes book she had sent to me via Sarge. I looked at Dudley and told him we were going to make a pit stop. He said something but I wasn't sure of what, so I just assumed he was agreeable as we continued on.

CHAPTER THIRTY-EIGHT

Ten minutes later we pulled up to the bookstore. I parked the Power Wagon and turned her off. I unstrapped my seatbelt and turned toward Dudley. I looked him right in the eye and told him he had better stay in the truck or else. He looked at me, reached his head over, and started uncontrollably licking my face with his huge tongue.

"Oh, no, not this time," I told him. I pointed my index finger at him, told him to stay, and that I would be right back.

He moaned, whined, and groaned a bit but I was determined to see Maria again. She intrigued me, which if you think about it wasn't all that hard to do; but I was intrigued none the less. I jumped out of the Power Wagon and closed and locked the door behind me. I pointed my index finger at Dudley again, told him to stay, and that I would be watching him. Then I gave him the universal signal for watching someone by pointing my two fingers at my eyes and motioning the same hand back toward him while pointing my index finger to make sure he knew I was serious.

I walked slowly toward the bookstore entrance while occasionally glancing over my shoulder to see what kind of shenanigans he would try to pull, but he just sat there staring at me with a long face. At least he was listening this time.

The bookstore wasn't really too crowded so I headed for the coffee shop and looked feverishly for Maria. I was almost giddy with the thought of seeing her again and I can't believe I just wrote the word giddy. I did see several people working behind the counter, but Maria was nowhere to be found. I waited around for a few minutes trying my best not to appear to be a stalker. Finally, I walked around until I found someone that looked like he worked there. His back was turned to me but he was helping a customer so I assumed that either he did in fact work at the bookstore or he was a fellow stalker pretending to help someone so as not to appear to be a stalker.

I tapped him on the shoulder and asked, "Exscrews me, sir, do you work here?"

The man abruptly turned around and seemed kind of shocked that someone had asked him a question. "Yes, I do work here; how may I help you?"

He certainly looked familiar and I asked him if we had met before. He denied ever meeting me but just like that, it came to me. Could it be? Yes, of course, I blurted out, "You're Seth, store manager, aren't you?"

"Yes, sir, I am Seth, the store manager; do I know you?" he asked.

"The name's Careless."

I jogged his memory for him and told him he had kicked me and my friend, Dudley, out of the store yesterday. He promptly went on to lecture me about company policy of no animals allowed in the store. I asked him if he didn't serve "those kind," but he just gave me a stern look and was not amused.

I noticed that while talking to me, he appeared to be a bit nervous and was scanning the store for a crazed dog running up and down the aisles. That was so nice; he did remember me after all. Eventually, I asked him about Maria and he informed me that yesterday was her last day at the store and she had moved back home to take care of a family matter.

I inquired as to exactly where that was but Seth, store manager, was tight-lipped about employee information so that proved to be a dead-end. I was really bummed out because I thought that Maria had a real interest in me.

I thanked Seth, store manager, and turned to walk out of the store. As I did, Seth, store manager, cleared his throat in an obvious attempt to regain my attention. I turned back to see that he was directing his attention toward me and he hesitantly said, "Sir, she did leave this for you, just in case you came back looking for her," while handing me an envelope.

I took the envelope from Seth, store manager, as he turned and walked away in a huff. I sure hoped this was not my Dear Jane letter like the one E.D. recently received. I opened the envelope and pulled out a letter. It was folded into thirds so I unfolded it and read it. The following was written in very beautiful and meticulous handwriting using the same black India ink also used to write the note in the book she sent to me: "Careless, once I see you again, I will know just how good of a detective you really are. Until then, Maria."

That was the entire letter—short and sweet. Story of my life. This was a mystery I would take up in short order. Then, I, as well as Maria, will see if Careless is up to snuff, and I do believe I will be.

I was feeling a little down but probably not as bad as E.D. was after reading her Dear John letter. I figured at least I had a light at the end of my tunnel and one day soon I would see Maria again. I felt sure of that. I was deep in thought as I exited the bookstore and wandered over to the Power Wagon. I was trying to formulate a plan to find Maria, but I heard Dudley moaning like a cheap whore so it broke my concentration, which that sound is apt to do, especially if you are a man, but not necessarily. Not that there's anything wrong with that.

My friend was anxiously awaiting me even though I hadn't been gone more than five minutes. He had his moist nose pressed up tight against the glass of the driver's-side window. I could see right down his nostrils almost clear to his brain. It wasn't really his brain, it was probably just a big booger in the shape of a brain. At least he stayed put this time. I didn't think Seth, store manager, could take another visit from the D Man. As I reached for the door, Dudley backed up into the passenger's seat. Of course he left nose prints all over the inside of the driver's-side window.

I unlocked and opened the door to the Power Wagon and climbed inside. Before I could even close the door behind me Dudley lunged practically into my lap and started smothering me with his huge tongue as he licked my face. After what seemed like two days I finally told him to stop and tried to push him off just a little bit, but in Newton fashion he pushed back with an equal and opposite force. He finally calmed down and returned to his seat. Dudley acted as if he hadn't seen me in five years, let alone five minutes ago.

I cranked up the Power Wagon and Dudley and I headed home. Minutes later we arrived at Big Rock Lofts and I shut down the Power Wagon. I opened the door and Dudley jumped right over me and landed gracefully on the ground. I was willing to give him a nine-point-five because he really stuck the landing. He went about his business as I climbed out of the Power Wagon and closed the door behind me. Dudley and I headed toward the old iron door entrance.

I saw Betsy, E.D.'s big blue boat, parked out front so I assumed she was home. I was hoping she wasn't still angry about Dudley's indiscretions. After all, he's only human!

Dudley joined me by my side and we entered the building and went on to #158. Once safely in the loft, I poured myself a freshly cold-brewed iced coffee along with some Jack Daniels to make it interesting. I know what you're thinking, but I can stop whenever I want. I can give up coffee, no problem. Besides, I just thought of the name for my favorite beverage, Careless Coffee. I think one day it may become a best-seller, along with this book I hope. I took a few sips and was about to sit down on my sofa but quickly remembered I no longer had a sofa since Dudley made a morsel out of it. Dudley retired to my bed, rolled over on his back, and grabbed some shut-eye. My answering machine light was blinking so I hit the play button.

"Careless, it's L.D. Eckermann, after your visit, I think it might be wise for Dudley to get his heart murmur thoroughly checked out just to make sure we know exactly what we're dealing with. I made a call to the Texas A&M Veterinary School and they just had a cancellation so there is an opening in two days. I reserved it for you, but if you don't want to keep the appointment let me know. If you do want to proceed, you will have to drive Dudley up to College Station and let them run some tests on him. I am recommending this just to be safe, but the decision of course is yours. It could turn out to be nothing, so let's not worry prematurely about it."

But I did worry about it. I worried a lot.

CHAPTER THIRTY-NINE

I sat there drinking my iced coffee with just a splash of Jack Black and was thankfully, as well as unexpectedly, interrupted by Dudley who had woken up from a sound sleep and slinked past me, headed silently toward the door. He just stood there as still as a statue as if waiting for something or someone. At first I thought he needed to go outside to see a man about a horse, but then came the knock on the door and Dudley erupted in a loud and boisterous bark.

At least now I knew I didn't have to worry about stranger danger with Dudley, my new friend and guard dog. I walked toward the door and told Dudley to sit and be silent. He did sit but of course he couldn't remain completely silent. He grumbled just a bit. He was a low talker for sure.

I unlocked and opened the door. To my very pleasant surprise, it was E.D. from upstairs. Finally, she realized she was madly in love with me and had walked downstairs to express that. This was probably wishful thinking on my part. A guy can dream!

She had a big smile on her face until Dudley stood up and headed in her direction. Dudley was somewhat confused because it was only Monday but for some reason he thought it was Hump Day. Before Dudley could close in for the kill, E.D. pointed her index finger at him, sternly looked him in the eye, and forcefully said, "No, Dude, go sit your butt right down!"

She must have caught him off guard because to my amazement he stopped in his tracks and sat down before he could reach her. For him, that took some real will power, something I daresay I did not possess when it came to the lovely E.D.

E.D. walked in right past Dudley. She was wearing sweatpants, a tight white tee-shirt, and sandals. Her long, straight, golden hair was pulled up high in a ponytail.

I could definitely see why Dudley was attracted to her. He was a man of fine taste. She had a cardboard box in her arms and handed it to me. "I saw what Dude did to your sofa last night and since you were somewhat nice to me in my hour of need, I decided to help you out. It is obvious that someone needs to care for the dumb animal who lives here," she said.

At that point Dudley's eyebrows went up. I did take up for him and I told her that he was sitting right there and could hear every word she was saying. I also told her I resented her calling him an animal, at which point Dudley cocked his head and looked at me. It was almost as if he knew I was trying to be funny at his expense, which of course I was; but then E.D. told me she wasn't referring to Dudley. I guess the joke was on me.

"Look, Witless, the reason Dude dismantled your sofa was because you left him alone for too long, and he got bored. You are lucky the sofa was all he tore up. I took the liberty of going to the pet store and purchasing a few items I thought Dude would like so maybe next time he'll concentrate his energy on them instead of your personal belongings, which by the way need to take a one-way trip to the Goodwill store," she said.

"You are such a sweetie, E.D.; but the name's Careless, and his name is Dudley," I responded while hand gesturing in Dudley's direction. Now he looked happy. "Hey, I like the way that sounds. From now on, I think I'll call you E.D. Sweetie," I jokingly said.

"That's good, Hapless, because that is my name, but you already knew that didn't you?" she asked.

I actually did not know that, but I didn't act surprised in front of her because sometimes hiding your true feelings can give you the upper hand in a relationship; plus I didn't want to ruin her opinion of me.

"Okay, this is what I got for Dude," she said while pulling six items out of the cardboard box.

I wondered what would happen if Dudley didn't like what was behind door number one, and I don't think he was going to get a shot at what was behind door number two. The price is wrong, Dude! Where is Bob Barker when you need him? It really didn't matter because I had my own barker to deal with, and his name is Dudley.

E.D. held up one of the items and directed my attention toward it. "This is a bag of Greenies. They are cute little toothbrush-shaped green chewy treats that taste good and will keep Dude's teeth white," she explained.

While talking, she opened the re-sealable plastic bag the greenies were in. She pulled one out and held it forward for Dudley and me to see. It immediately caught Dudley's attention because he goose-stepped right over to E.D. and sat down at full attention directly in front of her. I wasn't sure if he smelled it, saw it, heard the bag crinkle, or all of the above, but his concentration was solely fixed on the Greenie in E.D.'s very beautiful and slender hand. I guess the way to a man's heart really is through his stomach. It certainly was in Dudley's case.

E.D. handed the Greenie over to Dudley and he quickly inhaled it. He definitely enjoyed it but it sure didn't last long. There were certainly going to be some white teeth in that golden head of his.

E.D. continued to pull out items from the box she had purchased at the pet store. There were a couple of squeaky balls, some rawhide chews, and a few other toys, but Dudley didn't seem particularly interested in any of them. I think his attention was beginning to wander until E.D. produced the final toy from the box. When she did, his gaze became fixed on it. "This is one I like to call Baby," E.D. said.

She held up something that looked like a gingerbread man except it was fluffy, white, and appeared to be made out of lamb's wool. It was approximately ten inches in length and two inches thick. I know what you're thinking but, let's keep this PG-13; I was describing the toy E.D. was holding up, okay?

E.D. noticed that Dudley couldn't take his eyes off of Baby so she tossed it to him. He caught it in his mouth and started masticating Baby with all of his might. Much like Birk, he was a top-notch masticator. Then, what he did next is really hard to describe and I feel certain it took E.D. by complete surprise. He dropped Baby from his mouth, grabbed it with both front legs, and starting emitting a new but highly unusual grunting noise I hadn't heard yet and yes, you guessed it, starting humping Baby. I was slightly embarrassed but E.D. almost fell over because she was laughing so hard.

"Dudley, cut that out," I said, but he was oblivious to the fact that anyone else was even there. After what seemed like days, Dudley finally tossed Baby up in the air and where it fell he did not care. Dudley retired back to my bed for some shut-eye. All that excitement really wore him out. He acted like he needed an afterwards cigarette right about now.

It was getting late so I thanked E.D. for the dog toys and told her that it was time for me to hit the hay. She reached over and kissed me on the cheek, turned around, and walked out. She is one real fine lady.

I drank a little more iced coffee and jumped in bed with my new life partner or, as he probably preferred it, my significant other, not that there's anything wrong with that. I was on my back and almost asleep when I felt Dudley's head gently come to rest on my chest. That's when the snoring began. I closed my eyes and went to my happy place.

CHAPTER FORTY

The next morning I woke up at five o'clock. I wake up almost every morning at five o'clock because Pappa brainwashed me into a routine when I was very young and a lot more fun. As I adjusted my eyes after opening them, I noticed Dudley's motionless head still resting on my chest, but now his eyes were wide open and he was staring at me.

On the bright side, his snoring had ceased. It was shower time. Dudley began licking my face non-stop, over and over. After what seemed like weeks, I finally had to tell him to stop. Once I told him to stop for the fifth time, he finally relented. Then, it was really shower time.

I jumped up, took a quick shower, and got dressed. Dudley and I left Big Rock Lofts to go to work, but first we would stop by Pappa's house to meet him and Ross the Boss for breakfast. On the way to Pappa's house via the Power Wagon, I don't know why but I started singing that famous Christmas song in my head, "Over the potholes and through the hood, to Grandpa's house we go."

A few minutes later, at Pappa's house we found Ross the Boss and Pappa already at the breakfast table. Dudley walked around to both of them to receive his pat on the head and sat down next to me for breakfast. There was an old steel percolator coffeemaker probably from the 1950s, warming up on the stove. Hell, it looked like it might have been made in the Bronze Age but, then again, Pappa may have smuggled it over from the old country. I wasn't really sure. It made a good cup of jo but it used a pretty backwards technology. The water was poured into the bottom of the pot, the coffee sat on top of the water in a little steel tray, and when closed up and heated to a boil on the stove, the hot water would shoot up over the coffee, run through it, and drip back down to the bottom of the pot through small holes in the steel tray. There was a glass knob on the top that the coffee jumped up and down in so it was visible when the coffee was percolating. It was kind of fun to watch but left a lot of coffee grounds in the coffee.

Pappa had already made some Jimmy Dean's sausage patties and scrambled eggs. There was a box of cereal out for anyone who wanted to eat healthy. The box has remained unopened for years. The cereal was probably past the expiration date but really, aren't we all at some point? We sat around and ate breakfast for fifteen minutes or so and I fed Dudley a leftover sausage patty. He seriously liked it and breakfast really is the most important meal of the day, so it was all good. Dudley was in agreement. Once the four of us were finished, we picked all of the percolated coffee grinds out of our teeth, put all of the dirty dishes in the sink to wash later, and headed out of the door for another glorious, fun-filled day at work.

Dudley and I jumped in the Power Wagon while Ross the Boss and Pappa got in my grandfather's Buick LeSabre. My grandfather liked his Buick LeSabre because it was big and roomy. Ross the Boss drove him to work every morning because he was getting up there in years and enjoyed being chauffeured around. Ross the Boss also liked the Buick LeSabre because it had a huge V-8 engine in it so it really had some get up and go. He punched the gas pedal and a loud whoosh sound came from the four-barrel carburetor sucking in gas and air while the car took off like a rocket.

By 5:45 a.m. we were at the pipe yard on the east side of Houston. It was a little rough on the east side but we never really had any problems to speak of. I loved it at the pipe yard early in the morning because we were very close to the Anheuser Busch Brewery and they brewed the beer early in the morning. The smell of hops and barley filled the air. It was quite a powerful and distinct aroma, one that I looked forward to every morning.

Ross the Boss got out of the Buick LeSabre and opened the front entrance gate. We all drove in, parked, and went into the office to begin our day. We all assumed the position. Dudley had scoped out the office ahead of us and went through his doggie door to his outside paradise. Ross the Boss went out into the pipe yard to direct the trucks and employees. I sat down at my desk and began working on our account payables and waiting for phone calls. Pappa had a seat in the front office and began his morning smoke, El Producto style. He often says the only things that keep him alive are work and cigars, and I have no reason to doubt him.

CHAPTER FORTY-ONE

Trucks were already lined up to be loaded and unloaded in the pipe yard. There were five eighteen-wheel trucks in line. The front door to our office building has an alarm on it so every time it is opened, a little chirping sound is made. This way whenever someone enters the office, we know about it.

Our lobby is unmanned but we do have a window that connects the lobby to the front office, which we use to see who's there and to communicate with whoever comes into the office. It is similar to a doctor's office, just not as nice.

Dudley had come back in from his doggie paradise. I was amazed because he was already accustomed to our office and everyone in it. Of course he already had a key to the executive washroom. I was working on our accounts payable when I heard Dudley start a low growl. He was standing at the window in my office, watching something. I couldn't see much because the sun had barely begun to rise. Then I saw a truck driver pass by the window and Dudley's growl turned up a notch. It wasn't really until the front door opened and the chirping alarm sounded that Dudley went into red alert protection mode.

He ran off to the front office and started barking in a loud, deep, menacing manner. By the time I got there, the truck driver had taken a few steps back from the window even though there was no way Dudley could leap his big butt through it, especially since it was closed. He had a large amount of goober dripping from his oversized jowls. If I didn't know him the way I did, I would have thought he was a rabid dog. Who needs an alarm when you have Dudley? At least now I knew he would protect us.

I passed by Pappa, who was watching the whole thing, but I couldn't tell if he was amused or not liking it too much. He just looked at me, took a puff of his cigar, and pointed toward the window with his hand holding the smoking cigar.

I told Dudley to simmer down and I put my hand on his head. He immediately went silent and sat by my side. I pushed open the window and asked the truck driver how I could help him.

He said, "Your dog really scared the crap out of me. I've never seen a Black Mouth Cur behave like that." He went on to tell me he was certain Dudley was a Blackmouth Cur.

I had no idea what type of dog Dudley was. It had never really crossed my mind because I just assumed he was a mutt from the SPCA, but now I began to wonder.

The truck driver told me he was here to drop off a load of twenty-four-inch pipe we had purchased from a pipe mill in Baton Rouge, Louisiana. I signed his paperwork and sent him out to the pipe yard to see Ross the Boss to get unloaded. I realized now Dudley would always notify me when someone was entering the office. I hope he doesn't ask for a raise.

This routine repeated itself every time the front door opened or Dudley saw someone he didn't know in the window. Sometimes he rested on his green leather sofa and sometimes he went out to his doggie paradise to have some fun in the sun. The only incident that could possibly be viewed as negative occurred when Ross the Boss came running into my office as white as a ghost. He was so skinny he could be a ghost. He started whining and complaining about how he went into the restroom and was sitting on his throne, nice and peacefully, when Dudley decided to zip into the restroom like a freight train going through the doggie door. Ross the Boss had forgotten we had installed the doggie door in the restroom and Dudley was already outside before the restroom was occupado.

When he mentioned that it wasn't funny and how it literally scared the crap out of him, we looked at one another and both started cracking up laughing. It was all good in the hood after that. I told him that for future reference I would make and hang a sign above the doggie door in the restroom that read: Warning, doggie door in use. Stay a safe distance back and expect sudden, unexpected entrances and exits. I'll get to work on that later.

The Blackmouth Cur is a working breed of dog, meaning they are bred and raised as dogs that will fulfill a certain desired purpose. They can be many colors and even combinations of colors ranging from fawn, brown, black, red, and brindle. They can grow up to ninety-five pounds and their hair is usually short, shiny, and coarse. Originally they were bred for herding but they are fierce hunters with a keen sense of smell. They are known to track their prey with their nose in the air, moving from side to side as they close in. This is a little different than other types of dogs that track their prey by keeping their nose to the ground to pick up a scent. Blackmouth Curs have very sensitive noses. They are fast, agile, muscular, and very intelligent. They are quick learners and will protect their territory and family vigorously. They have webbed feet and are great swimmers. Their roots can be traced back in history from Europe, Australia, and America, but Dudley's roots can be traced back only as far as the SPCA. They are great family dogs and while bred for a purpose, they do like to clown around all over town and will turn your frown upside down. It has been long rumored that a Blackmouth Cur was used in the Disney film, *Old Yeller*.

It was almost lunchtime and that could only mean one thing at our office and that was poker time. On most afternoons Pappa set up our conference table with several decks of cards along with delicatessen food from Kenny & Ziggy's Delicatessen. Pappa and several older gentlemen in the business community played high stakes poker for an hour during lunch. It was always the same guys and they were all respected business owners or oil company executives.

This ritual has been going on for over thirty years. It's something Pappa and his friends really look forward to. I know I will miss that one day when Pappa is no longer here. I never really know how much money they play for, but I do remember seeing piles of one-hundred-dollar bills sitting on the table on more than one occasion. After the card game and lunch were over, everyone went back to work and it was as if the card game had never even occurred.

Later that afternoon, my friend Rik, who works at Allbritton Drilling, came by for a visit and to inspect some pipe he was going to purchase. I have known him for many years. He came into my office where Dudley sized him up pretty quickly and warmed up to him. Rik was a dog person, so there were no problems to speak of. He was ready to have a look at the pipe so we left Dudley with Pappa inside of the office and we went outside. As we walked toward the pipe and past the dog run, I noticed something new and not necessarily something I liked. White paper was scattered all over Dudley's beautiful grassy dog run and there was a lot of it. Rik looked at it and then looked at me and asked me why we never clean up Dudley's dog run.

I really had no answer for this but after closer inspection I did notice there was a paper trail leading around to the back side of the office where the doggie door was located. I explained to Rik that it had just happened and it would be cleaned up shortly. He inspected the pipe he was going to purchase and everything was fine. Rik and I shook hands, said goodbye, and he took off in his pickup truck. The most popular motor vehicle in Texas is the Ford F150 pickup truck. In Texas, we love our pickup trucks. Don't mess with Texas or our pickup trucks.

I walked back into the office as a man on a mission. I had a sneaky suspicion as to what all of the garbage was in Dudley's dog run but I needed to be certain; and if I was correct, then someone was sure going to be hurtin' for certain.

I walked through my office, through Ross the Boss's office, and past Pappa in the front office. Sure enough, when I got to the restroom, Dudley was walking out of it. I sure hope he remembered to wash his hands. He saw me and his tail started spinning around like a helicopter rotor. I pet him and walked into the restroom. Dudley had grabbed all the rolls of toilet paper from the shelves and had taken them outside through the doggie door and into his dog run where he had been toying around and shredding them.

Normally I wouldn't have blamed him right off the bat but, unfortunately for him, he left a telltale trail of unrolled toilet paper from inside the restroom, through the doggie door, and outside to the dog run. The doggie door was closed on top of the toilet paper trail. If the doggie door hadn't been made out of transparent plastic then the toilet paper trail would have looked like it ended right at the wall. I could see right through it and there was a clear trail of toilet paper leading from inside the restroom to Dudley's dog run outside. Dudley would certainly not make a good criminal. He left too many loose ends.

Ross the Boss walked in and saw what had happened. He started laughing at us and told me to have fun cleaning up the mess. I looked at Dudley and visually reprimanded him. He just smiled sheepishly. I couldn't stay mad at him because I loved him too much and he was pretty cute. I would however be moving the toilet paper dispenser much higher and moving the extra rolls of toilet paper higher so we wouldn't have a repeat performance.

I cleaned up the toilet paper trail in the restroom and went outside to clean up his doggie run. When I finally finished my trash detail I went back inside to continue to work. The rest of the day went pretty smoothly. I made a few sales and talked to customers while Dudley continued to bark and act like a rabid dog whenever anyone entered our lobby. Other than the toilet paper incident, things were going pretty smoothly at the office.

CHAPTER FORTY-TWO

It was almost closing time so I went in Ross the Boss' office and told him I wouldn't be coming to work tomorrow because I had to take Dudley to the Texas A&M Veterinary school in the morning. I explained that L.D. from the Westbury Animal Hospital had left me a message that Dudley needed his ticker checked out. He seemed okay with that. He and Pappa could handle the business for a day without me or, as I like to think of it, as a day without sunshine.

Ross the Boss asked me if I would lock the front gate because he had a tennis game he needed to get to. I told him that was no problem and we all packed up and left the office together. I soon found out how wrong I was; there would be a little problem.

Ross the Boss and Pappa took off in the Buick LeSabre and Dudley and I hopped in the Power Wagon as I pulled outside of the main gate and shifted the Power Wagon into park. I got out, closed my door behind me, and closed the gate. As I was placing the lock on the gate, I noticed that the Power Wagon appeared to be rolling backwards. When I looked up, Dudley was in the driver's seat and the Power Wagon was indeed moving backwards. I know I left it in park so I wasn't sure how this was possible.

I will admit I got a little nervous because Dudley didn't have his driver's license with him so he could really get himself into some trouble. Quick as a jackrabbit, I ran to the Power Wagon, flung the driver's side door open and jumped in. Dudley moved over in rapid fashion. Just as I hit the brakes, the Power Wagon backed into a fire hydrant with a loud sounding thud. We looked at each other in disbelief.

I shifted into drive and drove the Power Wagon forward just a little bit so I could get out and assess the damage. Luckily the fire hydrant didn't sustain any damage but there was a nice fist-sized dent in the Power Wagon bumper. Apparently Dudley had jumped from the passenger seat to the driver's seat and while doing so his front leg must have landed on the column-mounted stick shift, placing it in reverse. It could have been a lot worse and, since I had already reprimanded him once today, I decided to let him off the hook.

I opened the driver's side door and jumped back in. He was being awfully quiet. I turned to him and said, "It's all right, boy. You want to drive home?"

Of course he said something, while turning his head sideways. He looked at me and muttered a few sounds. Then he started licking my face. Maybe Birk and Dudley should take a defensive drivers' class. I gave him a hug and we drove toward Big Rock. Damn fire hydrant rear-ended him! Hugs not fire plugs!

A few minutes later we were in front of Big Rock Lofts. I parked the new and improved, dented Power Wagon in the parking lot and we got out and entered the loft through the old iron door. As Dudley and I passed through the entryway we saw Sarge sitting on the sofa with his head buried in a book. He was so enthralled that he didn't even notice us. Dudley walked over to him and without even looking up, Sarge reached his hand out and patted Dudley on the head.

Dudley mumbled something towards him. We started to walk past him and he said, "Hey, man, han, han, han, han. How's it going man, han, han, han, han?"

I told him we were doing fine and we were just going upstairs to grab a bite to eat and then hit the hay.

"Yeah, heh, heh, heh, heh, heh. Mardi Gras 2000, man, han, han, han, han, han, han," I heard him say in the distance as we headed up the stairs to #158.

We got to the door and went inside. I gave Dudley some dog food and water and poured myself a Careless Coffee. *Mmm, mmm,* good.

I sat down to relax but my red-and-white HEB telephone chose to start expressing itself that very moment. I debated whether to pick it up or not, but my curiosity got the better of me so I reluctantly picked it up and said, "Crisis hotline, state your emergency."

"Careless, it's Birk," the voice at the other end said. I was so glad that he informed me as to who he was because I may have never figured that one out. "I don't have an emergency but my truck won't start so I need to take it to the shop. I need you to pick me up from there so I can go rent a car until it's fixed. There's one other thing, Careless, and this is a big one that might be right up your alley," he said as he took a long pause as if waiting for me to say something. Of course I didn't say anything because I knew he wanted me to. I'm just passive aggressive that way.

"I have a friend at the Houston Police Department. His name is Detective Blake Present and he told me that Jake Harm of Jake Harm and the Holdouts may be missing. He wouldn't give me any of the details, but don't you think we should help out if Jake has gone missing? If we find him and help solve the case he might let us go backstage and listen to a concert, and maybe even give us some free autographed CDs. Careless, did you hear anything I said?" Birk moaned on.

"I'm sorry, sir, but for non-emergencies please hang up and dial the city information line," I answered back.

Leave it up to Birk to try to solve an official police case just so he could get some free stuff. After a moment of silence I said, "I think we should talk. Come on over."

"I just told you my truck won't start. How am I supposed to get over there?" he asked, all exasperated. I actually had already thought of that but I just wanted to give him a hard time. There goes my passive aggressive behavior rearing its ugly head again.

"I'll be along shortly to collect you. Where are you?" I asked.

Birk was at his house and his Cowboy Cadillac was sitting in front of it as dead as a doorknob. He told me he was getting it towed to a shop just off of Loop 610 and I should meet him there. I downed my iced coffee and told Dudley I had to step out for a few minutes. He grumbled a little bit but I left out all of the toys E.D. had so kindly purchased for him and I told him not to eat any furniture, walls, or appliances while I was gone. He was a little sad, but I had to go take care of business.

I left the loft and headed downstairs. Not surpisingly, Sarge was still sitting on the sofa in the entryway reading a book. "See you later, Sarge," I said, while walking past him.

"Later man, han, han, han, han, han, han," he replied.

I left the building and headed for the fire-hydrantly challenged Power Wagon.

Shortly after leaving Big Rock I was pulling up in front of the Ford repair shop where Birk had his truck towed. He was talking to the service manager while the tow truck operator was lowering the Cowboy Cadillac to the ground.

A few minutes later Birk jumped up in the Power Wagon's passenger seat. The first words that came out of his mouth were when he asked me if I knew there was a fist-sized dent in my back bumper. I just ignored that as best as I could. Birk had an irritating knack for stating the obvious.

Birk asked me to take him to a car rental place so he wouldn't be without a vehicle. After another twenty minutes of driving, Birk guided me to the rental car place. He had been jabbering away about Jake Harm and the Holdouts the whole way there, but I chose to not participate. I really didn't think it was a good idea to encourage him. He asked me to come in to the car rental place with him, which I reluctantly agreed to do. We walked in and were the only people in the place except for the gentleman behind the counter who looked us over and asked Birk if he could be of service.

I looked at Birk and motioned him forward with a sweeping hand gesture. Birk walked up to the counter and explained to the man that his truck had broken down and he needed something for a day or two until his truck was running again. Being a tightwad, he explained that he wanted the very cheapest automobile available, but something really nice and roomy.

"Would you and your partner prefer one of the best values we are presently offering at a very low rate of just thirty-nine dollars and ninety-nine cents per day plus a fuel surcharge?" the man behind the counter asked as he pointed to a picture of a car on a clear plastic lined chart on top of the counter.

I briefly looked at it and all I could think about were those clown cars at the circus about the size of a soda can and fifty to one hundred clowns exiting when the doors opened. I was pretty sure Birk was not going to fit his big ass in that tin can. I looked at Birk and he seemed perplexed. He told the man behind the counter that he wanted something just a tad bit bigger but still as inexpensive as possible. Then Birk was told there was a special running today and he could save a ton of money on an SUV for just twenty dollars per day.

Birk liked that until the contract was written up at fifty-nine dollars and ninety-nine cents per day. That's when all hell broke loose as Birk and the rental car man began screaming at one another. As it turned out, twenty dollars was in addition to the everyday very low price of just thirty-nine dollars and ninety-nine cents per day, but the rental car man used a little wordplay on Birk, which is fairly easy to do; but nonetheless, he was not too happy. Birk was definitely not a superstar with rental cars.

After everyone calmed down, Birk told the rental car man to just rent him the very cheapest car and, in addition, that he and I were not "partners," and that we barely knew one another. A closet homosexual in the making if ever I saw one, not that there's anything wrong with that.

We were almost finished when the man behind the counter looked at me and asked Birk, "What type of protection do you prefer?" I looked at Birk and he looked at me. I couldn't hold it together any longer and burst out laughing. I laughed so hard I almost fell to the floor. Birk was turning a little red around the gills so I knew he was not even the slightest bit amused.

I gradually stopped my hysterical laughing and toned it down to a quiet little smirk. Oh sure, I was tempted to break out laughing again but I used all of my strength to hold it together. It wasn't easy but I gutted it out. Birk finally leased the car and we headed out to the parking lot to find it. It was probably going to be a Victor Yugo, Mitsufuji, Hiawatha, or something of that nature.

I always thought of Birk as more of a sidekick rather than a partner. Partner can mean oh-so-many things and let's face it, I didn't need to have a Brokeback moment with Birk, so I'm sticking with sidekick.

Birk found his leased clown car, got in it, and drove off. He gave me the country wave, which is while your hands are on the steering wheel you briefly lift your index finger from the hand at the 12:00 position. I think he may have been a little embarrassed to be demoted from the Cowboy Cadillac to a clown car, but we all have our moments and this was one I probably wouldn't soon let Birk forget.

I walked over to the Power Wagon, jumped in, cranked her up, and headed back to Big Rock where I hoped Dudley was entertaining himself in a non-destructive manner. Kids today! I got back home, parked the Power Wagon and walked through the old iron door entrance. I passed through the empty entryway and headed up the stairs to #158 where I unlocked the door and went in.

It appeared that everything was still in one piece. The sheetrock walls were still standing and all the appliances appeared to be unchanged in nature. Dudley had his back turned to me and was playing with Baby, the white, wooly stuffed toy resembling a gingerbread man. He was making a very bizarre almost whining sound while holding Baby between his front legs and chomping down on it with his mouth. When he heard me, he dropped Baby, turned, and galloped toward me. Once he reached me he sat down in front of me so I would pet him.

As I did so, he started licking my hands and that's right when I knew something was terribly wrong. To my horror, I noticed Dudley's whole head, face, and quite oversized jowls were green in color. It really looked like his circulation had been cut off to his head. Because of the way Birk acted, I sometimes thought that had happened to him as well, but I didn't know for sure. This was just mere speculation on my part.

CHAPTER FORTY-THREE

I was very worried about Dudley. I thought maybe he was getting gangrene and it was distressing. I looked him over pretty well and, other than the green discoloration of his face, I couldn't find anything wrong with him. He appeared to be in no pain but the green color of his head had me a little spooked. I grabbed the red-and-white HEB telephone and dialed up the Westbury Animal Hospital.

"Westbury Animal Hospital," the voice of a young lady answered on the other end of the telephone.

I frantically asked if L.D. was in, but the young lady informed me that it was after hours and there were no veterinarians in. That begged the question of why *she* was there if it was after hours. She informed me that there is someone at the animal hospital twenty-four hours a day to watch over the sick animals in their charge, but there was always a veterinarian on call.

I asked if she would give me L.D.s' telephone number because Dudley was having an emergency. She told me to calm down and started asking me a bunch of questions. I thought she was wasting my and Dudley's valuable time with the question-answer session, but after asking a lot of mundane questions, she asked me one last thing that turned out to be quite helpful. "Has he eaten anything green?" she posed to me.

When she said green, a little light bulb went off in my head and I began to closely inspect the toys E.D. bought for Dudley. They were all laid out on the floor in a haphazard pattern so I knew Dudley had been playing with them all, and that's when I saw it. The Greenie bag had been shredded and was lying on the ground. I told the young lady at the animal hospital that Dudley had indeed eaten some green food items.

She went on to tell me that if Dudley was acting normal (like he ever acted normal) and didn't appear to have any symptoms, other than having a green head, then the green color had probably rubbed off onto his head. He most likely had gotten into the Greenies and, after goobering on them, rolled his head around on them while playing before he ate them.

That actually did make perfect sense and in fact Dudley did have an overactive goober gland. It appeared that Dudley was in good health so I thanked the young lady at the animal clinic and hung up the telephone. If this would just last until Saint Patrick's Day, maybe Dudley might be allowed to march in the Saint Patty's Day Parade. For all I know, he could be Irish.

Just then he started licking my face. Oh great, now I suppose he's going to start wearing a shirt that says: Kiss Me, I'm Irish. I felt a smile of comfort and relief coming on.

I showered and jumped in bed. I was going to get up early the next day for Dudley's check up at the Texas A&M Veterinary School. It would take us several hours to get there and I was afraid it was going to be a long day. I turned on my side and started to drift off. I felt a disturbance in the force and more specifically on the bed. I felt footsteps pressing down on the mattress moving ever so close to me. The serial spooner leaned up against me and his head came to rest on my side. I don't know what the heck was wrong with me (generally speaking) but I was really starting to enjoy having him there when I went to sleep, except of course when he snored. There could be symphonies written with all of the scales Dudley's snoring took him through. Still, there was something about having him there that was comforting to me. All went silent as Dudley and I went to our respective happy places.

The next coherent moment I had was at 5:00 a.m. Dudley was milling around and lying on his back. He was wriggling around like a Mexican jumping bean with his legs sporadically going up and down in a pattern somewhat resembling pistons going up and down in a motor. It was the craziest thing I had ever seen. My guess was that he was scratching his back but he did look like a bit of a dumbass. All I could think of at that very moment was Curly, of the Three Stooges fame, dancing and bouncing up and down like a yo-yo exclaiming, "Moe, Larry, the cheese, Moe, Larry, the cheese. Moe, Larry, the cheese!"

I rolled out of bed and got dressed while Dudley sat on the bed upright with his two front legs fully extended looking like an Egyptian sphinxter, watching my every move. Maybe he knew that today we weren't going to the office and that might have worried him a bit. He appeared to be a creature of habit so if the slightest thing was out of place or our activities varied whatsoever, he would probably notice it instantly. I made a cup of Careless Coffee and called for Dudley to come with me. We walked out of the loft together; and as always, he was at my side. I just hoped it wouldn't be for the last time.

Dudley and I walked downstairs, through the entryway, and out of Big Rock Lofts. He stopped a few times to take care of business after which we both hopped in the Power Wagon and headed for the Texas A&M Veterinary School in College Station. It was going to take several hours traveling west on Highway 290. Dudley stretched out on his seat facing me and put his head on my leg. He closed his eyes and went to sleep and I prayed the Lord his soul to keep, just in case.

He was placing his life in my hands but little did he know I had done the same with him, for it was with him I finally felt complete. Not that my life was bad before him, it was just so much better with him, and I was determined to keep it that way. Jake Harm and the Holdouts started playing one of their hit songs on the radio as we drove along. My mind shifted into detective mode and I started wondering about what Birk had said when he told me Jake had disappeared. Something in my mind had me curious about the disappearance. I just knew that I knew something but it wasn't clear to me what it was yet. Throw in the fact that it was early in the morning and I was not particularly a morning person; it wasn't all that surprising that I was having a brain freeze.

"Wild Turkey at sunrise, Wild Turkey with my friend in sight...." Jake sang his newest hit song while we went down the road to have our fate determined together.

CHAPTER FORTY-FOUR

We finally reached College Station after a very ho hum drive. It definitely was not very scenic. College Station is a college town centered around the Texas A&M University. We pulled up to the veterinary school. I parked the Power Wagon and as I got out I called to Dudley to follow me. He wasn't budging. For the first time since I rescued him from the SPCA, I had to put a leash on him and lead him into the veterinary school. He was visibly unhappy, as was I, just not as outwardly noticeable. His hair went up on his back and his big, oversized jowls curled up just a little bit into what I would classify as a mini-snarl.

We walked into the lobby together and were greeted by the receptionist. The young lady asked if she could help us. She was most likely a student at the college and she was very pleasant, but Dudley of course was on red alert and having none of this.

I told the young lady who we were and she said we were the first appointment of the day and the doctor would be with us shortly. Sure enough, a few minutes later the doctor, surrounded by a team of younger doctors all in white lab coats, walked out toward us in the lobby. Aggies are very precision-oriented so it wasn't surprising at all that the doctor was on time, but I was starting to get a bad feeling about this and wondering if I had made the correct decision. I almost felt like Lucy from the Peanuts cartoon was about to turn the sign around to say "The doctor is in," while all the lab coats were there to "help" Dudley take his medicine.

While my mind was wandering, and not in a particularly good direction, the words broke in, "Hello, Mr. Robinson, my name is Dr. Gordon and these are my student doctors. Texas A&M Veterinary School is a teaching hospital and my students will be assisting me in evaluating Dudley. Is Dudley friendly? He appears to be a little agitated."

That was an understatement!

I told her that, for Dudley, this definitely wasn't even near agitated and in fact he was usually moderately friendly, but that he had a ruff day at the office and I also told her the name was Careless.

"Okay, Careless, if you don't mind, I'm just going to look Dudley over for a minute, and then we'll talk about how to proceed. Is that okay with you?" she asked in a very soothing tone.

I told her that was fine with me and she quickly turned her attention to Dudley, who was not liking what he was seeing.

"Is that okay with you, Dudley?" Dr. Gordon asked while she gave Dudley the once over and said a few more kind words to him in a soothing manner. He grumbled a little bit but she placed her hand on his back just above his shoulders anyway. I thought for sure she was making a big mistake but to my amazement Dudley simmered down as she stroked her hand across his back. As she did this, his hair went back down to its normal position as did everyone's blood pressure.

I had to admit she was good. Dogs can always tell what is in a person's heart and the character of that person. I'm not sure how they do it but they always seem to know when to trust and when not to trust. Perhaps it's a survival instinct. That's why they are so attracted to young children whose hearts are still pure. I'm not a dog so, unfortunately for me, I trust no one. It's a curse really, but one that serves me well.

Dr. Gordon was now rubbing Dudley all up and down and I could tell he was liking it by the crocodile smile he was sporting. She whipped out her stethoscope and listened to his heart.

After a few minutes she stopped her examination and quietly said a few things to her student doctors who all turned around in unison and walked back to where they had come from. I just knew this wasn't going to be good. Dr. Gordon stood up and said, "Careless, Dudley definitely has a heart murmur. I can't be sure of what is really going on until we do some extensive testing. I recommend we do some procedures so we can correctly address the problem. This won't be without risks. What we will do may injure him further, or worse. There is always a risk of death, especially when we put him under anesthesia or from the procedure itself. That will probably not happen but I do want you to be aware of every possibility. Do you need to take some time to make up your mind, Careless?" she asked.

There was no need. Time was the one thing Dudley and I hadn't had enough of together and I was hoping my next decision would garner us both a little more. I reluctantly decided to go forward and I told her so.

She told me the procedure would take a while and Dudley would be heavily sedated so afterwards he would need to be monitored for another several hours before he could be released.

I told her I understood and knelt down to grab his face, hopefully not for the last time, and tell him what a good boy he was and that I loved him. I rubbed his long floppy ears, looked him in the eye, and gave him a big hug.

Dr. Gordon took the leash that was still around his neck and began to walk away from me. Unfortunately for her, Dudley did not. He wasn't budging and the hair on his back was beginning to bristle again. It was clear he didn't want to leave my side. He probably thought he was protecting me. I just hoped the man upstairs would be protecting him because it was completely out of my hands and, for once, I was helpless instead of Careless.

The doctor called for a couple of assistants and they began to pull Dudley away forcefully. He looked back at me and his eyes were wide open with fright. He started a menacing growl. There was nothing I could do, but I felt my heart beginning to break and for the first time I could remember I felt tears swelling up in my eyes.

I turned away to make sure no one would see me cry. This was something I would never forget. Dudley was alone and afraid and I was emotionally paralyzed. Then he was gone and all went quiet. Now I was alone. I was alone before I met Dudley; and while I thought I liked it, I now realized I didn't, and I don't recommend it to anyone. I was alone.

CHAPTER FORTY-FIVE

I sat there stunned for a few minutes. The young lady behind the counter was asking me something, but I couldn't hear a word she said. Mentally, I was somewhere else. After a while, I gained my composure and asked the young lady if there was somewhere I could go to take my mind off of things while waiting for Dudley. While talking with her, I pretended to have something in my eye as I wiped away the tears with my hands.

She offered up the George Bush Presidential Library and Museum on the Texas A&M University campus and she gave me directions. I just couldn't understand how I had fallen so in love with a dog I had just recently met. Was this normal? Was I missing something in my life until he came along? The answer of course was yes and yes. I left the veterinary school with a heavy heart. I jumped into the Power Wagon and gunned it towards the George Bush Library. For the first time in a while, I had no co-pilot.

Ten minutes later I was pulling up in front of the George Bush Library. It was a beautiful building with exquisite landscaping surrounding it. There were eight flagpoles with American flags arranged in a big circle in the front with a huge bronze horse sculpture just before the entrance. It was quite a sight to see from the outside.

I parked in the front parking lot. It didn't appear to be too crowded. I wondered if President Bush was out skydiving again. I remember reading that he enjoyed skydiving and at his age that was truly amazing. I started skydiving in college at Tulane University when I took the class as an elective and later joined the Tulane Skydiving Team. I thought when I first tried skydiving that it should probably be named skydying. I figured if I didn't die from the act of skydiving itself, then I would probably die of fear from jumping out of a perfectly good airplane. The only close call I ever had was when I did my first night dive and landed on a barn, slid down the metal roof, and landed in a pile of lumber. It took several days to get the splinters out of my ass but still, it was fun. I don't remember a whole lot afterwards because one of my friends immediately ran up to me with two six packs of Dixie beer that we proceeded to down once I extracted myself from the lumber pile. Nature took its course after that so my memory is a little cloudy from that point forward.

Skydiving is exhilarating, followed by a natural high that lasts for several days. Of course the natural high is really your mind and body thanking you for not killing yourself. The thing is that it's not the jumping out of the airplane that might kill you, it's the sudden stop when you hit the ground after a malfunction. That is what is affectionately termed as bouncing, which is a bit misleading because you do anything but.

I walked into the Bush Library and it was just as fantastic inside as it was outside, but frankly, I wasn't in the mood for sightseeing. I might as well have been on Uranus because I was only thinking of one thing and that was the well-being of my friend Dudley. The cost to tour the library was seven dollars. I paid the fee but instead of seeing a short film in the theater and walking around with earphones on while taking the tour, I made like the wind and blew out of the back door of the library.

It was really beautiful in the back of the library. Just as in the front, the landscaping was impeccable. Not a leaf or blade of grass was out of place. It was so perfect it almost looked like a beautiful painting. There was also a nice-sized pond right in the middle of the property with benches sporadically placed around it. Shade trees were strategically planted to block out the sun while sitting on the benches and made for a picture perfect setting. It was breathtakingly beautiful and peaceful. Not a soul was there. I picked a bench to sit down on for a moment while deep in thought.

After a short time, I felt a little nudge and a rather large pair or nostrils snorting warm air on my arm. Without looking, I instinctively lifted my arm up and reached over to rub Eagle's forehead. His face was as soft as ever, just as I remembered. He nudged me a little more until I stood up and faced him. I patted him repeatedly on his strong, muscular neck and he started bobbing his head up and down in approval.

He was so beautiful with his chestnut brown hair and his jet-black mane and tail. I climbed on him and he started prancing around as happy as can be.

"I've missed you, old friend," I told him and then we took off like a bolt of lightning, flying down the mountain and treelined flats of the Texas Hill Country.

The wind was cool, brisk, and blowing as if we were in a wind tunnel. For the first time today my mind was at ease and it was a welcome change. We finally slowed down and came up to Wallace Creek. Eagle put his head down for a drink and when he was finished we walked into the clear beautiful bluish-green water. Wallace Creek is completely spring fed and is so clear it's like looking through a sheet of glass.

Eagle and I walked out into the water and when it became too deep to walk he began swimming. Swimming on a horse is a unique experience. They are actually very good swimmers and it is a lot of fun to swim with them. It involves a good degree of trust from both parties. I trusted Eagle and he trusted me. We finally reached the other side of Wallace Creek and I swung my leg over and slid off of Eagle. We both knew we had reached the time to say goodbye, at least for a while. It was the time we both dreaded the most.

I rubbed his forehead for a bit longer and he bobbed his head up and down as if to say goodbye. Sadly, my eyes opened and I was still sitting on that bench, under that shade tree at the George Bush Library at Texas A&M University. I wasn't sure how long I had been out for but I did feel a little bit better. Judging from the position of the sun in the sky, it was later than I thought. I looked at my watch and it was already three o'clock. My mind turned back toward Dudley and I stood up and walked to the back door of the library. I went into the library and quickly passed through the onslaught of visitors.

A young man working at the library asked me if I had a good visit but I just quickly waved to him and nodded as I walked through the front exit to get back to the Power Wagon in the parking lot. No time to chitchat; I had to go face the music but it was a good visit. It's always a good visit when I get to go back to a time and place that now lives only in my heart. It was a good visit.

CHAPTER FORTY-SIX

I jumped into the Power Wagon, cranked her up, and drove like a madman to the veterinary school. I got there and power-walked from the Power Wagon until I was inside the veterinary school. There was a different young lady working at the desk and she asked if she could help me.

I told her who I was and that I was there for Dudley. I anxiously asked her how Dudley had done and she told me the doctor would be with me shortly and to have a seat. I paced around like a nervous father expecting his first child. My mind was racing. *Was he okay? How did he do? Was he even still on this Earth or was he now on Uranus?* These are the questions I needed answered and needed them answered now. That was when my heart melted because I saw him slowly walking toward me on a leash held by Dr. Gordon.

When Dudley saw me his tail began slowly spinning around like a helicopter rotor. I walked toward them both, bent down, and gave him a big hug. The way Dudley was acting, it was as if he hadn't seen me in years. While we were both acting like idiots, I had forgotten the doctor was still there; and that's when she lowered the boom on me.

"Careless, we need to talk about Dudley. Let's go sit down over here so we can be comfortable," she said as we walked over to an area with a table and chairs. I removed the leash from around Dudley's neck, and the three of us walked over to the chairs. Dr. Gordon and I sat in the chairs and Dudley sat down next to me.

"Careless, Dudley has a condition known as aortic stenosis. He was probably born with this condition. When his blood leaves the lower chamber of his heart called the left ventricle, it passes through a little valve called the aortic valve, and into the aorta. Dudley's aortic valve is not functioning properly and it is not fully opening. Therefore a ballooning effect occurs from the pressure just in front of the valve. Are you with me so far, Careless?" she asked.

I nodded my head to acknowledge that I understood.

She continued on, "This can be quite serious. Dudley is still young so it hasn't affected him yet. The only reason we even caught it was because his heart murmur was detected. Some dogs may live with this condition their entire life and not be affected and for some it really takes a toll. In Dudley's case, we will not be able to operate on him to fix the problem for a whole host of reasons, one of which is that the operation itself is likely to injure him even more, or possibly kill him. In my opinion, it is not worth the risk. I will tell you that Dudley is a very strong dog with a strong will to live. My feeling is that if he makes it past two years of age, he will live a normal life. He must never be exercised to the point of exhaustion. If he starts having problems, he can be put on medications, which should help him. I'm sorry to have to be the one to tell you this, Careless. I really believe judging from this dog's behavior he is going to be just fine and will continue to have a normal life. You just need to be aware of all the scenarios."

She asked me if I had any further questions and I told her I didn't. I thanked her. She was very thorough and caring. Dudley and I left the veterinary school. We walked out together and it was as if nothing had happened.

Obviously Dudley chose not to hear what the good doctor said and that was probably a good thing; but unfortunately I did hear it and while his heart may have been in bad shape, now mine was as well. I opened the driver's side of the Power Wagon. Dudley jumped in and sat in the passenger's seat. *Not bad for a cardiac patient*, I thought to myself.

We started the long drive back and once again, I had my co-pilot. It's really nice to have a partner in crime or, as I would later find out, a partner in crime-solving. Dudley was still a little tired from the procedure so he stretched out and placed his head in my lap. I rested my hand on his large golden head and drove with the other hand. I then decided we would just take it one day at a time and live every precious day as if it were our last. I would definitely be making a donation to the Heart Trust at http://vetmed. tamu.edu/giving.

After hours of driving, we finally made it back to Big Rock Lofts. I parked the Power Wagon right next to E.D.'s car, Betsy, and turned off the motor. As soon as I did, Dudley woke up. He seemed refreshed and, whether good or bad, was back to his old self again. We jumped out of the

Power Wagon and walked up to the entrance of Big Rock.

Dudley stopped for what seemed like a very long time to drain the lizard. It was getting late and there was nobody around. After he finished doing his business, Dudley and I walked up to the old iron door and entered the building. We went up the stairs together. I wondered if he should be taking the elevator in his condition, but he was having none of that and, besides, we didn't have an elevator. He stayed with me stride for stride up to #158. It was like a ghost town at Big Rock. I guess everyone had settled in for the evening and we were about to do the same.

Once I unlocked the door and we entered the loft, Dudley went straight over to his food and water and began eating and drinking. It was like he had been in the desert for a while because he made his food and water go bye bye in a hurry. It was really funny watching him drink. His head bobbed up and down like he was bobbing for an apple in an apple-bobbing contest, and his unusually large and long tongue slurped up the water and brought it into his oversized, goobering jowls. Watching that never failed to put a smile on my face but, then again, I'm entertained rather easily.

Dudley went to the bed, climbed in, stretched out with his head on the pillow, and grabbed some shut-eye. He was still a little tired from his daytime adventure. I went to the refrigerator and poured myself a Careless Coffee. I reached over to the cabinet for my favorite topping and placed a little Jack Black in the iced coffee for good measure. It was kind of like the beer commercial: Tastes great but less feeling. Of course, it did taste great and the more I drank, the less I would feel.

Before I lost all feeling, I decided to turn on the television. I sat down in a chair since I no longer had a sofa, thanks to Dudley. I really do miss that sofa. While drinking my iced coffee, I began to mindlessly watch the idiot tube. That's when I saw something that began firing up my brain cells. It was either that or the Careless Coffee had started to kick in. I wasn't sure which. No, this was definitely something else.

The Houston SPCA was having a telethon and it was going on right at this very moment. It was entertaining but some of the stories were a little sad. Most of them had happy endings. That's when the red-and-white HEB telephone began singing like a really bad contestant on one of those reality television shows I never watch.

"Ciro's Pizza, may I hava your order?" I answered.

Speaking of happy endings, it was the lovely E.D. from upstairs. "How's Dudley, Witless?" she asked.

That was awful nice of her for checking on Dudley. If I couldn't make her fall in love with me, at least she was obviously head over heels in love with one of us. She probably made the right choice. Dudley did have good character and he most likely would keep his hair in his elderly years.

"It's Careless, honey, and the patient is doing just fine. He's resting in bed right now," I responded.

"Is he okay? Is he comfortable?" she asked.

"Well, I think he makes a living but you can bring that up with him the next time you see him," I said.

She told me to quit being a smartass and she would be seeing him real soon because tonight was the Jake Harm and the Holdouts concert at the Hide Out and Birk had asked her to go with us. So much for the dates Birk promised to get us for the concert. E.D. said she would be down in about forty-five minutes and I should make myself presentable. Then she hung up.

Because of my adventure today with Dudley, I had forgotten all about the concert. I was tired but still a little excited to go. I loved watching Jake in concert; it was always entertaining when he was on stage. He is quite the performer and an excellent songwriter. I always got a good feeling watching him. I hung up my telephone and was about to get up, shower, and slap on some smell good when my brain began alerting me that I need-ed to see something on the television. I suppose I caught something out of the corner of my eye because when I turned my full attention toward the television I noticed something very interesting. There were four women at the SPCA sitting around on a sofa and each one of them was holding a really cute dog they were trying to get viewers to adopt.

I was a little jealous because I kind of wished I still had a sofa but that's not where my interest was directed. I do really miss that sofa. My eyes and brain honed in behind the set where the women were sitting with the dogs. There, blending in with the background was a constable in full uniform with a sidearm strapped to his belt. He was most likely barely noticeable to most people, but not to me. Most viewers only focused on the main event just as when a magician distracts you by having you focus on only what he wants you to see while he secretly does his magic trick. It is pretty common to have security at the SPCA telethon, especially when local celebrities make guest appearances to help the shelter out. The constable in the background became very recognizable to me as I closely studied him. It was definitely Richard, from China Gardens. What was he doing there? He must have been a constable in his former life. That's just when things began to click in my mind and something told me there was indeed a mystery about to unfold.

The SPCA telethon scene on the television changed the location being viewed and they were now showing the corral in the back where the rescued horses and farm animals were kept. I thought this would be an excellent time to get myself all gussied up for the concert tonight. I quickly showered up, slapped on some Aqua Lavanda smell-good, and threw on some old blue jeans and a Western wear shirt. There is nothing like a worn pair of blue jeans for comfort. It really takes years to get them just right.

I walked out of the bathroom and found Dudley standing at the front door just staring at it, not making a sound. His tail was wagging around in a big circular motion just like that of the orbit of the moon around the Earth. I bet Uranus had a moon but really, enough about Uranus. Dudley either needed a mental health day off or there was something or someone of interest behind door number one. I went to the door with Dudley by my side and opened it. Dudley's spidey senses must have been tingling, if not something else, because the door opened wide to reveal a true vision of loveliness.

Standing in the hallway was a cowgirl named E.D. She was wearing a very tight, extremely short, blue jean denim skirt, a tight black Western wear shirt with white snaps down the front, tied up at the bottom and revealingly unbuttoned at the top, and a pair of black leather Lucchese boots. Her golden hair was long and feathered, neatly tucked underneath a beautiful black felt Resistol cowboy hat with a feather band around it. Once again, I didn't know what to say because when you stare beauty directly in the face it can be quite overwhelming.

"Nothing to say, smartass?" she quipped with a wicked little smile on her face.

It's not like me to go braindead at any particular moment in time so, as not to be a total disappointment, I mustered a few jumbled up words to the effect of something like, "Save a horse, ride a cowboy."

She was not amused. She knelt down and called to Dudley who promptly walked right up to her. She began rubbing his big head and telling him how worried she was about him today.

"Let's get a move on, Hitless, I don't want to be late for the Jake Harm and the Holdouts concert. Now there's a man a girl could fall in love with," she said.

"It's Careless," I said as I walked off to get my boots and hat so we could head out.

CHAPTER FORTY-SEVEN

We both said our goodbyes to Dudley and I threw a couple of treats and other chewy things down on the floor for him to entertain himself with. He would need that since we no longer had a sofa for him to chew on. He left the treats where they were and went to his bowl of water to grab a drink. His head bobbed up and down as his overly large tongue drew the water into his mouth. It was just some slobbery goodness that amused E.D. and me as we watched. After he finished, he grabbed his favorite white wool gingerbread-man-shaped toy we had nicknamed Baby and he put himself to bed, in my bed, with Baby. I guess it was probably our bed now.

E.D. and I let ourselves out of the loft as I closed and locked the door behind us.

"Yeah, heh, heh, heh, heh," I heard Sarge's familiar voice sing out in the background. Sarge had quietly walked up behind us without us even noticing him. "Hey man, han, han, han, han, let's get going or we'll miss Jake Harm and the Holdouts. He's one of my favorite singers," Sarge said as he started humming one of Jake's new hit songs, "Marathons," in octaves I was pretty certain I hadn't heard since I was in the womb. So much for the dates Birk had promised.

The three of us marched down the stairs, though the front entryway, and out of the front old iron door. As we walked outside, I noticed Birk was waiting for us in the parking lot. He had his Cowboy Cadillac back so I'm sure he was happy and I was certain he most likely had established what type of protection he preferred. Birk has a Type A personality and when I say Type A, I mean Type A-Hole. When he finally saw us walking out of Big Rock he starting honking his horn. I wasn't sure whether he did this to hurry us up or whether he thought we didn't see him. Either way, he was still a Type A-Hole.

The three of us walked to the truck and Birk started mouthing something to the effect that he wasn't getting any younger and we needed to get a move on to the Houston Livestock Show and Rodeo to watch Jake Harm and the Holdouts perform.

I mentioned to him that he wasn't getting any more handsome or intelligent either and we were only human. I often use that explanation when I need to make a point that is foolproof. It is really hard to argue with someone once they say they are only human. There is really no way to prove otherwise. The trick is to apply this strategy to something you may or may not want to do, so your opponent has no snappy comeback and honestly, I usually use it to avoid something I don't want to do.

I opened the front passenger side door for E.D. and that hot little cowgirl jumped up in the truck just as easily as she would have jumped up on a horse. She pushed the middle console up to make a middle seat available and moved over to the middle, looked at me, and patted her hand down on the passenger seat. "Come on, Careless, I'm not getting any younger," she said amusingly while mocking Birk.

"Well, you sure are getting prettier, if that's even possible," I responded as a big smile formed on her lovely face.

Maybe there was still hope for me. Only time will tell. Maybe some of Dudley's boyish charm was starting to rub off on me. Sarge opened the back door and climbed into the backseat. Before he could completely get the door shut, Birk had already put it in gear and hit the gas, or shall I say diesel, as the Powerstroke engine hummed along. No worries, the centripetal force from the curving motion of the truck closed the door for him. Sarge was not amused. Birk had one of Jake Harm and the Holdout's new songs playing on the stereo, "Hill Country Blues."

It seemed to me that country-western and blues songs were usually about the wife or woman that left, something to do with drinking, a dog, or a truck. Jake always seemed to find a nice balance in his songs involving implications of the universe. We drove on.

Some fifteen minutes later we had arrived at the Astrodome. The outdoor carnival was completely lit up like the Las Vegas Strip. There were all kinds of rides and a huge Ferris wheel with different colored blinking neon lights making it glow in the evening sky. I would not be going on that, unless of course E.D. asked me to and then I would reluctantly go. It is very difficult to turn down the wishes of a beautiful woman. At least for me it is. It's just a weakness I'll have to live with.

There was a long line of cars and busses waiting to enter the parking areas in and around the Astrodome. Normally, it would take thirty minutes to an hour to park and go inside because it was so crowded but we had Birk on our side. He set his anger management aside and turned a knob on the dash of his truck to place the vehicle in four-wheel drive. We noticed right away that the ride had gotten much rockier as well as did our relationship with Birk. Birk mumbled something about not waiting in line with all those people and, before we knew it, Birk had his Cowboy Cadillac hop a few curbs, jump a few esplanades, and trench a few yards.

Sooner, much sooner, than we had expected, we had navigated our way through an angry bunch of spectators and were trying to park in the lot right next to the Astrodome. Through no fault of their own, the people waiting in line to park, the very same people who were driving cars instead of trucks, had been bypassed by an angry, slightly aggressive driver named Birk.

I suppose he did cut in line, but what could I do? I wasn't driving and I had no control over what Birk was doing. He drove so fast I thought I saw myself behind me for a moment when I looked back. Before we knew what he was doing, it was already done. In Texas we have a saying: Wherever you go, there you are. And there we were, at the Astrodome.

CHAPTER FORTY-EIGHT

All four of us got out of the Cowboy Cadillac and started walking through the crowd as Birk pushed his alarm button and locked the truck. We walked through the carnival and, as we did, I noticed the distinct smell of cotton candy, candied apples, popcorn, barbeque, and roasted turkey legs all rolled into one aroma. If only someone could bottle that smell, it would probably sell like hotcakes.

Speaking of hotcakes, I thought I smelled something resembling them but it turned out to be fried Oreos, fried Twinkies, and fried Snickers bars. As disgusting as that sounds, it sure smelled pretty good and most of the young teenagers and kids at the carnival usually ate these tasty delights until they were sick. We finally made our way through the carnival and the crowd as we walked toward the Astrodome.

There was a line of people waiting to get in the Astrodome; and looking around I distinctly noticed that everyone entering the Astrodome, where the Hide Out was located, was wearing a golden-colored badge with the Houston Live Stock Show and Rodeo logo etched into it. Everyone had them pinned somewhere on their person. Most people had them pinned to their shirts; but there were those who most likely had been drinking adult beverages, who were quite creative as to where their golden badges were placed. I won't elaborate but suffice it to say that some of these folks definitely looked like they had just returned from a long trip to Uranus. That word really never gets old.

As the line steadily moved forward, we got closer to the entrance. A big white sign with black letters informed us that no one was allowed to enter the Astrodome without a golden badge. I looked at Birk with a quizzical expression and wondered where our golden badges were. Birk looked a little confused so I helped him out and directed his attention to the large sign at the entrance by pointing my index finger at it, while shrugging my shoulders.

I saw a lightbulb go off in his head as if he were remembering something and, with Birk, that can sometimes be dangerous. He reached into his front pants pocket and produced four golden badges for each of us to wear while we waited in line to enter the Astrodome. Birk told me, "Don't ask!" as he passed out the golden badges. He muttered something about a friend of a friend and that was good enough for me.

We all started to pin the golden badges onto our shirts just before the doorman checked for them. I asked E.D. if she needed help pinning on her badge but, her eyes closed slightly while she said to me, "Nice try, but that's not happenin', Captain."

"I was just trying to be a gentleman, E.D.," I justified to her.

Honestly, it was probably a good thing she didn't accept my offer to help because she would have definitely been felt up from the belt up, if you know what I mean. E.D.'s shirt was so tight it looked like it had been painted on her. I guess I couldn't blame her for the rejection but then again she couldn't blame me for being an overachiever, or perhaps just a frustrated future TSA agent. She just smirked and pinned on her badge as we were waved through Checkpoint Charlie. We entered the massive structure of the Astrodome.

CHAPTER FORTY-NINE

As the four of us entered the Astrodome, we walked through the big tunnels the NFL football players used to go from the locker rooms to the field. It was very crowded but everyone was pretty orderly. I was sure that after the concert and a few truckloads of beer were consumed, the crowd might not be as well behaved, but that was the nature of the yeast.

Everyone walking in with us was well dressed in their finest Western wear duds. It was a handsome crowd. The men were all well groomed and the cowgirls were all decked out and looking good, just as they should. We walked down a few ramps and finally found our way to the end of the tunnel where we were spit out onto the massive floor of the Astrodome. This was the actual field where The Houston Astros played baseball and where The Houston Oilers played football.

Originally, the Astros were named the Colt .45s in 1962 and played baseball in Colt .45 Stadium. In 1965 they became the Astros and started playing baseball in the Astrodome. At that point in time they were owned by Judge Roy Hofheinz. They currently play in Minute Maid Park, which was formerly known as Enron Stadium. The Astros produced great legends such as Joe Morgan, Rusty Staub, Cesar Cedano, J. R. Richards, Larry Dierker, Joe Niekro, Mike Scott, Alan Ashby, Jose Cruz, Enos Cabel, Nolan Ryan, Craig Biggio, Mark Portugal, Ken Caminiti, and Jeff Bagwell, to name a few. The Astros made playoff appearances in 1980, 1981, and 1986. In 2005 the Astros lost the World Series to the Chicago White Sox.

In 1960 The Houston Oilers started playing football at Jeppesen Stadium and were owned by Bud Adams. They moved to Rice Stadium in 1965 and in 1968 they finally moved to their permanent home in the Astrodome. The Oilers made their way into the playoffs in 1960, 1961, 1962, 1978, 1979, 1980, 1987, 1989, 1990, and 1992, until 1996 when the team moved to Nashville, Tennessee, where they became The Tennessee Titans. The Oilers produced great players such as George Blanda, Billy Cannon, Earl Campbell, Kenny Burroughs, Dan Pastorini, Billy White Shoes Johnson, Bruce Mathews, and Mike Munchak.

A stage was set up at one end of the Astrodome with plenty of room to watch, sing along, or dance to the music. There was already plenty of drinking going on so I was certain the singing and dancing would follow shortly, very shortly. In the meantime I began scanning the area. I always like to know where everything and everyone is.

As a bonus, with my keen memory, I am almost always able to find a restroom or bar wherever I go. I try to concentrate on just the valuable information that may come in handy when needed or perhaps at a later time.

For instance, upon entering the Hide Out, I had already noticed there was one main entrance and exit but five emergency exits dimly lit up scattered along the back walls, approximately thirty feet apart from one another. There were eight bars, cash only, scattered haphazardly around the outskirts of the dance floor and one food court just to the left of the tunnel entrance we had just come through. There were six restrooms, four women's and two men's, located between the eight bars. My guess is they would be heavily used before the end of the concert; but, as I would soon find out, that would not be the case.

A cover band named the Copperhead Crashers was already playing when we walked up to the stage and the lead singer had long flowing reddish-orange hair hanging out of the back and sides of his cowboy hat. They sounded pretty good. They were playing Western swing music and people were starting to hit the dance floor for a boot-scoot.

Sarge snuck off to grab beers for everyone. Shiner Bach beer was available and is brewed right here in Texas. This was definitely my favorite beverage, right behind Careless Coffee. Sarge came back and handed out the beers to everyone. We set them down on a table, which was really just an old wooden barrel. The barrels were scattered around for people to put their drinks on and if you must know there were thirty-eight of them.

We were all watching and listening to the band as people danced right past us. It was very festive and hopefully none of the people having a good time were any of the ones that Birk had sidestepped to park in front of in the parking lot. If they were, I was sincerely hoping they wouldn't recognize us. I took a few sips of my beer and enjoyed the music while waiting for Jake to come out and perform. It would be a long wait.

Shiner Bach beer is made at the Spoetzl Brewery in the little town of Shiner, Texas, just east of San Antonio. Originally formed as the Shiner Brewing Association in 1909, it is one of the oldest breweries in Texas. It became the Spoetzl Brewery when Kosmo Spoetzl began brewing Bavarian beer in 1914. The brewery made it through America's Prohibition period, the Great Depression, and has become very successful. They produce many fine beers such as Bach, Light, Blonde, Hefeweizen, and my personal favorite, Black Lager. The brewery offers tours and uses imported copper vessels to brew their beer. Seasonal beers such as Holiday Cheer, Smokehaus, and Frost are also made. You know you're in a fine establishment when Shiner beer is served.

CHAPTER FIFTY

As the festivities continued I noticed there was someone moving through the crowd, heading in our direction. He zigged and zagged a few times but he was still coming at us. I didn't know who he was, but I didn't like it. My guess was that he was either a bouncer about to throw us all out, because Birk had possibly provided us with counterfeit golden Houston Livestock Show and Rodeo badges, or an undercover police officer. Either way, I sized him up pretty quickly and was a little concerned. As he got closer I lightly and inconspicuously kicked the back of Birk's boot in a manner that no one would notice except him. He turned and looked at me with a puzzled expression on his face and I directed his attention with just my eyes, so as to not alert anyone else that there was an oncoming stranger headed directly toward us.

He looked at the approaching man, smiled, and raised his hand up slightly into the air to wave to him. "That's my friend, Detective Present. I told you about him earlier," Birk informed me.

"Super," I responded.

Detective Present walked up to us just as the Copperhead Crashers finished their last set. He shook hands with Birk and they spoke for a few minutes. Unlike Birk, he was a handsome man and appeared to be in his early forties. He was about five-foot-seven, slim, and had light-brown hair. He was wearing blue jeans, a white button-down shirt, a brown Western jacket, and a pair of black dress shoes. By my best estimate he was carrying a Glock, Model 23, which is a mostly polymer .40 caliber semi-automatic pistol that is standard issue for a lot of Houston Police Department officers and detectives.

I noticed the slight bulge just inside his jacket tucked neatly away in a holster on his hip. It also appeared that he had a small Smith & Wesson snub nose .38 caliber tucked away in an ankle holster on his right leg just above his shoe and under his pant leg. I noticed that slight bulge as well and that was also standard issue for a lot Houston Police Department officers and detectives as the backup weapon of choice. I could be wrong but I probably wasn't. It's always good to know when someone around you is armed. Most people would never notice that Detective Present was armed and undercover, which is as it should be.

While all of this was going on, I was still scanning my surroundings for anything out of the ordinary. I felt something was not right and with a police detective milling about, there was sure to be something going on. I did notice there were at least seven other undercover police officers blending in with the crowd. People were really streaming in now because Jake Harm and the Holdouts were scheduled to start their gig any minute as the headliner. Everyone was cramming forward to get closer to the stage, get a glimpse of Jake, and hear his music. There definitely wouldn't be any dancing tonight once Jake started playing. There wouldn't be any room on the dance floor and frankly I was a little happy about that because I knew E.D. would want me to dance with her and I didn't want to do the white-man shuffle in front of her for fear of chasing her off, especially before she had the opportunity to fully fall in love with me, after which all bets were off. At least I hoped she would want me to dance with her. A guy can dream, and E.D. was really every man's dream.

It was really getting crowded and people were still coming in. No one was leaving, or at least no one should have been. That's when I noticed something very strange and it gave me a very bad feeling.

CHAPTER FIFTY-ONE

The road crew for the Copperhead Crashers were packing up the band's instruments and taking them off of the stage to get ready for the next performance. The crowd was getting excited and a little impatient. When you drink heavily, everything tends to move a little slower than you might like. Birk introduced Officer Present to E.D., Sarge, and lastly to me.

He was pleasant to everyone but when he got to me he stuck his hand out for me to shake as he introduced himself. I knew he was sizing me up, but I really had no need of an undercover detective getting to know me. I had already sized him up while he had been walking towards us earlier. I extended my hand and shook hands with him.

He had a pretty firm handshake and I liked that. I can't stand shaking hands with someone who has a limp-dick handshake. I find it irritating and it tells me in advance all I need to know about that person. Of course, I matched Officer Present's firmness of his handshake and added a little extra so he knew who he was dealing with.

He asked me if I had a concealed handgun license to carry the sidearm tucked away inside my pants in a holster covered up by my shirt. I thought that was pretty impressive, but declined to offer up any information about what I had determined concerning any weapons he was carrying or where they were strategically located. My feeling was, why give away useful information when it wasn't really necessary or pertinent? Some things are better left unsaid unless needed at a future date. That's why I never mentioned that I carry a concealed handgun earlier. I mean really, do you need to know every little detail about me? If so, then the answer is yes, I do have a concealed handgun license and, yes, I usually have at least one weapon on my person, sometimes two. You never know when you're going to need a gun.

In Texas, our rule of thumb when it comes to handguns is to never carry anything for defense that doesn't have a 4 in the caliber. No, Texans don't run around shooting guns in the air while riding up and down the streets on our horses. In Texas, after passing extensive testing and training, citizens are allowed to conceal handguns on their person as well as keep them in our automobiles and homes. In Texas, we refer to that as "crimestoppers" and thankfully I have not yet had to introduce anyone to my two friends, Smith & Wesson. Hey, wait a minute, maybe I do have friends! I told Detective Present that I had no idea what he was referring to. He was not amused.

Jake's road crew and band were setting up the stage with all of their instruments. The detective and I made some small talk, but I could tell something was up. He was constantly scanning the surroundings for something, but I was pretty sure he hadn't noticed what I had noticed, because I could tell he was still searching for something.

He stopped looking around and directed his attention toward me. He told me my friend Birk told him I was always figuring out mysteries and that I took notice of every detail around me, great and small. He asked me if I was an amateur sleuth and I told him I wasn't, but that I did save a lot of money with Geico Insurance. Again, he was not amused.

I suppose Birk had warned him about me but all work and no play made Detective Present a dull boy. I told him I was running a little dry and I needed to go grab another brewsky. I turned and walked off toward the nearest bar but I had something else or, should I say, someone else in mind. I'll get to that shortly.

A few minutes later I rejoined the group along with Detective Present. I had a Shiner Bach beer in one hand and my cell phone in the other hand, holding it up to my ear while talking in a very loving tone. "I really love you and I miss you so much. I'll be home soon. I can't wait to see you."

E.D. was rolling her very beautiful blue eyes while listening to me talk on my cell phone. She was so cute when she was aggravated. I finally ended the conversation, closed the phone, and stuck it in my front right pants pocket. It was pretty small and thin so it definitely didn't create a rise in my Levis.

Detective Present asked me how long I had been married.

I asked him why he wanted to know, and he told me I must have a really nice wife by the way I was talking to her on my cell phone. At that point E.D. started to laugh out loud as I told Detective Present I had never been married and that I was talking to my dog, Dudley. I knew he was probably just sitting around the loft waiting for me to get back and the answering machine plays the message being recorded out loud so he could take some comfort when hearing my voice. I do miss him terribly when we're apart.

Again, Detective Present was not amused. He asked me to stick around for a while because he would have something more to talk to me about.

I told him I would.

Something definitely did not feel right. The road crew had set up the band's instruments but it was taking an unusually long time for the band to come out. That's when Detective Present hit me with a bombshell. He told me Jake Harm had disappeared that very day and no one had heard from him since. No one knew if it was a kidnapping or worse. He just disappeared with no warning and it was as if he had never existed. The police had no leads and no ransom notes had been received.

Detective Present told me he might be able to use a little help with the disappearance of Jake, especially with what Birk had told him about me. He asked if I wanted to help out with the investigation.

I wasn't sure what to say because to date I had only used my considerable powers of observation for fun things. I thought about it for a moment and told him I would be glad to help out to the best of my ability. To be honest, in my mind, I had already solved the case but I needed a little more time to gather some facts. I had to be very careful because, if I didn't play my cards right, harm could definitely come to Jake Harm, or worse.

We shook on it and this time Detective Present's grip had become a little more firm. I was starting to like this guy, just a little.

Just as I agreed to help Detective Present, a middle-aged man in a cowboy hat walked out on stage to make an announcement to the already impatient and somewhat beer-laden crowd. As he started speaking, I had a few words with Detective Present. I informed him that the culprit was in the Hide Out earlier, but had slipped away and was no longer here. I told him if he wanted to catch the person who had most likely kidnapped Jake then he needed to act quickly and to go up on the stage and announce to the crowd that Jake had been taken ill and would not be able to play tonight. I told him he should tell the crowd that while he was really sorry for the inconvenience, Jake would definitely be here tomorrow night at the same time and everyone would be welcome back for that concert.

He told me he didn't have the authority to do that.

I looked him squarely in the eye and asked him if he was the MFIC (rhymes with fother mucker in charge) or not.

The man on the stage told the crowd the Jake Harm and the Holdouts concert had been cancelled. The crowd began to grumble and boo.

I looked at Detective Present and again told him to climb up on the stage and make the announcement if he wanted to see Jake Harm again. I added that he had best do this to control the crowd and to mention that the beer would be on the house for the Jake Harm and the Holdouts concert tomorrow night.

Detective Present saw that the crowd was turning a little nasty and impatient, so quick as a jackrabbit he climbed up on the stage and edged the microphone away from the man making the announcement. He told the audience he was terribly sorry, Jake had taken ill and was in too bad of shape to play. The booing and discontent got louder.

It was not looking good for Detective Present. Sensing the crowd was getting a little unruly, he finally did as I instructed and announced that Jake would put on a concert tomorrow night. He told everyone they were welcome to come back tomorrow night at the very same time.

Things became a little quieter in the Hide Out, but there were still some angry onlookers. That's when he made an executive decision and announced that the beer for everyone would be on the house tomorrow night (just as I had instructed him to say).

Everyone cheered and whistled and the ugliness that had been building up subsided. Thankfully, the crowd began to disperse.

The man on the stage looked very confused until Detective Present told him not to worry because this was official police business as he showed him his badge. Detective Present had been contacted earlier by the Holdouts because they were concerned that they hadn't seen Jake for a while and he wasn't answering his phone. They decided to go forward with the concert tonight because sometimes in the past, Jake had gone on a bender but always managed to return in time to perform, sometimes, just in time. The show must go on; but this time, for the first time, it didn't.

Detective Present went backstage and had a brief conversation with the Holdouts. My guess is that he asked them for their cooperation and tried to assure them that Jake would be found unharmed. I'm sure he was also hoping Jake would make his way to the concert before it started. No such luck, and I had a pretty good idea as to why.

He reappeared and jumped off of the stage as he walked back over to

Birk, Sarge, E.D., and me. They all looked a little confused.

"I hope you know what you're doing," Detective Present said as he gave me a stern look.

"I just solved the case for you but I will need you to do one thing for me," I said.

"What would that be?" he asked.

"I'm going to need the police department to pay for the beer tomorrow night," I responded.

He thought about that for a moment and reluctantly said the department would expense the cost of the beer if and only if I solved the case to his satisfaction.

I informed him it had already been solved and the culprit would be revealed at the concert tomorrow night.

He asked me how I could possibly know that or how there would be a concert tomorrow night if Jake was still missing. I asked him to walk with me for a moment and as we left the gang standing there, I explained a few things to him and informed him of what I would need to solve the case and to get Jake back. He seemed fairly agreeable.

We finished talking and walked back to the others who looked just a little confused. I told Detective Present I would contact him tomorrow, but that right now, I had to leave because I had a loved one waiting for me at home, and I did.

What an exciting night. I never thought of myself as a crime fighter and I never thought I would be called upon to help solve a case by a police detective. This was my very first case and possibly my last if I didn't solve it without getting Jake hurt or killed.

I did have great confidence in myself, but that beer might be very costly if everything didn't pan out to Detective Present's liking. That would certainly leave me a little light in the wallet and frankly I didn't need any help with that.

We all walked together out of the Hide Out and out of the Astrodome. The carnival was still going strong and people, mostly kids, were running about like maniacs. Detective Present wished us good night and walked off. I watched as he got into an unmarked police car and drove off. You can always tell when there is an unmarked police car around because they look just like an unmarked police car. That's just a little trick I have learned that

I'm sharing with you.

Birk and Sarge decided they couldn't leave without having a bag of fried Oreos. We all stopped while the two of them each purchased a bag and wolfed them down. There were one dozen of those little fried, crispy beauties in each bag. I was fairly certain they both would be sick to their stomachs when they got home, if in fact they actually made it that far.

We made our way to the parking lot and to Birk's Cowboy Cadillac. The four of us jumped in and drove off. After a few minutes of Birk's driving, two of the four us were turning nice shades of green (not my favorite color, which is black, by the way), thanks to a little something called fried Oreos. People say the grease is what gives them their great flavor. It certainly seemed not to be a gastronomical pleasure for Birk and Sarge.

We finally arrived at Big Rock Lofts, and Birk slowed down for about two seconds and told us it was go time. Similar to paratroopers, Sarge, E.D. and I opened our respective doors and bailed out of the Cowboy Cadillac. Thankfully we all hit the ground safely on our feet and, by the time we looked back up, there was no trace of Birk. He most likely had an urgent appointment with a toilet.

E.D. and I looked at Sarge scurrying along ahead of us. All we heard was, "Oh man, han, han, han, han, han, han," while he vanished inside the building.

E.D. and I looked at each other and started cracking up laughing. I put my arm around her as we walked up the sidewalk from the parking lot to the Big Rock Lofts entrance, and I thanked her.

She told me she had an exciting evening but wanted to know why I was thanking her. I thought to myself for a moment and wondered if I should thank her for agreeing to marry me, even though she hadn't, or should I tell her the truth? I opted for the truth and told her I was thanking her for helping me solve the case.

She looked a bit puzzled as I opened the old iron door. We entered the building together. Unfortunately for me, that was the last thing we would do together that night.

CHAPTER FIFTY-TWO

I went to loft #158 and before I could get my keys out to unlock the door I heard Dudley on the other side of the door grunting and mumbling something because he knew I was there. I don't know if he heard me with his keen sense of hearing or had caught my scent with his ultra-sensitive nose, but he was waiting for me nonetheless.

I unlocked the door, opened it, and entered the loft. Just as I had suspected, Dudley was waiting at the door for me. He jumped up on me, curved his paws around my shoulders, and started licking my face over and over, which really made it a little hard to breathe. While this was going on, he was grunting and moaning in several different octaves varying from low, high, and in between. This boy should have been a singer.

As the lovefest continued, Dudley's eyebrows rose up and I heard someone behind me throat an "uh hum" in a questioning manner. Well, of course it was the lovely E.D. who had cleverly slipped down the staircase and back to #158 without Dudley or me noticing her. In our defense, we were a little busy making up for lost time.

"I just came down for a nightcap, but I can see you boys are busy so I'll just see you tomorrow at the Jake Harm and the Holdouts concert, if there actually is one," she said. Before I could complain or explain she had turned and walked away.

I looked at Dudley and he looked at me, and we continued the lovefest, for just a few more minutes. I had been foiled again by my love for a dog, dang it.

Dudley and I walked out of the loft as I closed and locked the door. We went down the stairwell and out of the back door of Big Rock. I figured he probably needed to use the facilities. After he did his business I called him and he came running back to me. We went back into the building and back up to our loft. Once inside, I poured myself a Careless Coffee, drank it down, and hit the hay. I was tired. It had been a long and exciting day and I had a lot to think about if the case was going to get solved in a way that was beneficial to everyone, except for the kidnapper of course.

Yes, indeed there was a kidnapper and I knew just who it was, but I would have to make that person reveal to us what had been done and where Jake was located, if he was even still alive. I believed he was still alive. I went to bed and a few minutes later I had Dudley's head resting on my chest while he was staring at me, waiting for me to go to sleep so he could do the same. He is a good boy.

The next morning, after getting thoroughly spooned by Dudley all night, I woke up, showered, got dressed, and Dudley and I left the loft to head over to Pappa's for breakfast. As we arrived, Pappa had just finished frying up some Jimmy Dean sausage, scrambled eggs, and something from the old country he referred to as matzah brei. Matzah brei is simply matzah, which is an unleavened bread similar to a cracker, crunched up, mixed with egg, and fried up with butter in a frying pan.

It's a real colon pleaser from the mother country and I'm pretty sure it's good for your cholesterol as well. At this time of the morning I didn't much care to ask. I would eat just about anything and wash it down with some of Pappa's crunchy coffee he made in his old stove-top coffee percolator.

Friend, if you haven't had a breakfast like that, trust me, it's the breakfast of champions, especially if you're from the old country. We finished up and I gave Dudley some leftover matzah brei. He'll eat anything, and since I never really knew where he grew up, it is possible he may be from the old country as well. We all cleaned up and left. Ross the Boss took Pappa, and I took Dudley to work.

CHAPTER FIFTY-THREE

We all got to the office and I opened Dudley's doggie door for him, which he promptly took advantage of. I sat down at my desk and began going over some sales figures. Pappa sat down in the front office and lit up his early morning cigar, and Ross the Boss jettisoned himself out into the pipe yard to make sure everything was going smoothly.

I was having a problem concentrating because I kept mentally going over all of the details of the elaborate trap I was setting tonight for Jake Harm's kidnapper. I must have planned it over a hundred times in my mind so I would be prepared for any variance whatsoever. A man's life probably depended on it and I wasn't sure if it would be Jake's or mine if Detective Present became dissatisfied.

I kept on working and about an hour later Dudley's head was resting on my leg. He had finished his sunbath outside and had snuck back to my desk without me noticing. I just kept working and put one hand on his unusually large golden-colored head. I pet him a couple of times and he retired to his green leather sofa where he promptly laid down, turned upside down on his back, stuck his legs straight up in the air, and began sawing logs. His massive jowls were pulled down by gravity and flopped down on the sofa, exposing his gums and teeth. It appeared from my vantage point that he did have good oral hygiene. He probably did some brushing and flossing after he ate my sofa. It was pretty busy in the office but some people can sleep through anything and I was beginning to suspect Dudley was one of those people.

Ross the Boss came into my office and told me our twenty-four-inch pipe beveling machine had just broken down and needed to be taken to the repair shop because we were going to need it soon. Our pipe beveling machine is an aluminum machine that is strapped down on top of the pipe and has a hand crank and some gears, allowing it to pass around the outside of the pipe while either putting a square cut or a bevel cut on the end of the pipe with a very hot burning flame. We used it pretty regularly at the pipe yard, so a repair was in order and pretty routine, due to everyday wear and tear.

Since Dudley had already proved he was a crappy driver and Pappa didn't drive anymore, it appeared I was the odd man out. I told Dudley to behave himself and I said goodbye to Pappa who I was pretty sure was taking a catnap with a lit cigar in his mouth. I began to walk out of the door but first I reached over and gently took Pappa's cigar out of his mouth. He didn't notice because he was asleep. I set it in the ashtray on a table next to him so he could resume smoking it later. They're really just as good the second go round.

I went outside and lifted up the beveling machine. The beveling machine didn't look like much, but it weighed well over a hundred pounds. No problem for a man of my great strength. I placed it in the back of the Power Wagon. Once it was secure with tie-down straps, I got in, cranked her up, and left for the repair shop.

It took me about twenty minutes to get from my office to the repair shop. Once there, I dropped off the beveling machine and headed back toward the office, but all I kept really thinking about was my plan of action for tonight. As I approached my exit, I was feeling a little thirsty. I decided to stop at Jack in the Box for an iced coffee. I would have to enhance the Jack in the Box coffee with some Jack in the Bottle once I returned to my office.

Jack in the Box is a fast-food restaurant similar to McDonald's or Burger King but their spokesperson is a Jack in the Box. The funny thing is that all three of these fast-food restaurants are usually located pretty close to one another. Jack in the Box's television commercials are some of the most clever and funniest I have ever seen.

I pulled around the drive-through and the person in the building asked me if he could take my order. I noticed they were advertising something called the Ultimate Cheeseburger. I asked the person on the other end if I could order one cheeseburger without the cheese and a large iced coffee decaf.

"Sir, if you order a cheeseburger without the cheese then it would just be a hamburger. Is that what you want? And we don't serve iced coffee," the person said.

Who said our young people aren't as smart as they look? "In that case,

I'll have an Ultimate Cheeseburger and a large decaf coffee dumped in a big cup of ice, can you do that?"

I heard an uninspired, "Uh huh, please pull around to the window."

I pulled around to the drive-through window and two minutes and five dollars later I was on my way back to the office. I liked my own iced coffee much better but any port in a storm, I always say.

I got back to the office, parked, and walked in. Pappa greeted me in the front office and Ross the Boss was on the telephone in his office. I waved to him and kept on walking. Little white tufts of cigar smoke were dancing their way up towards the ceiling.

Dudley was waiting for me in my office and his nostrils were flaring as he took in the smell of his soon-to-be new favorite snack, the Ultimate Cheeseburger from Jack in the Box. That would be two quarter-pound beef patties and four slices of different kinds of cheeses on a sesame seed bun. Sounds like a little slice of heaven to me, if I ate that sort of thing.

I'm sure it was plenty tasty because as soon as I unwrapped it, I held it out to Dudley and he inhaled it in one bite. As I double-checked to make sure I still had all of my fingers, I saw his big tongue come out of his massive mouth and lick his lips, so I was pretty sure it was a culinary pleasure for him. After his rather large and tasty lunch, Dudley went through the doggie door and headed outside to his happy place. I wasn't sure but I may have to get his cholesterol checked after that meal. I went back to my desk and tried to finish out my day, which was not very easy.

I reached down to the bottom drawer of my desk and opened it. I pulled out a bottle of Jack Daniels and threw a few shots into my Jack in the Box iced coffee to flavor it up a bit. It seemed I now had several Jacks in my life. I put the bottle back in the drawer and closed it. I took a few sips and got to work but all I could think about was tonight and I kept going over every detail in my mind to make sure there would be no screw-ups. Jake's life may depend upon my plan to actually work and since I had never done anything like this before, I needed to make sure all of my bases were covered.

I looked up and noticed Ross the Boss was sitting in a chair directly across from me. He was just staring at me and I was a little startled because normally I am very observant so people usually have a hard time sneaking up on me. He asked me what I was thinking about and why I wasn't paying attention to anything in particular.

I explained to him what had transpired and how I was concentrating on tonight. He looked at me, shook his head from side to side for a bit, and told me I needed to learn how to multitask. I made a fist, held it up, and told him to multitask that.

He smiled a little and so did I as he told me he understood how important this was. He told me he had everything under control and to take the rest of the day off while adding, "Since you weren't going to get anything done anyway!"

I thanked him, grabbed my iced coffee, and started to leave the office. Multitask, indeed! I walked up to the front office and it looked like Dudley and Pappa were enjoying a smoke together. Great, now I found another bad habit my dog has.

Pappa was sitting in his chair, smoking his El Producto cigar with one hand and resting his other hand on Dudley's big head. They were just sitting there together, not talking or doing anything while staring up at the ceiling lost in thought. They were just enjoying a good smoke and life in general.

I told Pappa I was taking the rest of the day off and said goodbye to him. He acted as if he already knew. It seemed that nothing ever really surprised Pappa, even if he was from the old country. I walked past Pappa and Dudley stood up and walked right next to me. We walked out of the office together, jumped in the Power Wagon, and made our way back to Big Rock.

CHAPTER FIFTY-FOUR

Several minutes later, Dudley and I were back in front of Big Rock Lofts or as I like to call it, home. Big Rock is my home and where Dudley and I feel most at home. I opened my door and Dudley and I jumped out of the Power Wagon. We quickly went through the old iron door entrance, up the stairs, and into the loft. Dudley and I had a busy day at work but tonight we were going to be even busier. Dudley didn't know it yet but my plan included him and in fact, as it would turn out, he would play a crucial role in the solving of the kidnapping.

Dudley began drinking water from his bowl and I watched his head bob up and down while his tongue slurped up the water. That really just never gets old and always brings a smile to my face. Once he had finished, he retired to my bed, which was good because he was going to need his rest for helping to solve the case tonight.

While he slept I made a few phone calls, tied up a few loose ends, and made my final preparations for this evening. I called Birk and told him to pick me up at six-thirty sharp for the Jake Harm and the Holdouts concert at the Hide Out. I also told him to come alone and to tell no one. He seemed a bit confused but I assured him everything was under control.

I poured myself a Careless Coffee and sat, waiting for the clock to tick off a little time. You know, it's just like they say, it's good to the last drop. After the last drop was consumed, it was go time. I called for Dudley and he came marching in. I opened the door to the loft and we exited together. We walked downstairs and before we made it to the old iron door, Sarge, E.D., and Birk were all waiting in the entryway. They were standing up with their arms folded, giving me the evil eye.

E.D. snapped, "You most certainly didn't think you were going to the concert and trying to solve this case without all of us did you, Clueless?"

I was pretty sure she was asking a rhetorical question. "Honey, if I didn't want you all to come, I wouldn't have told Birk to tell no one and to come alone," I retorted. Everyone knows Birk has the biggest mouth in the

241

West. Birk played his role flawlessly. "Besides, this case is already solved and the name's Careless," I said with some confidence.

The five of us saddled up and left Big Rock Lofts on what should prove to be one very exciting night. We headed out to the parking lot and climbed into Birk's Cowboy Cadillac. It was more than capable of seating the five of us, and then some. Birk was behind the wheel, E.D. sat in the middle of the front seat, I sat next to E.D. in the front seat, and Sarge sat in the backseat with Dudley who was already sticking his humongous head out of the sunroof. Birk fired her up and we were back at the Astrodome in no time.

This time since we were early, there was almost no traffic so Birk didn't have to pull another Evel Knievel and jump a few curbs to get us to the parking lot. Birk parked the truck and we all got out and headed toward the Astrodome, and to the Hide Out for the concert. Birk reminded us all to pin on our golden badges he had given us from the night before so we could enter the Hide Out.

We walked through the carnival and it almost seemed as if the same people and kids from the night before were running around and riding the rides. Delicious smells came from all of the cooking foods. I looked at E.D. and said, "I know, déjà vu."

She seemed a little surprised that I knew what she was thinking and also that I knew how to speak French, but it was quite obvious by the look on her face what she was thinking. Dudley on the other hand had his nose in the air and was swinging his head from side to side so he wouldn't miss a smell. He had a great nose, which if I was correct, we would probably need tonight. He continued to walk by my side.

When we reached the Astrodome entrance, I pulled out a pair of sunglasses and put them on. My companions looked at me like I was nuts because it was already starting to get dark outside. I reached my hand down and grabbed Dudley's collar while we continued to walk. We didn't miss a beat. Before anyone could ask what the hell I was doing, the doorman looked at me and told me no pets were allowed. I informed him that Dudley was not a pet but he was in fact my seeing-eye dog and I was here with my friends who were all high-powered attorneys. The doorman waved us all through. I thanked him and waved to him just to the left of where he was actually standing to complete the charade.

Normally, I hate to pretend to be handicapped, but getting Dudley in the Hide Out was going to be crucial to solve the case and perhaps save Jake's life. In my defense, E.D. has said on more than one occasion that I am mentally handicapped so technically it was possible that I wasn't really lying.

We all walked down the ramp toward the floor of the Astrodome. As we reached the entrance to the floor, I took Dudley a few paces to the side and told him to sit and stay, which he promptly did. I petted him on the head and the four of us walked on toward the stage. It was already getting a little crowded and the smell of beer was in the air. That would be free beer, a tin roof, on the house. In Texas, if you have free beer and a good band to listen to, well, we just call that heaven and usually it involves a stampede of folks trying to get in. Tonight would be no different.

We walked closer to the stage and Detective Present was already there waiting for us. He told me everything I had asked him to do was done and everything had better go accordingly or there was going to be hell to pay. I told him to have no fear; the kidnapper was already here.

Of course he wanted to know who it was but I told him to have some patience and the villain would be revealed to us in due time. I was about to give everyone a task they would have to follow to a tee, with no variations. I told them a man's life may very well be in jeopardy if there were any mistakes.

CHAPTER FIFTY-FIVE

We were all about halfway between the stage and the exit. "Now, everyone, continue to look at me. Do not look around. We do not want to create suspicion. While we continue to talk and look at one another, there is a young lady to the right of the stage approximately thirty feet away from where we are. Do not look around! She has blonde hair down to the middle of her back. She has blue eyes and is wearing a red Western wear shirt and a mid-length blue jean denim skirt with brown cowboy boots. She appears to be about five-foot-one. Detective Present, I want you to slowly and inconspicuously circle around the outside of the crowd towards the back. Locate yourself just to the side of her and once the concert starts, I want you to walk directly towards her and make certain she sees you and knows you are walking directly towards her. Birk, I want you to do the exact same thing but from the other side of the Hide Out. Sarge, I want you to go to the back of the Hide Out and move directly towards her. E.D., I want you to go to the stage and directly approach her from there. Make sure she sees you coming for her. We will surround her and it will become very obvious who you are looking for, because she will run like the wind once she knows you are on to her," I directed them.

They all agreed to their roles but wanted to know what I would be doing while all of this was going on. I told them I would be observing and waiting. "Now, ladies and gentlemen, it's show time," I said as they all scattered to play their parts.

The stage was still set up from the night before and just then the same man from the night before wearing a cowboy hat came out on the stage to announce the band, and the crowd erupted with cheers. "Ladies and gentlemen, what you've all been waiting for. One of our very own, please welcome Jake Harm and the Holdouts," he excitedly screamed.

The cheers got even louder. The band walked out, picked up their instruments, and started to play. The crowd was going wild and then, Jake Harm came out to join the Holdouts. He picked up his guitar and began

244

strumming and singing. Everyone was loving it, or at least almost everyone. I heard an older gentlemen next to me say to his friend, "Hey, that doesn't look like Jake Harm. He sure looks a little different than I remembered."

Indeed, he did look a little different and that's just when my plan was set into motion. While pretending to watch the concert, I could see from the corner of my eye the little blonde-headed girl had figured out that she had walked into a trap and she was moving rather rapidly through the crowd in the opposite direction of Detective Present who she had noticed was walking in her direction, straight toward her. Unfortunately like a mouse moving toward a mouse trap, she was headed directly toward me as I pretended to watch the concert.

Her wild eyes were wide open. She looked in the opposite direction and saw Birk moving in on her as well. She looked around and saw Sarge moving toward her. She looked in the other direction and noticed E.D. gaining on her. Her flight instinct had taken over and she was now very close to me. She looked behind her one last time and made a beeline toward me, away from Detective Present.

Just as she reached me, I quickly turned, opened my arms, and grabbed her with all my strength, so she would understand there was no escape for her. She had no clue I was lying in wait for her, just as I had planned. I held her there while the others caught up.

"Surprised?" I asked her. I knew she was by the expression on her face, although I would not underestimate her.

She said nothing. Most criminals are very foolish and get caught because they do foolish things, but some are quite intelligent and it is with those you must be especially cautious. Only time would tell which type of criminal we were dealing with. The band continued to play and very few people even noticed the commotion. The free beer turned out to be a great idea after all.

CHAPTER FIFTY-SIX

Once Detective Present, E.D., Birk, and Sarge rolled up, Detective Present pulled out his handcuffs to place on the young lady. I told him that would not be necessary, releasing the kidnapper with one hand and waving him off with the other. I had her in my kung fu grip and she wasn't going anywhere. He was about to call in the other plain-clothes policemen he had stationed around the Hide Out but I asked him to hold off for just a little while. He complied, for now.

She made no effort to get away because she knew her number had been pulled.

Sarge just kept saying, "Wow, how, how, how, how, man, han, han, han, han! That was awesome man, han, han, han, han."

I think everyone was on an adrenalin rush right now. It was all very exciting but we still had a man to find and save. Thankfully, Detective Present was allowing me to be the MFIC and to continue on with the investigation.

I told everyone to walk to a quieter place where we could question our little kidnapper who had ventured into our mouse trap and was now just as quiet as a mouse.

The six of us walked off of the floor of the Astrodome, back through a tunnel, and into an open area where it was nice and quiet and devoid of people. I saw a large cardboard box and asked Birk to turn it over and to push it up against the wall. I finally turned the young lady loose and, giving her a very serious look, I told her to sit on the box. I could tell from her demeanor that she knew she had been beaten at her own game and she was presently not a flight risk, especially since we had her surrounded.

Little did she know my secret weapon was waiting in the wings to be called upon if and when needed. She compliantly sat down and I asked her for her name. She had a blank look on her face, but that changed quickly as she looked up at me and raised her two arms, bent at the elbows and bent at the wrists. She began moving her arms back and forth and up and down in unison, much like Michael Jackson in his famous *Thriller* music video.

I thought for a minute she was joking around and that she might stand up and start doing the *Thriller* dance or perhaps the moonwalk, but she didn't. She continued to look at me while making the motions with her arms and began making a noise in a high-pitched, squeaky voice that sounded something like, "Eh, eh, eh, eh, eh, eh," in quick, rapid bursts with a short pause in between each outburst.

It was almost funny but I was certain she wasn't faking it so I felt like we were probably dealing with someone who might be a little dangerous. We would have to tread lightly.

Once the kidnapper began this strange behavior with her arm motions and noises I could see Detective Present was getting irritated. It was clear from his facial expression that he was not going to stand for much more of this. I quickly turned and shot him a look to back off and thankfully he simmered down, at least for the time being. I turned my attention back to the kidnapper and sternly asked, "What's your name, honey?"

She stopped the *Thriller* arm movement, continued looking at me with her wild blue eyes, and started giggling in a very strange manner.

"Honey, if you don't tell me your name and everything else I want to know, I'm going to turn my partner loose on you and believe me he's not near as nice as I am," I said.

She stopped giggling for a moment, stopped looking at me, and looked around at my friends and Detective Present. I'm sure she thought my partner was Detective Present, not that there's anything wrong with that. Since we had not rehearsed this, everyone looked a little confused by what I had just said, and that made the kidnapper even bolder than she already had been. Most people at this point would have considered this a setback but this was actually part of my plan, and I was about to spring something on her that she didn't expect. I was pretty sure she wouldn't like it. I was quite certain this would be her breaking point.

"Last chance," I warned her. She continued her strange giggle.

"Fair enough," I said and I whistled as loud as I could. Initially nothing happened and the kidnapper was not impressed whatsoever. In less than a minute a very large golden streak was seen running into the area we were occupying. This large golden streak also had a very large golden head with some very large jowls. Needless to say, the giggling quickly stopped.

The arm twitching stopped. The wild, wide eyes returned. Someone was not a happy camper.

Dudley stopped right by my side and sat down, not taking his eyes off of the kidnapper; and, trust me when I tell you, she did not take her eyes off of him either. She had a frozen stare on her face I would not soon forget. Since Dudley had been excited and running to get to us, he had an over-abundance of goober steadily dripping from his jowls. Normally, I would get a towel and do the quicker picker upper on him, but seeing the expression on the kidnapper's face made me want to wait a bit. Dudley didn't mind and he was still sitting motionless with a fixed gaze on the kidnapper.

After a minute or two, Dudley began a low menacing growl at the kidnapper and that was right when she snapped. "No, no, moist, keep him away; I hate moist! No moist! No moist! Keep him away," she screamed while breaking down in tears.

"I won't be able to keep him away for much longer if you don't tell me what I want to know and if he really doesn't like you then he will stick his head right on your face and the goober will run like a wide open faucet. Do you know what I mean?" I asked her point blank.

"Okay, okay, my name's Evelyn Slack and I kidnapped Jake. I only did it because I love him so and he loves me, only me. No one else! We're going to get married, you'll see. Moist, I hate moist. Keep that thing away from me!" she screamed at the top of her lungs.

I placed my hand on Dudley's head and he looked up at me. "Good boy," I said while patting his head. He was a good boy! I turned my head for a moment to see the others and they all had astonished looks on their faces, even Detective Present. I nodded my head up and down a couple of times to show them I was in control of the kidnapper and then turned my attention right back toward her. "Now, young lady, you will tell us where Jake Harm is," I commanded.

"No, Jake's mine. You can't have him. He's mine and he'll always be mine," she said while refusing to give us Jake's whereabouts.

"That's fine, honey, no problem. I'm just going to turn you over to my very moist friend here and he's going to want to have a face-to-face conversation with you. You won't mind that, will you?" I asked.

I started walking toward her and Dudley stood up and started walking toward her as well, while not taking his eyes off her. He was still growling and much to my benefit he was leaving a nice trail of goober on the floor as he walked forward, and the growling became gradually louder.

"No, moist, no moist! I hate moist! Keep him away! The storage closet in the back of the food court. Please make him stop," she begged.

I stopped walking toward her and so did my friend Dudley. He stopped and promptly sat by my side. He most certainly did not like Evelyn and it showed.

CHAPTER FIFTY-SEVEN

Once Evelyn gave us the information we needed, I instructed Detective Present to handcuff her to a four-inch steel pipe protruding from the floor to somewhere over the rainbow, way up high. He did so and I instructed everyone to follow me as we headed toward the food court.

As we were all walking off, Evelyn started screaming at the top of her lungs that Jake was all hers, that no one else could have him, and he could only love her. It was sad really, but on we went to find Jake. An obsession gone bad, I suppose. I was sure Detective Present would find Evelyn the help she needed once we found Jake and the case was solved.

We continued our short walk to the food court. There were no people around as they were all enjoying the Jake Harm and the Holdouts concert, or so they thought. You might say the concert was sold out without the holdout. That would be a great title for my very first case and I was well on the way to solving it. I'll have to remember that for later. Fortunately, no one in the audience figured out that I hired an impersonator to fill in for Jake to draw his kidnapper out into the open. I hope the police department will pay for him as well.

Of course Evelyn thought Jake was still her captive but she had to make sure, and the curiosity was just too much for her to not show up and check it out. That is what I had banked on and, fortunately for me, it worked out. Most of the people at the concert were so buzzed from the free beer that I probably could have put Dudley up there wearing a cowboy hat and no one would have noticed the difference. I think he would look very handsome wearing a cowboy hat. We finally made it to the food court and there were five guys working behind the counter.

Detective Present flashed his HPD badge and ordered a young man to unlock and open the door so we could all go into the food court. As we entered, one of the men behind the counter was holding a hot dog in his hand. He was getting it ready just in case a customer came by to order it. The problem was that while watching us walk in he had frozen in his tracks. It seemed his curiosity had gotten the better of him. The other problem was that a hungry dog who happened to love hotdogs was on red alert and unfortunately for the man, Dudley inhaled the hotdog while he was still holding it.

I smiled because, frankly, I found it humorous but I also thought the man might go into shock so I asked him what the damage was. He informed me that I owed him seven bucks. I pulled out my fairly empty wallet, opened it up, and whipped out a ten dollar bill. "Here you go my good man and keep the change. Oh, and you may want to check your fingers just to make sure they're all still where they're supposed to be," I said as I amused myself.

In my defense and I may have already mentioned this but I get amused rather easily. Dudley and I chuckled as we walked to the back of the food court to find the storage closet door. There it was, right in front of us just as Evelyn had described.

"Now I must inform you all that I don't want you to get your hopes up that Jake Harm is in the storage closet. We're dealing with a very clever and slightly warped individual but nonetheless very clever. Let's just take it one step at a time," I said to my friends and Detective Present.

There was no way Evelyn was going to make this easy or obvious for us, so I thought this might be a mere stepping stone to finding Jake, but a positive stepping stone nonetheless.

As we got closer to the storage closet door, we all noticed there were several large boxes stacked up in front of it and since the hinges were on the outside of the door, it was clear the door opened to the outside. Evelyn had obviously stacked the boxes up against the door to make it look like no one had been in the storage closet for some time, if in fact she was telling the truth about Jake being in there.

I slid the boxes away rather easily as they moved across the slick concrete floor. The storage closet probably hadn't been used in years. It was the perfect hiding place. With the boxes moved aside, I grabbed the doorknob, turned it, and opened the storage closet door. That's when I heard Sarge say, "Wow, how, how, how, how, how, man, han, han, han, han, han, han!"

Jake was not in the storage closet but what we did find was very interesting and even more mysterious.

CHAPTER FIFTY-EIGHT

Once we had all crammed ourselves into the closet, I realized some very important things. Jake Harm was not in the closet, we could all stand to lose a few pounds except for Dudley and the very lovely E.D. of course, and at the end of the small closet was a small elevator door. It appeared to not have been used in years and my guess was that anyone who had ever known about it had not been in the Astrodome for a very long time.

Of course appearances can be deceiving and that is why I never base my decisions on appearances. No one should. Only the facts need to be considered no matter how unlikely they may be. This must be the elevator rumored to be used by Judge Roy Hofheinz to get to his secret penthouse somewhere above us. It truly did exist and my guess was that Evelyn had somehow discovered it while scheming to kidnap Jake before his concert. I wasn't sure how she did it but I believed she had stashed Jake up in the penthouse.

I turned to the others, who seemed dismayed that Jake was not found in the storage closet. Birk said, "What are we going to do now? How are we going to find Jake? That psycho obviously lied to us. Let's you and I go back and have a good ole' Texas chat with her, Careless."

I wasn't quite sure what that meant, but then again I'm not quite sure he even knew what he meant. I told him to hold the wedding because it wasn't yet clear to me that Evelyn had lied to us. She probably just hadn't fully disclosed all of the information we needed. I knew something like this may happen with Evelyn and the mental state she was in. She was probably just trying to measure her intelligence against ours, but unfortunately for her she had met her match and his name was Dudley.

While everyone else was about to leave, I walked forward and pushed the elevator button to open the door. It was a very old, dusty elevator and it did not appear to be operational. When I pushed the button the light did not come on and there were no sounds coming from it. Perhaps it was out of order. I just knew there had to be more to this than met the eye, but we appeared to be at a dead end.

I was about to give up hope and started to turn around to walk off with the others who were well ahead of me. That's when something big happened, something that just might lead us to Jake. Without lights and without any sound announcing the arrival of the elevator, the elevator door suddenly opened. Someone had disabled the lights and the sound. I believe that same someone was now handcuffed to a pipe, and her name was Evelyn.

I called out to my friends and Detective Present to come back when I discovered the elevator was in fact working. They all came hustling back to check out this latest development. I knew in my heart we were now about to officially solve the case even though I had mentally already done so yesterday.

The elevator was pretty small and could only fit four people at the most. I walked in the elevator with Dudley, Detective Present, and E.D. Sarge and Birk would have to wait until we sent the elevator back down for them. It was only fair that Dudley and I should take the first ride up since we had solved the case. E.D. was the only hottie so of course she had to ride up with us. Never leave a hottie waiting. I think I'm going to make that my motto from now on. Detective Present was a police detective so he definitely had to ride up on the first go round. That left Birk and Sarge the odd men out, and frankly they were both a little odd so perhaps they should be left out or at least left to come up after us.

The four of us climbed aboard the elevator. There was only a down and an up button, so I pushed the up button. There were no stops in between. Nothing happened for a minute until the elevator door began to slowly close. Once shut, it got very dark in there. It smelled a little musty but upward we went.

"Witless, that better not be your hand on my butt," I heard E.D. say in my direction.

I checked both of my hands and sure enough I wasn't touching E.D. although I wish I had thought of that before my friend Dudley began acting up and beating me to the punch. "That's Careless, honey, and both of my hands are well accounted for," I replied.

E.D. said, "That's an understatement!"

That's when Dudley began to mumble something under his breath.

"That mangy dog better stop feeling on me if you like living, Heartless," E.D. said and everyone in the elevator broke out in laughter.

A moment later, the elevator came to an abrupt stop and the elevator door slowly creaked opened.

CHAPTER FIFTY-NINE

We exited the elevator and walked out into an elegant stateroom. It was completely lit up as if someone had just left. I pushed the down button so the elevator returned to the bottom floor to pick up our two cohorts waiting downstairs. We walked around for a while and it was quite the setup. Behind a big desk stood a huge floor-to-ceiling bookshelf filled with all types of law books. To the right of that was a full-size pool table, and further over from that was a nice, plush leather sofa that looked like it could seat at least eight people.

That made me a little sad because it reminded me of how my favorite sofa bit the dust after Dudley devoured it. I'm not sure I ever found all the material and pieces of my dear departed sofa, but suffice it to say I did give it a proper burial.

Across from the large desk was a big opening that looked down on the playing field. It was almost like a window without glass and it was used to watch the sporting events from up high, away from the crowds. The funny thing was that because of the angle and shape of the opening, it was almost undetectable from any vantage point in the Astrodome. That was pretty clever.

"Wow, how, how, how, how, how, man, han, han, han, han, han, han," I heard Sarge say behind me as he exited the elevator that had just made its way back up to the penthouse. Birk and Sarge went straight for the pool table and began to play a game of pool. Two fools playing pool. Just what we needed! At least they would stay out of our way while we searched for Jake.

The rest of us walked around the penthouse but there was no sign of Jake. Detective Present looked at me and said, "I thought you had this case solved. Where is Jake Harm? I don't see him anywhere. I should have never listened to you."

Impatience is not a good character trait, especially if you want to solve a crime. Sometimes you must let the facts come to you on their own accord. When giving in to impatience, many things can happen and few of them are ever good. I could see Detective Present was at his wits end, so I announced to everyone, including and especially to Detective Present that in fact, Jake Harm was here. He was here in this very room. That's when the two boneheads stopped playing pool and started listening to what I was saying.

Detective Present was mildly interested but still displayed a willing suspension of disbelief. Everyone began looking around and yet Jake was nowhere to be found. That's when I decided to call in the big gun.

"Dudley, come here, boy," I called to him. He came over to me from across the room and sat by my side. I produced a bandana from my pocket and held it in front of Dudley's nose for a few seconds. He sniffed at it several times and then I placed it back in my pocket. I looked at him and told him, "Go get him, boy!"

Dudley stood up and stuck his nose in the air and moved it from side to side as he began tracking Jake. Earlier I had asked one of Jake's Holdouts for a piece of clothing from Jake that he had recently worn so Dudley could pick up his scent and track him. It was working like a charm. Dudley had Jake's scent imprinted on his brain after he smelled the bandana Jake had worn two nights earlier.

Dudley walked across the room, still sniffing with his nose in the air and turning his head slightly from side to side to make sure he was on the right path. He was using his exceptional tracking abilities and made it all the way across the room, just past the large desk, and stopped right at the bookshelf.

Everyone thought Dudley had failed and lost Jake's scent, everyone except his best friend, me. They were all looking at Dudley and wondering what in blazes was going on, and I exclaimed, "Ah ha, just as I suspected!"

That's when they took their attention off of Dudley and placed it on me. I walked over to the bookshelf and touched a few books until I found the one I was looking for. As I pulled, it shifted backward toward me at a forty-five degree angle and popped right back into its original position. This was followed by loud clanking sounds similar to lock tumblers on a safe moving around when being opened.

The bookshelf swung open just a little bit toward me. Dudley was still standing there as if he knew the bookshelf would open and as if he knew the man we had been searching for was behind it. I grabbed the edge of the bookshelf and swung it the rest of the way open. There behind the bookshelf in a secret room, about a quarter of the size of the penthouse, was Jake. He was tied into a chair and had tape over his mouth. Dudley, Detective Present, and I walked over to him. Detective Present gently pulled the tape off of Jake's mouth and began to untie him. Everyone seemed dazzled and went silent.

Jake and Dudley were not.

"Thank God, you're here! Some crazy little blonde girl drugged me, kidnapped me, and I found myself here in this room tied up in this chair. How long have I been here? What day is it?" Jake asked.

I assured him that everything was okay and that we were here to help him. I told him his kidnapper was no longer a threat to him and I introduced him to Detective Present who finished untying Jake.

While Detective Present spoke with Jake, Dudley stood next to him, mumbling something, and Jake began petting him. At first I thought this was a mistake because Dudley didn't really cotton to strangers but it turned out that Dudley loved Jake immediately. That was a nice surprise, for everyone.

Once Jake was untied, he stood up and stretched. He was in pretty good shape so I was guessing he hadn't been held against his will for long. I quickly filled him in on how we trapped his kidnapper and how I had set up an elaborate plan to catch her at the Jake Harm and the Holdouts concert that was going on as we spoke.

Jake was impressed and amused that I hired an impersonator to replace him at the concert, but then he looked at me and said, "Son, I've gotta a gig to get to, so let's get a move on." He walked out of the secret room behind the bookshelf, through the penthouse, and to the elevator. He looked at me and Dudley, waved his hand motioning us to come with him and said, "You boys coming, or what? And bring that pretty little filly over there with you."

Dudley, E.D., and I walked over to the elevator and, when the door opened up, we walked in with Jake and hit the down button. The others would follow behind us.

Once on the bottom floor, the elevator door slowly creaked opened and we walked out and back into the storage closet. As we emerged from the storage closet in a single line, the people working at the food court looked at us in disbelief. They couldn't figure out how we had all fit in that small storage closet much less figure out what we were doing in there in the first place.

CHAPTER SIXTY

We walked back down the hallway to where we left Evelyn handcuffed to the pipe protruding from the ground. She was nowhere to be found but the handcuffs were sitting on the ground next to the pipe. She had managed to free herself. I have no idea how she did that unless she had a key on her person. Perhaps she did and perhaps it was just as well. Now that Jake was free and we all knew who she was, she wouldn't chance coming after him ever again. He would be expecting it if she ever did.

Maybe Detective Present would be able to track her down. Something told me however that she had disappeared and would only be found if she wanted us to find her. There was a piece of paper crumpled up on the ground next to the pipe. I picked it up and straightened it out. It was a note written in chicken-scratch handwriting. It was from Evelyn and the only thing written on it was, "I'll get you, my puppy!"

Someone had watched the *Wizard of Oz* too many times and fortunately for me there was no place like home, which is just where I was about to head off to after my first case had been successfully solved. I folded up the note and stuck it in my pocket to keep for my first case file.

As I was about to split off from the group, Jake turned to me and said, "Son, let's go, we've got a performance to put on, and since you helped me out I want you and your boy over there to come backstage and watch me put on a show."

The "boy" he was referring to was Dudley. I nodded my head to oblige him and we walked out on the Hide Out floor and around to the back of the stage. Talk about perfect timing, the band had just hit a break and the two Jakes traded places. Once they saw Jake, the Holdouts started to cheer and had big smiles on their faces. They all ran up and hugged one another. They shared a few beers, had a few laughs, and twenty minutes later the real Jake Harm and the Holdouts took the stage and started with Jake's new single, "Wild Turkey at Sunrise."

The crowd went nuts and Jake played on into the night, just as he should have. Dudley and I scanned the crowd for Evelyn but she was long gone and hopefully we had seen the last of her. Birk, Sarge, and Detective Present came strolling up and joined E.D. who had been watching the concert from the Hide Out floor.

After the concert, Jake thanked me again and he and the band packed up and left. The crowd was now gone and the only people left were me, Dudley, E.D., Birk, Sarge, and Detective Present, as well as a bunch of empty beer bottles. Detective Present thanked me and, after what he just witnessed, wanted to know if I would be interested in doing some consulting work for the police department.

I asked him if the department would pick up the tab for the Jake Harm impersonator I hired, and he said they would.

I told him it was a pleasure doing business with him and I would be in touch soon. We shook hands and he turned and left.

The five of us walked out of the Hide Out together. It had been a good night. My first case was solved and Jake lived to sing another day. We were all very happy about that. As we left the Astrodome, I felt a real sense of pride and accomplishment. I was especially grateful to have Dudley by my side. He was an invaluable member of my team and was crucial to the solving of the case. I dare say it wouldn't have ended the way it did without him. He was also my best friend. Real friends, mister or sister, you probably only need one hand to count on and I knew I could always count on Dudley.

As we walked back through the carnival, I noticed it was mostly deserted. There were only a few people left who were cleaning up, shutting down the rides, and getting ready for the surge of people that would arrive the next day. No more fried Oreos for Birk and Sarge. Frankly, I didn't know how their stomachs tolerated that but they seemed no worse for the wear.

The carnival was closing down for the night just as the case was now closed. We made our way back to Birk's Cowboy Cadillac and once he unlocked the door, we all jumped into our designated spots, buckled up, and left the Astrodome. Birk, E.D., and I sat in the front while Sarge and Dudley sat in the backseat. Dudley had managed to prop himself up on the back of E.D.'s seat with his back legs firmly planted on the backseat while his rather large golden head protruded from the sunroof Birk had opened.

Birk hit the gas and away we sped. Being the white-knuckled driver he was, we were back at Big Rock in a flash.

Birk pulled up in the parking lot and we all said goodnight. Everyone exited the truck and Dudley walked off to drain the main vein. I turned to thank Birk but before I could utter a sound, he was speeding off. All he left was a trail of dust.

I turned back around and we all walked toward the entrance. I unlocked and opened the old iron door as we entered Big Rock. As we passed through the entryway and up the stairs, I turned to E.D. and, before a word was even uttered from my mouth, she looked at me with a devilish smile and said, "No, I won't marry you and no, I don't want to come have a nightcap with you and Dudley. Does that answer your question, Halfless?"

Frankly, I was a little stunned because I thought I was the most observant person there, but E.D. had just correctly anticipated my thought process. Perhaps I was getting a bit too predictable. I would have to change that. She would definitely never marry me if I didn't make it more interesting for her. My work was definitely cut out for me.

Sarge and I exited the stairwell on the second floor and E.D. reached over and kissed me on the cheek and reached down and patted Dudley on the head as she kept walking up the stairs. She sure smelled good, even better than fried Oreos.

Dudley and I made it to #158 and stopped in front of the door. Sarge kept on walking. "Goodnight, Sarge," I said.

"Yeah, heh, heh, heh, heh, heh, heh, man, han, han, han, han, han, han," echoed somewhere faraway as he disappeared down the long hallway. That Sarge, he is a real character.

I unlocked the door and Dudley and I entered the loft for a well-deserved rest. It had been a ruff day but my excitement from earlier in the evening prevented me from feeling tired. Dudley went over to his bowls and inhaled his food and he swallowed a bowl of water. I watched his head bob up and down as his huge tongue slurped up the water. All I kept thinking of was "moist." Moist had saved the day, and I smiled.

I poured myself a Careless Coffee and added a heaping helping of Jack Daniels. I began to drink my coffee as I almost sat down on my sofa that no longer existed thanks to someone in the room, but I won't bother to mention any names. Damn, I miss that sofa.

I finished my coffee and retired to the bedroom. I got undressed and got into bed. As I lay there, I felt the usual disturbance in the force, or a disturbance in the bed. Dudley had jumped on the bed behind me and was walking around looking for his sweet spot so he could hit the sack. He finally found it after two years of life and it was by my side. He settled down and placed his head on my chest, looked at me one last time, and closed his eyes to go to his happy place.

I wondered if his happy place was as nice as mine. I bet it was. I placed my hand on his head, looked at him one last time, and closed my eyes. It was *siesta* time.

EL FIN

Suddenly, while in the middle of a huge green flat surrounded by beautiful green hills, I was cutting up some carrots on the open tailgate of the Power Wagon. In the distance I heard a snorting sound and the clip-clops of steel horseshoes pounding the ground. The sound got louder as he approached me. Without seeing him, I instinctively reached my right hand out to place it on his face, between his nostrils and his forehead. Eagle always enjoyed that. I felt his soft face in my hand and his hot breath exiting his nostrils. I was home again and all was well.

I fed Eagle the carrots I had just cut up for him by placing them one at a time in the palm of my hand as his lips grabbed them, and he crunched them up with his teeth. He loved eating carrots from my hand and I enjoyed feeding them to him. He was a great, majestic horse, full of energy and stamina. I loved watching him prance around with his neck curved upward and his head held high. He was so beautiful.

After Eagle finished the carrots he lowered his head and wanted me to scratch him behind his ears. He loved that as well. I patted his very muscular neck a few times, jumped up on him and we galloped off. We went flying down the flat and into a cedar forest so thick the sunlight barely penetrated it and the air was freshly filtered, smelling like fresh cut cedar. It was so exhilarating. I loved that horse and loved our moments together, but our moment had passed and once we reached the end of the forest Eagle came to a sliding stop.

Our time together was at an end, for now, but he would stay with me until my time came to an end and then, then there would be plenty of carrots, plenty of green flats, and plenty of cedar forests. Until then, my friend. I jumped down and as he lowered his head, I began petting him. He nudged me a couple of times and I reluctantly said goodbye.

As I woke up in my bed, I was being nudged by Dudley in the same spot Eagle was nudging me. Was my mind playing tricks on me or was this just a coincidence? Did they share the same spirit? I wonder. I'll probably never know for sure but what I did know is that it was 5:00 a.m. and we needed to leave for breakfast at Pappa's house. I was a little tired. All that detective work had mentally worn me out.

I jumped out of bed, showered up, and got dressed for work. I asked Dudley if he was ready to go to work, but he was no longer there so once again I ended up talking to myself. I walked toward the front door and there he was waiting to go have breakfast with Pappa and to go to the office. I guess I had brainwashed him just like Pappa had brainwashed me. We were both hardworking, valued employees. We left Big Rock, Dudley did his thing outside, and we took the Power Wagon to Pappa's house.

We ate breakfast with Ross the Boss and Pappa, went to work, and put in a full day. I must say, it went by very quickly and I was still on a high from solving the disappearance of Jake Harm. It was all good in the hood. The day rushed by quickly and we found ourselves back at Big Rock by 5:00 p.m.

Once we were settled in for the night at Big Rock, I fed and watered Dudley. A few minutes later I noticed Dudley was frozen and eyeballing the door. A few seconds later, there was a banging on the door.

"Careless, open up, we know you're in there," a voice from the hallway called out. It sounded like Birk.

Dudley and I went to the door and I opened it. It was Birk, along with the lovely E.D., and Sarge. I was not expecting anyone, but they all walked in and Birk and Sarge were carrying a sofa. It looked very similar to the yellow-and-orange vinyl sofa Dudley had eaten for a snack, except it was different shades of brown. They carried it in and placed it in the same exact spot where the other sofa had met its match.

While this was going on, E.D. rolled in a covered large rectangular-shaped object on a dolly. Once the sofa was in place, Sarge took over for E.D. and placed the object next to my desk but left it covered.

Dudley immediately went over to the sofa and turned his head to look back at me. I shook my head from side to side, indicating to him that this sofa was not a chew toy. He just sat on it and waited patiently for me to come join him, which I did. I came over and sat right next to him and he began pressing his large body up against me. You couldn't fit a dime between us.

I loved my new sofa. I asked the gang where the new sofa came from and they told me it wasn't from them; it was a gift from Detective Present. He had learned of what technically could have been considered my very first case, *The Case of the Disappearing Sofa*. They had informed him of my sofa situation and he apparently had this particular sofa in his house, which he was about to haul off to the dump because his wife, Rachel, thought it was the ugliest thing she had ever laid eyes on. There's no accounting for taste really.

E.D. told me since I had solved the case that Detective Present wanted me to have the sofa and the other object they had rolled in. I asked them what the rectangular object was under the cover but in truth I already had ascertained what it was when they walked in with it.

E.D. said they would tell me what the object was under the cover only if I did something for them first. I asked her if what she wanted involved walking down the aisle with me, but she just gave me the "in your dreams, Hapless" look, so I asked her what the request was.

She told me they all wanted to know how I solved the case.

At that point, I smiled, got up, poured myself a Careless Coffee, took a few sips, and, while looking at her, said, "Elementary, my dear E.D."

Now, they were all listening with anticipation.

"My first clue was when I was at the library studying E.D.'s very beautiful photo exhibit. There was one picture of the Astrodome that was quite nice but I noticed a small detail in it that at the time I couldn't reconcile in my mind. The top of the Astrodome is made out of many small windows. Those windows are there to let light into the Astrodome so it is not completely dark inside. They all uniformly reflect light on the outside, however there was one small window not reflecting the same amount of light the other windows were, almost as if there was something behind it other than the large opening of the Astrodome. It was something perhaps such as a secret room or a penthouse that had a different light source than the rest of the Astrodome. The brightness of the reflection on that one window was very slight and almost undetectable to the human eye, but it did catch my attention."

I paused for a sip of Careless Coffee. "Then there was Richard at China Gardens. When Birk and I pulled up to go eat at the restaurant, I noticed Richard was talking to a strange-looking bearded man outside in front of the restaurant. I knew he looked familiar but I couldn't quite place him.

This man looked a little nervous and left almost as soon as we got there. Later, while watching the SPCA telethon on television, I noticed Richard standing in the background and he was actually a constable. Again, most people would not have noticed him because they would be focusing on the ladies holding the pets at center stage. It became clear to me that the strange bearded man was none other than Jake Harm, who was in disguise so as not to be recognized. My guess was that he and Richard are friends and Jake may have been receiving threats or was worried about something or someone. Jake probably went to Richard, asking for help and possibly some lemon chicken."

It was very quiet in the loft as everyone was now listening to me and hanging on my every word.

"My next clue was when we were all at the first Jake Harm and the Holdouts concert. The crowd was very excited to see Jake play but once the cover band finished and Jake Harm and the Holdouts were about to take the stage, I noticed that everyone was crowding in to see Jake. There were throngs of people streaming in from the outside because they knew the concert was about to start. All but one person. I noticed a blonde young lady fighting against the flow of people, trying to make her way *out* of the Hide Out. Now why would she be leaving if everyone else was heading in to watch the much-anticipated concert? I asked myself that and then it became clear to me. She knew something no one else there knew. She knew Jake wasn't going to be at that concert so there was no reason for her to stick around. She was the only one there who could have known that, and right then she became the culprit in my mind. I also got a brilliant idea when I had dinner with the lovely E.D. at Lucio's. Since I had been mistaken for Damian Mandola by the doorman at the restaurant, I realized everyone probably has a double somewhere so all I had to do next was hire a Jake Harm impersonator, get the band in on the plan, and draw her back out into the open. I figured her curiosity would get the better of her and she would show up back at the scene of the crime—and she did."

E.D. got a very interested look on her face as one of her eyebrows raised up and she put her right hand under her chin as she listened on in anticipation.

"Finally, my last clue happened at work the other day. While Dudley went to his outdoor happy place through the doggie door, he was acting like a goofball and grabbed a roll of toilet paper to play with, which really could have technically been my second case known as *The Toilet Paper Caper*, but I digress. As he dragged the toilet paper through the doggie door he left a trail. It appeared as if the toilet paper just stopped right at the doggie door but in fact, it continued on to the outside. Had the doggie door not been transparent, I would not have been able to see it from my vantage point because the doggie door closed on top of it. Once we had discovered the secret penthouse in the Astrodome where Jake was nowhere to be found and Dudley led us to the bookcase, I noticed a very small circular wear pattern on the carpet next to the bookcase as if something had rubbed up against the carpet and just stopped at the bookcase. It was also almost undetectable to the naked eye, but it did catch my attention and reminded me of how Dudley's toilet paper trail just seemed to stop at the wall even though I knew it continued on the other side. That's when I realized there was a secret, hidden room behind the bookshelf."

"When I employed my secret weapon, Dudley, the case, or shall I say the bookcase, cracked wide open," I said as I finished my explanation and my Careless Coffee.

The three of them sat there astonished in silence for a few moments while they absorbed how I had arrived at my conclusions to solve the case.

When the gang finally came to their senses, E.D. stood up, walked over to the covered object, and uncovered it. It was an old metal file cabinet. I had already assumed it was a file cabinet from its shape and by the metal clanking noise it made when it was rolled in, but I still needed to think of a name to put on the label.

I stood up, grabbed a black marker from the desk, and wrote on the front label of the filing cabinet: *The Dudley Files*. I liked that. It was catchy. *The Dudley Files*. Dudley was my partner in crime-fighting so it seemed only fitting and really, without him, the case most likely would not have been solved.

E.D. and the gang told me I was now an amateur investigator and Detective Present wanted to consult me on some future cases.

I agreed and told them I would do so as long as I could depend upon them for help from time to time. They readily agreed, and so my first case was solved, *The Dudley Files: Sold Out Without the Holdout.*

I opened the filing cabinet and dropped my case notes into it. I closed it and the gang wanted to know what my next case would be.

I thought for a moment, sat down on my new and improved sofa, started petting Dudley, and said, "I think the next mystery to solve may take me down to Mexico." And so it might.

Dudley agreed and mumbled something as he wagged his tail around in helicopter fashion.

ABOUT THE AUTHOR

People often ask me, "Careless, how did it come about that you have written this fabulous literary masterpiece?" and I always tell them the same thing: One day during my extensive travels in the Middle East (Houston) I came across a store named Hung Dong Market. At that point my perspective and direction in life was profoundly and forever changed. I might also add that I get amused and become inspired rather easily.

Lastly, since you have obviously made it through the whole book, I can now be honest and admit I in fact did not actually write it. Dudley is the true author. I merely typed it for him because frankly his typing, much like his driving, really sucks.